DICK FRANCIS

"is one of the world's best tellers of tales, particularly in his field of mayhem and English horse racing, and *Banker* is one of *his* best . . . fraught with violence, conspiracy and, of course, horses."

The Boston Globe

BANKER

"has perhaps the most elaborate plot Francis has yet devised."

The Washington Post Book World

"For those who have read and enjoyed the work of Francis, merely the announcement that another effort is out is usually enough to send them to the library or book store. Those who have not read him before are in for a treat."

Houston Chronicle

"The problem (the hero) confronts . . . is a masterpiece of ingenious complication."

The Atlantic Monthly

Fawcett Crest Books
by Dick Francis

REFLEX

TWICE SHY

DICK FRANCIS
BANKER

FAWCETT CREST • NEW YORK

A Fawcett Crest Book
Published by Ballantine Books

Library of Congress Catalog Card Number: 82-18122

ISBN: 0-449-20262-3

This edition published by arrangement with G.P. Putnam's Sons

Manufactured in the United States of America

First International Edition: November 1983

First Ballantine Books Edition: April 1984

My sincere thanks for the
generous help of
JEREMY H. THOMPSON
M.D., F.R.C.P.I.
Professor of Pharmacology
University of California
Los Angeles

and of
MICHAEL MELLUISH
and
JOHN COOPER.

Contents

Introduction

It's difficult to say where disaster begins, to point to one particular happening as the first significant step towards distant cataclysm. Tim Ekaterin, looking back, saw the beginning as the day his boss stepped into a fountain. Onwards from there he came across people and events as yet unconnected but which when woven together by time and chance led towards violent explosive action and the threat of death.

Set in the worlds of thoroughbred racing and merchant banking, *Banker* covers a span of three years, growing from quiet harmless-seeming seeds to a wholly horrific harvest.

The First Year

May

Gordon Michaels stood in the fountain with all his clothes on.

"My God," Alec said. "What is he doing?"

"Who?"

"Your boss," Alec said. "Standing in the fountain."

I crossed to the window and stared downwards: down two floors to the ornamental fountain in the forecourt of the Paul Ekaterin merchant bank. Down to where three entwining plumes of water rose gracefully into the air and fell in a glittering circular curtain. To where, in the bowl, calf-deep, stood Gordon in his navy pin-striped suit . . . in his white shirt and sober silk tie . . . in his charcoal socks and black shoes . . . in his gold cufflinks and onyx ring . . . in his polished City persona . . . soaking wet.

It was his immobility, I thought, which principally alarmed. Impossible to interpret this profoundly uncharacteristic behavior as in any way an expression of lightheartedness, of celebration or of joy.

I whisked straight out of the deep-carpeted office, through the fire doors, down the flights of gritty stone staircase and across the marbled expanse of entrance hall. The uniformed man at the security desk was staring towards the wide glass front doors with his fillings showing and two arriving visitors were looking stunned. I went past them at a rush into the open air and slowed only in the last few strides before the fountain.

"Gordon!" I said.

His eyes were open. Beads of water ran down his forehead from his dripping black hair and caught here and there on his lashes. The main fall of water slid in a crystal sheet just behind his shoulders with scatterings of drops spraying forwards on to him like rain. Gordon's eyes looked at me unblinkingly with earnest vagueness as if he were not at all sure who I was.

"Get into the fountain," he said.

"Er . . . why, exactly?"

"They don't like water."

"Who don't?"

"All those people. Those people with white faces. They don't like water. They won't follow you into the fountain. You'll be all right if you're wet."

His voice sounded rational enough for me to wonder wildly whether this was not after all a joke: but Gordon's jokes were normally small, civilized, glinting commentaries on the stupidities of mankind, not whooping, gusty, practical affairs smacking of the surreal.

"Come out of there, Gordon," I said uneasily.

"No, no. They're waiting for me. Send for the police. Ring them up. Tell them to come and take them all away."

"But *who*, Gordon?"

"All those people, of course. Those people with white faces." His head slowly turned from side to side, his eyes focused as if on a throng closely surrounding the whole fountain. Instinctively I too looked from side to side, but all I could see were the more distant stone and glass walls of Ekaterin's, with, now, a growing chorus of heads appearing disbelievingly at the windows.

I clung still to a hope of normality. "They work here," I said. "Those people work here."

"No, no. They came with me. In the car. Only two or three of them, I thought. But all the others, they were here, you know. They want me to go with them, but they can't reach me here, they don't like the water."

He had spoken fairly loudly throughout so that I should hear him above the noise of the fountain, and the last of these remarks reached the chairman of the bank, who came striding briskly across from the building.

"Now, Gordon, my dear chap," the chairman said authoritatively, coming to a purposeful halt at my side. "What's all this about, for God's sake?"

"He's having hallucinations," I said.

The chairman's gaze flicked to my face, and back to Gordon, and Gordon seriously advised him to get into the fountain, because the people with white faces couldn't reach him there, on account of disliking water.

"Do something, Tim," the chairman said, so I stepped into the fountain and took Gordon's arm.

"Come on," I said. "If we're wet they won't touch us. We don't have to stay in the water. Being wet is enough."

"Is it?" Gordon said. "Did they tell you?"

"Yes, they did. They won't touch anyone who's wet."

"Oh. All right. If you're sure."

"Yes, I'm sure."

He nodded understandingly and with only slight pressure from my arm took two sensible-seeming paces through the water and stepped over the knee-high coping onto the paving slabs of the forecourt. I held on to him firmly and hoped to heaven that the people with white faces would keep their distance; and although Gordon looked around apprehensively it appeared that they were not so far trying to abduct him.

The chairman's expression of concern was deep and genuine, as he and Gordon were firm and long-time friends. Except in appearance they were much alike; essentially clever, intuitive, and with creative imaginations. Each in normal circumstances had a manner of speaking that expressed even the toughest commands in gentle politeness, and both had a visible appetite for their occupation. They were both in their fifties, both at the top of their powers, both comfortably rich.

Gordon dripped onto the paving stones.

"I think," the chairman said, casting a glance at the inhabited windows, "that we should go indoors. Into the boardroom, perhaps. Come along, Gordon."

He took Gordon Michaels by his other sodden sleeve, and between us one of the steadiest banking brains in London walked obediently in its disturbing fog.

"The people with white faces," I said as we steered a calm course across the marble entrance hall between clearly human open-mouthed watchers, "are they coming with us?"

"Of course," Gordon said.

It was obvious also that some of them came up in the elevator with us. Gordon watched them dubiously all the time. The others, as we gathered from his reluctance to step out into the top-floor hallway, were waiting for our arrival.

"It's all right," I said to Gordon encouragingly. "Don't forget, we're still wet."

"Henry isn't," he said, anxiously eyeing the chairman.

"We're all together," I said. "It will be all right."

Gordon looked doubtful, but finally allowed himself to be drawn from the elevator between his supporters. The white faces apparently parted before us, to let us through.

The chairman's personal assistant came hurrying along the corridor but the chairman waved him conclusively to a stop and said not to let anyone disturb us in the boardroom until he rang the bell; and Gordon and I in our wet shoes sloshed across the deep-piled green carpet to the long glossy mahogany boardroom table. Gordon consented to sit in one of the comfortable leather armchairs that surrounded it with me and the chairman alongside, and this time it was the chairman who asked if the people with white faces were still there.

"Of course," Gordon said, looking around. "They're

sitting in all the chairs round the table. And standing behind them. Dozens of them. Surely you can see them?''

"What are they wearing?" the chairman asked.

Gordon looked at him in puzzlement, but answered simply enough. "White suits of course. With black buttons. Down the front, three big black buttons."

"All of them?" the chairman asked. "All the same?"

"Oh, yes, of course."

"Clowns," I exclaimed.

"What?"

"White-faced clowns."

"Oh, no," Gordon said. "They're not clowns. They're not funny."

"White-faced clowns are sad."

Gordon looked troubled and wary, and kept a good eye on his visitations.

"What's best to do?" wondered the chairman; but he was talking principally to himself. To me directly, after a pause, he said, "I think we should take him home. He's clearly not violent, and I see no benefit in calling in a doctor here, whom we don't know. I'll ring Judith and warn her, poor girl. I'll drive him in my car, as I'm perhaps the only one who knows exactly where he lives. And I'd appreciate it, Tim, if you'd come along, sit with Gordon on the back seat, keep him reassured."

"Certainly," I agreed. "And incidentally, his own car's here. He said that when he drove in he thought there were two or three of the white faces with him. The rest were waiting here."

"Did he?" The chairman pondered. "He can't have been hallucinating when he actually left home. Surely Judith would have noticed."

"But he seemed all right in the office when he came in," I said. "Quiet, but, all right. He sat at his desk for nearly an hour before he went out and stood in the fountain."

"Didn't you talk with him?"

"He doesn't like people to talk when he's thinking."

The chairman nodded. "First thing, then," he said,

"see if you can find a blanket. Ask Peter to find one. And . . . er . . . how wet are you, yourself?"

"Not soaked, except for my legs. No problem, honestly. It's not cold."

He nodded, and I went on the errand. Peter, the assistant, produced a red blanket with "Fire" written across one corner for no good reason that I could think of, and with this wrapped snugly round his by now naked chest Gordon allowed himself to be conveyed discreetly to the chairman's car. The chairman himself slid behind the wheel and with the direct effectiveness that shaped his whole life drove his still half-damp passengers southwards through the fair May morning.

Henry Shipton, chairman of Paul Ekaterin Ltd., was physically a big-framed man, whose natural bulk was kept short of obesity by raw carrots, mineral water and will power. Half visionary, half gambler, he habitually subjected every soaring idea to rigorous analytic test: a man whose powerful instinctive urges were everywhere harnessed and put to work.

I admired him. One had to. During his twenty-year stint (including ten as chairman) Paul Ekaterin Ltd. had grown from a moderately successful banking house into one of the senior league, accepted worldwide with respect. I could measure almost exactly the spread of public recognition of the bank's name, since it was mine also: Timothy Ekaterin, great-grandson of Paul the founder. In my school days people always said "Timothy *who*? E-*kat*-erin? How do you spell it?" Quite often now they simply nodded—and expected me to have the fortune to match, which I hadn't.

"They're very peaceful, you know," Gordon said after a while.

"The white faces?" I asked.

He nodded. "They don't say anything. They're just waiting."

"Here in the car?"

He looked at me uncertainly. "They come and go."

At least they weren't pink elephants, I thought irreverently: but Gordon, like the chairman, was abstemious beyond doubt. He looked pathetic in his red blanket, the sharp mind confused with dreams, the well-groomed businessman a pre-fountain memory, the patina stripped away. This was the warrior who dealt confidently every day in millions, this huddled mass of delusions going home in wet trousers. The dignity of man was everywhere tissue-paper thin.

He lived, it transpired, in leafy splendor by Clapham Common, in a late-Victorian family pile surrounded by head-high garden walls. There were high cream-painted wooden gates, which were shut, and which I opened, and a short graveled driveway between tidy lawns.

Judith Michaels erupted from her opening front door to meet the chairman's car as it rolled to a stop, and the first thing she said, aiming it variously between Henry Shipton and myself, was "I'll throttle that bloody doctor."

After that she said, "How is he?" and after that, in compassion, "Come along, love, it's all right, come along in, darling, we'll get you warm and tucked into bed in no time."

She put sheltering arms round the red blanket as her child of a husband stumbled out of the car, and to me and to Henry Shipton she said again in fury, "I'll kill him. He ought to be struck off."

"They're very bad these days about house calls," the chairman said doubtfully. "But surely . . . he's coming?"

"No, he's not. Now you lambs both go into the kitchen —there's some coffee in the pot—and I'll be down in a sec. Come on Gordon, my dear love, up those stairs . . . ." She helped him through the front door, across a Persian-rugged hall and towards a paneled wood staircase, with me and the chairman following and doing as we were told.

Judith Michaels, somewhere in the later thirties, was a brown-haired woman in whom the life-force flowed strongly and with whom I could easily have fallen in love. I'd met her several times before that morning (at the bank's various social gatherings) and had been conscious freshly each time of the warmth and glamour

that were as normal to her as breathing. Whether I in
return held the slightest attraction for her I didn't
know and hadn't tried to find out, as entangling oneself
emotionally with one's boss's wife was hardly best for
one's prospects. All the same I felt the same old tug, and
wouldn't have minded taking Gordon's place on the
staircase.

With these thoughts, I hoped, decently hidden, I went
with Henry Shipton into the friendly kitchen and
drank the offered coffee.

"A great girl, Judith," the chairman said with feeling, and I looked at him in rueful surprise and agreed.

She came to join us after a while, still more annoyed
than worried. "Gordon says there are people with white
faces sitting all round the room and they won't go away.
It's really too bad. It's infuriating. I'm so angry I could
spit."

The chairman and I looked bewildered.

"Didn't I tell you?" she said, observing us. "Oh, no, I
suppose I didn't. Gordon hates anyone to know about
his illness. It isn't very bad, you see. Not bad enough for
him to have to stop working, or anything like that."

"Er . . ." said the chairman. "What illness?"

"Oh. I suppose I'll have to tell you, now this has happened. I could kill that doctor, I really could." She took
a deep breath and said, "Gordon's got mild Parkinson's
disease. His left hand shakes a bit now and then. I don't
expect you've noticed. He tries not to let people see."

We blankly shook our heads.

"Our normal doctor's just retired, and this new man,
he's one of those frightfully bumptious people who
think they know better than everyone else. So he's
taken Gordon off the old pills, which were fine as far as
I could see, and put him on some new ones. As of the day
before yesterday. So when I rang him just now in an absolute *panic* thinking Gordon had suddenly gone raving
mad or something and I'd be spending the rest of my life
visiting mental hospitals he says lightheartedly not to
worry, this new drug quite often causes hallucinations,
and it's just a matter of getting the dosage right. I tell

you, if he hadn't been at the other end of a telephone
wire, I'd have *strangled* him."

Both Henry Shipton and I, however, were feeling
markedly relieved.

"You mean," the chairman asked, "that this will all
just . . . wear off?"

She nodded. "That bloody doctor said to stop taking
the pills and Gordon would be perfectly normal in thirty-six hours. I *ask* you! And after that he's got to start
taking them again, but only half the amount, and to see
what happens. And if we were *worried*, he said pity-
ingly, as if we'd no right to be, Gordon could toddle
along to the surgery in a couple of days and discuss it
with him, though as Gordon would be perfectly all right
by tomorrow night we might think there was no need."

She herself was shaking slightly with what still
looked like anger but was more probably a release of
tension, because she suddenly sobbed, twice, and said,
"Oh, God," and wiped crossly at her eyes.

"I was so frightened, when you told me," she said,
half apologetically. "And when I rang the surgery I got
that damned obstructive receptionist and had to argue
for ten minutes before she let me even *talk* to the doctor."

After a brief sympathetic pause the chairman, going
as usual to the heart of things, said, "Did the doctor say
how long it would take to get the dosage right?"

She looked at him with a defeated grimace. "He said
that as Gordon had reacted so strongly to an average
dose it might take as much as six weeks to get him thoroughly stabilized. He said each patient was different,
but that if we would persevere it would be much the
best drug for Gordon in the long run."

Henry Shipton drove me pensively back to the City.

"I think," he said, "that we'll say—in the office—that
Gordon felt 'flu' coming on and took some pills that
proved hallucinatory. We might say simply that he
imagined that he was on holiday, and felt the need for a
dip in a pool. Is that agreeable?"

"Sure," I said mildly.

"Hallucinatory drugs are, after all, exceedingly common these days."

"Yes."

"No need, then, Tim, to mention white-faced clowns."

"No," I agreed.

"Nor Parkinson's disease, if Gordon doesn't wish it."

"I'll say nothing," I assured him.

The chairman grunted and lapsed into silence; and perhaps we both thought the same thoughts along the well-worn lines of drug-induced side effects being more disturbing than the disease.

It wasn't until we were a mile from the bank that Henry Shipton spoke again, and then he said, "You've been in Gordon's confidence for two years now, haven't you?"

"Nearly three," I murmured, nodding.

"Can you hold the fort until he returns?"

It would be dishonest to say that the possibility of this offer hadn't been in my mind since approximately ten-fifteen, so I accepted it with less excitement than relief.

There was no rigid hierarchy in Ekaterin's. Few explicit ranks: to be "in so and so's confidence," as house jargon put it, meant one would normally be on course for more responsibility, but unlike the other various thirty-two-year-olds who crowded the building with their hopes and expectations I lived under the severe disadvantage of my name. The whole board of directors, consistently afraid of accusations of nepotism, made me double-earn every step.

"Thank you," I said neutrally.

He smiled a shade. "Consult," he said, "whenever you need help."

I nodded. His words weren't meant as disparagement. Everyone consulted, in Ekaterin's, all the time. Communication between people and between departments was an absolute priority in Henry Shipton's book, and it was he who had swept away a host of small-room offices to form opened-up expanses. He himself sat always at one (fairly opulent) desk in a room that contained eight similar, his own flanked on one side by the vice-chairman's and on the other by that of the head of Corporate Finance. Further senior directors from other departments occupied a row of desks opposite, all of them within easy talking earshot of each other.

As with all merchant banks, the business carried on by Ekaterin's was different and separate from that conducted by the High Street chains of clearing banks. At Ekaterin's one never actually saw any money. There were no tellers, no clerks, no counters, no deposits, no withdrawals and hardly any check books.

There were three main departments, each with its separate function and each on its own floor of the building. Corporate Finance acted for major clients on mergers, takeovers and the raising of capital. Banking, which was where I worked with Gordon, loaned money to enterprise and industry. And Investment Management, the oldest and largest department, aimed at producing the best possible returns from the vast investment funds of charities, companies, pensions, trusts and trade unions.

There were several small sections, like Administration, which did everyone's paperwork; Property, which bought, sold, developed and leased; Research, which dug around; Overseas Investments, growing fast; and Foreign Exchange, where about ten frenetic young wizards bought and sold world currencies by the minute, risking millions on decimal-point margins and burning themselves out by forty.

The lives of all the three hundred and fifty people who worked for Ekaterin's were devoted to making money work. To the manufacture, in the main, of business, trade, industry, pensions and jobs. It wasn't a bad thing to be convinced of the worth of what one did, and certainly there was a tough basic harmony in the place, which persisted unruffled by the surface tensions and jealousies and territorial defenses of everyday office life.

Events had already moved on by the time the chairman and I returned to the hive. The chairman was pounced upon immediately in the entrance hall by a worriedly waiting figure from Corporate Finance, and upstairs in Banking Alec was giggling into his blotter.

Alec, my own age, suffered, professionally speaking, from an uncontrollable bent for frivolity. It brightened up the office no end, but as court jesters seldom made it to the throne his career path was already observably sideways and erratic. The rest of us were probably hopelessly stuffy. Thank God, I often thought, for Alec.

He had a well-shaped face of scattered freckles on cream-pale skin; a high forehead, a mat of tight tow-colored curls. Stiff blond eyelashes blinked over alert blue eyes behind gold-framed spectacles, and his mouth twitched easily as he saw the funny side. He was liked on sight by almost everybody, and it was only gradually that one came to wonder whether the examiner who had awarded him a First in law at Oxford had been suffering from critical blindness.

"What's up?" I said, instinctively smiling to match the giggles.

"We've been leaked." He lifted his head but tapped the paper that lay on his desk. "My *dear*," he said with mischievous pleasure, "this came an hour ago and it seems we're leaking all over the place like a punctured bladder. Like a baby. Like the *Welsh*."

Leeking like the Welsh . . . ah well.

He lifted up the paper, and all, or at least a great deal, was explained. There had recently appeared a slim bi-monthly publication called *What's Going On Where It Shouldn't*, which had fast caught the attention of most of the country and was reportedly read avidly by the police. Descendant of the flood of investigative journalism spawned by the tidal wave of Watergate, *What's Going On* was said to be positively bombarded by informers telling *precisely* what was going on, and all the investigating the paper had to do was into the truth of the information: which task it had been known to perform less than thoroughly.

"What does it say?" I asked; as who wouldn't.

"Cutting out the larky innuendo," he said, "it says that someone at Ekaterin's has been selling inside information."

"*Selling* . . ."

"Quite so."

"About a takeover?"

"How did you guess?"

I thought of the man from Corporate Finance hopping from leg to leg with impatience while he waited for the chairman to return and knew that nothing but extreme urgency would have brought him down to the doorstep.

"Let's see," I said, and took the paper from Alec's outstretched hand.

The piece, headed merely "Tut tut," was only four paragraphs long, and the first three of those were taken up with explaining with seductive authority that in merchant banks it was possible for the managers of investment funds to learn at an early stage about a takeover being organized by their colleagues. It was strictly illegal, however, for an investment manager to act on this private knowledge, even though by doing so he might make a fortune for his clients.

The shares of a company about to be taken over were likely to rise in value. If one could buy them at a low price before even a rumor of takeover started, the gain could be huge.

Such unprofessional behavior by a merchant bank would be instantly recognized simply *because of* the profits made, and no investment manager would invite personal disaster in that way.

However, asked the article, *What's Going On in the merchant bank of Paul Ekaterin Ltd.? Three times in the past year takeovers managed by this prestigious firm have been "scooped" by vigorous buying beforehand of the shares concerned. The buying itself cannot be traced to Ekaterin's investment managers, but we are informed that the information did come from within Ekaterin's, and that someone there has been selling the golden news, either for straight cash or a slice of the action.*

"It's a guess," I said flatly, giving Alec back the paper. "There are absolutely no facts."

"A bucket of cold water," he complained, "is a sunny day compared with you."

"Do you *want* it to be true?" I asked curiously.

"Livens the place up a bit."

And there, I thought, was the difference between

Alec and me. For me the place was alive all the time, even though when I'd first gone there eight years earlier it had been unwillingly; a matter of being forced into it by my uncle. My mother had been bankrupt at that point, her apartment stripped to the walls by the bailiffs of everything except a telephone (property of the Post Office) and a bed. My mother's bankruptcy, as both my uncle and I well knew, was without doubt her own fault, but it didn't stop him applying his blackmailing pressure.

"I'll clear her debts and arrange an allowance for her if you come and work in the bank."

"But I don't want to."

"I know that. And I know that you're stupid enough to try to support her yourself. But if you do that she'll ruin you like she ruined your father. Just give the bank a chance, and if you hate it after three months I'll let you go."

So I'd gone with mulish rebellion to tread the path of my great-grandfather, my grandfather and my uncle, and within three months you'd have had to prize me loose with a crowbar. I suppose it was in my blood. All the snooty teenage scorn I'd felt for "money-grubbing," all the supercilious disapproval of my student days, all the negative attitudes bequeathed by my failure of a father, all had melted into comprehension, interest and finally delight. The art of money management now held me as addicted as any junkie, and my working life was as fulfilling as any mortal could expect.

"Who do you think did it?" Alec said.

"If anyone did."

"It must have happened," he said positively. "Three times in the last year . . . that's more than a coincidence."

"And I'll bet that that coincidence is all the paper's working on. They're dangling a line. Baiting a hook. They don't even say which takeovers they mean, let alone give figures."

True or not, though, the story itself was bad for the bank. Clients would back away fast if they couldn't trust, and *What's Going On* was right often enough to instill disquiet. Henry Shipton spent most of the afternoon in the boardroom conducting an emergency meeting of the directors, with ripples of unease spreading outwards from there through all the departments. By going-home time that evening practically everyone in the building had read the bombshell, and although some took it as lightheartedly as Alec it had the effect of almost totally deflecting speculation from Gordon Michaels.

I explained only twice about flu and pills: only two people asked. When the very reputation of the bank was being rocked, who cared about a dip in the ornamental fountain, even if the bather had had all his clothes on and was a director in Banking.

On the following day I found that filling Gordon's job was no lighthearted matter. While he had gradually given me power of decision over loans up to certain amounts, anything larger was in his own domain entirely. This meant that, within my bracket, I could arrange any loan if I believed the client was sound and could repay principal and interest at an orderly rate: but if I judged wrong and the client went bust, the lenders lost both their money and their belief in my common sense. As the lenders were quite often the bank itself, I couldn't afford for it to happen too often.

With Gordon there, the ceiling of my possible disasters had at least been limited. For him, though, the ceiling hardly existed, except that with loans incurring millions it was normal for him to consult with others on the board.

These consultations, already easy and informal because of the open-plan layout, also tended to stretch over lunch, which the directors mostly ate together in their own private dining room. It was Gordon's habit to look with a pleased expression at his watch at five to one and take himself amiably off in the direction of a tomato juice and roast lamb; and he would return an hour later with his mind clarified and made up.

I'd been loaned Gordon's job but not his seat on the board, so I was without the benefit of the lunches; and

as he himself had been the most senior in our own green
pasture of office expanse, there was no one else of his
stature immediately at hand. Alec's advice tended to
swing between the brilliantly perceptive and the mani-
acally reckless, but one was never quite sure which was
which at the time. All high-risk Cinderellas would have
gone to the ball under Alec's wand: the trick was in
choosing only those who would keep an eye on the clock
and deliver the crystal goods.

Gordon tended therefore to allocate only cast-iron certainties to Alec's care and most of the Cinderella type to
me, and he'd said once with a smile that in this job one's
nerve either toughened or broke, which I'd thought
faintly extravagant at the time. I understood, though,
what he meant when I faced without him a task that
lay untouched on his desk: a request for financial back-
ing for a series of animated cartoon films.

It was too easy to turn things down . . . and perhaps
miss Peanuts or Mickey Mouse. A large slice of the
bank's profits came from the interest paid by borrowers. If we didn't lend, we didn't earn. A toss-up. I picked
up the telephone and invited the hopeful cartoonist to
bring his proposals to the bank.

Most of Gordon's projects were halfway through, his
biggest at the moment being three point four million
for an extension to a cake factory. I had heard him
working on this one for a week, so I merely took on
where he had left off, telephoning people who sometimes had funds to lend and asking if they'd be interested in underwriting a chunk of Home-made Heaven.
The bank itself, according to Gordon's list, was lending
three hundred thousand only, which made me wonder
whether he privately expected the populace to go back
to eating bread.

There was also, tucked discreetly in a folder, a glossy-
prospectus invitation to participate in a multi-million
project in Brazil, whereon Gordon had doodled in pencil
an army of question marks and a couple of queries: *Do
we or don't we? Remember Brasilia! Is coffee enough??*
On the top of the front page, written in red, was a jump-
to-it memo: *Preliminary answer by Friday.*

It was already Thursday. I picked up the prospectus and went along to the other and larger office at the end of the passage, where Gordon's almost-equal sat at one of the seven desks. Along there the carpet was still lush and the furniture still befitting the sums dealt with on its tops, but the view from the windows was different. No fountain, but the sunlit dome of St. Paul's Cathedral rising like a Fabergé egg from the white stone lattice of the City.

"Problem?" asked Gordon's almost-equal. "Can I help?"

"Do you know if Gordon meant to go any further with this?" I asked. "Did he say?"

Gordon's colleague looked the prospectus over and shook his head. "Who's along there with you today?"

"Only Alec. I asked him. He doesn't know."

"Where's John?"

"On holiday. And Rupert is away because of his wife."

The colleague nodded. Rupert's wife was imminently dying: cruel at twenty-six.

"I'd take it around," he said. "See if Gordon's put out feelers in Research, Overseas, anywhere. Form a view yourself. Then if you think it's worth pursuing you can take it to Val and Henry." Val was head of Banking and Henry was Henry Shipton. I saw that to be Gordon was a big step up indeed, and was unsure whether to be glad or sorry that the elevation would be temporary.

I spent all afternoon drifting round with the prospectus and in the process learned less about Brazil than about the tizzy over the report in *What's Going On.* Soul-searching appeared to be fashionable. Long faces inquired anxiously, "Could one possibly . . . without knowing . . . have mentioned a takeover to an interested party?" And the short answer to that, it seemed to me, was No, one couldn't. Secrecy was everywhere second nature to bankers.

If the article in the paper were true there had to be three people involved; the seller, the buyer and the informant; and certainly neither the buyer nor the informant could have acted in ignorance or by chance.

Greed and malice moved like worms in the dark. If one were infested by them, one knew.

Gordon seemed to have asked no one about Brazil, and for me it was make-up-your-mind time. It would have been helpful to know what the other merchant banks thought, the sixteen British accepting houses like Schroders, Hambro's, Morgan Grenfell, Kleinwort Benson, Hill Samuel, Warburg's, Robert Fleming, Singer and Friedlander . . . all permitted, like Paul Ekaterin's, to assume that the Bank of England would come to their aid in a crisis.

Gordon's opposite numbers in those banks would all be pursing mouths over the same prospectus, committing millions to a fruitful enterprise, pouring millions down the drain, deciding not to risk it either way.

Which?

One could hardly directly ask, and finding out via the grapevine took a little time.

I carried the prospectus finally to Val Fisher, head of Banking, who usually sat at one of the desks facing Henry Shipton, two floors up.

"Well, Tim, what's your own view?" he said. A short man, very smooth, very charming, with nerves like toughened ice.

"Gordon had reservations, obviously," I said. "I don't know enough, and no one else here seems to. I suppose we could either make a preliminary answer of cautious interest and then find out a bit more, or just trust to Gordon's instinct."

He smiled faintly. "Which?"

Ah, which?

"Trust to Gordon's instinct, I think," I said.

"Right."

He nodded and I went away and wrote a polite letter to the Brazil people expressing regret. And I wouldn't know for six or seven years, probably, whether that decision was right or wrong.

The gambles were all long term. You cast your bread on the waters and hoped it would float back in the future with butter and jam.

Mildew . . . too bad.

June

Gordon telephoned three weeks later sounding thoroughly fit and well. I glanced across to where his desk stood mute and tidy, with all the paper action now transferred to my own.

"Judith and I wanted to thank you . . ." he was saying.

"Really no need," I said. "How are you?"

"Wasting time. It's ridiculous. Anyway . . . we've been offered a half-share in a box at Ascot next Thursday. We thought it might be fun . . . We've six places. Would you like to come? As our guest, of course. As a thank-you."

"I'd love it," I said. "But . . ."

"No buts," he interrupted. "If you'd like to, Henry will fix it. He's coming himself. He agreed you'd earned a day off, so all you have to do is decide."

"Then I'd like to, very much."

"Good. If you haven't a morning coat, don't worry. We're not in the Royal Enclosure."

"If you're wearing one . . . I inherited my father's."

"Ah. Good. Yes, then. One o'clock Thursday, for

lunch. I'll send the entrance tickets to you in the office. Both Judith and I are very pleased you can come. We're very grateful. Very." He sounded suddenly half-embarrassed, and disconnected with a click.

I wondered how much he remembered about the white faces, but with Alec and Rupert and John all in earshot it had been impossible to ask. Maybe at the races he would tell me. Maybe not.

Going racing wasn't something I did very often nowadays, although as a child I'd spent countless afternoons waiting around the Tote lines while my mother in pleasurable agony backed her dozens of hunches and bankers and third strings and savers and lost money by the ton.

"I've won!" she would announce radiantly to all about her, waving an indisputably winning ticket: and the bunch of losses on the same race would be thrust into a pocket and later thrown away.

My father at the same time would be standing drinks in the bar, an amiable open-fisted lush with more good nature than sense. They would take me home at the end of the day giggling happily together in a hired chauffeur-driven Rolls, and until I was quite old I never questioned but that this contented affluence was built on rock.

I had been their only child and they'd given me a very good childhood, to the extent that when I thought of holidays it was of yachts on warm seas or Christmas in the Alps. The villain of those days was my uncle, who descended on us occasionally to utter Dire Warnings about the need for his brother (my father) to find a job.

My father, however, couldn't shape up to "money-grubbing" and in any case had no real ability in any direction; and with no habit of working he quietly scorned people who had. He never tired of his life of aimless ease, and if he earned no one's respect, few detested him either. A weak, friendly, unintelligent man. Not bad as a father. Not good at much else.

He dropped dead of a heart attack when I was nineteen and it was then that the point of the Dire Warnings became apparent. He and mother had lived on the capital inherited from grandfather, and there wasn't a great deal left. Enough just to see me through college; enough, with care, to bring mother a small income for life.

Not enough to finance her manner of betting, which she wouldn't or couldn't give up. A lot more of the Dire Warnings went unheeded, and finally, while I was trying to stem a hopeless tide by working (of all things) for a bookmaker, the bailiffs knocked on the door.

In twenty-five years, it seemed, my mother had gambled away the best part of half a million pounds; all gone on horses, fast and slow. It might well have sickened me altogether against racing, but in a curious way it hadn't. I remembered how much she and father had enjoyed themselves: and who was to say that it was a fortune ill spent?

"Good news?" Alec said, eyeing my no doubt ambivalent expression.

"Gordon's feeling better."

"Hm," he said judiciously, "so he should be. Three weeks off for flu . . ." He grinned. "Stretching it a bit."

I made a noncommittal grunt.

"Be glad, shall we, when he comes back?"

I glanced at his amused, quizzical face and saw that he knew as well as I did that when Gordon reappeared to repossess his kingdom, I wouldn't be glad at all. Doing Gordon's job, after the first breath-shortening initial plunge, had injected me with great feelings of vigor and good health; had found me running up stairs and singing in the bath and showing all the symptoms of a love affair: and like many a love affair it couldn't survive the return of the husband. I wondered how long I'd have to wait for such a chance again, and whether next time I'd feel as high.

"Don't think I haven't noticed," Alec said, the eyes electric blue behind the gold-rimmed specs.

"Noticed what?" Rupert asked, raising his head above papers he'd been staring blindly at for ninety minutes.

Back from his pretty wife's death and burial poor Rupert still wore a glazed, otherwhere look and tended too late to catch up with passing conversations. In the two days since his return he had written no letters, made no telephone calls, reached no decisions. Out of compassion one had had to give him time, and Alec and I continued to do his work surreptitiously without him realizing.

"Nothing," I said.

Rupert nodded vaguely and looked down again, an automaton in his living grief. I'd never loved anyone, I thought, as painfully as that. I think I hoped that I never would.

John, freshly returned also, but from his vacation, glowed with a still-red sunburn and had difficulty in fitting the full lurid details of his sexual adventures into Rupert's brief absences to the washroom. Neither Alec nor I ever believed John's sagas, but at least Alec found them funny, which I didn't. There was an element lurking there of a hatred of women, as if every boasted possession (real or not) was a statement of spite. He didn't actually use the word possession. He said "made" and "screwed" and "had it off with the little cow." I didn't like him much and he thought me a prig: we were polite in the office and never went together to lunch. And it was he alone of all of us who actively looked forward to Gordon's return, he who couldn't disguise his dismay that it was I who was filling the empty shoes instead of himself.

"Of course, if I'd been here . . ." he said at least once a day; and Alec reported that John had been heard telling Gordon's almost-equal along the passage that now he, John, was back, Gordon's work should be transferred from me to him.

"Did you hear him?" I asked, surprised.

"Sure. And he was told in no uncertain terms that it was the Old Man himself who gave you the green light, and there was nothing John could do about it. Proper miffed was our Lothario. Says it's all because you are who you are, and all that."

"Sod him."

"Rather you than me." He laughed gently into his blotter and picked up the telephone to find backers for a sewage and water purification plant in Norfolk.

"Did you know," he said conversationally, busy dialing a number, "that there are so few sewage farms in West Berlin that they pay the East Berliners to get rid of the extra?"

"No, I didn't." I didn't especially want to know, either, but as usual Alec was full of useless information and possessed by the urge to pass it on.

"The East Berliners take the money and dump the stuff out on the open fields. Untreated, mind you."

"Do shut up," I said.

"I saw it," he said. "And smelled it. Absolutely disgusting."

"It was probably fertilizer," I said, "and what were you doing in East Berlin?"

"Calling on Nefertiti."

"She of the one eye?"

"My God, yes, isn't it a shock? Oh . . . hello . . ." He got through to his prospective money-source and for far too long and with a certain relish explained the need for extra facilities to reverse the swamp of effluent which had been killing off the Broads. "No risk involved, of course, with a water authority." He listened. "I'll put you in, then, shall I? Right." He scribbled busily and in due course disconnected. "Dead easy, this one. Ecology and all that. Good emotional stuff."

I shuffled together a bunch of papers of my own that were very far from dead easy and went up to see Val Fisher, who happened to be almost alone in the big office. Henry Shipton, it seemed, was out on one of his frequent walkabouts through the other departments.

"It's a cartoonist," I said. "Can I consult?"

"Pull up a chair." Val nodded and waved hospitably, and I sat beside him, spread out the papers, and explained about the wholly level-headed artist I had spent three hours with two weeks earlier.

"He's been turned down by his own local bank, and so far by three other firms like ourselves," I said. "He's got no realizable assets, no security. He rents an apartment and is buying a car on HP. If we financed him, it would be out of faith."

"Background?" he asked. "Covenant?"

"Pretty solid. Son of a sales manager. Respected at art school as an original talent: I talked to the Principal. His bank manager gave him a clean bill but said that his head office wouldn't grant what he's asking. For the past two years he's worked for a studio making animated commercials. They say he's good at the job; understands it thoroughly. They know he wants to go it alone, they think he's capable and they don't want to lose him."

"How old?"

"Twenty-four."

Val gave me an "Oh ho ho" look, knowing, as I did, that it was the cartoonist's age above all that had invited negative responses from the other banks.

"What's he asking?" Val said, but he too looked as if he were already deciding against.

"A studio, properly equipped. Funds to employ ten copying artists, with the expectation that it will be a year before any films are completed and can expect to make money. Funds for promotion. Funds for himself to live on. These sheets set out the probable figures."

Val made a face over the pages, momentarily rearranging the small neat features, slanting the tidy dark moustache, raising the arched eyebrows towards the black cap of hair.

"Why haven't you already turned him down?" he asked finally.

"Um," I said. "Look at his drawings." I opened another file and spread out the riotously colored progression of pages that established two characters and told a funny story. I watched Val's sophisticated world-weary face as he leafed through them: saw the awakening interest, heard the laugh.

"Exactly," I said.

"Hmph." He leaned back in his chair and gave me an assessing stare. "You're not saying you think we should take him on?"

"It's an unsecured risk, of course. But yes, I am. With a string or two, of course, like a cost accountant to keep tabs on things and a first option to finance future expansion."

"Hm." He pondered for several minutes, looking again at the drawings, which still seemed funny to me even after a fortnight's close acquaintance. "Well, I don't know. It's too like aiming at the moon with a bow and arrow."

"They might watch those films one day on space shuttles," I said mildly, and he gave me a fast amused glance while he squared up the drawings and returned them to their folder.

"Leave these all here, then, will you?" he said. "I'll have a word with Henry over lunch," and I guessed in a swift uncomfortable moment of insight that what they would discuss would be not primarily the cartoonist but the reliability or otherwise of my judgment. If they thought me a fool I'd be back behind John in the promotion line in no time.

At four-thirty, however, when my interoffice telephone rang, it was Val at the other end.

"Come up and collect your papers," he said. "Henry says this decision is to be yours alone. So sink or swim, Tim, it's up to you."

One's first exposure to the Royal Ascot meeting was, according to one's basic outlook, either a matter of surprised delight or of puritanical disapproval. Either the spirits lifted to the sight of emerald grass, massed flowers, bright dresses, fluffy hats and men elegant in gray formality, or one despised the expenditure, the frivolity, the shame of champagne and strawberries while some in the world starved.

I belonged, without doubt, to the hedonists, both by upbringing and inclination. The Royal meeting at Ascot was, as it happened, the one racing event from which my parents had perennially excluded me, children in any case being barred from the Royal Enclosure for three of the four days, and mother more interested on this occasion in socializing than betting. School, she had said firmly every year, must come first: though on other days it hadn't, necessarily. So it was with an extra sense of pleasure that I walked through the gates in my father's resurrected finery and made my way through the smiling throng to the appointed, high-up box.

"Welcome to the charade," Gordon said cheerfully, handing me a bubbling glass, and "Isn't this *fun?*" Judith exclaimed, humming with excitement in yellow silk.

"It's great," I said, and meant it; and Gordon, looking sunburned and healthy, introduced me to the owner of the box.

"Dissdale, this is Tim Ekaterin. Works in the bank. Tim—Dissdale Smith."

We shook hands. His was plump and warm, like his body, like his face. "Delighted," he said. "Got a drink? Good. Met my wife? No? Bettina, darling, say hello to Tim." He put an arm round the thin waist of a girl less than half his age whose clinging white black-dotted dress was cut low and bare at neck and armholes. There was also a wide black hat, beautiful skin and a sweet and practiced smile.

"Hello, Tim," she said. "So glad you could come." Her voice, I thought, was like the rest of her: manufactured, processed, not natural top drawer but a long way from gutter.

The box itself was approximately five yards by three, most of the space being filled by a dining table laid with twelve places for lunch. The far end wall was of windows looking out over the green course, with a glass door opening to steps going down to the viewing balcony. The walls of the box were covered, as if in a house, with pale blue hessian, and a soft blue carpet, pink flowers and pictures lent an air of opulence far greater than the actual expense. Most of the walls of the boxes into which I'd peered on the way along to this one were of builders' universal margarine color, and I wondered fleetingly whether it was Dissdale or Bettina who had the prettying mind.

Henry Shipton and his wife were standing in the doorway to the balcony, alternately facing out and in, like a couple of Januses. Henry across the room lifted his glass to me in a gesture of acknowledgment, and Lorna as ever looked as if faults were being found.

Lorna Shipton, tall, over-assured, and dressed that frilly day in repressive tailored gray, was a woman from whom disdain flowed outward like a tide, a woman who seemed not to know that words could wound and saw no reason not to air each ungenerous thought. I had met her about the same number of times as I'd met Judith Michaels and mostly upon the same occasions, and if I smothered love for the one it was irritation I had to hide for the other. It was, I supposed, inevitable, that of the two it was Lorna Shipton I was placed next to at lunch.

More guests arrived behind me, Dissdale and Bettina greeting them with whoops and kisses and making the sort of indistinct introductions that one instantly forgets. Dissdale decided there would be less crush if everyone sat down and so took his place at the top of the table with Gordon, his back to the windows, at the foot. When each had arranged their guests around them there were two empty places, one next to Gordon, one up Dissdale's end.

Gordon had Lorna Shipton on his right, with me beside her: the space on his left, then Henry, then Judith. The girl on my right spent most of her time leaning forward to speak to her host Dissdale, so that although I grew to know quite well the blue chiffon back of her shoulder, I never actually learned her name.

Laughter, chatter, the study of race cards, the refilling of glasses: Judith with yellow silk roses on her hat and Lorna telling me that my morning coat looked a size too small.

"It was my father's," I said.

"Such a stupid man."

I glanced at her face, but she was merely expressing her thoughts, not positively trying to offend.

"A beautiful day for racing," I said.

"You should be working. Your Uncle Freddie won't like it, you know. I'm certain that when he bailed you out he made it a condition that you and your mother should both stay away from racecourses. And now look at you. It's really too bad. I'll have to tell him, of course."

I wondered how Henry put up with it. Wondered, as one does, why he'd married her. He, however, his ear attuned across the table in a husbandly way, said to her pleasantly, "Freddie knows that Tim is here, my dear. Gordon and I obtained a dispensation, so to speak." He gave me a glimmer of a smile. "The wrath of God has been averted."

"Oh." Lorna Shipton looked disappointed and I noticed Judith trying not to laugh.

Uncle Freddie, ex-vice-chairman, now retired, still owned enough of the bank to make his unseen presence felt, and I knew he was in the habit of telephoning Henry two or three times a week to find out what was going on. Out of interest, one gathered, not from desire to meddle; as certainly, once he had set his terms, he never meddled with mother and me.

Dissdale's last guest arrived at that point with an unseen flourish of trumpets, a man making an entrance as if well aware of newsworthiness. Dissdale leaped to his feet to greet him and pumped him warmly by the hand.

"Calder, this is great. Calder Jackson, everybody."

There were yelps of delight from Dissdale's end and polite smiles round Gordon's. "Calder Jackson," Dissdale said down the table, "you know, the miracle-worker. Brings dying horses back to life. You must have seen him on television."

"Ah yes," Gordon responded. "Of course."

Dissdale beamed and returned to his guest, who was lapping up adulation with a show of modesty.

"Who did he say?" Lorna Shipton asked.

"Calder Jackson," Gordon said.

"Who?"

Gordon shook his head, his ignorance showing. He raised his eyebrows in a question to me, but I fractionally shook my head also. We listened, however, and we learned.

Calder Jackson was a shortish man with a head of hair designed to be noticed. Designed literally, I guessed. He had a lot of dark curls going attractively gray, cut short towards the neck but free and fluffy on top of his head and over his forehead; and he had let his

beard grow in a narrow fringe from in front of his ears
round the line of his jaw, the hairs of this being also
bushy and curly but gray to white. From in front his
weathered face was thus circled with curls: from the
side he looked as if he were wearing a helmet. Or a coal
scuttle, I thought unflatteringly. Once seen, in any
case, never forgotten.

"It's just a gift," he was saying deprecatingly in a
voice that had an edge to it more compelling than loud-
ness: an accent very slightly of the country but of no
particular region; a confidence born of acclaim.

The girl sitting next to me was ecstatic. "How *divine*
to meet you. One has heard so *much* . . . Do tell us, now
do tell us your secret."

Calder Jackson eyed her blandly, his gaze sliding for
a second beyond her to me and then back again. Myself
he quite openly discarded as being of no interest, but to
the girl he obligingly said, "There's no secret, my dear.
None at all. Just good food, good care and a few age-old
herbal remedies. And of course . . . well . . . the laying
on of hands.

"But *how*," asked the girl, "how do you do that to
horses?"

"I just . . . touch them." He smiled disarmingly.
"And then sometimes I feel them quiver, and I know
the healing force is going from me into them."

"Can you do it infallibly?" Henry asked politely, and
I noted with interest that he'd let no implication of
doubt sound in his voice: Henry whose gullibility could
be measured in micrograms, if at all.

Calder Jackson took his seriousness for granted and
slowly shook his head. "If I have the horse in my care
for long enough, it usually happens in the end. But not
always. No, sadly, not always."

"How fascinating," Judith said, and earned another
of those kind bland smiles. Charlatan or not, I thought,
Calder Jackson had the mix just right: an arresting appearance, a modest demeanor, no promise of success.
And for all I knew, he really could do what he said.
Healers were an age-old phenomenon, so why not a
healer of horses?

"Can you heal people too?" I asked in a mirror-image of Henry's tone. No doubts. Just inquiry.

The curly head turned my way with more civility than interest and he patiently answered the question he must have been asked a thousand times before. Answered in a sequence of words he had perhaps used almost as often. "Whatever gift it is that I have is especially for horses. I have no feeling that I can heal humans, and I prefer not to try. I ask people not to ask me, because I don't like to disappoint them."

I nodded my thanks, watched his head turn away and listened to him willingly answering the next question, from Bettina, as if it too had never before been asked. "No, the healing very seldom happens instantaneously. I need to be near the horse for a while. Sometimes for only a few days. Sometimes for a few weeks. One can never tell."

Dissdale basked in the success of having hooked his celebrity and told us all that two of Calder's ex-patients were running that very afternoon. "Isn't that right, Calder?"

The curly head nodded. "Cretonne, in the first race, she used to break blood vessels, and Molyneaux, in the fifth, he came to me with infected wounds. I feel they are my friends now. I feel I know them."

"And shall we back them, Calder?" Dissdale asked roguishly. "Are they going to win?"

The healer smiled forgivingly. "If they're fast enough, Dissdale."

Everyone laughed. Gordon refilled his own guests' glasses. Lorna Shipton said apropos of not much that she had occasionally considered becoming a Christian Scientist and Judith wondered what color the Queen would be wearing. Dissdale's party talked animatedly among themselves, and the door from the corridor tentatively opened.

Any hopes I might have had that Gordon's sixth place was destined for a Bettina-equivalent for my especial benefit were immediately dashed. The lady who appeared and whom Judith greeted with a kiss on the cheek was nearer forty than twenty-five and more solid than lissome. She wore a brownish-pink linen suit and a small white straw hat circled with a brownish-pink ribbon. The suit, I diagnosed, was an old friend: the hat, new in honor of the occasion.

Judith in her turn introduced the newcomer: Penelope Warner—Pen—a good friend of hers and Gordon's. Pen Warner sat where invited, next to Gordon, and made small talk with Henry and Lorna. I half-listened and took in few desultory details like no rings on the fingers, no polish on the nails, no gray in the short brown hair, no artifice in the voice. Worthy, I thought. Well-intentioned; slightly boring. Probably runs the church.

A waitress appeared with an excellent lunch, during which Calder could from time to time be heard extolling the virtues of watercress, for its iron content, and garlic, for the treatment of fever and diarrhea.

"And of course in humans," he was saying, "garlic is literally a life-saver in whooping-cough. You make a poultice and bind it onto the bottom of the feet of the child every night, in a bandage and a sock, and in the morning you'll smell the garlic on the breath of the child, and the cough will abate. Garlic, in fact, cures almost everything. A truly marvelous life-giving plant."

I saw Pen Warner lift her head to listen and I thought that I'd been wrong about the church. I had missed the worldliness of the eyes, the long sad knowledge of human frailty. A magistrate, perhaps? Yes, perhaps.

Judith leaned across the table and said teasingly, "Tim, can't you forget you're a banker even at the races?"

"What?" I said.

"You look at everyone as if you're working out just how much you can lend them without risk."

"I'd lend you my soul," I said.

"For me to pay back with interest?"

"Pay in love and kisses."

Harmless stuff, as frivolous as her hat. Henry, sitting next to her, said in the same vein, "You're second in the line, Tim. I've a first option, eh, Judith? Count on me, dear girl, for the last drop of blood."

She patted his hand affectionately and glowed a little from the deep truth of our idle protestations: and Calder Jackson's voice came through with "Comfrey heals tissues with amazing speed and will cause chronic ulcers to disappear in a matter of days, and of course it mends fractures in half the time considered normal. Comfrey is miraculous."

There was a good deal of speculation after that all round the table about a horse called Sandcastle that had won the 2,000 Guineas six weeks earlier and was hot favorite for the King Edward VII Stakes, the top Ascot race for three-year-old colts, due to be run that afternoon.

Dissdale had actually seen the Guineas at Newmarket and was enthusiastic. "Daisy-cutter action. Positively eats up the ground." He sprayed his opinions good-naturedly to the furthest ear. "Big rangy colt, full of courage."

"Beaten in the Derby, though," Henry said, judiciously responding.

"Well, yes," Dissdale allowed. "But fourth, you know. Not a total disgrace, would you say?"

"He was good as a two-year-old," Henry said, nodding.

"Glory, yes," said Dissdale fervently. "And you can't fault his breeding. By Castle out of an Ampersand mare. You can't get much better than that."

Several heads nodded respectfully in ignorance.

"He's my banker," Dissdale said and then spread his arms wide and half-laughed. "OK, we've got a roomful of bankers. But Sandcastle is where I'm putting my money today. Doubling him with my bets in every other race. Trebles. Accumulators. The lot. You all listen to your Uncle Dissdale. Sandcastle is the soundest banker at Ascot." His voice positively shook with evangelical belief. "He simply can't be beaten."

"Betting is out for you, Tim," Lorna Shipton said severely in my ear.

"I'm not my mother," I said mildly.

"Heredity," Lorna said darkly. "And your father drank."

I smothered a bursting laugh and ate my strawberries in good humor. Whatever I'd inherited from my parents it wasn't an addiction to their more expensive pleasures: rather a firm intention never again to lose my record collection to the bailiffs. Those stolid men had taken even the rocking horse on which at the age of six I'd ridden my fantasy Grand Nationals. They'd taken my books, my skis and my camera. Mother had fluttered around in tears saying those things were mine, not hers, and they should leave them, and the men had gone on marching out with all our stuff as if they were deaf. About her own disappearing treasures she had been distraught, her distress and grief hopelessly mixed with guilt.

I had been old enough at twenty-four to shrug off our actual losses and more or less replace them (except for the rocking horse) but the fury of that day had affected my whole life since: and I had been silent when it happened, white and dumb with rage.

Lorna Shipton removed her disapproval from me long enough to tell Henry not to have cream and sugar on his strawberries or she would have no sympathy if he put on weight, had a heart attack, or developed pimples. Henry looked resignedly at the forbidden delights, which he wouldn't have eaten anyway. God preserve me, I thought, from marrying a Lorna Shipton.

By the coffee-brandy-cigar stage the tranquil seating pattern had broken up into people dashing out to back their hopes in the first race, and I, not much of a gambler whatever Mrs. Shipton might think, had wandered out onto the balcony to watch the Queen's procession of sleek horses, open carriages, gold, glitter and fluttering feathers trotting like a fairy tale up the green course.

"Isn't it *splendid*," said Judith's voice at my shoulder, and I glanced at the characterful face and met the straight smiling eyes. Damn it to hell, I thought, I'd like to live with Gordon's wife.

"Gordon's gone to bet," she said. "So I thought I'd take the opportunity . . . He's appalled at what happened . . . and we're really grateful to you, you know, for what you did that dreadful day."

I shook my head. "I did nothing, believe me."

"Well, that's half the point. You *said* nothing. In the bank, I mean. Henry says there hasn't been a whisper."

"But . . . I wouldn't."

"A lot of people *would,*" she said. "Suppose you had been that Alec."

I smiled involuntarily. "Alec isn't unkind. He wouldn't have told."

"Gordon says he's as discreet as a town crier."

"Do you want to go down and see the horses?" I asked.

"Yes. It's lovely up here, but too far from life."

We went down to the paddock, saw the horses walk at close quarters round the ring and watched the jockeys mount ready to ride out onto the course. Judith smelled nice. Stop it, I told myself. Stop it.

"That horse over there," I said, pointing, "is the one Calder Jackson said he cured. Cretonne. The jockey in bright pink."

"Are you going to back it?" she asked.

"If you like."

She nodded the yellow silk roses and we lined up in good humor to make the wager. All around us in gray toppers and frothy dresses the Ascot crowd swirled, a feast to the eye in the sunshine, a ritual in make-believe, a suppression of gritty truth. My father's whole life had been a pursuit of the spirit I saw in those Royal Ascot faces; the pursuit and entrapment of happiness.

"What are you thinking?" Judith said. "So solemnly."

"That lotus-eaters do no harm. Let terrorists eat lotus."

"As a steady diet," she said, "it would be sickening."

"On a day like this one could fall in love."

"Yes, one could." She was reading her race card over-intently. "But should one?"

After a pause I said, "No, I don't think so."

"Nor do I." She looked up with seriousness and understanding and with a smile in her mind. "I've known you six years."

"I haven't been faithful," I said.

She laughed and the moment passed, but the declaration had quite plainly been made and in a way accepted. She showed no awkwardness in my continued presence but rather an increase of warmth, and in mutual contentment we agreed to stay in the paddock for the first short race rather than climb all the way up and find it was over by the time we'd reached the box.

The backs of the jockeys disappeared down the course as they cantered to the start, and I said, as a way of conversation, "Who is Dissdale Smith?"

"Oh." She looked amused. "He's in the motor trade. He loves to make a splash, as no doubt you saw, but I don't think he's doing as well as he pretends. Anyway, he told Gordon he was looking for someone to share the expense of this box here and asked if Gordon would be interested in buying half the box for today. He's sold halves for the other days as well. I don't think he's supposed to, actually, so better say nothing to anyone else."

"No."

"Bettina's his third wife," she said. "She's a model."

"Very pretty."

"And not as dumb as she looks."

I heard the dryness in her voice and acknowledged that I had myself sounded condescending.

"Mind you," Judith said forgivingly, "his second wife was the most gorgeous thing on earth, but without two thoughts to rub together. Even Dissdale got tired of the total vacancy behind the sensational violet eyes. It's all very well to get a buzz when all men light up on meeting your wife, but it rather kicks the stilts away when the same men diagnose total dimness within five minutes and start pitying you instead."

"I can see that. What became of her?"

"Dissdale introduced her to a boy who'd inherited millions and had an IQ on a par with hers. The last I heard they were in a fog of bliss."

From where we stood we couldn't see much of the race, only a head-on view of the horses as they came up to the winning post. In no way did I mind that, and when one of the leaders proved to carry bright pink Judith caught hold of my arm and shook it.

"That's Cretonne, isn't it?" She listened to the announcement of the winner's number. "Do you realize, Tim, that we've damned well won?" She was laughing with pleasure, her face full of sunshine and wonder.

"Bully for Calder Jackson."

"You don't trust him," she said. "I could see it in all your faces, yours and Henry's and Gordon's. You all have the same way of peering into people's souls: you too, though you're so young. You were all being incredibly polite so that he shouldn't see your reservations."

I smiled. "That sounds disgusting."

"I've been married to Gordon for nine years," she said.

There was again a sudden moment of stillness in which we looked at each other in wordless question and answer. Then she shook her head slightly, and after a pause I nodded acquiescence: and I thought that with a woman so straightforwardly intelligent I could have been content forever.

"Do we collect our winnings now or later?" she asked.

"Now if we wait awhile."

Waiting together for the jockeys to weigh in and the all-clear to be given for the payout seemed as little hardship for her as for me. We talked about nothing much and the time passed in a flash; and eventually we made our way back to the box to find that everyone there too had backed Cretonne and was high with the same success. Calder Jackson beamed and looked modest, and Dissdale expansively opened more bottles of excellent Krug, champagne of kings.

Escorting one's host's wife to the paddock was not merely acceptable but an expected civility, so that it was with a benign eye that Gordon greeted our return. I was both glad and sorry, looking at his unsuspecting friendliness, that he had nothing to worry about. The jewel in his house would stay there and be his alone. Unattached bachelors could lump it.

The whole party, by now markedly carefree, crowded the box's balcony for the big race. Dissdale said he had staked his all on his banker, Sandcastle; and although he said it with a laugh I saw the tremor in his hands, which fidgeted with the race glasses. He's in too deep, I thought. A bad way to bet.

Most of the others, fired by Dissdale's certainty, happily clutched tickets doubling Sandcastle every which way. Even Lorna Shipton, with a pink glow on each bony cheekbone, confessed to Henry that just for once, as it was a special day, she had staked five pounds in forecasts.

"And you, Tim?" Henry teased. "Your shirt?"

Lorna looked confused. I smiled. "Buttons and all," I said cheerfully.

"No, but . . ." Lorna said.

"Yes, but," I said, "I've dozens more shirts at home."

Henry laughed and steered Lorna gently away, and I found myself standing next to Calder Jackson.

"Do you gamble?" I asked, for something to say.

"Only on certainties." He smiled blandly in the way that scarcely warmed his eyes. "Though on certainties it's hardly a gamble."

"And is Sandcastle a certainty?"

He shook his curly head. "A probability. No racing bet's a certainty. The horse might feel ill. Might be kicked at the start."

I glanced across at Dissdale, who was faintly sweating, and hoped for his sake that the horse would feel well and come sweetly out of the stalls.

"Can you tell if a horse is sick just by looking at him?" I inquired. "I mean, if you just watched him walk round the parade ring, could you tell?"

Calder answered in the way that revealed it was again an often-asked question. "Of course sometimes you can see at once, but mostly a horse as ill as that wouldn't have been brought to the races. I prefer to look at a horse closely. To examine for instance the color inside the eyelid and inside the nostril. In a sick horse, what should be a healthy pink may be pallid." He stopped with apparent finality, as if that were the appointed end of that answer, but after a few seconds, during which the whole huge crowd watched Sandcastle stretch out in the sun in the canter to the post, he said almost with awe, "That's a superb horse. Superb." It sounded to me like his first spontaneous remark of the day and it vibrated with genuine enthusiasm.

"He looks great," I agreed.

Calder Jackson smiled as if with indulgence at the shallowness of my judgment compared with the weight of his inside knowledge. "He should have won the Derby," he said. "He got shut in on the rails, couldn't get out in time."

My place at the great man's side was taken by Bettina, who threaded her arm through his and said, "Dear Calder, come down to the front, you can see better than here at the back." She gave me a photogenic little smile and pulled her captive after her down the steps.

In a buzz that rose to a roar the runners covered their mile-and-a-half journey; longer than the 2,000 Guineas, the same length as the Derby. Sandcastle, in scarlet and white, was making no show at all to universal groans and lay only fifth as the field swept round the last bend, and Dissdale looked as if he might have a heart attack.

Alas for my shirt, I thought. Alas for Lorna's forecasts. Bang goes the banker that can't lose.

Dissdale, unable to watch, collapsed weakly onto one of the small chairs that dotted the balcony, and in the next-door boxes people were standing on top of theirs and jumping up and down and screaming.

"Sandcastle making his move . . ." the commentator's voice warbled over the loudspeakers, but the yells of the crowd drowned the rest.

The scarlet-and-white colors had moved to the outside. The daisy-cutter action was there for the world to see. The superb horse, the big rangy colt full of courage was eating up his ground.

Our box in the grandstand was almost a furlong down the course from the winning post, and when he reached us Sandcastle still had three horses ahead. He was flying, though, like a streak, and I found the sight of this fluid valor, this all-out striving, most immensely moving and exciting. I grabbed Dissdale by his despairing shoulder and hauled him forcefully to his feet.

"Look," I shouted in his ear. "Watch. Your banker's going to win. He's a marvel. He's a dream."

He turned with a gaping mouth to stare in the direc-

tion of the winning post and he saw . . . he saw Sandcastle among the tumult going like a javelin, free now
of all the others, aiming straight for the prize.

"He's won," Dissdale's mouth said slackly, though
amid the noise I could hardly hear him. "He's bloody
won."

I helped him up the steps into the box. His skin was
gray and damp and he was stumbling.

"Sit down," I said, pulling out the first chair I came
to, but he shook his head weakly and made his shaky
way to his own place at the head of the table. He almost
fell into it, heavily, and stretched out a trembling hand
to his champagne.

"My God," he said, "I'll never do that again. Never
on God's earth."

"Do what?"

He gave me a flickering glance over his glass and
said, "All on one throw."

All. He'd said it before. "All on the banker . . ." He
surely couldn't, I thought, have meant literally *all;* but
not much else could have produced such physical symptoms.

Everyone else piled back into the room with balloon-
ing jollity. Everyone without exception had backed
Sandcastle, thanks to Dissdale. Even Calder Jackson,
when pressed by Bettina, admitted to "a small something on the Tote. I don't usually, but just this once."
And if he'd lost, I thought, he wouldn't have confessed.

Dissdale, from near fainting, climbed rapidly to a
pulse-throbbing high, the color coming back to his
plump cheeks in a hectic red. No one seemed to have noticed his near-collapse, certainly not his wife, who
flirted prettily with the healer and got less than her due
response. More wine easily made its way down every
throat, and there was no doubt that for the now com-
mingled party the whole day was a riotous success.

In a while Henry offered to take Judith to the paddock. Gordon to my relief invited Lorna, which left me
with the mystery lady, Pen Warner, with whom I'd so
far exchanged only the thrilling words "How do you do."

"Would you like to go down?" I asked.

"Yes, indeed. But you don't need to stay with me if it's too much bother."

"Are you so insecure?"

There was a quick widening of the eyes and a visible mental shift. "You're damned rude," she said. "And Judith said you were nice."

I let her go past me out onto the landing and smiled as she went. "I should like to stay with you," I said, "if it's not too much bother."

She gave me a dry look, but as we more or less had to walk in single file along the narrow passageway owing to people going in the opposite direction she said little more until we had negotiated the elevators, the escalators and the pedestrian tunnel and had emerged into the daylight of the paddock.

It was her first time at Ascot, she said. Her first time, in fact, at the races.

"What do you think of it?"

"Very beautiful. Very brave. Quite mad."

"Does sanity lie in ugliness and cowardice?" I asked.

"Life does, pretty often," she said. "Haven't you noticed?"

"And some aren't happy unless they're desperate."

She quietly laughed. "Tragedy inspires, so they say."

"They can stick it," I said. "I'd rather lie in the sun."

We stood on the raised tiers of steps to watch the horses walk round the ring, and she told me that she lived along the road from Judith in another house fronting the common. "I've lived there all my life, long before Judith came. We met casually, as one does, in the local shops, and just walked home together one day several years ago. Been friends ever since."

"Lucky," I said.

"Yes."

"Do you live alone?" I asked conversationally.

Her eyes slid my way with inner amusement. "Yes, I do. Do you?"

I nodded.

"I prefer it," she said.

"So do I."

Her skin was clear and still girlish, the thickened figure alone giving an impression of years passing. That and the look in the eyes, the "I've seen the lot" sadness.

"Are you a magistrate?" I asked.

She looked startled. "No, I'm not. What an odd thing to ask."

I made an apologetic gesture. "You just look as if you might be."

She shook her head. "Wouldn't have time, even if I had the urge."

"But you do do good in the world."

She was puzzled. "What makes you say so?"

"I don't know. The way you look." I smiled to take away any seriousness and said, "Which horse do you like? Shall we choose one and bet?"

"What about Burnt Marshmallow?"

She liked the name, she said, so we stopped briefly at a Tote window and invested some of the winnings from Cretonne and Sandcastle.

During our slow traverse of the paddock crowds on our way back to the box we came towards Calder Jackson, who was surrounded by respectful listeners and didn't see us.

"Garlic is as good as penicillin," he was saying. "If you scatter grated garlic onto a septic wound it will kill all the bacteria . . ."

We slowed a little to hear.

". . . and comfrey is miraculous," Calder said. "It knits bones and cures intractable skin ulcers in half the time you'd expect."

"He said all that upstairs," I said.

Pen Warner nodded, faintly smiling. "Good sound herbal medicine," she said. "You can't fault him. Comfrey contains allantoin, a well-known cell proliferant."

"Does it? I mean . . . do you know about it?"

"Mm." We walked on, but she said nothing more until we were high up again in the passageway to the box. "I don't know whether you'd think I do good in the world . . . but basically I dole out pills."

"Er . . . ?" I said.

She smiled. "I'm a lady in a white coat. A pharmacist."

I suppose I was in a way disappointed, and she sensed it.

"Well," she sighed, "we can't all be glamorous. I told you life was ugly and frightening, and from my point of view that's often what it is for my customers. I see fear every day . . . and I know its face."

"Pen," I said. "Forgive my frivolity. I'm duly chastened."

We reached the box to find Judith alone there, Henry having loitered to place a bet.

"I told Tim I'm a pharmacist," Pen said. "He thinks it's boring."

I got no further than the first words of protestation when Judith interrupted.

"She's not just 'a' pharmacist," she said. "She owns her own place. Half the medics in London recommend her. You're talking to a walking gold mine with a heart like a wet sponge."

She put her arm around Pen's waist and the two of them together looked at me, their eyes shining with what perhaps looked like liking, but also with the mischievous feminine superiority of being five or six years older.

"Judith!" I said compulsively. "I . . . I . . ." I stopped. "Oh *damn* it," I said. "Have some Krug."

Dissdale's friends returned giggling to disrupt the incautious minute and shortly Gordon, Henry and Lorna crowded in. The whole party pressed out onto the balcony to watch the race, and because it was a time out of reality Burnt Marshmallow romped home by three lengths.

The rest of the afternoon slid fast away. Henry at some point found himself alone out on the balcony beside me while inside the box the table was being spread with a tea that was beyond my stretched stomach entirely and a temptation from which the ever-hungry Henry had bodily removed himself.

"How's your cartoonist?" he said genially. "Are we staking him, or are we not?"

"You're sure . . . I have to decide . . . all alone?"

"I said so. Yes."

"Well . . . I got him to bring some more drawings to the bank. And his paints."

"His *paints?*"

"Yes. I thought if I could see him at work, I'd know . . ." I shrugged. "Anyway, I took him into the private interview room and asked him to paint the outline of a cartoon film while I watched; and he did it, there and then, in acrylics. Twenty-five outline sketches in bright color, all within an hour. Same characters, different story, terrifically funny. That was on Monday. I've been . . . well . . . dreaming about those cartoons. It sounds absurd. Maybe they're too much on my mind."

"But you've decided?"

After a pause I said, "Yes."

"And?"

With a sense of burning bridges I said, "To go ahead."

"All right." Henry seemed unalarmed. "Keep me informed."

"Yes, of course."

He nodded and smoothly changed the subject. "Lorna and I have won quite a bit today. How about you?"

"Enough to give Uncle Freddie fits about the effect on my unstable personality."

Henry laughed aloud. "Your Uncle Freddie," he said, "knows you better than you may think."

At the end of that splendid afternoon the whole party descended together to ground level and made its way to the exit; to the gate that opened onto the main road, and across that to the car park and to the covered walk that led to the station.

Calder just ahead of me walked in front, the helmet curls bent kindly over Bettina, the strong voice thanking her and Dissdale for "a most enjoyable time." Dissdale himself, not only fully recovered but incoherent with joy as most of his doubles, trebles and accumulators had come up, patted Caldor plumply on the shoulder and invited him over to "my place" for the weekend.

Henry and Gordon, undoubtedly the most sober of the party, were fiddling in their pockets for car keys and throwing their race cards into wastebins. Judith and

Pen were talking to each other and Lorna was graciously unbending to Dissdale's friends. It seemed to be only I, with unoccupied eyes, who saw at all what was to happen.

We were out on the pavement, still in a group, half-waiting for a chance to cross the road, soon to break up and scatter. All talking, laughing, busy; except me.

A boy stood there on the pavement, watchful and still. I noticed first the fixed, burning intent in the dark eyes, and quickly after that the jeans and faded shirt, which contrasted sharply with our Ascot clothes, and then finally with incredulity the knife in his hand.

I had almost to guess at whom he was staring with such deadly purpose, and no time even to shout a warning. He moved across the pavement with stunning speed, the stab already on its upward travel.

I jumped almost without thinking; certainly without assessing consequences or chances. Most unbankerlike behavior.

The steel was almost in Calder's stomach when I deflected it. I hit the boy's arm with my body in a sort of flying tackle and in a flashing view saw the weave of Calder's trousers, the polish on his shoes, the litter on the pavement. The boy fell beneath me and I thought in horror that somewhere between our bodies he still held that wicked blade.

He writhed under me, all muscle and fury, and tried to heave me off. He was lying on his back, his face just under mine, his eyes like slits and his teeth showing between drawn-back lips. I had an impression of dark eyebrows and white skin and I could hear the breath hissing between his teeth in a tempest of effort.

Both of his hands were under my chest and I could feel him trying to get space enough to up-end the knife. I pressed down onto him solidly with all my weight and in my mind I was saying "Don't do it, don't do it, you bloody fool"; and I was saying it *for his sake,* which seemed crazy to me at the time and even crazier in retrospect. He was trying to do me great harm and all I thought about was the trouble he'd be in if he succeeded.

We were both panting but I was taller and stronger

and I could have held him there for a good while longer but for the two policemen who had been out on the road directing traffic. They had seen the mêlée; seen as they supposed a man in morning dress attacking a pedestrian, seen us struggling on the ground. In any case the first I knew of their presence was the feel of viselike hands fastening onto my arms and pulling me backwards.

I resisted with all my might. I didn't know they were policemen. I had eyes only for the boy: his eyes, his hands, his knife.

With peremptory strength they hauled me off, one of them anchoring my upper arms to my sides by encircling me from behind. I kicked furiously backwards and turned my head, and only then realized that the new assailants wore navy blue.

The boy comprehended the situation in a flash. He rolled over onto his feet, crouched for a split second like an athlete at the blocks and without lifting his head above waist-height slithered through the flow of the crowds still pouring out of the gates and disappeared out of sight inside the racecourse. Through there they would never find him. Through there he would escape to the cheaper rings and simply walk out of the lower gate.

I stopped struggling but the policemen didn't let go. They had no thought of chasing the boy. They were incongruously calling me "sir" while treating me with contempt, which if I'd been calm enough for reflection I would have considered fairly normal.

"For God's sake," I said finally to one of them. "What do you think that knife's doing on the pavement?"

They looked down to where it lay; to where it had fallen when the boy ran. Eight inches of sharp steel kitchen knife with a black handle.

"He was trying to stab Calder Jackson," I said. "All I did was stop him. Why do you think he's gone?"

By this time Henry, Gordon, Laura, Judith and Pen were standing round in an anxious circle continually assuring the law that never in a million years would their friend attack anyone except out of direst need, and Calder was looking dazed and fingering a slit in the waistband of his trousers.

The farce slowly resolved itself into duller bureau-
cratic order. The policemen relinquished their hold and
I brushed the dirt off the knees of my father's suit and
straightened my tangled tie. Someone picked up my
tumbled top hat and gave it to me. I grinned at Judith.
It all seemed such a ridiculous mixture of death and
pathos.

The aftermath took half of the evening and was boring in the extreme: police station, hard chairs, polysty-
rene cups of coffee.

No, I'd never seen the boy before.

Yes, I was sure the boy had been aiming at Calder
specifically.

Yes, I was sure he was only a boy. About sixteen,
probably.

Yes, I would know him again. Yes, I would help with
an Identikit picture.

No. My fingerprints were positively not on the knife.
The boy had held on to it until he ran.

Yes, of course they could take my prints, in case.

Calder, wholly mystified, repeated over and over that
he had no idea who could want to kill him. He seemed
scandalized, indeed, at the very idea. The police persisted: most people knew their murderers, they said,
particularly when as seemed possible in this case the
prospective killer had been purposefully waiting for his
victim. According to Mr. Ekaterin the boy had known
Calder. That was quite possible, Calder said, because of
his television appearances, but Calder had *not* known
him.

Among some of the police there was a muted quality,
among others a sort of defiant aggression, but it was
only Calder who rather acidly pointed out that if they
hadn't done such a good job of hauling me off, they
would now have the boy in custody and wouldn't need
to be looking for him.

"You could have asked first," Calder said, but even I
shook my head.

If I had indeed been the aggressor I could have killed
the boy while the police were asking the onlookers just
who was fighting whom. Act first, ask questions after

was a policy full of danger, but getting it the wrong way round could be worse.

Eventually we both left the building, Calder on the way out trying his best with unrehearsed words. "Er . . . Tim . . . Thanks are in order . . . If it hadn't been for you . . . I don't know what to say."

"Say nothing," I said. "I did it without thinking. Glad you're OK."

I had taken it for granted that everyone else would be long gone, but Dissdale and Bettina had waited for Calder, and Gordon, Judith and Pen for me, all of them standing in a group by some cars and talking to three or four strangers.

"We know you and Calder both came by train," Gordon said, walking towards us, "but we decided we'd drive you home."

"You're extraordinarily kind," I said.

"My dear Dissdale . . ." Calder said, seeming still at a loss for words. "So grateful, really."

They made a fuss of him; the endangered one, the lion delivered. The strangers round the cars turned out to be gentlemen of the press, to whom Calder Jackson was always news, alive or dead. To my horror they announced themselves, producing notebooks and a camera, and wrote down everything anyone said, except they got nothing from me because all I wanted to do was shut them up.

As well try to stop an avalanche with an outstretched palm. Dissdale and Bettina and Gordon and Judith and Pen did a diabolical job, which was why for a short time afterwards I suffered from public notoriety as the man who had saved Calder Jackson's life.

No one seemed to speculate about his assailant setting out for a second try.

I looked at my photograph in the papers and wondered if the boy would see it, and know my name.

October

Gordon was back at work with his faintly trembling left hand usually out of sight and unnoticeable.

During periods of activity, as on the day at Ascot, he seemed to forget to camouflage, but at other times he had taken to sitting forwards in a hunched way over his desk with his hand anchored down between his thighs. I thought it a pity. I thought the tremor so slight that none of the others would have remarked on it, either aloud or to themselves, but to Gordon it was clearly a burden.

Not that it seemed to have affected his work. He had come back in July with determination, thanked me briskly in the presence of the others for my stopgapping and taken all major decisions off my desk and back to his.

John asked him, also in the hearing of Alec, Rupert and myself, to make it clear to us that it was he, John, who was the official next-in-line to Gordon, if the need should occur again. He pointed out that he was older and had worked much longer in the bank than I had. Tim, he said, shouldn't be jumping the line.

Gordon eyed him blandly and said that if the need
arose no doubt the chairman would take every factor
into consideration. John made bitter and audible remarks under his breath about favoritism and unfair
privilege, and Alec told him ironically to find a merchant bank where there *wasn't* a nephew or some such
on the force.

"Be your age," he said. "Of *course* they want the next
generation to join the family business. Why shouldn't
they? It's natural." But John was unplacated, and
didn't see that his acid grudge against me was wasting
a lot of his time. I seemed to be continually in his
thoughts. He gave me truly vicious looks across the
room and took every opportunity to sneer and deni-
grate. Messages never got passed on, and clients were
given the impression that I was incompetent and only
employed out of family charity. Occasionally on the
telephone people refused to do business with me, saying
they wanted John, and once a caller said straight out,
"Are you that playboy they're shoving ahead over better men's heads?"

John's gripe was basically understandable; in his
place I'd have been cynical myself. Gordon did nothing
to curb the escalating hate campaign and Alec found it
funny. I thought long and hard about what to do and decided simply to work harder. I'd see it was very difficult
for John to make his allegations stick.

His aggression showed in his body, which was round-
edly muscular and looked the wrong shape for a city
suit. Of moderate height, he wore his wiry brown hair
very short so that it bristled above his collar, and his
voice was loud, as if he thought volume equaled authority: and so it might have done in schoolroom or on bar-
racks square, instead of on a civilized patch of carpet.

He had come into banking via business school with
high ambitions and good persuasive skills. I sometimes
thought he would have made an excellent export sales-
man, but that wasn't the life he wanted. Alec said that
John got his kicks from saying "I am a merchant
banker" to pretty girls and preening himself in their
admiration.

Alec was a wicked fellow, really, and a shooter of perceptive arrows.

There came a day in October when three whirlwind things happened more or less simultaneously. The cartoonist telephoned; *What's Going On Where It Shouldn't* landed with a thud throughout the City; and Uncle Freddie descended on Ekaterin's for a tour of inspection.

To begin with, the three events were unconnected, but by the end of the day, entwined.

I heard the cartoonist's rapid opening remarks with a sinking heart. "I've engaged three extra animators and I need five more," he said. "Ten isn't nearly enough. I've worked out the amount of increased loan needed to pay them all."

"Wait," I said.

He went right on. "I also need more space, of course, but luckily that's no problem, as there's an empty warehouse next to this place. I've signed a lease for it and told them you'll be advancing the money, and of course more furniture, more materials . . ."

"Stop," I said distractedly, "you *can't.*"

"What? I can't what?" He sounded, of all things, bewildered.

"You can't just keep on borrowing. You've a limit. You can't go beyond it. Look, for heaven's sake come over here quickly and we'll see what can be undone."

"But you said," his voice said plaintively, "that you'd want to finance later expansion. That's what I'm doing. Expanding."

I thought wildly that I'd be licking stamps for a living as soon as Henry heard. Dear *God* . . .

"Listen," the cartoonist was saying, "we all worked like hell and finished one whole film. Twelve minutes long, dubbed with music and sound effects, everything, titles, the lot. And we did some rough cuts of three others, no music, no frills, but enough . . . and I've sold them."

"You've what?"

"Sold them." He laughed with excitement. "It's solid, I promise you. That agent you sent me to, he's fixed the

sale and the contract. All I have to do is sign. It's a
major firm that's handling them, and I get a big perpetual royalty. Worldwide distribution, that's what
they're talking about, and the BBC are taking them.
But we've got to make twenty films in a year from now,
not seven like I meant. Twenty! And if the public like
them, that's just the start. Oh, heck, I can't believe it.
But to do twenty in the time I need a lot more money. Is
it all right? I mean . . . I was so sure . . ."

"Yes," I said weakly. "It's all right. Bring the contract when you've signed it, and new figures, and we'll
work things out."

"Thanks," he said. "Thanks, Tim Ekaterin, God
bless your darling bank."

I put the receiver down feebly and ran a hand over my
head and down the back of my neck.

"Trouble?" Gordon asked, watching.

"Well no, not exactly . . ." A laugh like the cartoonist's rose in my throat. "I backed a winner. I think perhaps I backed a bloody geyser." The laugh broke out
aloud. "Did you ever do that?"

"Ah yes," Gordon nodded, "of course."

I told him about the cartoonist and showed him the
original set of drawings, which were still stowed in my
desk: and when he looked through them, he laughed.

"Wasn't that application on my desk," he said,
wrinkling his forehead in an effort to remember, "just
before . . . er . . . I was away?"

I thought back. "Yes, it probably was."

He nodded. "I'd decided to turn it down."

"Had you?"

"Mm. Isn't he too young, or something?"

"That sort of talent strikes at birth."

He gave me a brief assessing look and handed the
drawings back. "Well," he said. "Good luck to him."

The news that Uncle Freddie had been spotted in the
building rippled through every department and stif-
fened a good many slouching backbones. Uncle Freddie
was given to growling out devastatingly accurate judg-
ments of people in their hearing, and it was not only I

who'd found the bank more peaceful (if perhaps also more complacent) when he retired.

He was known as "Mr. Fred" as opposed to "Mr. Mark" (grandfather) and "Mr. Paul," the founder. No one ever called me "Mr. Tim"; sign of the changing times. If true to form Uncle Freddie would spend the morning in Investment Management, where he himself had worked all his office life, and after lunch in the boardroom would put at least his head into Corporate Finance, to be civil, and end with a march through Banking. On the way, by some telepathic process of his own, he would learn what moved in the bank's collective mind; sniff, as he had put it, the prevailing scent on the wind.

He had already arrived when the copies of *What's Going On* hit the fan.

Alec as usual slipped out to the local paper shop at about the time they were delivered there and returned with the six copies the bank officially sanctioned. No one in the City could afford not to know about What was Going On on their own doorstep.

Alec shunted around delivering one copy to each floor and keeping ours to himself to read first, a perk he said he deserved.

"Your uncle," he reported on his return, "is beating the shit out of poor Ted Lorrimer in Investments for failing to sell Winkler Consolidated when even a squint-eyed baboon could see it was overstretched in its Central American operation, and a neck sticking out asking for the comprehensive chop."

Gordon chuckled mildly at the verbatim reporting, and Alec sat at his desk and opened the paper. Normal office life continued for perhaps five more minutes before Alec shot to his feet as if he'd been stung.

"Jes-us *Christ,*" he said.

"What is it?"

"Our leaker is at it again."

"What?" Gordon said.

"You'd better read it." He took the paper across to Gordon, whose preliminary face of foreboding turned slowly to anger.

"It's disgraceful," Gordon said. He made as if to pass the paper to me, but John, on his feet, as good as snatched it out of his hand.

"I should come first," he said forcefully, and took the paper over to his own desk, sitting down methodically and spreading the paper open on the flat surface to read. Gordon watched him impassively and I said nothing to provoke. When John at his leisure had finished, showing little reaction but a tightened mouth, it was Rupert he gave the paper to, and Rupert, who read it with small gasps and widening eyes, who brought it eventually to me.

"It's bad," Gordon said.

"So I gather." I lolled back in my chair and lifted the offending column to eye level. Under a heading of *"Dinky Dirty Doings"* it said:

It is perhaps not well known to readers that in many a merchant bank two thirds of the annual profits come from interest on loans. Investment and Trust management and Corporate Finance departments are the public faces and glamour machines of these very private banks. Their investments (of other people's money) in the stock market and their entrepreneurial role in mergers and takeovers earn the spotlight year by year in the City Pages.

Below stairs, so to speak, lies the tail that wags the dog, the secretive Banking department, which quietly lends from its own deep coffers and rakes in vast profits in the shape of interest at rates they can set to suit themselves.

These rates are not necessarily high.

Who in Paul Ekaterin Ltd. has been effectively lending to himself small fortunes from these coffers at FIVE percent? Who in Paul Ekaterin Ltd. has set up private companies, which are NOT carrying on the business for which the money has ostensibly been loaned? Who has not declared that these companies are his?

The man-in-the-street (poor slob) would be delighted to get unlimited cash from Paul Ekaterin Ltd. at five percent so that he could invest it in something else for more.

Don't Bankers have a fun time?

I looked up from the damaging page and across at Alec, and he was, predictably, grinning.

"I wonder who's had his hand in the cookie jar," he said.

"And who caught it there?" I asked.

"Wow, yes."

Gordon said bleakly, "This is very serious."

"If you believe it," I said.

"But this paper . . ." he began.

"Yeah," I interrupted. "It had a dig at us before, remember? Way back in May. Remember the flap everyone got into?"

"I was at home . . . with the flu."

"Oh, yes. Well, the furor went on here for ages and no one came up with any answers. This column today is just as unspecific. So . . . supposing all it's designed to do is stir up trouble for the bank? Who's got it in for us? To what raving nut have we for instance refused a loan?"

Alec was regarding me with exaggerated wonder. "Here we have Sherlock Holmes to the rescue," he said admiringly. "Now we can all go out to lunch."

Gordon, however, said thoughtfully, "It's perfectly possible, though, to set up a company and lend it money. All it would take would be paperwork. I could do it myself. So could anyone here, I suppose, up to his authorized ceiling, if he thought he could get away with it."

John nodded. "It's ridiculous of Tim and Alec to make a joke of this," he said importantly. "The very reputation of the bank is at stake."

Gordon frowned, stood up, took the paper off my desk, and went along to see his almost-equal in the room facing St. Paul's. Spreading consternation, I thought; bringing out cold sweats from palpitating banking hearts.

I ran a mental eye over everyone in the whole department who could possibly have had enough power along with the opportunity, from Val Fisher all the way down to myself; and there were twelve, perhaps, who could theoretically have done it.

But . . . not Rupert, with his sad mind still grieving,

because he would not have had the appetite or energy
for fraud.

Not Alec, surely; because I liked him.

Not John: too self-regarding.

Not Val, not Gordon, unthinkable. Not myself.

That left the people along in the other pasture, and I
didn't know them well enough to judge. Maybe one of
them did believe that a strong fiddle on the side was
worth the ruin of discovery, but all of us were already
generously paid, perhaps for the very reason that temp-
tations would be more likely to be resisted if we weren't
scratching around for the money for the gas.

Gordon didn't return. The morning limped down to
lunchtime, when John bustled off announcing he was
seeing a client, and Alec encouraged Rupert to go out
with him for a pie and pint. I'd taken to working
through lunch because of the quietness, and I was still
there alone at two o'clock when Peter, Henry's assistant, came and asked me to go up to the top floor, because I was wanted.

Uncle Freddie, I thought. Uncle Freddie's read the
rag and will be exploding like a warhead. In some way
he'll make it out to be my fault. With a gusty sigh I left
my desk and took the elevator to face the old warrior,
with whom I had never in my life felt easy.

He was waiting in the top-floor hallway, talking to
Henry. Both of them, at six foot three, overtopped me by
three inches. Life would never have been as ominous, I
thought, if Uncle Freddie had been small.

"Tim," Henry said when he saw me, "go along to the
small conference room, will you?"

I nodded and made my way to the room next to the
boardroom where four or five chairs surrounded a
square polished table. A copy of *What's Going On* lay
there, already dog-eared from many thumbs.

"Now Tim," said my uncle, coming into the room behind me, "do you know what all this is about?"

I shook my head and said "No."

My uncle growled in his throat and sat down, waving
Henry and myself to seats. Henry might be chairman,
might indeed in office terms have been Uncle Freddie's

boss, but the whitehaired old tyrant still personally owned the leasehold of the building itself and from long habit treated everyone in it as guests.

Henry absently fingered the newspaper. "What do you think?" he said to me. "*Who* . . . do you think?"

"It might not be anyone."

He half-smiled. "A stirrer?"

"Mm. Not a single concrete detail. Same as last time."

"Last time," Henry said, "I asked the paper's editor where he got his information from. Never reveal sources, he said. Useless asking again."

"Undisclosed sources," Uncle Freddie said, "never trust them."

Henry said, "Gordon says you can find out, Tim, how many concerns, if any, are borrowing from us at five percent. There can't be many. A few from when interest rates were low. The few who got us in the past to agree to a long-term fixed rate." The few, though he didn't say so, from before his time, before he put an end to such unprofitable straightjackets. "If there are more recent ones among them, could you spot them?"

"I'll look," I said.

We both knew it would take days rather than hours and might produce no results. The fraud, if it existed, could have been going on for a decade. For half a century. Successful frauds tended to go on and on unnoticed, until someone tripped over them by accident. It might almost be easier to find out who had done the tripping, and why he'd told the paper instead of the bank.

"Anyway," Henry said, "that isn't primarily why we asked you up here."

"No," said my uncle, grunting. "Time you were a director."

I thought: I didn't hear that right.

"Er . . . what?" I said.

"A director. A director," he said impatiently. "Fellow who sits on the board. Never heard of them, I suppose."

I looked at Henry, who was smiling and nodding.

"But," I said, "so soon . . ."

"Don't you want to, then?" demanded my uncle.

"Yes, I do."

"Good. Don't let me down. I've had my eye on you since you were eight."

I must have looked as surprised as I felt.

"You told me then," he said, "how much you had saved, and how much you would have if you went on saving a pound a month at four percent compound interest for forty years, by which time you would be very old. I wrote down your figures and worked them out, and you were right."

"It's only a formula," I said.

"Oh, sure. You could do it now in a drugged sleep. But at *eight*? You'd inherited the gift, all right. You were just robbed of the inclination." He nodded heavily. "Look at your father. My little brother. Got drunk nicely, never a mean thought, but hardly there when the brains were handed out. Look at the way he indulged your mother, letting her gamble like that. Look at the life he gave you. All pleasure, regardless of cost. I despaired of you at times. Thought you'd been ruined. But I knew the gift was there somewhere, might still be dormant, might grow if forced. So there you are, I was right."

I was pretty well speechless.

"We all agree," Henry said. "The whole board was unanimous at our meeting this morning that it's time another Ekaterin took his proper place."

I thought of John, and of the intensity of rage my promotion would bring forth.

"Would you," I said slowly, "have given me a directorship if my name had been Joe Bloggs?"

Henry levelly said, "Probably not this very day. But soon, I promise you, yes. You're almost thirty-three, after all, and I was on the board here at thirty-four."

"Thank you," I said.

"Rest assured," Henry said. "You've earned it." He stood up and formally shook hands. "Your appointment officially starts as of the first of November, a week today. We will welcome you then to a short meeting in the boardroom, and afterwards to lunch."

They must both have seen the depth of my pleasure, and they themselves looked satisfied. Hallelujah, I thought, I've made it. I've got there . . . I've barely started.

Gordon went down with me in the elevator, also smiling.

"They've all been dithering about it on and off for months," he said. "Ever since you took over from me when I was ill, and did OK. Anyway I told them this morning about your news from the cartoonist. Some of them said it was just lucky. I told them you'd now been lucky too often for it to be a coincidence. So there you are."

"I can't thank you . . ."

"It's your own doing."

"John will have a fit."

"You've coped all right so far with his envy."

"I don't like it, though," I said.

"Who would? Silly man, he's doing his career no good."

Gordon straightaway told everyone in the office, and John went white and walked rigidly out of the room.

I went diffidently a week later to the induction and to the first lunch with the board, and then in a few days, as one does, I got used to the change of company and to the higher level of information. In the departments one heard about the decisions that had been made: in the dining room one heard the decisions being reached. "Our daily board meeting," Henry said. "So much easier this way when everyone can simply say what they think without anyone taking notes."

There were usually from ten to fifteen directors at lunch, although at a pinch the elongated oval table could accommodate the full complement of twenty-three. People would vanish at any moment to answer telephone calls, and to deal. Dealing, the buying and selling of stocks, took urgent precedence over food.

The food itself was no great feast, though perfectly presented. "Always lamb on Wednesdays," Gordon said at the buffet table as he took a couple from a row of trimmed lean cutlets. "Some sort of chicken on Tuesdays, beef wellington most Thursdays. Henry never eats the crust." Each day there was a clear soup before and fruit and cheese after. Alcohol if one chose, but most of them didn't. No one should deal in millions whose brain wanted to sleep, Henry said, drinking Malvern water steadily. Quite a change, all of it, from a rough-hewn sandwich at my desk.

They were all polite about my failure to discover "paper" companies to whom the bank had been lending at five percent, although Val and Henry, I knew, shared my own view that the report originated from malice and not from fact.

I had spent several days in the extra-wide office at the back of our floor, where the more mechanical parts of the banking operation were carried on. There in the huge expanse (gray carpet, this time) were row upon row of long desks whose tops were packed with telephones, adding machines and above all computers.

From there went out our own interest checks to the depositors who had lent us money for us to lend to things like "Home-made Heaven cakes" and "Water Purification" plants in Norfolk. Into there came the interest paid *to* us by cakes and water and cartoonists and ten thousand such. Machines clattered, phone bells rang, people hurried about.

Many of the people working there were girls, and it had often puzzled me why there were so few women among the managers. Gordon said it was because few women wanted to commit their whole lives to making money and John (in the days when he was speaking to me) said with typical contempt that it was because they preferred to spend it. In any case, there were no female managers in Banking, and none at all on the board.

Despite that, my best helper in the fraud search proved to be a curvy redhead called Patty who had taken the *What's Going On* article as a personal affront, as had many of her colleagues.

"No one could do that under our noses," she protested.

"I'm afraid they could. You know they could. No one could blame any of you for not spotting it."

"Well . . . where do we start?"

"With all the borrowers paying a fixed rate of five percent. Or perhaps four percent, or five point seven five, or six or seven. Who knows if five is right?"

She looked at me frustratedly with wide amber eyes. "But we haven't got them sorted like that."

Sorted, she meant, on the computer. Each loan transaction would have its own agreement, which in itself could originally range from one single slip of paper to a contract of fifty pages, and each agreement should say at what rate the loan interest was to be levied, such as two above the current official minimum. There were thousands of such agreements typed onto and stored on computer discs. One could retrieve any one transaction by its identifying number, or alphabetically, or by the dates of commencement, or full term, or by the date when the next payment was due, but if you asked the computer who was paying at what percent you'd get a blank screen and the microchip version of a raspberry.

"You can't sort them out by rates," she said. "The rates go up and down like seesaws."

"But there must still be some loans being charged interest at a fixed rate."

"Well . . . yes."

"So when you punch in the new interest rate the computer adjusts the interest due on almost all the loans but doesn't touch those with a fixed rate."

"I suppose that's right."

"So somewhere in the computer there must be a code which tells it when not to adjust the rates."

She smiled sweetly and told me to be patient, and half a day later produced a cheerful-looking computer programmer to whom the problem was explained.

"Yeah, there's a code," he said. "I put it there myself. What you want, then, is a program that will print out all the loans that have the code attached. That right?"

We nodded. He worked on paper for half an hour with a much-chewed pencil and then typed rapidly onto the computer, pressing buttons and being pleased with the results.

"You leave this program on here," he said. "Then feed in the discs, and you'll get the results on that line-printer over there. And I've written it all out for you tidily in pencil, in case someone switches off your machine. Then just type it all in again, and you're back in business."

We thanked him and he went away whistling, the aristocrat among ants.

The line printer clattered away on and off for hours as we fed through the whole library of discs, and it finally produced a list of about a hundred of the ten-digit numbers used to identify an account.

"Now," Patty said undaunted, "do you want a complete printout of all of the original agreements for those loans?"

"I'm afraid so, yes."

"Hang around."

It took two days even with her help to check through all the resulting paper and by the end I couldn't spot any companies there that had no known physical existence, though short of actually tramping to all the addresses and making an on-the-spot inquiry, one couldn't be sure.

Henry, however, was against the expenditure of time. "We'll just be more vigilant," he said. "Design some more safeguards, more tracking devices. Could you do that, Tim?"

"I could, with that programmer's help."

"Right. Get on with it. Let us know."

I wondered aloud to Patty whether someone in her own department, not one of the managers, could set up such a fraud, but once she got over her instinctive indignation she shook her head.

"Who would bother? It would be much simpler . . . in fact it's almost dead easy . . . to feed in a mythical firm who has lent *us* money, and to whom we are paying interest. Then the computer goes on sending out interest checks forever, and all the crook has to do is cash them."

Henry, however, said we had already taken advice on that one, and the "easy" route had been plugged by systematic checks by the auditors.

The paper-induced rumpus again gradually died down and became undiscussed if not forgotten. Life in our plot went on much as before with Rupert slowly recovering, Alec making jokes and Gordon stuffing his left hand anywhere out of sight. John continued to suffer from his obsession, not speaking to me, not looking at me if he could help it, and apparently telling clients outright that my promotion was a sham.

"Cosmetic, of course," Alec reported his saying on the telephone. "Makes the notepaper heading look impressive. Means nothing in real terms, you know. Get through to me, I'll see you right."

"He said all that?" I asked.

"Word for word." Alec grinned. "Go and bop him on the nose."

I shook my head, however, and wondered if I should get myself transferred along to the St. Paul's–facing office. I didn't want to go, but it looked as if John wouldn't recover his balance unless I did. If I tried to get John himself transferred, would it make things that much worse?

I was gradually aware that Gordon, and behind him Henry, were not going to help, their thought being that I was a big boy now and should be able to resolve it myself. It was a freedom that brought responsibility, as all freedoms do, and I had to consider that for the bank's sake John needed to be a sensible member of the team.

I thought he should see a psychiatrist. I got Alec to say it to him lightly as a joke, out of my hearing ("what you need, old pal, is a friendly shrink"), but to John his own anger appeared rational, not a matter for treatment.

I tried saying to him straight, "Look, John, I know how you feel. I know you think my promotion isn't fair. Well, maybe it is, maybe it isn't, but either way I can't help it. You'll be a lot better off if you just face things and forget it. You're good at your job, we all know it, but you're doing yourself no favors with all this bellyaching. So shut up, accept that life's bloody, and let's lend some money."

- It was a homily that fell on a closed mind, and in the end it was some redecorating that came to the rescue. For a week while painters rewhitened our walls the five of us in the fountain-facing office squeezed into the other one, desks jammed together in every corner, phone calls made with palms pressed to ears against the noise and even normally placid tempers itching to snap. Overcrowd the human race, I thought, and you always got a fight. In distance lay peace.

Anyway, I used the time to do some surreptitious persuasion and shuffling, so that when we returned to our own patch both John and Rupert stayed behind. The two oldest men from the St. Paul's office came with Gordon, Alec and myself, and Gordon's almost-equal obligingly told John that it was great to be working again with a younger team of bright energetic brains.

November

Val Fisher said at lunch one day, "I've received a fairly odd request." (It was a Friday: grilled fish.)

"Something new?" Henry asked.

"Yes. Chap wants to borrow five million pounds to buy a racehorse."

Everyone at the table laughed except Val himself.

"I thought I'd toss it at you," he said. "Kick it around some. See what you think."

"What horse?" Henry said.

"Something called Sandcastle."

Henry, Gordon and I all looked at Val with sharpened attention; almost perhaps with eagerness.

"Mean something to you three, does it?" he said, turning his head from one to the other of us.

Henry nodded. "That day we all went to Ascot. Sandcastle ran there, and won. A stunning performance. Beautiful."

Gordon said reminiscently, "The man whose box we were in saved his whole business on that race. Do you remember Dissdale, Tim?"

"Certainly do."

"I saw him a few weeks ago. On top of the world. God knows how much he won."

"Or how much he staked," I said.

"Yes, well," Val said. "Sandcastle. He won the 2,000 Guineas, as I understand, and the King Edward VII Stakes at Royal Ascot. Also the 'Diamond' Stakes in July, and the Champion Stakes at Newmarket last month. This is, I believe, a record second only to winning the Derby or the Arc de Triomphe. He finished fourth, incidentally, in the Derby. He could race next year as a four-year-old, but if he flopped his value would be less than it is at the moment. Our prospective client wants to buy him now and put him to stud."

The rest of the directors got on with their filets of sole while listening interestedly with eyes and ears. A stallion made a change, I supposed, from chemicals, electronics and oil.

"Who is our client?" Gordon asked. Gordon liked fish. He could eat it right-handed with his fork, in no danger of shaking it off between plate and mouth.

"A man called Oliver Knowles," Val said. "He owns a stud farm. He got passed along to me by the horse's trainer, whom I know slightly because of our wives' being distantly related. Oliver Knowles wants to buy, the present owner is willing to sell. All they need is the cash." He smiled. "Same old story."

"What's your view?" Henry said.

Val shrugged his well-tailored shoulders. "Too soon to have one of any consequence. But I thought, if it interested you at all, we could ask Tim to do a preliminary look-see. He has a background, after all, a lengthy acquaintance, shall we say, with racing."

There was a murmur of dry amusement round the table.

"What do you think?" Henry asked me.

"I'll certainly do it if you like."

Someone down the far end complained that it would be a waste of time and that merchant banks of our stature should not be associated with the Turf.

"Our own dear Queen," someone said ironically, "is

associated with the Turf. And knows the Stud Book backwards, so they say."

Henry smiled. "I don't see why we shouldn't at least look into it." He nodded in my direction. "Go ahead, Tim. Let us know."

I spent the next few working days alternately chewing pencils with the computer programmer and joining us to a syndicate with three other banks to lend twelve point four million pounds short term at high interest to an international construction company with a gap in its cash flow. In between those I telephoned around for information and opinions about Oliver Knowles, in the normal investigative preliminaries to any loan for anything, not only for a hair-raising price for a stallion.

Establishing a covenant, it was called. Only if the covenant was sound would any loan be further considered.

Oliver Knowles, I was told, was a sane, sober man of forty-one with a stud farm in Hertfordshire. There were three stallions standing there with ample provision for visiting mares, and he owned the one hundred and fifty acres outright, having inherited them on his father's death.

When talking to local bank managers one listened attentively for what they left out, but Oliver Knowles' bank manager left out not much. Without in the least discussing his client's affairs in detail he said that occasional fair-sized loans had so far been paid off as scheduled and that Mr. Knowles' business sense could be commended. A rave notice from such a source.

"Oliver Knowles?" a racing acquaintance from the long past said. "Don't know him myself. I'll ask around," and an hour later called back with the news. "He seems to be a good guy but his wife's just buggered off with a Canadian. He might be a secret wife-beater, who can tell? Otherwise the gen is that he's as honest as any horse-breeder, which you can take as you find it, and how's your mother?"

"She's fine, thanks. She remarried last year. Lives in Jersey."

"Good. Lovely lady. Always buying us ice creams. I adored her."

I put the receiver down with a smile and tried a credit rating agency. No black marks, they said: the Knowles credit was good.

I told Gordon across the room that I seemed to be getting nothing but green lights, and at lunch that day repeated the news to Henry. He looked around the table, collecting a few nods, a few frowns and a great deal of indecision.

"We couldn't carry it all ourselves, of course," Val said. "And it isn't exactly something we could go to our regular sources with. They'd think us crackers."

Henry nodded. "We'd have to canvass friends for private money. I know a few people here or there who might come in. Two million, I think, is all we should consider ourselves. Two and a half at the outside."

"I don't approve," a dissenting director said. "It's madness. Suppose the damn thing broke its leg?"

"Insurance," Henry said mildly.

Into a small silence I said, "If you felt like going into it further I could get some expert views on Sandcastle's breeding, and then arrange blood and fertility tests. And I know it's not usual with loans, but I do think someone like Val should go and personally meet Oliver Knowles and look at his place. It's too much of a risk to lend such a sum for a horse without going into it extremely carefully."

"Just listen to who's talking," said the dissenter, but without ill-will.

"Mm," Henry said, considering. "What do you think, Val?"

Val Fisher smoothed a hand over his always smooth face. "Tim should go," he said. "He's done the groundwork, and all I know about horses is that they eat grass."

The dissenting director almost rose to his feet with the urgency of his feelings.

"Look," he said, "all this is ridiculous. How can we possibly finance a *horse?*"

"Well, now," Henry answered. "The breeding of thor-

oughbreds is big business, tens of thousands of people
round the world make their living from it. Look upon it
as an industry like any other. We gamble here on ship-
builders, motors, textiles, you name it, and all of those
can go bust. And none of them," he finished with a
near-grin, "can procreate in their own image."

The dissenter heavily shook his head. "Madness. Utter madness."

"Go and see Oliver Knowles, Tim," Henry said.

Actually I thought it prudent to bone up on the fi-
nances of breeding in general before listening to Oliver
Knowles himself, as I would then have a better idea
whether what he was proposing was sensible or not.

I didn't myself know anyone who knew much on the
subject, but one of the beauties of merchant banking
was the ramification of people who knew people who
knew people who could find someone with the information that was wanted. I sent out the question-mark
smoke signal and from distant out-of-sight mountain-
tops the answer puff-puffed back.

Ursula Young, I was told, would put me right. "She's
a bloodstock agent. Very sharp, very talkative, knows
her stuff. She used to work on a stud farm, so you've got
it every which way. She says she'll tell you anything
you want, only if you want to see her in person this
week it will have to be at Doncaster races on Saturday,
she's too busy to spend the time else."

I went north to Doncaster by train and met the lady
at the racecourse, where the last Flat meeting of the
year was being held. She was waiting as arranged by
the entrance to the Members' Club and wearing an
identifying red velvet beret, and she swept me off to a
secluded table in a bar where we wouldn't be interrupted.

She was fifty, tough, good-looking, dogmatic and in-
clined to treat me as a child. She also gave me a patient
and invaluable lecture on the economics of owning a
stallion.

"Stop me," she said to begin with, "if I say something
you don't understand."

I nodded.

" All right. Say you own a horse that's won the Derby and you want to capitalize on your gold mine. You judge what you think you can get for the horse, then you divide that by forty and try to sell each of the forty shares at that price. Maybe you can, maybe you can't. It depends on the horse. With Troy, now, they were lining up. But if your winner isn't frightfully well bred or if it made little show *except* in the Derby you'll get a cool response and have to bring the price down. OK so far?"

"Um," I said. "Why only forty shares?"

She looked at me in amazement. "You don't know a *thing*, do you?"

"That's why I'm here."

"Well, a stallion covers forty mares in a season, and the season, incidentally, lasts roughly from February to June. The mares come to *him*, of course. He doesn't travel, he stays put at home. Forty is just about average; physically, I mean. Some can do more, but others get exhausted. So forty is the accepted number. Now, say you have a mare and you've worked out that if you mate her with a certain stallion you might get a top-class foal, you try to get one of those forty places. The places are called nominations. You apply for a nomination, either directly to the stud where the stallion is standing, or through an agent like me, or even by advertising in a breeders' newspaper. Follow?"

"Gasping," I nodded.

She smiled briefly. "People who invest in stallion shares sometimes have broodmares of their own they want to breed from." She paused. "Perhaps I should have explained more clearly that everyone who owns a share automatically has a nomination to the stallion every year."

"Ah," I said.

"Yes. So say you've got your share and consequently your nomination but you haven't a mare to send to the stallion, then you sell your nomination to someone who *has* a mare, in the ways I already described.

"I'm with you."

"After the first three years the nominations may

vary in price and in fact are often auctioned, but of course for the first three years the price is fixed."

"Why of course?"

She sighed and took a deep breath. "For three years no one knows whether the progeny on the whole are going to be winners or not. The gestation period is eleven months, and the first crop of foals don't race until they're two. If you work it out, that means that the stallion has stood for three seasons, and therefore covered a hundred and twenty mares, before the crunch."

"Right."

"So to fix the stallion fee for the first three years you divide the price of the stallion by one hundred and twenty, and that's it. That's the fee charged for the stallion to cover a mare. That's the sum you receive if you sell your nomination."

I blinked.

"That means," I said, "that if you sell your nomination for three years you have recovered the total amount of your original investment?"

"That's right."

"And after that . . . every time, every year you sell your nomination, it's clear profit?"

"Yes. But taxed, of course."

"And how long does that go on?"

She shrugged. "Ten to fifteen years. Depends on the stallion's potency."

"But that's . . ."

"Yes," she said. "One of the best investments on earth."

The bar had filled up behind us with people crowding in, talking loudly, and breathing on their fingers against the chill of the raw day outside. Ursula Young accepted a warmer in the shape of whisky and ginger wine, while I had coffee.

"Don't you drink?" she asked with mild disapproval.

"Not often in the daytime."

She nodded vaguely, her eyes scanning the company, her mind already on her normal job. "Any more questions?" she asked.

"I'm bound to think of some the minute we part."

She nodded. "I'll be here until the end of racing. If you want me, you'll see me near the weighing room after each race."

We were on the point of standing up to leave when a man whose head one could never forget came into the bar.

"Calder Jackson!" I exclaimed.

Ursula casually looked. "So it is."

"Do you know him?" I asked.

"Everyone does." There was almost a conscious neutrality in her voice, as if she didn't want to be caught with her thoughts showing. The same response, I reflected, that he had drawn from Henry and Gordon and me.

"You don't like him?" I suggested.

"I feel nothing either way." She shrugged. "He's part of the scene. From what people say, he's achieved some remarkable cures." She glanced at me briefly. "I suppose you've seen him on television, extolling the value of herbs?"

"I met him," I said, "at Ascot, back in June."

"One tends to." She got to her feet, and I with her, thanking her sincerely for her help.

"Think nothing of it," she said. "Any time." She paused. "I suppose it's no use asking what stallion prompted this chat?"

"Sorry . . . no. It's on behalf of a client."

She smiled slightly. "I'm here if he needs an agent."

We made our way towards the door, a path, I saw, which would take us close to Calder. I wondered fleetingly whether he would know me, remember me after several months. I was after all not as memorable as himself, just a standard-issue six foot with eyes, nose and mouth in roughly the right places, dark hair on top.

"Hello Ursula," he said, his voice carrying easily through the general din. "Bitter cold day."

"Calder." She nodded acknowledgment.

His gaze slid to my face, dismissed it, focused again on my companion. Then he did a classic double-take, his eyes widening with recognition.

"Tim," he said incredulously. "Tim . . ." he flicked his fingers to bring the difficult name to mind ". . . Tim Ekaterin!"

I nodded.

He said to Ursula, "Tim, here, saved my life."

She was surprised until he explained, and then still surprised I hadn't told her. "I read about it, of course," she said. "And congratulated you, Calder, on your escape."

"Did you ever hear any more," I asked him. "From the police, or anyone?"

He shook his curly head. "No, I didn't."

"The boy didn't try again?"

"No."

"Did you really have no idea where he came from?" I said. "I know you told the police you didn't know, but . . . well . . . you just might have done."

He shook his head very positively, however, and said, "If I could help to catch the little bastard I'd do it at once. But I don't know who he was. I hardly saw him properly, just enough to know I didn't know him from Satan."

"How's the healing?" I said. "The tingling touch."

There was a brief flash in his eyes as if he had found the question flippant and in bad taste, but perhaps mindful that he owed me his present existence he answered civilly. "Rewarding," he said. "Heartwarming."

Standard responses, I thought. As before.

"Is your yard full, Calder?" Ursula asked.

"Always a vacancy if needed," he replied hopefully. "Have you a horse to send me?"

"One of my clients has a two-year-old that looks ill and half-dead all the time, to the despair of the trainer, who can't get it fit. She—my client—was mentioning you."

"I've had great success with that sort of general debility."

Ursula wrinkled her forehead in indecision. "She feels Ian Pargetter would think her disloyal if she sent you her colt. He's been treating him for weeks, I think, without success."

Calder smiled reassuringly. "Ian Pargetter and I are on good terms, I promise you. He's even persuaded owners himself sometimes to send me their horses. Very good of him. We talk each case over, you know, and act in agreement. After all, we both have the recovery of the patient as our prime objective." Again the swift impression of a statement often needed.

"Is Ian Pargetter a vet?" I asked incuriously.

They both looked at me.

"Er . . . yes," Calder said.

"One of a group practice in Newmarket," Ursula added. "Very forward-looking. Tries new things. Dozens of trainers swear by him."

"Just ask him, Ursula," Calder said. "Ian will tell you he doesn't mind owners sending me their horses. Even if he's a bit open-minded about the laying on of hands, at least he trusts me not to make the patient worse." It was said as a self-deprecating joke, and we all smiled. Ursula Young and I in a moment or two walked on and out of the bar, and behind us we could hear Calder politely answering another of the everlasting questions.

"Yes," he was saying, "one of my favorite remedies for a prolonged cough in horses is licorice root boiled in water with some figs. You strain the mixture and stir it into the horse's normal feed . . ."

The door closed behind us and shut him off.

"You'd think he'd get tired of explaining his methods," I said. "I wonder he never snaps."

The lady said judiciously, "Calder depends on television fame, good public relations and medical success, roughly in that order. He owns a yard with about thirty boxes on the outskirts of Newmarket—it used to be a regular training stables before he bought it—and the yard's almost always full. Short-term and long-term crocks, all sent to him either from true belief or as a last resort. I don't pretend to know anything about herbalism, and as for supernatural healing powers . . ." She shook her head. "But there's no doubt that whatever his methods, horses do usually seem to leave his yard in a lot better health than when they went in."

"Someone at Ascot said he'd brought dying horses back to life."

"Hmph."

"You don't believe it?"

She gave me a straight look, a canny businesswoman with a lifetime's devotion to thoroughbreds.

"Dying," she said, "is a relative term when it doesn't end in death."

I made a nod into a slight bow of appreciation.

"But to be fair," she said, "I know for certain that he totally and permanently cured a ten-year-old broodmare of colitis X, which has a habit of being fatal."

"They're not all horses in training, then, that he treats?"

"Oh, no, he'll take anybody's pet from a pony to an event horse. Show jumpers, the lot. But the horse has to be worth it, to the owner, I mean. I don't think Calder's hospital is terribly cheap."

"Exorbitant?"

"Not that I've heard. Fair, I suppose, if you consider the results."

I seemed to have heard almost more about Calder Jackson than I had about stallion shares, but I did after all have a sort of vested interest. One tended to want a life one had saved to be of positive use in the world. Illogical, I daresay, but there it was. I was pleased that it was true that Calder cured horses, albeit in his own mysterious unorthodox ways: and if I wished that I could warm to him more as a person, that was unrealistic and sentimental.

Ursula Young went off about her business, and although I caught sight of both her and Calder during the afternoon, I didn't see them again to speak to. I went back to London on the train, spent two hours of Sunday morning on the telephone, and early Sunday afternoon drove off to Hertfordshire in search of Oliver Knowles.

He lived in a square hundred-year-old stark red brick house that to my taste would have been friendlier if softened by trailing creeper. Blurred outlines, however, were not in Oliver Knowles' soul: a crisp bare tidiness was apparent in every corner of his spread.

His land was divided into a good number of paddocks of various sizes, each bordered by an immaculate fence of white rails; and the upkeep of those, I judged, as I pulled up on the weedless gravel before the front door, must alone cost a fortune. There was a scattering of mares and foals in the distance in the paddocks, mostly heads down to the grass, sniffing out the last tender shoots of the dying year. The day itself was cold with a muted sun dipping already towards distant hills, the sky quiet with the grayness of coming winter, the damp air smelling of mustiness, wood smoke and dead leaves.

There were no dead leaves as such to be seen. No flower beds, no ornamental hedges, no nearby trees. A barren mind, I thought, behind a business whose aim was fertility and the creation of life.

Oliver Knowles himself opened his front door to my knock, proving to be a pleasant lean man with an efficient, cultured manner of authority and politeness. Accustomed to command, I diagnosed. Feels easy with it; second nature. Positive, straightforward, self-controlled. Charming also, in an understated way.

"Mr. Ekaterin?" he shook hands, smiling. "I must confess I expected someone . . . older."

There were several answers to that, such as "time will take care of it" and "I'll be older tomorrow," but nothing seemed appropriate. Instead I said "I report back" to reassure him, which it did, and he invited me into his house.

Predictably the interior was also painfully tidy, such papers and magazines as were to be seen being squared up with the surface they rested on. The furniture was antique, well-polished, brass handles shining, and the carpets venerably from Persia. He led me into a sitting room, which was also office, the walls thickly covered with framed photographs of horses, mares and foals, and the window giving on to a view of, across a further expanse of gravel, an archway leading into an extensive stable yard.

"Boxes for mares," he said, following my eyes. "Beyond them, the foaling boxes. Beyond those, the breeding pen, with the stallion boxes on the far side of that again. My stud groom's bungalow and the lads' hostel, those roofs you can see in the hollow, they're just beyond the stallions." He paused. "Would you care, perhaps, to look round?"

"Very much," I said.

"Come along, then." He led the way to a door at the back of the house, collecting an overcoat and a black retriever from a mud room on the way. "Go on then, Squibs, old fellow," he said, fondly watching his dog squeeze ecstatically through the opening outside door. "Breath of fresh air won't hurt you."

We walked across to the stable arch with Squibbs circling and zigzagging nose-down to the gravel.

"It's our quietest time of year, of course," Oliver Knowles said. "We have our own mares here, of course, and quite a few at livery." He looked at my face to see if I understood and decided to explain anyway. "They belong to people who own broodmares but have nowhere of their own to keep them. They pay us to board them."

I nodded.

"Then we have the foals born to the mares this past spring, and of course the three stallions. Total of seventy-eight at the moment.

"And next spring," I said, "the mares coming to your stallions will arrive?"

"That's right." He nodded. "They come here a month or five weeks before they're due to give birth to the foals they are already carrying, so as to be near the stallion within the month following. They have to foal here, because the foals would be too delicate straight after birth to travel."

"And . . . how long do they stay here?"

"About three months altogether, by which time we hope the mare is safely in foal again."

"There isn't much pause then," I said. "Between . . . er . . . pregnancies?"

He glanced at me with civil amusement. "Mares come into use nine days after foaling, but normally we would think this a bit too soon for breeding. The es-trus—heat you would call it—lasts six days, then there's an interval of fifteen days, then the mare comes into use again for six days, and this time we breed her. Mind you," he added, "nature being what it is, this cycle doesn't work to the minute. In some mares the estrus will last only two days, in some as much as eleven. We try to have the mare covered two or three times while she's in heat, for the best chance of getting her in foal. A great deal depends on the stud groom's judgment, and I've a great chap just now, he has a great feel for mares, a sixth sense, you might say."

He led me briskly across the first big oblong yard, where long dark equine heads peered inquisitively from over half-open stable doors, and through a passage on the far side that led to a second yard of almost the same size but whose doors were fully shut.

"None of these boxes is occupied at the moment," he said, waving a hand around "We have to have the ca-pacity, though, for when the mares come."

Beyond the second yard lay a third, a good deal smaller and again with closed doors.

"Foaling boxes," Oliver Knowles explained. "All empty now, of course."

The black dog trotted ahead of us, knowing the way. Beyond the foaling boxes lay a wide path between two small paddocks of about half an acre each, and at the end of the path, to the left, rose a fair-sized barn with a row of windows just below its roof.

"Breeding shed," Oliver Knowles said economically, producing a heavy key ring from his trouser pocket and unlocking a door set into a large roll-aside entrance. He gestured to me to go in, and I found myself in a bare concrete-floored expanse surrounded by white walls topped with the high windows, through which the dy-ing sun wanly shone.

"During the season of course the floor in here is cov-ered with peat," he said.

I nodded vaguely and thought of life being generated purposefully in that quiet place, and we returned prosa-

ically to the outer world with Oliver Knowles locking
the door again behind us.

Along another short path between two more small
paddocks we came to another small stable yard, this
time of only six boxes, with feed room, tack room, hay
and peat storage alongside.

"Stallions," Oliver Knowles said.

Three heads almost immediately appeared over the
halfdoors, three sets of dark liquid eyes turning inquisitively our way.

"Rotaboy," my host said, walking to the first head
and producing a carrot unexpectedly. The black mobile
lips whiffled over the outstretched palm and sucked the
goodie in: strong teeth crunched a few times and Rotaboy nudged Oliver Knowles for a second helping. Oliver
Knowles produced another carrot, held it out as before,
and briefly patted the horse's neck.

"He'll be twenty next year," he said. "Getting old,
eh, old fella?"

He walked along to the next box and repeated the carrot routine. "This one is Diarist, rising sixteen."

By the third box he said, "This is Parakeet," and delivered the treats and the pat. "Parakeet turns twelve
on January first."

He stood a little away from the horse so that he could
see all three heads at once and said, "Rotaboy has been
an outstanding stallion and still is, but one can't realistically expect more than another one or two seasons.
Diarist is successful, with large numbers of winners
among his progeny, but none of them absolutely top
rank like those of Rotaboy. Parakeet hasn't proved as
successful as I'd hoped. He turns out to breed better
stayers than sprinters, and the world is mad nowadays
for very fast two-year-olds. Parakeet's progeny tend to
be better at three, four, five and six. Some of his first
crops are now steeplechasing and jumping pretty well."

"Isn't that good?" I asked, frowning, since he spoke
with no great joy.

"I've had to reduce his fee," he said. "People won't
send their top flat-racing mares to a stallion who breeds
jumpers."

"Oh."

After a pause he said, "You can see why I need new blood here. Rotaboy is old, Diarist is middle rank, Parakeet is unfashionable. I will soon have to replace Rotaboy, and I must be sure I replace him with something of at least equal quality. The *prestige* of a stud farm, quite apart from its income, depends on the drawing power of its stallions."

"Yes," I said. "I see."

Rotaboy, Diarist and Parakeet lost interest in the conversation and hope in the matter of carrots, and one by one withdrew into the boxes. The black retriever trotted around smelling unimaginable scents and Oliver Knowles began to walk me back towards the house.

"On the bigger stud farms," he said, "you'll find stallions that are owned by syndicates."

"Forty shares?" I suggested.

He gave me a brief smile. "That's right. Stallions are owned by any number of people between one and forty. When I first acquired Rotaboy it was in partnership with five others. I bought two of them out—they needed the money—so now I own half. This means I have twenty nominations each year, and I have no trouble in selling all of them, which is most satisfactory." He looked at me inquiringly to make sure I understood, which, thanks to Ursula Young, I did.

"I own Diarist outright. He was as expensive in the first place as Rotaboy, and as he's middle rank, so is the fee I can get for him. I don't always succeed in filling his forty places, and when that occurs I breed him to my own mares, and sell the resulting foals as yearlings."

Fascinated, I nodded again.

"With Parakeet it's much the same. For the last three years I haven't been able to charge the fee I did to begin with, and if I fill his last places these days it's with mares from people who *prefer* steeplechasing, and this is increasingly destructive of his flat-racing image."

We retraced our steps past the breeding shed and across the foaling yard.

"This place is expensive to run," he said objectively. "It makes a profit and I live comfortably, but I'm not getting any further. I have the capacity here for another stallion—enough accommodation, that is to say, for the extra forty mares. I have a good business sense and excellent health, and I feel underextended. If I am ever to achieve more I must have more capital . . . and capital in the shape of a world-class stallion."

"Which brings us," I said, "to Sandcastle."

He nodded. "If I acquired a horse like Sandcastle this stud would immediately be more widely known and more highly regarded."

Understatement, I thought. The effect would be galvanic. "A sort of overnight stardom?" I said.

"Well, yes," he agreed with a satisfied smile. "I'd say you might be right."

The big yard nearest the house had come moderately to life, with two or three lads moving about carrying feed scoops, hay nets, buckets of water and sacks of muck. Squibs, with madly wagging tail, went in a straight line towards a stocky man who bent to fondle his black ears.

"That's Nigel, my stud groom," Oliver Knowles said. "Come and meet him." And as we walked across he added, "If I can expand this place I'll up-rate him to stud manager; give him more standing with the customers."

We reached Nigel, who was of about my own age, with crinkly light-brown hair and noticeably bushy eyebrows. Oliver Knowles introduced me merely as "a friend" and Nigel treated me with casual courtesy but not as the possible source of a future fortune. He had a Gloucestershire accent, but not pronounced, and I would have placed him as a farmer's son, if I'd had to.

"Any problems?" Oliver Knowles asked him, and Nigel shook his head.

"Nothing except that Floating mare with the discharge."

His manner to his employer was confident and without anxiety but at the same time diffident, and I had a strong impression that it was Nigel's personality that suited Oliver Knowles, as much as any skill he might have with mares. Oliver Knowles was not a man, I judged, to surround himself with awkward, unpredictable characters: the behavior of everyone around him had to be as tidy as his place.

I wondered idly about the wife who had "just buggered off with a Canadian," and at that moment a horse trotted into the yard with a young woman aboard. A girl, I amended, as she kicked her feet from the stirrups and slid to the ground. A noticeably curved young girl in jeans and heavy sweater with her dark hair tied in a pony tail. She led her horse into one of the boxes and presently emerged carrying the saddle and bridle, which she dumped on the ground outside the box before closing the bottom half of the door and crossing the yard to join us.

"My daughter," Oliver Knowles said.

"Ginnie," added the girl, holding out a polite brown hand. "Are you the reason we didn't go out to lunch?"

Her father gave an instinctive repressing movement and Nigel looked only faintly interested.

"I don't know," I said. "I wouldn't think so."

"Oh, I would," she said. "Dad really doesn't like parties. He uses any old excuse to get out of them, don't you, Dad?"

He gave her an indulgent smile while looking as if his thoughts were elsewhere.

"I didn't mind missing it," Ginnie said to me, anxious not to embarrass. "Twelve miles away and people all Dad's age . . . but they do have frightfully good canapés, and also a lemon tree growing in their greenhouse. Did you know that a lemon tree has everything all at once—buds, flowers, little green knobbly fruit and big fat lemons, all going on all the time?"

"My daughter," Oliver Knowles said unnecessarily, "talks a lot."

"No," I said, "I didn't know about lemon trees."

She gave me an impish smile and I wondered if she was even younger than I'd first thought: and as if by telepathy she said, "I'm fifteen."

"Everyone has to go through it," I said.

Her eyes widened. "Did you hate it?"

I nodded. "Spots, insecurity, a new body you're not yet comfortable in, self-consciousness . . . terrible."

Oliver Knowles looked surprised. "Ginnie isn't self-conscious, are you, Ginnie?"

She looked from him to me and back again and didn't answer. Oliver Knowles dismissed the subject as of no importance anyway and said he ought to walk along and see the mare with the discharge. Would I care to go with him?

I agreed without reservation and we all set off along one of the paths between the white-railed paddocks, Oliver Knowles and myself in front, Nigel and Ginnie following, Squibs sniffing at every fencing post and marking his territory. In between Oliver Knowles explaining that some mares preferred living out of doors permanently, others would go inside if it snowed, others went in at night, others lived mostly in the boxes. I could hear Ginnie telling Nigel that school this term was a dreadful drag owing to the new headmistress being a health fiend and making them all do jogging.

"How do you know what mares prefer?" I asked.

Oliver Knowles looked for the first time nonplussed. "Er . . ." he said. "I suppose . . . by the way they stand. If they feel cold and miserable they put their tails to the wind and look hunched. Some horses never do that, even in a blizzard. If they're obviously unhappy we bring them in. Otherwise they stay out. Same with the foals." He paused. " A lot of mares are miserable if you keep them inside. It's just . . . how they are."

He seemed dissatisfied with the loose ends of his answer, but I found them reassuring. The one thing he had seemed to me to lack had been any emotional contact with the creatures he bred: even the carrots for the stallions had been slightly mechanical.

The mare with the discharge proved to be in one of the paddocks at the boundary of the farm, and while Oliver Knowles and Nigel peered at her rump end and made obscure remarks like "With any luck she won't slip," and "It's clear enough, nothing yellow or bloody," I spent my time looking past the last set of white rails to the hedge and fields beyond.

The contrast from the Knowles land was dramatic. Instead of extreme tidiness, a haphazard disorder. Instead of short green grass in well-tended rectangles, long unkempt brownish stalks straggling through an army of drying thistles. Instead of rectangular brick-built stable yards, a ramshackle collection of wooden boxes, light gray from old creosote and with tarpaulins tied over patches of roof.

Ginnie followed my gaze. "That's the Watcherleys' place," she said. "I used to go over there a lot but they're so grimy and gloomy these days, not a laugh in sight. And all the patients have gone, practically, and they don't even have the chimpanzees anymore, they say they can't afford them."

"What patients?" I said.

"Horse patients. It's the Watcherleys' hospital for sick horses. Haven't you ever heard of it?"

I shook my head.

"It's pretty well known," Ginnie said. "Or at least it was until that razzamatazz man Calder Jackson stole the show. Mind you, the Watcherleys were no great shakes, I suppose, with Bob off to the boozer at all hours and Maggie sweating her guts out carrying muck sacks, but at least they used to be fun. The place was *cozy,* you know, even if bits of the boxes were falling off their hinges and weeds were growing everywhere, and all the horses went home blooming, or most of them, even if Maggie had her knees through her jeans and wore the same jersey for weeks and weeks on end. But Calder Jackson, you see, is the *in* thing, with all those chat shows on television and the publicity and such, and the Watcherleys have sort of got elbowed out."

Her father, listening to the last of these remarks, added his own view. "They're disorganized," he said. "No business sense. People liked their gypsy style for a while, but, as Ginnie says, they've no answer to Calder Jackson."

"How old are they?" I asked, frowning.

Oliver Knowles shrugged. "Thirties. Going on forty. Hard to say."

"I suppose they don't have a son of about sixteen, thin

and intense, who hates Calder ␣␣␣ckson obsessively for ruining his parents' business?"

"What an extraordinary question," said Oliver Knowles, and Ginnie shook her head. "They've never had any children," she said. "Maggie can't. She told me. They just lavish all that love on animals. It's really grotty, what's happening to them."

It would have been so neat, I thought, if Calder Jackson's would-be assassin had been a Watcherley son. Too neat, perhaps. But perhaps also there were others like the Watcherleys whose star had descended as Calder Jackson's rose. I said, "Do you know of any other places, apart from this one and Calder Jackson's, where people send their sick horses?"

"I expect there *are* some," Ginnie said. "Bound to be."

"Sure to be," said Oliver Knowles, nodding. "But of course we don't send away any horse that falls ill here. I have an excellent vet, great with mares, comes day or night in emergencies."

We made the return journey, Oliver Knowles pointing out to me various mares and foals of interest and distributing carrots to any head within armshot. Foals at foot, foals in utero; the fertility cycle swelling again to fruition through the quiet winter, life growing steadily in the dark.

Ginnie went off to see to the horse she'd been riding and Nigel to finish his inspections in the main yard, leaving Oliver Knowles, the dog and myself to go into the house. Squibs, poor fellow, got no farther than his basket in the mud room, but Knowles and I returned to the sitting room—office from which we'd started.

Thanks to my telephone calls of the morning I knew what the acquisition and management of Sandcastle would mean in the matter of taxation, and I'd also gone armed with sets of figures to cover the interest payable should the loan be approved. I found that I needed my knowledge not to instruct but to converse: Oliver Knowles was there before me.

"I've done this often, of course," he said. "I've had to arrange finance for buildings, for fencing, for buying

the three stallions you saw, and for another two before
them. I'm used to repaying fairly substantial bank
loans. This new venture is of course huge by compari-
son, but if I didn't feel it was within my scope I assure
you I shouldn't be contemplating it." He gave me a
brief charming smile. "I'm not a nut case, you know. I
really do know my business."

"Yes," I said. "One can see."

I told him that the maximum length of an Ekaterin
loan (if one was forthcoming at all) would be five years,
to which he merely nodded.

"That basically means," I insisted, "that you'd have
to receive getting on for eight million in that five years,
even allowing for paying off some of the loan every year
with consequently diminishing interest. It's a great
deal of money . . . Are you sure you understand how
much is involved?"

"Of course I understand," he said. "Even allowing for
interest payments and the ridiculously high insurance
premiums on a horse like Sandcastle, I'd be able to repay the loan in five years. That's the period I've used in
planning."

He spread out his sheets of neatly written calcula-
tions on his desk, pointing to each figure as he explained to me how he'd reached it. "A stallion fee of
forty thousand pounds will cover it. His racing record
justifies that figure, and I've been most carefully into
the breeding of Sandcastle himself, as you can imagine.
There is absolutely nothing in the family to alarm. No
trace of hereditary illness or undesirable tendencies.
He comes from a healthy blue-blooded line of winners,
and there's no reason why he shouldn't breed true." He
gave me a photocopied genealogical table. "I wouldn't
expect you to advance a loan without getting an expert
opinion on this. Please do take it with you."

He gave me also some copies of his figures, and I
packed them all into the briefcase I'd taken with me.

"Why don't you consider halving your risk to twenty-
one shares?" I asked. "Sell nineteen. You'd still outvote
the other owners—there'd be no chance of them whisk-

ing Sandcastle off somewhere else—and you'd be less
stretched."

With a smile he shook his head. "If I found for any
reason that the repayments were causing me acute difficulty, I'd sell some shares as necessary. But I hope in
five years' time to own Sandcastle outright, and also as
I told you to have attracted other stallions of that caliber, and to be numbered among the world's top-ranking
stud farms."

His pleasant manner took away any suggestion of
megalomania, and I could see nothing of that nature in
him.

Ginnie came into the office carrying two mugs, with
slightly anxious diffidence.

"I made some tea. Do you want some, Dad?"

"Yes, please," I said immediately, before he could answer, and she looked almost painfully relieved. Oliver
Knowles turned what had seemed like an incipient
shake of the head into a nod, and Ginnie, handing over
the mugs, said that if I wanted sugar she would go and
fetch some. "And a spoon, I guess."

"My wife's away," Oliver Knowles said abruptly.

"No sugar," I said. "This is great."

"You won't forget, Dad, will you, about me going
back to school?"

"Nigel will take you."

"He's got visitors."

"Oh . . . all right." He looked at his watch. "In half
an hour, then."

Ginnie looked even more relieved, particularly as I
could clearly sense the irritation he was suppressing.
"The school run," he said as the door closed behind his
daughter, "was one of the things my wife always did.
Does . . ." He shrugged. "She's away indefinitely. You
might as well know."

"I'm sorry," I said.

"Can't be helped." He looked at the tea mug in my
hand. "I was going to offer you something stronger."

"This is fine."

"Ginnie comes home on four Sundays a term. She's a
boarder, of course." He paused. "She's not yet used to

her mother not being here. It's bad for her, but there you are, life's like that."

"She's a nice girl," I said.

He gave me a glance in which I read both love for his daughter and a blindness to her needs. "I don't suppose," he said thoughtfully, "that you go anywhere near High Wycombe on your way home?"

"Well," I said obligingly, "I could do."

I consequently drove Ginnie back to her school, listening on the way to her views on the new headmistress's compulsory jogging program ("all our bosoms flopping up and down, bloody uncomfortable and absolutely *disgusting* to look at") and to her opinion of Nigel ("Dan thinks the sun shines out of his you-know-what and I daresay he is pretty good with the mares, they all seem to flourish, but what the lads get up to behind his back is nobody's business. They smoke in the feed sheds, I ask you! All that hay around . . . Nigel never notices. He'd make a rotten school prefect") and to her outlook on life in general. ("I can't wait to get out of school uniform and out of dormitories and being bossed around, and I'm no good at lessons; the whole thing's a *mess*. Why has everything *changed*? I used to be happy, or at least I wasn't *unhappy*, which I mostly seem to be nowadays, and no, it isn't because of Mum going away, or not especially, as she was never a lovey-dovey sort of mother, always telling me to eat with my mouth shut and so on . . . and you must be bored silly hearing all this.")

"No," I said truthfully. "I'm not bored."

"I'm not even *beautiful*," she said despairingly. "I can suck in my cheeks until I faint but I'll never look pale and bony and interesting."

I glanced at the still rounded child-woman face, at the peach-bloom skin and the worried eyes.

"Practically no one is beautiful at fifteen," I said. "It's too soon."

"How do you mean—too soon?"

"Well," I said, "say at twelve you're a child and flat and undeveloped and so on, and at maybe seventeen or eighteen you're a full-grown adult, just think of the terrific changes your body goes through in that time. Appearance, desires, mental outlook, everything. So at fifteen, which isn't much more than halfway, it's still too soon to know exactly what the end product will be like. And if it's of any comfort to you, you do now look as if you may be beautiful in a year or two, or at least not unbearable ugly."

She sat in uncharacteristic silence for quite a distance, and then she said, "Why did you come today? I mean, who are you? If it's all right to ask?"

"It's all right. I'm a sort of financial adviser. I work in a bank."

"Oh." She sounded slightly disappointed but made no further comment, and soon after that gave me prosaic and accurate directions to the school.

"Thanks for the lift," she said, politely shaking hands as we stood beside the car.

"A pleasure."

"And thanks . . ." she hesitated. "Thanks anyway."

I nodded, and she half-walked, half-ran to join a group of other girls going into the buildings. Looking briefly back she gave me a sketchy wave, which I acknowledged. Nice child, I thought, pointing the car homewards. Mixed up, as who wasn't at that age. Middling brains, not quite pretty, her future a clean stretch of sand waiting for footprints.

December

It made the headlines in the *Sporting Life (Oliver Knowles, King of the Sandcastle)* and turned up as the lead story under less fanciful banners on the racing pages of all the other dailies.

Sandcastle to go to stud, Sandcastle to stay in Britain, Sandcastle shares not for sale, Sandcastle bought privately for huge sum. The story in every case was short and simple. One of the year's top stallions had been acquired by the owner of a heretofore moderately ranked stud farm. "I am very happy," Oliver Knowles was universally reported as saying. "Sandcastle is a prize for British bloodstock."

The buying price, all the papers said, was "not unadjacent to five million pounds," and a few of them added, "the financing was private."

"Well," Henry said at lunch, tapping the *Sporting Life,* "not many of our loans make so much splash."

"It's a belly-flop," muttered the obstinate dissenter, who on that day happened to be sitting at my elbow.

Henry didn't hear and was anyway in good spirits. "If one of the foals runs in the Derby we'll take a party from the office. What do you say, Gordon? Fifty people on open-topped buses?"

Gordon agreed, with the sort of smile that hoped he wouldn't actually be called upon to fulfill his promise.

"Forty mares," Henry said musingly. "Forty foals. Surely one of them might be Derby material."

"Er," I said, from newfound knowledge. "Forty foals is stretching it. Thirty-five would be pretty good. Some mares won't 'take,' so to speak."

Henry showed mild alarm. "Does that mean that five or six fees will have to be returned? Doesn't that affect Knowles' program of repayment?"

I shook my head. "For a horse of Sandcastle's stature the fee is all up front. Payable for services rendered, regardless of results. That's in Britain, of course, and Europe. In America they have the system of no foal, no fee, even for the top stallions. A live foal, that is. Alive, standing on its feet and suckling."

Henry relaxed, leaning back in his chair and smiling. "You've certainly learned a lot, Tim, since this all started."

"It's absorbing."

He nodded. "I know it isn't usual, but how do you feel about keeping an eye on the bank's money at close quarters? Would Knowles object to you dropping in from time to time?"

"I shouldn't think so. Not out of general interest."

"Good. Do that, then. Bring us progress reports. I must say I've never been as impressed with any horse as I was that day with Sandcastle."

Henry's direct admiration of the colt had led in the end to Ekaterin's advancing three of the five million to Oliver Knowles, with private individuals subscribing the other two. The fertility tests had been excellent, the owner had been paid, and Sandcastle already stood in the stallion yard in Hertfordshire alongside Rotaboy, Diarist and Parakeet.

December was marching along towards Christmas, with trees twinkling all over London and sleet falling bleakly in the afternoons. On an impulse I sent a card embossed with tasteful robins to Calder Jackson, wishing him well, and almost by return of post received (in the office) a missive (Stubbs reproduction) thanking me sincerely and asking if I would be interested some time in looking round his place. If so, he finished, would I telephone—number supplied.

I telephoned. He was affable and far more spontaneous than usual. "Do come," he said, and we made a date for the following Sunday.

I told Gordon I was going. We were working on an interbank loan of nine and a half million for five days to a competitor, a matter of little more than a few telephone calls and a promise. My hair had almost ceased to rise at the size and speed of such deals, and with only verbal agreement from Val and Henry I had recently on my own loaned seven million for forty-eight hours. The trick was never to lend for a longer time than we ourselves were able to borrow the necessary funds: if we did, we ran the risk of having to pay a higher rate of interest than we were receiving on the loan, a process that physically hurt Val Fisher. There had been a time in the past when, owing to a client's repaying late, he had had to borrow several million for eighteen days at twenty-five percent, and he'd never got over it.

Most of our dealings weren't on such a heavy scale, and next on my agenda was a request for us to lend fifty-five thousand pounds to a man who had invented a wastepaper basket for use in cars and needed funds for development. I read the letter out to Gordon, who made a fast thumbs-down gesture.

"Pity," I said. "It's a sorely needed object."

"He's asking too little." He put his left hand hard between his knees and clamped it there. "And there are far better inventions dying the death."

I agreed with him and wrote a brief note of regret. Gordon looked up from his pages shortly after, and asked me what I'd be doing at Christmas.

"Nothing much," I said.

"Not going to your mother in Jersey?"

"They're cruising in the Caribbean."

"Judith and I wondered . . ." he cleared his throat

". . . if you'd care to stay with us. Come on Christmas Eve, stay three or four days? Just as you like, of course. I daresay you wouldn't find us too exciting . . . but the offer's there, anyway."

Was it wise, I wondered, to spend three or four days with Judith when three or four *hours* at Ascot had tempted acutely? Was it wise, when the sight of her aroused so many natural urges, to sleep so long—and so near—under her roof?

Most unwise.

"I'd like to," I said. "Very much," and I thought, you're a bloody stupid fool, Tim Ekaterin, and if you ache it'll be your own ridiculous fault.

"Good," Gordon said, looking as if he meant it. "Judith will be pleased. She was afraid you might have younger friends to go to."

"Nothing fixed."

He nodded contentedly and went back to his work, and I thought about Judith wanting me to stay, because if she hadn't wanted it I wouldn't have been asked.

If I had any sense I wouldn't go: but I knew I would.

Calder Jackson's place at Newmarket, seen that next Sunday morning, was a gem of public relations, where everything had been done to please those visiting the sick. The yard itself, an open-sided quadrangle, had been cosmetically planted with central grass and a graceful tree, and brightly painted tubs, bare now of flowers, stood at frequent intervals outside the boxes. There were park-bench type seats here and there, and ornamental gates and railings in black iron scrollwork, and a welcoming archway labeled "Comfort Room This Way."

Outside the main yard, and to one side, stood a small separate building painted glossy white. There was a large prominent red cross on the door, with, underneath it, the single word "Surgery."

The yard and the surgery were what the visitor first saw: beyond and screened by trees stood Calder Jackson's own house, more private from prying eyes than his business. I parked beside several other cars on a stretch of asphalt, and walked over to ring the bell. The front door was opened to me by a manservant in a white coat. Butler or nurse?

"This way, sir," he said deferentially, when I announced my name. "Mr. Jackson is expecting you."

Butler.

Interesting to see the dramatic haircut in its home setting, which was olde-worlde cottage on a grand scale. I had an impression of a huge room, oak rafters, stone-flagged floor, rugs, dark oak furniture, great brick fireplace with burning logs . . . and Calder advancing with a broad smile and outstretched arm.

"Tim!" he exclaimed, shaking hands vigorously. "This is a pleasure, indeed it is."

"Been looking forward to it," I said.

"Come along to the fire. Come and warm yourself. How about a drink? And . . . oh . . . this is a friend of mine . . ." he waved towards a second man already standing by the fireplace ". . . Ian Pargetter."

The friend and I nodded to each other and made the usual strangers-meeting signals, and the name tumbled over in my mind as something I'd heard somewhere before but couldn't quite recall.

Calder Jackson clinked bottles and glasses and upon consultation gave me a Scotch of noble proportions.

"And for you, Ian," he said. "A further tincture?"

Oh, yes, I thought. The vet. Ian Pargetter, the vet who didn't mind consorting with unlicensed practitioners.

Ian Pargetter hesitated but shrugged and held out his glass as one succumbing to pleasurable temptation.

"A small one, then, Calder," he said. "I must be off."

He was about forty, I judged; large and reliable-looking, with sandy graying hair, a heavy moustache and an air of being completely in charge of his life. Calder explained that it was I who had deflected the knife aimed at him at Ascot, and Ian Pargetter made predictable responses about luck, fast reactions and who could have wanted to kill Calder?

"That was altogether a memorable day," Calder said, and I agreed with him.

"We all won a packet on Sandcastle," Calder said. "Pity he's going to stud so soon."

I smiled. "Maybe we'll win on his sons."

There was no particular secret, as far as I knew, about where the finance for Sandcastle had come from, but it was up to Oliver Knowles to reveal it, not me. I thought Calder would have been interested, but bankers' ethics as usual kept me quiet.

"A superb horse," Calder said, with all the enthusiasm he'd shown in Dissdale's box. "One of the greats."

Ian Pargetter nodded agreement, then finished his drink at a gulp and said he'd be going. "Let me know how that pony fares, Calder."

"Yes, of course." Calder moved with his departing guest towards the door and slapped him on the shoulder. "Thanks for dropping in, Ian. Appreciate it."

There were sounds of Pargetter leaving by the front door, and Calder returned rubbing his hands together and saying that although it was cold outside, I might care to look round before his other guests arrived for lunch. Accordingly we walked across to the open-sided quadrangle, where Calder moved from box to box giving me a brief résumé of the illness and prospects of each patient.

"This pony only came yesterday . . . it's a prize show pony supposedly, and look at it. Dull eyes, rough coat, altogether droopy. They say it's had diarrhea on and off for weeks. I'm their last resort, they say." He smiled philosophically. "Can't think why they don't send me sick horses as a *first* resort. But there you are, they always try regular vets first. Can't blame them, I suppose."

We moved along the line. "This mare was coughing blood when she came three weeks ago. I was her owner's last resort." He smiled again. "She's doing fine now. The cough's almost gone. She's eating well, putting on condition." The mare blinked at us lazily as we strolled away.

"This is a two-year-old filly," Calder said, peering over a half-door. "She'd had an infected ulcer on her withers for six weeks before she came here. Antibiotics had proved useless. Now the ulcer's dry and healing. Most satisfactory."

We went on down the row.

"This is someone's favorite hunter, came all the way from Gloucestershire. I don't know what I can do for him, though of course I'll try. His trouble, truthfully, is just age."

Further on: "Here's a star three-day-eventer. Came to me with intermittent bleeding in the urine, intractable to antibiotics. He was clearly in great pain, and almost dangerous to deal with on account of it. But now he's fine. He'll be staying here for a while longer but I'm sure the trouble is cured."

"This is a three-year-old colt who won a race back in July but then started breaking blood vessels and went on doing it despite treatment. He's been here a fortnight. Last resort, of course!"

By the next box he said, "Don't look at this one if you're squeamish. Poor wretched little filly, she's so weak she can't hold her head up and all her bones are sharp under the skin. Some sort of wasting sickness. Blood tests haven't shown what it is. I don't know if I can heal her. I've laid my hands on her twice so far, but there's been nothing. No . . . feeling. Sometimes it takes a long time. But I'm not giving up with her, and there's always hope."

He turned his curly head and pointed to another box farther ahead. "There's a colt along there who's been here two months and is only just responding. His owners were in despair, and so was I, privately, but then just three days ago when I was in his box I could feel the force flowing down my arms and into him, and the next day he was mending."

He spoke with a far more natural fluency on his home ground and less as if reciting from a script, but all the same I felt the same reservations about the healing touch as I had at Ascot. I was a doubter, I supposed. I would never in my life have put my trust in a seventh son of a seventh son, probably because the only direct knowledge I had of any human seeking out "the touch" had been a close friend of mine at college who'd had hopeless cancer and gone to a woman healer as a last resort, only to be told that he was dying because he wanted to. I could vividly remember his anger, and mine on his behalf: and standing in Calder's yard I wondered if that same woman would also think that *horses* got sick to death because they wanted to.

"Is there anything you can't treat?" I asked. "Anything you turn away?"

"I'm afraid so, yes." He smiled ruefully. "There are some things, like advanced laminitis, with which I feel hopeless, and as for coryne . . ." he shook his head ". . . it's a killer."

"You've lost me," I said.

"So sorry. Well, laminitis is a condition of the feet where the bone eventually begins to crumble, and horses in the end can't bear the pain of standing up. They lie down, and horses can't live for more than a few days lying down." He spoke with regret. "And coryne," he went on, "is a frightful bacterial infection which is deadly to foals. It induces a sort of pneumonia with abcesses in the lungs. Terribly contagious. I know of one stud farm in America that lost seventy foals in one day."

I listened in horror. "Do we have it in England?" I asked.

"Sometimes, in pockets, but not widespread. It doesn't affect older horses. Foals of three months or over are safe." He paused. "Some very young foals do survive, of course, but they're likely to have scar tissue in the lungs, which may impair their breathing for racing purposes."

"Isn't there a vaccine?" I said.

He smiled indulgently. "Very little research is done into equine diseases, chiefly because of the cost but also because horses are so large, and can't be kept in a laboratory for any controlled series of tests."

I again had the impression that he had said all this many times before, but it was understandable and I was getting used to it. We proceeded on the hospital round (four-year-old with general debility, show jumper with festering leg) and came at length to a box with an open door.

"We're giving this one sun treatment," Calder said, indicating that I should look; and inside the box a thin youth was adjusting the angle of an ultraviolet lamp set on a head-high, wall-mounted bracket. It wasn't at the dappled gray that I looked, however, but at the lad, because in the first brief glimpse I thought he was the boy who had tried to attack Calder.

I opened my mouth . . . and shut it again.

He wasn't the boy. He was of the same height, same build, same litheness, same general coloring, but not with same eyes or jawline or narrow nose.

Calder saw my reaction and smiled. "For a split second, when I saw that boy move at Ascot, I thought it was Jason here. But it wasn't, of course."

I shook my head. "Alike but different."

Caldor nodded. "And Jason wouldn't want to kill me, would you, Jason?" He spoke with a jocularity to which Jason didn't respond.

"No, sir," he said stolidly.

"Jason is my right-hand man," said Calder heartily. "Indispensable."

The right-hand man showed no satisfaction at the flattery and maintained an impassive countenance throughout. He touched the gray horse and told it to shift over a bit in the manner of one equal to another, and the horse obediently shifted.

"Mind your eyes with that lamp," Calder said. "Where are your glasses?"

Jason fished into the breast pocket of his shirt and produced some ultra-dark sunglasses. Calder nodded. "Put them on," he said, and Jason complied. Where before there had already been a lack of mobility of expression, there was now, with the obscured eyes, no way at all of guessing Jason's thoughts.

"I'll be finished with this one in ten minutes," he said. "Is there anything else after that, sir?"

Calder briefly pondered and shook his head. "Just the evening rounds at four."

"Your invalids get every care," I said, complimenting them.

Jason's blacked-out eyes turned my way, but it was

Calder who said, "Hard work gets results." And you've said that a thousand times, I thought.

We reached the last box in the yard, the first one that was empty.

"Emergency bed," Calder said, jokingly, and I smiled and asked how much he charged for his patients.

He replied easily and without explanation or apology. "Twice the training fees currently charged for horses in the top Newmarket stables. When their rates go up, so do mine."

"Twice . . . ?"

He nodded. "I could charge more, you know. But if I charged less I'd be totally swamped by all those 'last resort' people, and I simply haven't the room or the time or the spiritual resources to take more cases than I do."

I wondered how one would ever get to the essence of the man behind the temperate, considerate public face, or indeed if the public face was not a façade at all but the essence itself. I looked at the physical strength of the shoulders below the helmet head and listened to the plain words describing a mystical force, considered the dominating voice and the mild manner, and still found him a man to admire rather than like.

"The surgery," he said, gesturing towards it as we walked that way. "My drug store!" He smiled at the joke (how often, I wondered, had he said it?) and produced a key to unlock the door. "There's nothing dangerous or illegal in here, of course, but one has to protect against vandals. So sad, don't you think?"

The surgery, which had no windows, was basically a large brick-built hut. The internal walls, like the outer, were painted white, and the floor was tiled in red. There were antiseptic-looking glass-fronted cabinets along the two end walls and a wide bench with drawers underneath along the wall facing the door. On the bench, a delicate-looking set of scales, a pestle and mortar and a pair of fine rubber gloves: behind the glass of the cabinets, rows of bottles and boxes. Everything very business-like and tidy: and along the wall that contained the door stood three kitchen appliances, refrigerator, stove and sink.

Calder pointed vaguely towards the cabinets. "In there I keep the herbs in pill and powder form. Comfrey, myrrh, sarsaparilla, golden seal, fo-ti-tieng, things like that."

"Er . . ." I said. "What do they do?"

He ran through them obligingly. "Comfrey knits bones and heals wounds, myrrh is antiseptic and good for diarrhea and rheumatism, sarsaparilla contains male hormones and increases physical strength, golden seal cures eczema, improves appetite and digestion, fo-ti-tieng is a revitalizing tonic second to none. Then there's licorice for coughs and papaya enzymes for digesting proteins and passiflora to use as a general pacifier and tranquilizer." He paused. "There's ginseng also, of course, which is a marvelous rejuvenator and invigorator, but it's really too expensive in the quantities needed to do a horse significant good. It has to be taken continuously, forever." He sighed. "Excellent for humans, though."

The air in the windowless room was fresh and smelled very faintly fragrant, and as if to account for it Calder started showing me the contents of the drawers.

"I keep seeds in here," he said. "My patients eat them by the handful every day." Three or four of the drawers contained large opaque plastic bags fastened by bulldog clips. "Sunflower seeds for vitamins, phosphorus and calcium, good for bones and teeth. Pumpkin seeds for vigor—they contain male hormones—and also for phosphorus and iron. Carrot seeds for calming nervous horses. Sesame seeds for general health."

He walked along a yard or two and pulled open an extra-large deep drawer that contained larger bags; more like sacks. "These are hops left after beer-making. They're packed full of all good things. A great tonic, and cheap enough to use in quantity. We have bagfuls of them over in the feed shed to grind up as chaff but I use these here as one ingredient of my special decoction, my concentrated tonic."

"Do you make it . . . on the stove?" I asked.

He smiled. "Like a chef." He opened the refrigerator door. "I store it in here. Want to see?"

I looked inside. Nearly the whole space was taken with gallon-sized plastic containers full of a brownish liquid. "We mix it in a bran mash, warmed of course, and the horses thrive."

I knew nothing about the efficiency of his remedies, but I was definitely impressed.

"How do you get the horses to take pills?" I said.

"In an apple, usually. We scoop out half the core, put in the tablet or capsule, or indeed just powder, and replace the plug."

So simple.

"And incidentally, I make most of my own pills and capsules. Some, like comfrey, are commercially available, but I prefer to buy the dried herbs in their pure form and make my own recipes." He pulled open one of the lower drawers under the workbench and lifted out a heavy wooden box. "This," he said, laying it on the work surface and opening the lid, "contains the makings."

I looked down at a whole array of brass dies, each a small square with a pill-sized cavity in its center. The cavities varied from tiny to extra large, and from round to oblong.

"It's an antique," he said with a touch of pride. "Early Victorian. Dates from when pills were always made by hand—and it's still viable, of course. You put the required drug in powder form into whatever sized cavity you want, and compress it with the rod that exactly fits." He lifted one of a series of short brass rods from its rack and fitted its end into one of the cavities, tamping it up and down: then picked the whole die out of the box and tipped it right over. "Hey presto," he said genially, catching the imaginary contents, "a pill!"

"Neat," I said, with positive pleasure.

He nodded. "Capsules are quicker and more modern." He pulled open another drawer and briefly showed me the empty tops and bottoms of a host of gelatin capsules, again of varying sizes, though mostly a little larger than those swallowed easily by humans. "Veterinary size," he explained.

He closed his gem of a pill-making box and returned

it to its drawer, straightening up afterwards and casting a caring eye around the place to make sure everything was tidy. With a nod of private satisfaction he opened the door for us to return to the outside world, switching off the fluorescent lights and locking the door behind us.

A car was just rolling to a stop on the asphalt, and presently two recognized figures emerged from it: Dissdale Smith and his delectable Bettina.

"Hello, hello," said Dissdale, striding across with ready hand. "Calder said you were coming. Good to see you. Calder's been showing you all his treasures, eh? The conducted tour, eh, Calder?" I shook the hand. "Calder's proud of his achievements here, aren't you, Calder?"

"With good reason," I said civilly, and Calder gave me a swift glance and a genuine-looking smile.

Bettina drifted more slowly to join us, a delight in high-heeled boots and cuddling fur, a white silk scarf round her throat and smooth dark hair falling glossily to her shoulders. Her scent traveled sweetly across the quiet cold air and she laid a decorative hand on my arm in an intimate touch.

"Tim the savior," she said. "Calder's hero."

The over-packaged charm unaccountably brought the contrasting image of Ginnie sharply to my mind, and I briefly thought that the promise was more beckoning than the performance, that child more interesting than that woman.

Calder took us all soon into his maxi-cottage sitting room and distributed more drinks. Dissdale told me that Sandcastle had almost literally saved his business and metaphorically his life, and we all drank a toast to the wonder horse. Four further guests arrived—a married couple with their two twentyish daughters—and the occasion became an ordinarily enjoyable lunch party, undemanding, unmemorable, good food handed round by the manservant, cigars offered with the coffee.

Calder at some point said he was off to America in the New Year on a short lecture tour.

"Unfortunately," he said, "I'll be talking to health

clubs, not horse people. American racehorse trainers aren't receptive to me. Or not yet. But then, it took a few years for Newmarket to decide I could make a contribution."

Everyone smiled at the skepticism of America and Newmarket.

Calder said, "January is often a quiet month here. We don't take any new admissions if I'm away, and of course my head lad just keeps the establishment routines going until I return. It works pretty well." He smiled. "If I'm lucky I'll get some skiing; and to be honest, I'm looking forward to the skiing much more than the talks."

Everyone left soon after three, and I drove back to London through the short darkening afternoon wondering if the herbs of antiquity held secrets we'd almost willfully lost.

"Caffeine," Calder had been saying towards the end, "is a get-up-and-go stimulant, tremendously useful. Found in coffee beans of course, and in tea and cocoa and in cola drinks. Good for asthma. Vigorous marvelous tonic. A life-saver after shock. And now in America, I ask you, they're casting caffeine as a villain and are busy taking it out of everything it's naturally *in.* You might as well take the alcohol out of bread."

"But Calder dear," Bettina said, "there's no alcohol in bread."

He looked at her kindly as she sat on his right. "Bread that is made with yeast definitely does contain alcohol before it's cooked. If you mix yeast with water and sugar you get alcohol and carbon dioxide, which is the gas that makes the dough rise. The air in a bakery smells of wine . . . simple chemistry, my dear girl, no magic in it. Bread is the staff of life and alcohol is good for you."

There had been jokes and lifted glasses, and I could have listened to Calder for hours.

The Christmas party at Gordon Michaels' home was in a way an echo, because Judith's apothecary friend Pen Warner was in attendance most of the time. I got to

know her quite well and to like her very much, which
Judith may or may not have intended. In any case, it
was again the fairy-tale day at Ascot that had led on to
friendly relations.

"Do you remember Burnt Marshmallow?" Pen said.
"I bought a painting with my winnings."

"I spent mine on riotous living."

"Oh yes?" She looked me up and down and shook her
head. "You haven't the air."

"What do I have the air of?" I asked curiously, and
she answered in amusement, "Of intelligent laziness
and boring virtue."

"All wrong," I said.

"Ho hum."

She seemed to me to be slightly less physically solid
than at Ascot, but it might have been only the change of
clothes; there were still the sad eyes and the ingrained
worthiness and the unexpected cast of humor. She had
apparently spent twelve hours that day—it was Christmas Eve—doling out remedies to people whose illnesses
showed no sense of timing, and proposed to go back at
six in the morning. Meanwhile she appeared at the Michaels' house in a long festive caftan with mood to
match, and during the evening the four of us ate quail
with our fingers, and roasted chestnuts, and played a
board game with childish gusto.

Judith wore rose pink and pearls and looked about
twenty-five. Gordon in advance had instructed me
"Bring whatever you like as long as it's informal" and
himself was resplendent in a plum velvet jacket and
bow tie. My own newly bought cream wool shirt, which
in the shop had looked fairly theatrical, seemed in the
event to be right, so that on all levels the evening
proved harmonious and fun, much more rounded and
easy than I'd expected.

Judith's housekeeping throughout my stay proved a
poem of invisibility. Food appeared from freezer and
cupboard, remnants returned to dishwasher and dust-
bin. Jobs were distributed when essential but sitting
and talking had priority: and nothing so smooth, I reflected, ever got done without hard work beforehand.

"Pen will be back soon after one tomorrow," Judith said at midnight on that first evening. "We'll have a drink then and open some presents, and have our Christmas feast at half past three. There will be breakfast in the morning, and Gordon and I will go to church." She left an invitation lingering in the air, but I marginally shook my head. "You can look after yourself, then, while we're gone."

She kissed me goodnight, with affection and on the cheek. Gordon gave me a smile and a wave, and I went to bed along the hall from them and spent an hour before sleep deliberately not thinking at all about Judith in or out of her nightgown—or not much.

Breakfast was taken in dressing gowns. Judith's was red, quilted and unrevealing.

They changed and went to church. Pray for me, I said, and set out for a walk on the common.

There were brightly wrapped gifts waiting around the base of the silver-starred Christmas tree in the Michaels' drawing room, and a surreptitious inspection had revealed one from Pen addressed to me. I walked across the windy grass, shoulders hunched, hands in pockets, wondering what to do about one for her, and as quite often happens came by chance to a solution.

A small boy was out there with his father, flying a kite, and I stopped to watch.

"That's fun," I said.

The boy took no notice but the father said, "There's no satisfying the little bleeder. I give him this and he says he wants roller skates."

The kite was a brilliant phosphorescent Chinese dragon with butterfly wings and a big frilly tail, soaring and circling like a joyful tethered spirit in the Christmas sky.

"Will you sell it to me?" I asked. "But the roller skates instead?" I explained the problem, the need for an instant present.

Parent and child consulted and the deal was done. I wound up the string carefully and bore the trophy home, wondering what on earth the sober pharmacist would think of such a thing: but when she unwrapped it from gold paper (cadged from Judith for the purpose) she pronounced herself enchanted, and back we all went onto the common to watch her fly it.

The whole day was happy. I hadn't had so good a Christmas since I was a child. I told them so, and kissed Judith uninhibitedly under some mistletoe, which Gordon didn't seem to mind.

"You were born sunny," Judith said, briefly stroking my cheek, and Gordon, nodding, said, "A man without sorrows, unacquainted with grief."

"Grief and sorrow come with time," Pen said, but not as if she meant it imminently. "They come to us all."

On the morning after Christmas Day I drove Judith across London to Hampstead to put flowers on her mother's grave.

"I know you'll think me silly, but I always go. She died on Boxing Day when I was twelve. It's the only way I have of remembering her . . . of feeling I had a mother at all. I usually go by myself. Gordon thinks I'm sentimental and doesn't like coming."

"Nothing wrong with sentiment," I said.

Hampstead was where I lived in the upstairs half of a friend's house. I wasn't sure whether or not Judith knew it, and said nothing until she'd delivered the pink chrysanthemums to the square marble tablet let in flush with the grass and communed for a while with the memories floating there.

It was as we walked slowly back towards the iron gates that I neutrally said, "My flat's only half a mile from here. This part of London is home ground."

"Is it?"

"Mm."

After a few steps she said, "I knew you lived somewhere here. If you remember, you wouldn't let us drive you all the way home from Ascot. You said Hampstead was too far."

"So it was."

"Not for Sir Galahad that starry night."

We reached the gates and paused for her to look back. I was infinitely conscious of her nearness and of my own

stifled desire; and she looked abruptly into my eyes and
said, "Gordon knows you live here, also."

"And does he know how I feel?" I asked.

"I don't know. He hasn't said."

I wanted very much to go that last half mile: that
short distance on wheels, that far journey in commitment. My body tingled . . . rippled . . . from hunger,
and I found myself physically clenching my back teeth.

"What are you thinking?" she said.

"For God's sake . . . you know damn well what I'm
thinking . . . and we're going back to Clapham right
this minute."

She sighed. "Yes, I suppose we must."

"What do you mean . . . you suppose?"

"Well, I . . ." she paused. "I mean, yes we must. I'm
sorry . . . it was just that . . . for a moment . . . I was
tempted."

"As at Ascot?" I said.

She nodded. "As at Ascot."

"Only here and now," I said, "we have the place and
the time and the opportunity to do something about it."

"Yes."

"And what we're going to do . . . is . . . nothing." It
came out as half a question, half a statement: wholly an
impossibility.

"Why do we *care?*" she said explosively. "Why don't
we just get into your bed and have a happy time? Why is
the whole thing so tangled up with bloody concepts like
honor?"

We walked down the road to where I'd parked the car
and I drove southwards with careful observance at
every red light: stop signals making round eyes at me
all the way to Clapham.

"I'd have liked it," Judith said as we pulled up outside her house.

"So would I."

We went indoors in a sort of deprived companionship,
and I realized only when I saw Gordon's smiling unsus-
picious face that I couldn't have returned there if it had
been in any other way.

* * *

It was at lunch that day, when Pen had again resurfaced from her stint among the pills, that I told them about my visit to Calder. Pen, predictably, was acutely interested and said she'd dearly like to know what was in the decoction in the refrigerator.

"What's a decoction?" Judith asked.

"A preparation boiled with water. If you dissolve things in alcohol, that's a tincture."

"One lives and bloody well learns!"

Pen laughed. "How about carminative, anodyne and vermifuge . . . effects of drugs. They simply roll off the tongue with grandeur."

"And what do they mean?" Gordon asked.

"Getting rid of gas, getting rid of pain, getting rid of worms."

Gordon too was laughing. "Have some anodyne tincture of grape." He poured wine into our glasses. "Do you honestly believe, Tim, that Calder cures horses by touch?"

"I'm sure *he* believes it." I reflected. "I don't know if he will let anyone watch. And if he did, what would one see? I don't suppose with a horse it's a case of 'take up your bed and walk.' "

Judith said in surprise, "You sound as if you'd like it to be true. You, that Gordon and Harry have trained to doubt!"

"Calder's impressive," I admitted. "So is his place. So are the fees he charges. He wouldn't be able to set his prices so high if he didn't get real results."

"Do the herbs come extra?" Pen said.

"I didn't ask."

"Would you expect them to?" Gordon said.

"Well . . ." Pen considered. "Some of those that Tim mentioned are fairly exotic. Golden seal—that's hydrastis—said to cure practically anything you can mention, and often used nowadays in tiny amounts in eye drops. Has to be imported from America. And fo-ti-tieng—which is *Hydrocotyle asiatica minor,* also called the source of the elixir of long life—that only grows as far as I know in the tropical jungles of the far east. I mean, I would have thought that giving things like that to horses would be wildly expensive."

If I'd been impressed with Calder I was probably more so with Pen. "I didn't know pharmacists were so clued up on herbs," I said.

"I was just interested so I learned their properties," she explained. "The age-old remedies are hardly even hinted at in the official pharmacy courses, though considering digitalis and pencillin one can't exactly see why. A lot of chemists' shops don't sell nonprescription herbal remedies, but I do, and honestly for a stack of people they seem to work."

"And do you advocate garlic poultices for the feet of babies with whooping-cough?" Gordon asked.

Pen didn't. There was more laughter. If one believed in Calder, Judith said firmly, one believed in him, garlic poultices and all.

The four of us spent a comfortable afternoon and evening together, and when Judith and Gordon went to bed I walked along with Pen to her house, filling my lungs with the fresh air off the common.

"You're going home tomorrow, aren't you?" she said, fishing out her keys.

I nodded. "In the morning."

"It's been great fun." She found the keys and fitted one in the lock. "Would you like to come in?"

"No . . . I'll just walk for a bit."

She opened the door and paused there. "Thank you for the kite . . . it was brilliant. And goodbye for this time, though I guess if Judith can stand it I'll be seeing you again."

"Stand what?" I asked.

She kissed me on the cheek. "Goodnight," she said. "And believe it or not, the herb known as passion flower is good for insomnia."

Her grin shone out like the Cheshire Cat's as she stepped inside her house and closed the door, and I stood hopelessly on her pathway wanting to call her back.

The Second Year

February

Ian Pargetter was murdered at about one in the morning on February first.

I learned about his death from Calder when I telephoned that evening on impulse to thank him belatedly for the lunch party, invite him for a reciprocal dinner in London and hear whether or not he had enjoyed his American tour.

"Who?" he said vaguely when I announced myself. "Who? Oh . . . Tim . . . Look, I can't talk now, I'm simply distracted, a friend of mine's been killed and I can't think of anything else."

"I'm so sorry," I said inadequately.

"Yes . . . Ian Pargetter . . . but I don't suppose you know . . ."

This time I remembered at once. The vet; big, reliable, sandy moustache.

"I met him," I said, "in your house."

"Did you? Oh, yes. I'm so upset I can't concentrate. Look, Tim, ring some other time, will you?"

"Yes, of course."

"It's not just that he's been a friend for years," he

said, "but I don't know . . . I really don't know how my
business will fare without him. He sent so many horses
my way . . . such a good friend . . . I'm totally distraught . . . Look, ring me another time . . . Tim, so
sorry." He put his receiver down with the rattle of a
shaking hand.

I thought at the time that he meant Ian Pargetter
had been killed in some sort of accident, and it was only
the next day when my eye was caught by a paragraph
in a newspaper that I realized my mistake.

Ian Pargetter, said the report, *well known, much respected Newmarket veterinary surgeon, was yesterday
morning found dead in his home. Police suspect foul
play. They state that Pargetter suffered head injuries
and that certain supplies of drugs appear to be missing.
Pargetter's body was discovered by Mrs. Jane Halson, a
daily cleaner. The vet is survived by his wife and three
young daughters, all of whom were away from home at
the time of the attack. Mrs. Pargetter was reported last
night to be very distressed and under sedation.*

A lot of succinct bad news, I thought, for a lot of sad
bereft people. He was the first person I'd known who'd
been murdered, and in spite of our very brief meeting I
found his death most disturbing: and if I felt so unsettled about a near-stranger, how, I wondered, did one
ever recover from the murder of someone one knew well
and loved? How did one deal with the anger? Come to
terms with the urge to revenge?

I'd of course read reports of husbands and wives who
pronounced themselves "not bitter" over the slaughter
of a spouse, but I'd never understood it. I felt furious on
Ian Pargetter's behalf that anyone should have had the
arrogance to wipe him out.

Because of Ascot and Sandcastle my long-dormant interest in racecourses seemed thoroughly to have re-
awakened, and on three or four Saturday afternoons
that winter I'd trekked to Kempton or Sandown or
Newbury to watch the jumpers. Ursula Young had
become a familiar acquaintance, and it was from

this brisk well-informed lady bloodstock agent that I learned most about Ian Pargetter and his death.

"Drink?" I suggested at Kempton, pulling up my coat collar against a biting wind.

She looked at her watch (I'd never seen her do anything without checking the time) and agreed to a quick one. Whisky-mac for her, coffee for me, as at Doncaster.

"Now tell me," she said, hugging her glass and yelling in my ear over the general din of the bar packed with other cold customers seeking inner warmth, "when you asked all those questions about stallion shares, was it for Sandcastle?"

I smiled without actually answering, shielding my coffee inadequately from adjacent nudging elbows.

"Thought so," she said. "Look—there's a table. Grab it."

We sat down in a corner with the racket going on over our heads and the closed-circuit television playing reruns of the last race fortissimo. Ursula bent her head towards mine. "A wow-sized coup for Oliver Knowles."

"You approve?" I asked.

She nodded. "He'll be among the greats in one throw. Smart move. Clever man."

"Do you know him?"

"Yes. Meet him often at the sales. He had a snooty wife who left him for some Canadian millionaire or other, and maybe that's why he's aiming for the big time; just to show her." She smiled fiendishly. "She was a real pain and I hope he makes it."

She drank half her whisky and I said it was a shame about Ian Pargetter, that I'd met him once at Calder's house.

She grimaced with a stronger echo of the anger I had myself felt. "He'd been out all evening saving the life of a classic-class colt with colic. It's so beastly. He went home well after midnight, and they reckon whoever killed him was already in the house stealing whatever he could lay his hands on. Ian's wife and family were away visiting her mother, you see, and the police think the killer thought the house would be empty for the night." She swallowed. "He was hit on the back of the head with a brass lamp off one of the tables in the sitting room. Just casual. Unpremeditated. Just . . . *stupid.*" She looked moved, as I guessed everyone must have been who had known him. "Such a waste. He was a really nice man, a good vet, everyone liked him. And all for practically nothing. . . . The police found a lot of silver and jewelry lying on a blanket ready to be carried away, but they think the thief just panicked and left it when Ian came home . . . all that anyone can think of that's missing is his case of instruments and a few drugs that he'd had with him that evening . . . nothing worth killing for . . . not even for an addict. Nothing in it like that." She fell silent and looked down into her nearly empty glass, and I offered her a refill.

"No, thanks all the same, one's enough. I feel pretty maudlin as it is. I liked Ian. He was a good sort. I'd like to *throttle* the little beast who killed him."

"I think Calder Jackson feels much as you do," I said.

She glanced up, her good-looking fiftyish face full of general concern. "Calder will miss Ian terribly. There aren't that number of vets around who'd not only put up with a faith-healer on their doorstep but actually treat him as a colleague. Ian had no professional jealousy. Very rare. Very good man. Makes it all the worse."

We went out again into the raw air and I lost five pounds on the afternoon, which would have sent Lorna Shipton swooning to Uncle Freddie, if she'd known.

Two weeks later with Oliver Knowles' warm approval I paid another visit to his farm in Hertfordshire, and although it was again a Sunday and still winter, the atmosphere of the place had fundamentally changed. Where there had been quiet sleepy near-hibernation there was now a wakeful bustle and eagerness; where a scattering of dams and foals across the paddocks, now a crowd of mares moving alone and slowly with big bellies.

The crop had come to the harvest. Life was ripening into the daylight, and into the darkness the new seed would be sown.

I had not been truly a country child (ten acres of wooded hill in Surrey) and to me the birth of animals still seemed a wonder and joy: to Oliver Knowles, he said, it meant constant worry and profit and loss. His grasp of essentials still rang out strong and clear, but there were lines on his forehead from the details.

"I suppose," he said frankly, walking me into the first of the big yards, "that the one thing I hadn't mentally prepared myself for was the value of the foals now being born here. I mean . . ." he gestured around at the patient heads looking over the rows of half-doors ". . . these mares have been to the top stallions. They're carrying fabulous bloodlines. They're history." His awe could be felt. "I didn't realize, you know, what anxiety they would bring me. We've always done our best for the foals, of course we have, but if one died it wasn't a tragedy, but with this lot . . ." He smiled ruefully. "It's not enough just owning Sandcastle. I have to make sure that our reputation for handling top broodmares is good and sound."

We walked along beside one row of boxes with him telling me in detail the breeding of each mare we came to and of the foal she carried, and even to my ignorant ears it sounded as if every Derby and Oaks winner for the past half-century had had a hand in the coming generation.

"I had no trouble selling Sandcastle's nominations," he said. "Not even at forty thousand pounds a throw. I could even choose, to some extent, which mares to accept. It's been utterly amazing to be able to turn away mares that I considered wouldn't do him justice."

"Is there a temptation," I asked mildly, "to sell more than forty places? To . . . er . . . accept an extra fee . . . in untaxed cash . . . on the quiet?"

He was more amused than offended. "I wouldn't say it hasn't been done on every farm that ever existed. But I wouldn't do it with Sandcastle . . . or at any rate not this year. He's still young. And untested, of course. Some stallions won't look at as many as forty mares . . . though shy breeders do tend to run in families, and there's nothing in his pedigree to suggest he'll be anything but energetic and fertile. I wouldn't have embarked on all this if there had been any doubts."

It seemed that he was trying to reassure himself as much as me; as if the size and responsibility of his undertaking had only just penetrated, and in penetrating, frightened.

I felt a faint tremor of dismay but stifled it with the reassurance that come hell or high water Sandcastle was worth his buying price and could be sold again even at this late date for not much less. The bank's money was safe on his hoof.

It was earlier in the day than my last visit—eleven in the morning—and more lads than before were to be seen mucking out the boxes and carrying feed and water.

"I've had to take on extra hands," Oliver Knowles said matter-of-factly. "Temporarily, for the season."

"Has recruitment been difficult?" I asked.

"Not really. I do it every spring. I keep the good ones on for the whole year, if they'll stay, of course: these lads come and go as the whim takes them, the unmarried ones, that is. I keep the nucleus on and put them painting fences and such in the autumn and winter."

We strolled into the second yard, where the butty figure of Nigel could be seen peering over a half-door into a box.

"You remember Nigel?" Oliver said. "My stud manager?"

Nigel, I noted, had duly been promoted.

"And Ginnie?" I asked, as we walked over. "Is she home today?"

"Yes, she's somewhere about." He looked around as if expecting her to materialize at the sound of her name, but nothing happened.

"How's it going, Nigel?" he asked.

Nigel's hairy eyebrows withdrew from the box and aimed themselves in our direction. "Floradora's eating again," he said, indicating the inspected lady and sounding relieved. "And Pattacake is still in labor. I'm just going back there."

"We'll come," Oliver said. "If you'd like to?" he said, looking at me questioningly.

I nodded and walked on with them along the path into the third, smaller quadrangle, the foaling yard.

Here too, in this place that had been empty, there was purposeful life, and the box to which Nigel led us was larger than normal and thickly laid with straw.

"Foals usually drop at night," Oliver said, and Nigel nodded. "She started about midnight. She's just lazy, eh, girl?" He patted the brown rump. "Very slow. Same thing every year."

"She's not come for Sandcastle, then?" I said.

"No. She's one of mine," Oliver said. "The foal's by Diarist."

We hovered for a few minutes but there was no change in Pattacake. Nigel, running delicately knowledgeable hands over the shape under her ribs, said she'd be another hour, perhaps, and that he would stay with her for a while. Oliver and I walked onwards, past the still closed breeding shed and down the path between the two small paddocks towards the stallion yard. Everything, as before, meticulously tidy.

There was one four-legged figure in one of the paddocks, head down and placid. "Parakeet," Oliver said. "Getting more air than grass, actually. It isn't warm enough yet for the new grass to grow."

We came finally to the last yard, and there he was, the gilt-edged Sandcastle, looking over his door like any other horse.

One couldn't tell, I thought. True, there was a poise to the well-shaped head, and an interested eye and alertly pricked ears, but nothing to announce that this was the marvelous creature I'd seen at Ascot. No one ever again, I reflected, would see that arrowlike raking gallop, that sublime throat-catching valor: and it seemed a shame that he should be denied his ability in the hope that he would pass it on.

A lad, broom in hand, was sweeping scatterings of peat off the concrete apron in front of the six stallions' boxes, watched by Sandcastle, Rotaboy and Diarist with the same depth of interest as a bus line would extend to a street singer.

"Lenny," Oliver said, "you can take Sandcastle down

to the small paddock opposite to the one with Parakeet." He looked up at the sky as if to sniff the coming weather. "Put him back in his box when you return for evening stables."

"Yes, sir."

Lenny was well into middle age, small, leathery and of obviously long experience. He propped the broom against one of the empty boxes and disappeared into a doorway, to reappear presently carrying a length of rope.

"Lenny is one of my most trusted helpers," Oliver Knowles said. "Been with me several years. He's good with stallions and much stronger than he looks. Stallions can be quite difficult to handle, but Lenny gets on with them better than with mares. Don't know why."

Lenny clipped the rope onto the head collar that Sandcastle, along with every other equine resident, wore at all times. Upon the head collar was stapled a metal plate bearing the horse's name, an absolute essential for identification. Shuffle all those mares together without their head collars, I thought, and no one would ever sort them. I suggested the problem mildly to Oliver, who positively blanched. "God forbid! Don't suggest such things. We're very careful. Have to be. Otherwise, as you say, we could breed the wrong mare to the wrong stallion and never know it."

I wondered, but privately, how often that in fact had happened, or whether indeed it was possible for two mares or two foals to be permanently swapped. The opportunities for mistakes, if not for outright fraud, put computer manipulation in the shade.

Nigel arrived in the yard, and with his scarcely necessary help Lenny opened Sandcastle's door and led the colt out; and one could see in all their strength the sleek muscles, the tugging sinews, the spring-like joints. The body that was worth its weight in gold pranced and scrunched on the hard apron, wheeling round impatiently and tossing its uncomprehending head.

"Full of himself," Oliver explained. "We have to feed him well and keep him fairly fit, but of course he doesn't get the exercise he used to."

We stepped to one side with undignified haste to avoid Sandcastle's restless hindquarters. "Has he . . . er . . . started work yet?" I asked.

"Not yet," Oliver said. "Only one of his mares has foaled so far. She's almost through her foal-heat, so when she comes into use in fifteen or sixteen days' time, she'll be his first. After that there will be a pause—give him time to think!—then he'll be busy until into June."

"How often . . . ?" I murmured delicately.

Oliver fielded the question as if he, like Calder, had had to give the same answer countless times over.

"It depends on the stallion," he said. "Some can cover one mare in the morning and another in the afternoon and go on like that for days. Others haven't that much stamina or that much desire. Occasionally you get very shy and choosy stallions. Some of them won't go near some mares but will mate all right with others. Some will cover only one mare a fortnight, if that. Stallions aren't machines, you know, they're individuals like everyone else."

With Nigel in attendance Lenny led Sandcastle out of the yard, the long bay legs stalking in powerful strides beside the almost trotting little man.

"Sandcastle will be all right with mares," Oliver said again firmly. "Most stallions are."

We stopped for Oliver to give two carrots and a pat each to Rotaboy and Diarist, so that we didn't ourselves see the calamity. We heard a distant clatter and yell and the thud of fast hooves, and Oliver went white as he turned to run to the disaster.

I followed him, also sprinting.

Lenny lay against one of the white painted posts of the small paddock's rails, dazedly trying to pull himself up. Sandcastle, loose and excited, had found his way into one of the paths between the larger paddocks and from his bolting speed must have taken the rails to be those of a racecourse.

Nigel stood by the open gate of the small paddock, his mouth wide, as if arrested there by shock. He was still almost speechless when Oliver and I reached him, but had at least begun to unstick.

"For Christ's sake," Oliver shouted. "Get going. Get the Land Rover. He can get out onto the road that way through the Watcherleys'." He ran off in the direction of his own house, leaving a partially resurrected Nigel to stumble off toward the bungalow, half in sight beyond the stallion yard.

Lenny raised himself and began his excuses, but I didn't wait to listen. Unused to the problem and ignorant of how best to catch fleeing horses, I simply set off in Sandcastle's wake, following his path between the paddocks and seeing him disappear ahead of me behind a distant hedge.

I ran fast along the grassy path between the rails, past the groups of incurious mares in the paddocks, thinking that my brief January vacation skiing down the pistes at Gstaad might have its practical uses after all; there was currently a lot more muscle in my legs than was ever to be found by July.

Whereas on my last visit the hedge between Oliver Knowles' farm and the Watcherleys' run-down hospital for sick horses had been a thorny unbroken boundary, there were now two or three wide gaps, so that passing from one side to the other was easy. I pounded through the gap that lay straight ahead and noticed almost unconsciously that the Watcherleys' delapidation had been not only halted but partially reversed, with new fencing going up and repairs in hand on the roofs.

I ran towards the stable buildings across a thistly field in which there was no sign of Sandcastle, and through an as yet unmended gate that hung open on broken hinges on the far side. Beyond there, between piles of rubble and rusting iron, I reached the yard itself, to find Ginnie looking around her with unfocused anxiety and a man and a girl walking towards her inquiringly.

Ginnie saw me running, and her first instinctively cheerful greeting turned almost at once to alarm.

"What is it?" she said. "Is one of the mares out?"

"Sandcastle."

"Oh, no . . ." It was a wail of despair. "He can get on the road." She turned away, already running, and I ran after her; out of the Watcherleys' yard, round their ramshackle house and down the short, weedy, gateless drive to the dangerous outside world where a car could kill a horse without even trying.

"We'll never catch him," Ginnie said as we reached the road. "It's no use running. We don't know which way he went." She was in great distress: eyes flooding, tears on her cheeks. "Where's Dad?"

"I should think he's out in his car, looking. And Nigel's in a Land Rover."

"I heard a horse gallop through the Watcherleys'," she said. "I was in one of the boxes with a foal. I never thought . . . I mean, I thought it might be a mare . . ."

A speeding car passed in front of us, followed closely by two others doing at least sixty miles an hour, one of them dicily passing a heavy tractor-trailer rig, which should have been home in its nest on a Sunday. The thought of Sandcastle loose in that battlefield was literally goose-pimpling and I began for the first time to believe in his imminent destruction. One of those charging monsters would be sure to hit him. He would waver across the road into their path, swerving, rudderless, hopelessly vulnerable . . . a five-million-pound traffic accident in the making.

"Let's go this way," I said, pointing to the left. A motorcyclist roared from that direction, head down in a black visor, going too fast to stop.

Ginnie shook her head sharply. "Dad and Nigel will be on the road. But there's a track over there . . ." She pointed slantwise across the road. "He might just have found it. And there's a bit of a hill and even if he isn't up there at least we might see him from there . . . you can see the road in places . . . I often ride up there." She was off again, running while she talked, and I fell in beside her. Her face was screwed up with the intensity of her feelings and I felt as much sympathy for her as dismay about the horse. Sandcastle was insured—I'd examined and approved the policy myself—but Oliver Knowles' prestige wasn't. The escape and death of the first great stallion in his care would hardly attract future business.

The track was muddy and rutted and slippery from recent rain. There were also a great many hoofprints, some looking new, some overtrodden and old. I pointed to them as we ran and asked Ginnie pantingly if she knew if any of those were Sandcastle's.

"Oh." She stopped running suddenly. "Yes. Of course. He hasn't got shoes on. The blacksmith came yesterday, Dad said . . ." she peered at the ground dubiously ". . . he left Sandcastle without new shoes because he was going to make leather pads for under them . . . I wasn't really listening." She pointed. "I think that might be him. Those new marks . . . they could be, they really could." She began running again up the track, impelled by hope now as well as horror, fit in her jeans and sweater and jodhpur boots after all that compulsory jogging.

I ran beside her thinking that mud anyway washed easily from shoes, socks and trouser legs. The ground began to rise sharply and to narrow between barebranched scratchy bushes; and the jumble of hoofmarks inexorably led on and on.

"Please be up here," Ginnie was saying. "Please, Sandcastle, please be up here." Her urgency pumped in her legs and ran in misery down her cheeks. "Oh please . . . *please* . . ."

The agony of adolescence, I thought. So real, so overpowering . . . so remembered.

The track curved through the bushes and opened suddenly into a wider place where grass grew in patches beside the rutted mud; and there stood Sandcastle, head high, nostrils twitching to the wind, a brown-and-black creature of power and beauty and majesty.

Ginnie stopped running in one stride and caught my arm fiercely.

"Don't move," she said. "I'll do it. You stay here. Keep still. Please keep still."

I nodded obediently, respecting her experience. The colt looked ready to run again at the slightest untimely movement, his sides quivering, his legs stiff with tension, his tail sweeping up and down restlessly.

He's frightened, I thought suddenly. He's out here,

"Didn't it occur to you?" He sounded almost angry; the aftermath of fright. "Didn't you *think?*"

"No," I said truthfully. "I just did it."

"Never do it again," he said, "and thanks," he paused and swallowed and tried to make light of his own shattered state. "Thanks for taking care of my investment."

Lenny and Nigel had brought a different sort of head collar, which involved a bit in the mouth and a fierce-looking curb chain, and with these in place the captive (if not chastened) fugitive was led away. There seemed to me to be a protest in the stalking hindquarters, a statement of disgust at the injustices of life. I smiled at that fanciful thought; the pathetic fallacy, the ascribing to animals of emotions one felt only oneself.

Oliver drove Ginnie and me back in the Land Rover, traveling slowly behind the horse and telling how Nigel and Lenny had allowed him to go free.

"Sheer bloody carelessness," he said forthrightly. "Both of them should know better. They could see the horse was fresh and jumping out of his skin yet Lenny was apparently holding the rope with only one hand and stretching to swing the gate open with the other. He took his eyes off Sandcastle so he wasn't ready when Nigel made some sharp movement or other and the horse reared and ran backwards. I ask you! Lenny! Nigel! How can they be so bloody stupid after all these years?"

There seemed to be no answer to that so we just let him curse away, and he was still rumbling like distant thunder when the journey ended. Once home he hurried off to the stallion yard and Ginnie trenchantly said that if Nigel was as sloppy with discipline for animals as he was with the lads, it was no wonder any horse with spirit would take advantage.

"Accidents happen," I said mildly.

"Huh." She was scornful. "Dad's right. That accident *shouldn't* have happened. It was an absolute miracle that Sandcastle came to no harm at all. Even if he hadn't got out on the road he could have tried to jump the paddock rails—loose horses often do—and broken

his leg or something." She sounded as angry as her father, and for the same reason; the flooding release after
fear. I put my arm round her shoulders and gave her a
quick hug, which seemed to disconcert her horribly.
"Oh dear, you must think me so silly . . . and crying
like that . . . and everything."

"I think you're a nice dear girl who's had a rotten
morning," I said. "But all's well now, you know; it
really is."

I naturally believed what I said, but I was wrong.

April

Calder Jackson finally came to dinner with me while he was staying in London to attend a world conference of herbalists. He would be glad, he said, to spend one of the evenings away from his colleagues, and I met him in a restaurant, on the grounds that although my flat was civilized my cooking was not.

I sensed immediately a difference in him, though it was hard to define; rather as if he had become a figure still larger than life. Heads turned and voices whispered when we walked through the crowded place to our table, but because of television this would have happened anyway. Yet now, I thought, Calder really enjoyed it. There was still no overt arrogance, still a becoming modesty of manner, but something within him had intensified, crystallized, become a governing factor. He was now, I thought, even to himself, the Great Man.

I wondered what, if anything, had specifically altered him, and it turned out to be the one thing I would have least expected: Ian Pargetter's death.

Over a plateful of succulent smoked salmon Calder

apologized for the abrupt way he'd brushed me off on the telephone on that disturbing night, and I said it was most understandable.

"Fact is," Calder said, squeezing lemon juice, "I was afraid my whole business would collapse. Ian's partners, you know, never approved of me. I was afraid they would influence everyone against me, once Ian had gone."

"And it hasn't worked out that way?"

He shook his head, assembling a pink forkful. "Remarkably not. Amazing." He put the smoked salmon in his mouth and made appreciative noises, munching. I was aware, and I guessed he was, too, that the ears of the people at the tables on either side were almost visibly attuned to the distinctive voice, to the clear loud diction with its country edge. "My yard's still full. People have faith, you know. I may not get quite so many racehorses, that's to be expected, but still a few."

"And have you heard any more about Ian Pargetter's death? Did they ever find out who killed him?"

He looked regretful. "I'm sure they haven't. I asked one of his partners the other day, and he said no one seemed to be asking questions anymore. He was quite upset. And so am I. I suppose finding his murderer won't bring Ian back, but all the same one wants to *know.*"

"Tell me some of your recent successes," I said, nodding, changing the subject and taking a slice of paper-thin brown bread and butter. "I find your work tremendously interesting." I also found it about the only thing else to talk about, as we seemed to have few other points of contact. Regret it as I might, there was still no drift towards an easy personal friendship.

Calder ate some more smoked salmon while he thought. "I had a colt," he said at last, "a two-year-old in training. Ian had been treating him, and he'd seemed to be doing well. Then about three weeks after Ian died the colt started bleeding into his mouth and down his nose and went on and on doing it, and as Ian's partner couldn't find out the trouble the trainer persuaded the owner to send the horse to me."

"And did you discover what was wrong?" I asked.

"Oh, no." He shook his head. "It wasn't necessary. I laid my hands on him three succeeding days, and the bleeding stopped immediately. I kept him at my place for two weeks altogether, and returned him on his way back to full good health."

The adjacent tables were fascinated, as indeed I was myself.

"Did you give him herbs?" I asked.

"Certainly. Of course. And alfalfa in his hay. Excellent for many ills, alfalfa."

I had only the haziest idea of what alfalfa looked like, beyond its being some sort of grass.

"The one thing you can't do with herbs," he said confidently, "is *harm*."

I raised my eyebrows with my mouth full.

He gave the nearest thing to a grin. "With ordinary medicines one has to be so careful because of their power and their side effects, but if I'm not certain what's wrong with a horse I can give it all the herbal remedies I can think of all at once in the hope that one of them will hit the target, and it quite often does. It may be hopelessly unscientific, but if a trained vet can't tell exactly what's wrong with a horse, how can I?"

I smiled with undiluted pleasure. "Have some wine," I said.

He nodded the helmet of curls, and the movement I made towards the bottle in its ice-bucket was instantly forestalled by a watchful waiter who poured almost reverently into the healer's glass.

"How was the American trip," I asked, "way back in January?"

"Mm." He sipped his wine. "Interesting." He frowned a little and went back to finishing the salmon, leaving me wondering whether that was his total answer. When he'd laid down his knife and fork, however, he sat back in his chair and told me that the most enjoyable part of his American journey had been, as he'd expected, his few days on the ski slopes; and we discussed skiing venues throughout the roast beef and burgundy that followed.

With the crepes suzette I asked after Dissdale and Bettina and heard that Dissdale had been to New York on a business trip and that Bettina had been acting a small part in a British movie, which Dissdale hadn't known whether to be pleased about or not. "Too many gorgeous young studs around," Calder said, smiling. "Dissdale gets worried anyway, and he was away for ten days."

I pondered briefly about Calder's own seemingly non-existent sex life: but he'd never seen me with a girl either, and certainly there was no hint in him of the homosexual.

Over coffee, running out of subjects, I asked about his yard in general, and how was the right-hand man, Jason, in particular.

Calder shrugged. "He's left. They come and go, you know. No loyalty these days."

"And you don't fear . . . well, that he'd take your knowledge with him?"

He looked amused. "He didn't know much. I mean, I'd hand out a pill and tell Jason which horse to give it to. That sort of thing."

We finished amiably enough with a glass of brandy for each and a cigar for him, and I tried not to wince over the bill.

"A very pleasant evening," Calder said. "You must come out to lunch again one day."

"I'd like to."

We sat for a final few minutes opposite each other in a pause of mutual appraisal: two people utterly different but bonded by one-tenth of a second on a pavement in Ascot. Saved and saver, inextricably interested in each other; a continuing curiosity that would never quite lose touch. I smiled at him slowly and got a smile in return, but all surface, no depth, a mirror exactly of my own feelings.

In the office things were slowly changing. John had boasted too often of his sexual conquests and complained too often about my directorship, and Gordon's almost-equal had tired of such waste of time. I'd heard from Val Fisher in a perhaps edited version that at a small and special seniors' meeting (held in my absence and without my knowledge) Gordon's almost-equal had said he would like to boot John vigorously over St. Paul's. His opinion was respected. I heard from Alec one day merely that the mosquito that had stung me for so long had been squashed, and on going along the passage to investigate found John's desk empty and his bull-like presence but a quiver in the past.

"He's gone to sell air-conditioning to Eskimos," Alec said, and Gordon's almost-equal, smiling affably, corrected it more probably to a partnership with some brokers on the Stock Exchange.

Alec himself seemed restless, as if his own job no longer held him enthralled.

"It's all right for you," he said once. "You've the gift. You've the *sight.* I can't tell a gold mine from a pomegranate at five paces, and it's taken me all these years to know it."

"But you're a conjuror," I said. "You can rattle up outside money faster than anyone."

"Gift of the old gab, you mean." He looked uncharacteristically gloomy. "Syrup with a chisel in it." He waved his hand towards the desks of our new older colleagues, who had both gone out to lunch. "I'll end up like them, still here, still smooth-talking, part of the furniture, coming up to *sixty.*" His voice held disbelief that such an age could be achieved. "That isn't life, is it? That's not *all?*"

I said that I supposed it might be.

"Yes, but for you it's exciting," he said. "I mean, you love it. Your eyes *gleam.* You get your kicks right here in this room. But I'll never be made a director, let's face it, and I have this grotty feeling that time's slipping away, and soon it will be too late to start anything else."

"Like what?"

"Like being an actor. Or a doctor. Or an acrobat."

"It's been too late for that since you were six."

"Yeah," he said. "Lousy, isn't it?" He put his heart and soul ten minutes later, however, into tracking down a source of a hundred thousand for several years and lending it to a businessman at a profitable rate, knitting together such loan packages all afternoon with diligence and success.

I hoped he would stay. He was the yeast of the office: my bubbles in the dough. As for myself, I had grown accustomed to being on the board and had slowly found I'd reached a new level of confidence. Gordon seemed to treat me unreservedly as an equal, though it was not until he had been doing it for some time that I looked back and realized.

Gordon's hitherto uniformly black hair had grown a streak or two of gray. His right hand now trembled also, and his handwriting had grown smaller through his efforts to control his fingers. I watched his valiant struggles to appear normal and respected his privacy by never making even a visual comment: it had become second nature to look anywhere but directly at his hands. In the brain department he remained energetic, but physically over all he was slowing down.

I had only seen Judith once since Christmas, and that had been in the office at a retirement party given for the head of Corporate Finance, a golden-handshake affair to which all managers' wives had been invited.

"How are you?" she said amid the throng, holding a glass of wine and an unidentifiable canapé and smelling of violets.

"Fine. And you?"

"Fine."

She was wearing blue, with diamonds in her ears. I looked at her with absolute and unhappy love and saw the strain it put into her face.

"I'm sorry," I said.

She shook her head and swallowed. "I thought . . . it might be different . . . here in the bank."

"No."

She looked down at the canapé, which was squashy and yellow. "If I don't eat this damned thing soon it'll drop down my dress."

I took it out of her fingers and deposited it in an

ashtray. "Invest in a salami cornet. They stay rock-hard for hours."

"What's Tim telling you to invest in?" demanded Henry Shipton, turning to us a beaming face.

"Salami," Judith said.

"Typical. He loaned money to a seaweed processor last week. Judith, my darling, let me freshen your glass."

He took the glass away to the bottles and left us again looking at each other with a hundred ears around.

"I was thinking," I said, "when it's warmer, could I take you and Gordon, and Pen if she'd like it, out somewhere one Sunday? Somewhere not ordinary. All day."

She took longer than normal politeness required to answer, and I understood all the unspoken things, but finally, as Henry could be seen returning, she said, "Yes. We'd all like it. I'd like it . . . very much."

"Here you are," Henry said. "Tim, you go and fight for your own refill, and leave me to talk to this gorgeous girl." He put his arm around her shoulders and swept her off, and although I was vividly aware all evening of her presence, we had no more moments alone.

From day to day when she wasn't around I didn't precisely suffer: her absence was more of a faint background ache. When I saw Gordon daily in the office I felt no constant envy, nor hated him, nor even thought much of where he slept. I liked him for the good clever man he was, and our office relationship continued unruffled and secure. Loving Judith was both pleasure and pain, delight and deprivation, wishes withdrawn, dreams denied. It might have been easier and more sensible to have met and fallen heavily for some young glamorous unattached stranger, but the one thing love never did have was logic.

"Easter," I said to Gordon one day in the office. "Are you and Judith going away?"

"We had plans—they fell through."

"Did Judith mention that I'd like to take you both somewhere—and Pen Warner—as a thank-you for Christmas?"

"Yes, I believe she did."

"Easter Monday, then?"

He seemed pleased at the idea and reported the next day that Judith had asked Pen, and everyone was poised. "Pen's bringing her kite," he said. "Unless it's a day trip to Manchester."

"I'll think of something," I said, laughing. "Tell her it won't be raining."

What I did eventually think of seemed to please them all splendidly and also to be acceptable to others concerned, and I consequently collected Gordon and Judith and Pen (but not the kite) from Clapham at eight-thirty on Easter Bank Holiday morning. Judith and Pen were in fizzing high spirits, though Gordon seemed already tired. I suggested abandoning what was bound to be a fairly taxing day for him, but he wouldn't hear of it.

"I want to go," he said. "Been looking forward to it all week. But I'll just sit in the back of the car and rest and sleep some of the way." So Judith sat beside me while I drove and touched my hand now and then, not talking much but contenting me deeply by just being there. The journey to Newmarket lasted two and a half hours and I would as soon it had gone on forever.

I was taking them to Calder's yard, to the utter fascination of Pen. "But don't tell him I'm a pharmacist," she said. "He might clam up if he knew he had an informed audience."

"We won't tell," Judith assured her. "It would absolutely spoil the fun."

Poor Calder, I thought: but I wouldn't tell him either.

He greeted us expansively (making me feel guilty) and gave us coffee in the huge oak-beamed sitting room where the memory of Ian Pargetter hovered peripherally by the fireplace.

"Delighted to see you again," Calder said, peering at Gordon, Judith and Pen as if trying to conjure a memory to fit their faces. He knew of course who they were by name, but Ascot was ten months since, and although it had been an especially memorable day for him he had met a great many new people between then and now.

"Ah *yes*," he said with relief, his brow clearing. "Yellow hat with roses."

Judith laughed. "Well done."

"Can't forget anyone so pretty."

She took it as it was meant, but indeed he hadn't forgotten, as one tended never to forget people whose vitality brought out the sun.

"I see Dissdale and Bettina quite often," he said, making conversation, and Gordon agreed that he and Judith, also, sometimes saw Dissdale, though infrequently. As a topic it was hardly riveting, but served as an acceptable unwinding interval between the long car journey and the Grand Tour.

The patients in the boxes were all different but their ailments seemed the same: and I supposed surgeons could be excused their impersonal talk of "the appendix in bed 14," when the occupants changed week by week but the operation didn't.

"This is a star three-day-eventer who came here five weeks ago with severe muscular weakness and no appetite. Wouldn't eat. Couldn't be ridden. He goes home tomorrow, strong and thriving. Looks well, eh?" Calder patted the glossy brown neck over the half-door. "His owner thought he was dying, poor girl. She was weeping when she brought him here. It's really satisfying, you know, to be able to help."

Gordon said civilly that it must be.

"This is a two-year-old not long in training. Came with an intractably infected wound on his fetlock. He's been here a week, and he's healing. It was most gratifying that the trainer sent him without delay, since I'd treated several of his horses in the past."

"This mare," Calder went on, moving us all along, "came two or three days ago in great discomfort with blood in her urine. She's responding well, I'm glad to say." He patted this one too, as he did them all.

"What was causing the bleeding?" Pen asked, but with only an uninformed-member-of-the-public intonation.

Calder shook his head. "I don't know. His vet diagnosed a kidney infection complicated by crystalluria,

which means crystals in the urine, but he didn't know
the type of germ, and every antibiotic he gave failed to
work. So the mare came here. Last resort." He gave me
a wink. "I'm thinking of simply renaming this whole
place 'Last Resort.' "

"And you're treating her," Gordon asked, "with
herbs?"

"With everything I can think of," Calder said. "And
of course . . . with hands."

"I suppose," Judith said diffidently, "that you'd
never let anyone watch . . . ?"

"My dear lady, for you, anything," Calder said. "But
you'd see nothing. You might stand for half an hour,
and nothing would happen. It would be terribly boring.
And I might, perhaps, be *unable*, you know, if someone
was waiting and standing there."

Judith smiled understandingly and the tour continued, ending, as before, in the surgery.

Pen stood looking about her with sociable blankness
and then wandered over to the glass-fronted cabinets to
peer myopically at the contents.

Calder, happily ignoring her in favor of Judith, was
pulling out his antique tablet-maker and demonstrat-
ing it with pride.

"It's beautiful," Judith said sincerely. "Do you use it
much?"

"All the time," he said. "Any herbalist worth the
name makes his own pills and potions."

"Tim said you had a universal magic potion in the
fridge."

Calder smiled and obligingly opened the refrigerator
door, revealing the brown-filled plastic containers, as
before.

"What's in it?" Judith asked.

"Trade secret," he said, smiling. "Decoction of hops
and other things."

"Like beer?" Judith said.

"Yes, perhaps."

"Horses do drink beer," Gordon said. "Or so I've
heard."

Pen bent down to pick up a small peach-colored pill

that was lying unobtrusively on the floor in the angle of one of the cupboards, and put it without comment on the bench.

"It's all so *absorbing*," Judith said. "So tremendously kind of you to show us everything. I'll watch all your programs with more fervor than ever."

Calder responded to her warmly as all men did and asked us into the house again for a drink before we left. Gordon, however, was still showing signs of fatigue and now also hiding both hands in his pockets, which meant he felt they were trembling badly, so the rest of us thanked Calder enthusiastically for his welcome and made admiring remarks about his hospital and climbed into the car, into the same places as before.

"Come back any time you like, Tim," he said; and I said thank you and perhaps I would. We shook hands, and we smiled, caught in our odd relationship and unable to take it further. He waved, and I waved back as I drove away.

"Isn't he amazing?" Judith said. "I must say, Tim, I do understand why you're impressed."

Gordon grunted and said that theatrical surgeons weren't necessarily the best: but yes, Calder was impressive.

It was only Pen, after several miles, who expressed her reservations.

"I'm not saying he doesn't do a great deal of good for the horses. Of course he must do, to have amassed such a reputation. But I don't honestly think he does it all with herbs."

"How do you mean?" Judith asked, twisting round so as to see her better.

Pen leaned forward. "I found a pill on the floor. I don't suppose you noticed."

"I did," I said. "You put it on the bench."

"That's right. Well, that was no herb, it was plain straightforward warfarin."

"It may be plain straightforward war-whatever to you," Judith said. "But not to me."

Pen's voice was smiling. "Warfarin is a drug used in humans, and I daresay in horses, after things like heart attacks. It's a coumarin—an anticoagulant. Makes the blood less likely to clot and block up the veins and arteries. Widely used all over the place."

We digested the information in silence for a mile or two, and finally Gordon said, "How did you know it was warfarin? I mean, how can you tell?"

"I handle it every day," she said. "I know the dosages, the sizes, the colors, the manufacturers' marks. You see all those things so often, you get to know them at a glance."

"Do you mean," I said interestedly, "that if you saw fifty different pills laid out in a row you could identify the lot?"

"Probably. If they all came from major drug companies and weren't completely new, certainly, yes."

"Like a wine-taster," Judith said.

"Clever girl," Gordon said, meaning Pen.

"It's just habit." She thought. "And something else in those cupboards wasn't strictly herbal, I suppose. He had one or two bags of potassium sulfate, bought from Goodison's Garden Center, wherever that is."

"Whatever for?" Judith asked. "Isn't potassium sulfate a fertilizer?"

"Potassium's just as essential to animals as to plants," Pen said. "I wouldn't be surprised if it isn't one of the ingredients in that secret brew."

"What else would you put in it, if you were making it?" I asked curiously.

"Oh, heavens." She pondered. "Any sort of tonic. Perhaps licorice root, which he once mentioned. Maybe caffeine. All sorts of vitamins. Just a pepping-up mishmash."

The hardest part of the day had been to find somewhere decent to have lunch, and the place I'd chosen via the various gourmet guides turned out, as so often happens, to have changed hands and chefs since the books were written. The resulting repast was slow to arrive and disappointing to eat, but the mood of my guests forgave all.

"You remember," Gordon said thoughtfully over the coffee, "that you told us on the way to Newmarket that

Calder was worried about his business when that vet was killed?"

"Yes," I said. "He was, at the time."

"Isn't it possible," Gordon said, "that the vet was letting Calder have regular official medicines, like warfarin, and Calder thought his supplies would dry up, when the vet died?"

"Gordon!" Judith said. "How devious you are, darling."

We all thought about it, however, and Pen nodded. "He must have found another willing source, I should think."

"But," I protested, "would vets really do that?"

"They're not particularly brilliantly paid," Pen said. "Not badly by my standards, but they're never *rich*."

"But Ian Pargetter was very much liked," I said.

"What's that got to do with it?" Pen said. "Nothing to stop him passing on a few pills and advice to Calder in return for a fat untaxed fee."

"To their mutual benefit," Gordon murmured.

"The healer's feet of clay," Judith said. "What a shame."

The supposition seemed slightly to deflate the remembered pleasure of the morning, but the afternoon's visit put the rest of the day up high.

We went this time to Oliver Knowles' stud farm and found the whole place flooded with foals and mares and activity.

"How *beautiful*," Judith said, looking away over the stretches of white-railed paddocks with their colonies of mothers and babies. "How speechlessly *great*."

Oliver Knowles, introduced, was as welcoming as Calder and told Gordon several times that he would never, ever, be out of his debt of gratitude to Paul Ekaterin's, however soon he had paid off his loan.

The anxiety and misgivings to be seen in him on my February visit had all disappeared: Oliver was again, and more so, the capable and decisive executive I had met first. The foals had done well, I gathered. Not one from the mares coming to Sandcastle had been lost, and none of those mares had had any infection, a triumph of care. He told me all this within the first ten minutes, and also that Sandcastle had proved thoroughly potent and fertile and was a dream of a stallion. "He's tireless," he said. "Forty mares will be easy."

"I'm so glad," I said, and meant it from the bottom of my banking heart.

With his dog Squibs at his heels he showed us all again through the succession of yards, where since it was approximately four o'clock the evening ritual of mucking out and feeding was in full swing.

"A stud farm is not like a racing stable, of course," Oliver was explaining to Gordon. "One lad here can look after far more than three horses, because they don't have to be ridden. And here we have a more flexible system because the mares are sometimes in, sometimes out in the paddocks, and it would be impossible to assign particular mares to particular lads. So here a lad does a particular section of boxes, regardless of which animals are in them."

Gordon nodded, genially interested.

"Why are some foals in the boxes and some out in the paddocks?" Judith asked, and Oliver without hesitation told her it was because the foals had to stay with their dams, and the mares with foals in the boxes were due to come into heat, or were already in heat, and would go from their boxes to visit the stallion. When their heat was over they would go out into the paddocks, with their foals.

"Oh," Judith said, blinking slightly at this factory aspect. "Yes, I see."

In the foaling yard we came across Nigel and also Ginnie, who ran across to me when she saw me and gave me a great hug and a smacking kiss somewhere to the left of the mouth. Quite an advance in confidence, I thought, and hugged her back, lifting her off her feet and whirling her in a circle. She was laughing when I put her down, and Oliver watched in some surprise.

"I've never known her so demonstrative," he said.

Ginnie looked at him apprehensively and held on to my sleeve. "You didn't mind, did you?" she asked me worriedly.

"I'm flattered," I said, meaning it and also thinking that her father would kill off her spontaniety altogether if he wasn't careful.

Ginnie, reassured, tucked her arm into mine and said, "Come and look at the newest foal. It was born only about twenty minutes ago. It's a colt. A darling." She tugged me off, and I caught a fleeting glance of Judith's face, which was showing a mixture of all sorts of unreadable thoughts.

"Oliver's daughter," I said in explanation over my shoulder and heard Oliver belatedly introducing Nigel.

They all came to look at the foal over the half-door; a glistening little creature half-lying, half-sitting on the thick straw, all long nose, huge eyes and folded legs, new life already making an effort to balance and stand up. The dam, on her feet, alternately bent her head to the foal and looked up at us warily.

"It was an easy one," Ginnie said. "Nigel and I just watched."

"Have you seen many foals born?" Pen asked her.

"Oh, hundreds. All my life. Most often at night."

Pen looked at her as if she, as I did, felt the imagination stirred by such an unusual childhood: as if she, like myself, had never seen one single birth of any sort, let alone a whole procession by the age of fifteen.

"This mare has come to Sandcastle," Oliver said.

"And will that foal win the Derby?" Gordon asked, smiling.

Oliver smiled in return. "You never know. He has the breeding." He breathed deeply, expanding his chest. "I've never been able to say anything like that before this year. No foal born or conceived here has in the past won a Classic, but now . . ." he gestured widely with his arm ". . . one day, from these . . ." he paused. "It's a whole new world. It's . . . tremendous."

"As good as you hoped?" I asked.

"Better."

He had a soul after all, I thought, under all that tidy martial efficiency. A vision of the peaks, which he was reaching in reality. And how soon, I wondered, before the glossy became commonplace, the Classic winners a routine, the aristocrats the common herd. It would be what he'd aimed for; but in a way it would be blunting.

We left the foal and went on down the path past the breeding shed, where the main door was today wide open, showing the floor thickly covered with soft brown crumbly peat. Beyond succinctly explaining what went on in there when it was inhabited, Oliver made no comment, and we all walked on without stopping to the heart of the place, to the stallions.

Lenny was there, walking one of the horses round the small yard and plodding with his head down as if he'd been doing it for some time. The horse was dripping with sweat, and from the position of the one open empty box I guessed he would be Rotaboy.

"He's just covered a mare," Oliver said matter-of-factly. "He's always like that afterwards."

Judith and Gordon and Pen all looked as if the overt sex of the place was earthier than they'd expected, even without hearing, as I had at one moment, Oliver quietly discussing a vaginal disinfectant process with Nigel. They rallied valiantly, however, and gazed with proper awe at the head of Sandcastle, which swam into view from the inside-box shadows.

He held himself almost imperiously, as if his new role had basically changed his character; and perhaps it had. I had myself seen during my renewed interest in racing how constant success endowed some horses with definite "presence," and Sandcastle, even lost and frightened up on top of the hill, had perceptibly had it; but now, only two months later, there was a new quality one might almost call arrogance, a fresh certainty of his own supremacy.

"He's splendid," Gordon exclaimed. "What a treat to see him again after that great day at Ascot."

Oliver gave Sandcastle the usual two carrots and couple of pats, treating the king with familiarity. Neither Judith nor Pen, nor indeed Gordon or myself, tried even to touch the sensitive nose: afraid of getting our fingers bitten off at the wrist, no doubt. It was all right to admire, but distance had virtue.

Lenny put the calming-down Rotaboy back in his box and started mucking out Diarist next door.

"We have two lads looking after the stallions full time," Oliver said. "Lenny, here, and another much-trusted man, Don. And Nigel feeds them."

Pen caught the thought behind his words and asked, "Do you need much security?"

"Some," he said, nodding. "We have the yard wired for sound, so either Nigel or I, when we're in our houses, can hear if there are any irregular noises."

"Like hooves taking a walk?" Judith suggested.

"Exactly." He smiled at her. "We also have smoke alarms and massive extinguishers."

"And brick-built boxes and combination locks on these door bolts at night and lockable gates on all the ways out to the roads," Ginnie said, chattily. "Dad's really gone to town on security."

"Glad to hear it," Gordon said.

I smiled to myself at the classic example of bolting the stable door after the horse had done likewise, but indeed one could see that Oliver had learned a dire lesson and knew he'd been lucky to be given a second chance.

We began after a while to walk back towards the house, stopping again in the foaling yard to look at the new baby colt, who was now shakily on his feet and searching round for his supper.

Oliver drew me to one side and asked if I would like to see Sandcastle cover a mare, an event apparently scheduled for a short time hence.

"Yes, I would," I said.

"I can't ask them all—there isn't room," he said. "I'll get Ginnie to show them the mares and foals in the paddocks and then take them indoors for tea."

No one demurred at this suggested program, especially as Oliver didn't actually mention where he and I were going: Judith, I was sure, would have preferred to join us. Ginnie took them and Squibs off, and I could hear her saying, "Over there, next door, there's another yard. We could walk over that way if you like."

Oliver, watching them amble along the path that

Sandcastle had taken at a headlong gallop and I at a sprint, said, "The Watcherleys look after any delicate foals or any mares with infections. It's all worked out most satisfactorily. I rent their place and they work for me, and their expertise with sick animals comes in very useful."

"And you were mending their fences for them, I guess, when I came in February."

"That's right." He sighed ruefully. "Another week and the gates would have been up in the hedge and across their driveway, and Sandcastle would never have got out."

"No harm done," I said.

"Thanks to you, no."

We went slowly back towards the breeding shed. "Have you seen a stallion at work before?" he asked.

"No, I haven't."

After a pause he said, "It may seem strong to you. Even violent. But it's normal to them. Remember that. And he'll probably bite her neck, but it's as much to keep himself in position as an expression of passion."

"All right," I said.

"This mare, the one we're breeding, is receptive, so there won't be any trouble. Some mares are shy, some are slow to arouse, some are irritable, just like humans." He smiled faintly. "This little lady is a born one-nighter."

It was the first time I'd heard him make anything like a joke about his profession and I was almost startled. As if himself surprised at his own words he said more soberly, "We put her to Sandcastle yesterday morning, and all went well."

"The mares go more than once, then, to the stallion?" I asked.

He nodded. "It depends of course on the stud farm, but I'm very anxious, as you can guess, that all the mares here shall have the best possible chance of conceiving. I bring them all at least twice to the stallion during their heat, then we put them out in the paddocks and wait, and if they come into heat again it means they haven't conceived, so we repeat the breeding process."

"And how long do you go on trying?"

"Until the end of July. That means the foal won't be born until well on in June, which is late in the year for racehorses. Puts them at a disadvantage as two-year-olds, racing against March and April foals that have had more growing time." He smiled. "With any luck Sandcastle won't have any late-June foals. It's too early to be complacent, but none of the mares he covered three weeks or more ago has come back into use."

We reached and entered the breeding shed where the mare already stood, held at the head in a loose twitch by one lad and being washed and attended by another.

"She can't wait, sir," that lad said, indicating her tail, which she was holding high, and Oliver replied rather repressively, "Good."

Nigel and Lenny came with Sandcastle, who looked eagerly aware of where he was and what for. Nigel closed the door to keep the ritual private; and the mating that followed was swift and sure and utterly primeval. A copulation of thrust and grandeur, of vigor and pleasure, not without tenderness: remarkably touching.

"They're not all like that," Oliver remarked prosaically, as Sandcastle slid out and backwards and brought his forelegs to earth with a jolt. "You've seen a good one."

I thanked him for letting me be there, and in truth I felt I understood more about horses then than I'd ever imagined I would.

We walked back to the house, with Oliver telling me that with the four stallions there were currently six, seven or eight matings a day in the breeding shed, Sundays included. The mind stuttered a bit at the thought of all that rampaging fertility, but that, after all, was what the bank's five million pounds was all about. Rarely, I thought, had anyone seen Ekaterin's money so fundamentally at work.

We set off homewards fortified by tea, scones and

whisky, with Oliver and Gordon at the end competing over who thanked whom most warmly. Ginnie gave me another but more composed hug and begged me to come again, and Judith kissed her and offered female succor if ever needed.

"Nice child," she said as we drove away. "Growing up fast."

"Fifteen," I said.

"Sixteen. She had a birthday last week."

"You got on well with her," I said.

"Yes." She looked round at Pen and Gordon, who were again sitting in the back. "She told us about your little escapade here two months ago."

"She didn't!"

"She sure did," Pen said, smiling. "Why ever didn't you say?"

"I know why," Gordon said dryly. "He didn't want it to be known in the office that the loan he'd recommended had very nearly fallen under a truck."

"Is that right?" Judith asked.

"Very much so," I admitted wryly. "Some of the board were against the whole thing anyway, and I'd have never heard the end of the horse getting out."

"What a coward," Pen said, chuckling.

We pottered slowly back to Clapham through the stop-go end-of-Bank-Holiday traffic, and Judith and Pen voted it the best day they'd had since Ascot. Gordon dozed, I drove with relaxation and so we finally reached the tall gates by the common.

I went in with them for supper, as already arranged, but all of them, not only Gordon, were tired from the long day, and I didn't stay late. Judith came out to the car to see me off and to shut the gates after I'd gone.

We didn't really talk. I held her in my arms, her head on my shoulder, my head on hers, close in the dark night, as far apart as planets.

We stood away and I took her hand, lingering, not wanting all contact lost.

"A great day," she said, and I said "mm," and kissed her very briefly.

Got into the car and drove away.

October

Summer had come, summer had gone, sodden, cold and unloved. It had been overcast and windy during Royal Ascot week and Gordon and I, clamped to our telephones and pondering our options, had looked at the sullen sky and hardly minded that this year Dissdale hadn't needed to sell half-shares in his box.

Only with the autumn, far too late, had days of sunshine returned, and it was on a bright golden Saturday that I took the race train to Newbury to see the mixed meeting of two jump races and four flat.

Ursula Young was there, standing near the weighing room when I walked in from the station and earnestly reading her race card.

"Hello," she said when I greeted her. "Haven't seen you for ages. How's the money-lending?"

"Profitable," I said.

She laughed. "Are you here for anything special?"

"No. Just fresh air and a flutter."

"I'm supposed to meet a client." She looked at her watch. "Time for a quick sandwich, though. Are you on?"

I was on, and bought her and myself a thin pallid slice
of tasteless white meat between two thick pallid tasteless slices of soggy-crusted bread, the whole wrapped up
in cardboard and cellophane and costing a fortune.

Ursula ate it in disgust. "They used to serve proper
luscious sandwiches, thick, juicy handmade affairs that
came in a whole stack. I can't stand all this repulsive
hygiene." The rubbish from the sandwiches indeed lit-
tered most of the tables around us. "Every so-called advance is a retreat from excellence," she said, dogmatic
as ever.

I totally agreed with her and we chewed in joyless accord.

"How's trade with you?" I said.

She shrugged. "Fair. The cream of the yearlings are
going for huge prices. They've all got high reserves on
them because they've cost so much to produce—stallion
fees and the cost of keeping the mare and foal to start
with, let alone vet's fees and all the incidentals. My sort
of clients on the whole settle for second, third or fourth
rank, and many a good horse, mind you, has come from
the bargain counter."

I smiled at the automatic sales pitch. "Talking of
vets," I said, "is the Pargetter murder still unsolved?"

She nodded regretfully. "I was talking to his poor
wife in Newmarket last week. We met in the street.
She's only half the girl she was, poor thing, no life in
her. She said she asked the police recently if they were
still even trying, and they assured her they were, but
she doesn't believe it. It's been so long, nine months,
and if they hadn't any leads to start with, how can they
possibly have any now? She's very depressed, it's dreadful."

I made sympathetic murmurs, and Ursula went on,
"The only good thing you could say is that he'd taken
out decent life insurance and paid off the mortgage on
their house, so at least she and the children aren't pen-
niless as well. She was telling me how he'd been very
careful in those ways, and she burst into tears, poor
girl."

Ursula looked as if the encounter had distressed her also.

"Have another whisky-mac," I suggested. "To cheer you up."

She looked at her watch. "All right. You get it, but I'll pay. My turn."

Over the second drink, in a voice of philosophical irritation, she told me about the client she was presently due to meet, a small-time trainer of steeplechasers. "He's such a fool to himself," she said. "He makes hasty decisions, acts on impulse, and then when things go wrong he feels victimized and cheated and gets angry. Yet he can be perfectly nice when he likes."

I wasn't especially interested in the touchy trainer, but when I went outside again with Ursula he spotted her from a short distance away and practically pounced on her arm.

"There you are," he said, as if she'd had no right to be anywhere but at his side. "I've been looking all over."

"It's only just time," she said mildly.

He brushed that aside, a short wiry intense man of about forty with a pork-pie hat above a weatherbeaten face.

"I wanted you to see him before he's saddled," he said. "Do come on, Ursula. Come and look at his conformation."

She opened her mouth to say something to me but he almost forcefully dragged her off, holding her sleeve and talking rapidly into her ear. She gave me an apologetic look of long-suffering and departed in the direction of the pre-parade ring, where the horses for the first race were being led round by their lads before going off to the saddling boxes.

I didn't follow but climbed onto the steps of the main parade ring, round which walked several of the runners already saddled. The last of the field to appear some time later was accompanied by the pork-pie hat, and also Ursula, and for something to do I looked the horse up in the race card.

Zoomalong, five-year-old gelding, trained by F. Barnet.

F. Barnet continued his dissertation into Ursula's ear, aiming his words from approximately six inches away, which I would have found irritating but which she bore without flinching. According to the flickering numbers on the Tote board Zoomalong had a medium chance in the opinion of the public, so for interest I put a medium stake on him to finish in the first three.

I didn't see Ursula or F. Barnet during the race, but Zoomalong zoomed along quite nicely to finish third, and I walked down from the stands towards the unsaddling enclosure to watch the patting-on-the-back postrace routine.

F. Barnet was there, still talking to Ursula and pointing out parts of his now sweating and stomping charge. Ursula nodded noncommittally, her own eyes knowledgeably raking the gelding from stem to stern, a neat competent good-looking fifty in a rust-colored coat and a brown velvet beret.

Eventually the horses were led away and the whole cycle of excitement began slowly to regenerate towards the second race.

Without in the least meaning to I again found myself standing near Ursula, and this time she introduced me to the pork-pie hat, who had temporarily stopped talking.

"This is Fred Barnet," she said. "And his wife Susan." A rounded motherly person in blue. "And their son Ricky." A boy taller than his father, dark-haired, pleasant-faced.

I shook hands with all three, and it was while I was still touching the son that Ursula in her clear voice said my name, "Tim Ekaterin."

The boy's hand jumped in mine as if my flesh had burned him. I was astonished, and then I looked at his whitening skin, at the suddenly frightened dark eyes, at the stiffening of the body, at the rising panic: and I wouldn't have known him if he hadn't reacted in that way.

"What's the matter, Ricky?" his mother said, puzzled.

He said, "Nothing," hoarsely and looked around for

escape, but all too clearly I knew exactly who he was now and could always find him however far he ran.

"What do you think, then, Ursula?" Fred Barnet demanded, returning to the business in hand. "Will you buy him? Can I count on you?"

Ursula said she would have to consult her client.

"But he was third," Fred Barnet insisted. "A good third . . . in that company, a pretty good showing. And he'll win, I'm telling you. He'll win."

"I'll tell my client all about him. I can't say fairer than that."

"But you do like him, don't you? Look, Ursula, he's a good sort, easy to handle, just right for an amateur . . ." He went on for a while in this vein while his wife listened with a sort of aimless beam meaning nothing at all.

To the son, under cover of his father's hard sell, I quietly said, "I want to talk to you, and if you run away from me now I'll be telephoning the police."

He gave me a sick look and stood still.

"We'll walk down the course together to watch the next race," I said. "We won't be interrupted there. And you can tell me *why*. And then we'll see."

It was easy enough for him to drop back unnoticed from his parents, who were still concentrating on Ursula, and he came with me through the gate and out across the track itself to the center of the racecourse, stumbling slightly as if not in command of his feet. We walked down towards the last fence, and he told me why he'd tried to kill Calder Jackson.

"It doesn't seem real, not now, it doesn't really," he said first. A young voice, slightly sloppy accent, full of strain.

"How old are you?" I asked.

"Seventeen."

I hadn't been so far out, I thought, fifteen months ago.

"I never thought I'd see you again," he said explosively, sounding faintly aggrieved at the twist of fate. "I mean, the papers said you worked in a bank."

"So I do. And I go racing." I paused. "You remembered my name."

"Yeah. Could hardly forget it, could I? All over the papers."

We went a few yards in silence. "Go on," I said.

He made a convulsive gesture of frustrated despair. "All right. But if I tell you, you won't tell *them,* will you, not Mum and Dad?"

I glanced at him, but from his troubled face it was clear that he meant exactly what he'd said: it wasn't my telling the police he minded most, but my telling his parents.

"Just get on with it," I said.

He sighed. "Well, we had this horse. Dad did. He'd bought it as a yearling and ran it as a two-year-old and at three, but it was a jumper really, and it turned out to be good." He paused. "Indian Silk, that's what it was called."

I frowned. "But Indian Silk . . . didn't that win at Cheltenham this year, in March?"

He nodded. "The Gold Cup. The very top. He's only seven now and he's bound to be brilliant for years." The voice was bitter with a sort of resigned, stiffled anger.

"But he doesn't any longer belong to your father?"

"No, he doesn't." More bitterness, very sharp.

"Go on, then," I said.

He swallowed and took his time, but eventually he said, "Two years ago this month, when Indian Silk was five, like, he won the Hermitage 'Chase very easily here at Newbury, and everyone was tipping him for the Gold Cup *last* year, though Dad was saying he was still on the young side and to give him time. See, Dad was that proud of that horse. The best he'd ever trained, and it was his own, not someone else's. Don't know if you can understand that."

"I do understand it," I said.

He gave a split-second glance at my face. "Well, Indian Silk got sick," he said. "I mean, there was nothing you could put your finger on. He just lost his speed. He couldn't even gallop properly at home, couldn't beat the other horses in Dad's yard that he'd been running rings round all year. Dad couldn't run him in races. He could hardly train him. And the vet couldn't find out what was wrong with him. They took blood tests and all sorts, and they gave him antibiotics and purges, and they thought it might be worms or something, but it wasn't."

We had reached the last fence, and stood there on the rough grass beside it while in twos and threes other enthusiasts straggled down from the grandstand towards us to watch the horses in action at close quarters.

"I was at school a lot of the time, see," Ricky said. "I was home every night of course but I was taking exams and had a lot of homework and I didn't really want to take much notice of Indian Silk getting so bad or anything. I mean, Dad does go on a bit, and I suppose I thought the horse just had the virus or something and would get better. But he just got slowly worse and one day Mum was crying." He stopped suddenly, as if that part was the worst. "I hadn't seen a grownup cry before," he said. "Suppose you'll think it funny, but it upset me something awful."

"I don't think it funny," I said.

"Anyway," he went on, seeming to gather confidence, "it got so that Indian Silk was so weak he could barely walk down the road and he wasn't eating, and Dad was in real despair because there wasn't nothing anyone could do, and Mum couldn't bear the thought of him going to the knackers, and then some guy telephoned and offered to buy him."

"To buy a sick horse?" I said, surprised.

"I don't think Dad was going to tell him just how bad he was. Well, I mean, at that point Indian Silk was worth just what the knackers would pay for his carcass, which wasn't much, and this man was offering nearly twice that. But the man said he knew Indian Silk couldn't race anymore but he'd like to give him a good home in a nice field for as long as necessary, and it meant that Dad didn't have the expense of any more vets' bills and he and Mum didn't have to watch Indian Silk just getting worse and worse, and Mum wouldn't have to think of him going to the knackers for dog meat, so they let him go."

The horses for the second race came out onto the

course and galloped down past us, the jockeys' colors bright in the sun.

"And then what?" I said.

"Then nothing happened for weeks and we were getting over it, like, and then someone told Dad that Indian Silk was back in training and looking fine, and he couldn't believe it."

"When was that?" I asked.

"It was last year, just before . . . before Ascot."

A small crowd gathered on the landing side of the fence, and I drew him away down the course a bit further, to where the horses would set themselves right to take off.

"Go on," I said.

"My exams were coming up," he said. "And I mean, they were important, they were going to affect my whole life, see?"

I nodded.

"Then Dad found that the man who'd bought Indian Silk hadn't put him in any field, he'd sent him straight down the road to Calder Jackson."

"Ah," I said.

"And there was this man saying Calder Jackson had the gift of healing, some sort of magic, and had simply touched Indian Silk and made him well. I ask you . . . And Dad was in a frightful state because someone had suggested he should send the horse there, to Calder Jackson, while he was so bad, of course, and Dad had said don't be so ridiculous it was all a lot of rubbish. And then Mum was saying he should have listened to her, because she'd said why not try it, it couldn't do any harm, and he wouldn't do it, and they were having rows, and she was crying . . ." He gulped for air, the story now pouring out faster than he could speak. "And I wasn't getting any work done with it all going on, they weren't ever talking about anything else, and I took the first exam and just sat there and couldn't do it, and I knew I'd failed and I was going to fail them all because I couldn't concentrate . . . and then there was Calder Jackson one evening talking on television, saying he'd got a friend of his to buy a dying horse, because

the people who owned it would just have let it die because they didn't believe in healers, like a lot of people,
and he hoped the horse would be great again some day,
like before, thanks to him, and I knew he was talking
about Indian Silk. And he said he was going to Ascot on
that Thursday . . . and there was Dad screaming that
Calder Jackson had stolen the horse away, it was all a
filthy swindle, which of course it wasn't, but at the time
I believed him . . . and it all got so that I hated Calder
Jackson so much that I couldn't think straight. I mean,
I thought *he* was the reason Mum was crying and I was
failing my exams and Dad had lost the only really top
horse he'd have in his whole life, and I just wanted to
kill him."

The bedrock words were out, and the flood suddenly
stopped, leaving the echo of them on the October air.

"And did you fail your exams?" I asked, after a moment.

"Yeah. Most of them. But I took them again at
Christmas and got good passes." He shook his head,
speaking more slowly, more quietly. "I was glad even
that night that you'd stopped me stabbing him. I mean
. . . I'd've thrown my whole life away, I could see it afterwards, and all for nothing, because Dad wasn't going
to get the horse back whatever I did, because it was a
legal sale, like."

I thought over what he'd told me while in the distance the horses lined up and set off on their three-mile
steeplechase.

"I was sort of mad," he said. "I can't really understand it now. I mean, I wouldn't go around trying to kill
people. I really wouldn't. It seems like I was a different
person."

· Adolescence, I thought, and not for the first time,
could be hell.

"I took Mum's knife out of the kitchen," he said. "She
never could think where it had gone."

I wondered if the police still had it; with Ricky's fingerprints on file.

"I didn't know there would be so many people at Ascot," he said. "And so many gates into the course. Much

more than Newmarket. I was getting frantic because I thought I wouldn't find him. I meant to do it earlier, see, when he arrived. I was out on the road, running up and down the pavement, mad, you know, really, looking for him and feeling the knife kind of burning in my sleeve, like I was burning in my mind . . . and I saw his head, all those curls, crossing the road, and I ran, but I was too late, he'd gone inside, through the gate."

"And then," I suggested, "you simply waited for him to come out?"

He nodded. "There were lots of people around. No one took any notice. I reckoned he'd come up that path from the station, and that was the way he would go back. It didn't seem long, the waiting. Went in a flash."

The horses came over the next fence down the course like a multicolored wave and thundered towards the one where we were standing. The ground trembled from the thud of the hooves, the air rang with the curses of jockeys, the half-ton equine bodies brushed through the birch, the sweat and the effort and the speed filled eyes and ears and mind with pounding wonder and then were gone, flying away, leaving the silence. I had walked down several times before to watch from the fences, both there and on other tracks, and the fierce fast excitement had never grown stale.

"Who is it who owns Indian Silk now?" I asked.

"A Mr. Chacksworth, comes from Birmingham," Ricky answered. "You see him at the races sometimes, slobbering all over Indian Silk. But it wasn't him that bought him from Dad. He bought him later, when he was all right again. Paid a proper price for him, so we heard. Made it all the worse."

A sad and miserable tale, all of it.

"Who bought the horse from your father?" I said.

"I never met him . . . his name was Smith. Some funny first name. Can't remember."

Smith. Friend of Calder's.

"Could it," I asked, surprised, "have been *Dissdale* Smith?"

"Yeah. That sounds like it. How do you know?"

"He was there that day at Ascot," I said. "There on the pavement, right beside Calder Jackson."

"Was he?" Ricky looked disconcerted. "He was a dead liar, you know, all that talk about nice fields."

"Who tells the truth," I said, "when buying or selling horses?"

The runners were round again on the far side of the track, racing hard now on the second circuit.

"What are you going to do?" Ricky said. "About me, like? You won't tell Mum and Dad. You won't, will you?"

I looked directly at the boy-man, seeing the continuing anxiety but no longer the first panic-stricken fear. He seemed to sense now that I would very likely not drag him into court, but he wasn't sure of much else.

"Perhaps they should know," I said.

"No!" His agitation rose quickly. "They've had so much trouble and I would have made it so much worse if you hadn't stopped me, and afterwards I used to wake up sweating at what it would have done to them; and the only good thing was that I did learn that you can't put things right by killing people, you can only make things terrible for your family."

After a long pause I said, "All right. I won't tell them." And heaven help me, I thought, if he ever attacked anyone again because he thought he could always get away with it.

The relief seemed to affect him almost as much as the anxiety. He blinked several times and turned his head away to where the race was again coming round into the straight with this time an all-out effort to the winning post. There was again the rise and fall of the field over the distant fences but now the one wave had split into separate components, the runners coming home not in a bunch but a procession.

I watched again the fierce surprising speed of horse and jockey jumping at close quarters and wished with some regret that I could have ridden like that: but like Alec I was wishing too late, even strong and healthy and thirty-three.

The horses galloped off towards the cheers on the

grandstand and Ricky and I began a slow walk in their wake. He seemed quiet and composed in the aftermath of confession, the soul's evacuation giving him ease.

"What do you feel nowadays about Calder Jackson?" I asked.

He produced a lopsided smile. "Nothing much. That's what's so crazy. I mean, it wasn't his fault Dad was so stubborn."

I digested this. "You mean," I said, "that you think your father should have sent him the horse himself?"

"Yes, I reckon he should've, like Mum wanted. But he said it was rubbish and too expensive, and you don't know my Dad but when he makes his mind up he just gets fighting angry if anyone tries to argue, and he shouts at her, and it isn't fair."

"If your father had sent the horse to Calder Jackson, I suppose he would still own it," I said thoughtfully.

"Yes, he would, and don't think he doesn't know it, of course he does, but it's as much as anyone's life's worth to say it."

We trudged back over the thick grass, and I asked him how Calder or Dissdale had known that Indian Silk was ill.

He shrugged. "It was in the papers. He'd been favorite for the King George VI on Boxing Day, but of course he didn't run, and the press found out why."

We came again to the gate into the grandstand enclosure and went through it, and I asked where he lived.

"Exning," he said.

"Where's that?"

"Near Newmarket. Just outside." He looked at me with slightly renewed apprehension. "You meant it, didn't you, about not telling?"

"I meant it," I said. "Only . . ." I frowned a little, thinking of the hothouse effect of his living with his parents.

"Only what?" he asked.

I tried a different tack. "What are you doing now? Are you still in school?"

"No, I left once I'd passed those exams. I really

needed them, like. You can't get a halfway decent job without those bits of paper these days."

"You're not working for your father, then?"

He must have heard the faint relief in my voice because for the first time he fully smiled. "No, I reckon it wouldn't be good for his temper, and anyway I don't want to be a trainer, one long worry, if you ask me."

"What do you do, then?" I asked.

"I'm learning electrical engineering in a firm near Cambridge. An apprentice, like." He smiled again. "But not with horses, not me." He shook his head ruefully and delivered his young-Solomon judgment of life. "Break your heart, horses do."

November

To my great delight the cartoonist came up trumps, his twenty animated films being shown on television every weeknight for a month in the best time slot for that sort of humor, seven in the evening, when older children were still up and the parents home from work. The nation sat up and giggled, and the cartoonist telephoned breathlessly to ask for a bigger loan.

"I do need a proper studio, not this converted warehouse. And more animators, and designers, and recordists, and equipment."

"All right," I said into the first gap. "Draw up your requirements and come and see me."

"Do you *realize*," he said, as if he himself had difficulty, "that they'll take as many films as I can make? No limit. They said just go on making them for years and years . . . they said *please* go on making them."

"I'm very glad," I said sincerely.

"You gave me faith in myself," he said. "You'll never believe it, but you did. I'd been turned down so often, and I was getting depressed, but when you loaned me the money to start it was like being uncorked. The ideas just rushed out."

"And are they still rushing?"

"Oh, sure. I've got the next twenty films roughed out in drawings already and we're working on those, and now I'm starting on the batch after that."

"It's terrific," I said.

"It sure is. Brother, life's amazing." He put down his receiver and left me smiling into space.

"The cartoonist?" Gordon said.

I nodded. "Going up like a rocket."

"Congratulations." There was warmth and genuine pleasure in his voice. Such a generous man, I thought: so impossible to do him harm.

"He looks like turning into a major industry," I said.

"Disney, Hanna Barbera, eat your hearts out," Alec said from across the room.

"Good business for the bank." Gordon beamed. "Henry will be pleased."

Pleasing Henry, indeed, was the aim of us all.

"You must admit, Tim," Alec said, "that you're a fairish rocket yourself . . . so what's the secret?"

"Light the blue paper and retire immediately," I said good-humoredly, and he balled a page of jottings to throw at me, and missed.

At midmorning he went out as customary for the six copies of *What's Going On Where It Shouldn't,* and having distributed five was presently sitting back in his chair reading our own with relish.

Ekaterin's had been thankfully absent from the probing columns ever since the five-percent business, but it appeared that some of our colleagues along the road weren't so fortunate.

"Did you know," Alec said conversationally, "that some of our investment manager chums down on the corner have set up a nice little fiddle on the side, accepting payoffs from brokers in return for steering business their way?"

"How do you know?" Gordon asked, looking up from a ledger.

Alec lifted the paper. "The gospel according to this dicky bird."

"Gospel meaning good news," I said.

"Don't be so damned erudite." He grinned at me with mischief and went back to reading aloud. *"Contrary to popular belief the general run of so-called managers in merchant banks are not in the princely bracket."* He looked up briefly. "You can say that again." He went on, *"We hear that four of the investment managers in this establishment have been cozily supplementing their middle-incomes by steering fund money to three stockbrokers in particular. Names will be revealed in our next issue. Watch this space."*

"It's happened before," Gordon said philosophically. "And will happen again. The temptation is always there." He frowned. "All the same, I'm surprised their senior managers and the directors haven't spotted it."

"They'll have spotted it *now*," Alec said.

"So they will."

"It would be pretty easy," I said musingly, "to set up a computer program to do the spotting for Ekaterin's, in case we should ever find the pestilence cropping up here."

"Would it?" Gordon asked.

"Mm. Just a central program to record every deal done in the Investment Department with each stockbroker, with running totals, easy to see. Anything hugely unexpected could be investigated."

"But that's a vast job, surely," Gordon said.

I shook my head. "I doubt it. I could get our tame programmer to have a go, if you like."

"We'll put it to the others. See what they say."

"There will be screeches from Investment Management," Alec said. "Cries of outraged virtue."

"Guards them against innuendo like this, though," Gordon said, pointing to *What's Going On*.

The board agreed, and in consequence I spent another two days with the programmer, building dikes against future leaks.

Gordon these days seemed no worse, his illness not having progressed in any visible way. There was no means of knowing how he felt, as he never said and hated to be asked, but on the few times I'd seen Judith since the day at Easter, she had said he was as well as could be hoped for.

The best of those times had been a Sunday in July when Pen had given a lunch party at her house in Clapham; it was supposed to have been a lunch-in-the-garden party, but like so much that summer was frustrated by chilly winds. Inside was to me much better, as Pen had written place-cards for her long refectory table and put me next to Judith, with Gordon on her right hand.

The other guests remained a blur, most of them being doctors of some sort or another, or pharmacists like herself. Judith and I made polite noises to the faces on either side of us but spent most of the time talking to each other, carrying on two conversations at once, one with voice, one with eyes; both satisfactory.

When the main party had broken up and gone, Gordon and Judith and I stayed to supper, first helping Pen clear up from what she described as "repaying so many dinners at one go."

It had been a day when natural opportunities for touching people abounded, when kisses and hugs of greeting had been appropriate and could be warm, when all the world could watch and see nothing between Judith and me but an enduring and peaceful friendship: a day when I longed to have her for myself worse than ever.

Since then I'd seen her only twice, and both times when she'd come to the bank to collect Gordon before they went on to other events. On each of these occasions I'd managed at least five minutes with her, stiffly circumspect, Gordon's colleague being polite until Gordon himself was ready to leave.

It wasn't usual for wives to come to the bank: husbands normally joined them at wherever they were going. Judith said, the second time, "I won't do this often. I just wanted to see you, if you were around."

"Always here," I said.

She nodded. She was looking as fresh and poised as

ever, wearing a neat blue coat with pearls showing. The brown hair was glossy, the eyes bright, the soft mouth half-smiling, the glamour born in her and unconscious.

"I get . . . well . . . thirsty, sometimes," she said.

"Permanent state with me," I said lightly.

She swallowed. "Just for a moment or two . . ."

We were standing in the entrance hall, not touching, waiting for Gordon.

"Just to see you . . ." She seemed uncertain that I understood, but I did.

"It's the same for me," I assured her. "I sometimes think of going to Clapham and waiting around just to see you walk down the street to the baker's. Just to see you, even for seconds."

"Do you really?"

"I don't go, though. You might send Gordon to buy the bread."

She laughed a small laugh, a fitting size for the bank; and he came, hurrying, struggling into his overcoat. I sprang to help him and he said to her, "Sorry, darling, got held up on the telephone, you know how it is."

"I've been perfectly happy," she said, kissing him, "talking to Tim."

"Splendid. Splendid. Are we ready then?"

They went off to their evening smiling and waving and leaving me to hunger futilely for this and that.

In the office one day in November Gordon said, "How about you coming over to lunch on Sunday? Judith was saying it's ages since she saw you properly."

"I'd love to."

"Pen's coming, Judith said."

Pen, my friend; my chaperone.

"Great," I said positively. "Lovely."

Gordon nodded contentedly and said it was a shame we couldn't all have a repeat of last Christmas, he and Judith had enjoyed it so much. They were going this year to his son and daughter-in-law in Edinburgh, a visit long promised; to his son by his first long-dead wife, and his grandchildren, twin boys of seven.

"You'll have fun," I said regretfully.

"They're noisy little brutes."

His telephone rang, and mine also, and the money-lending proceeded. I would be dutiful, I thought, and spend Christmas with my mother in Jersey, as she wanted, and we would laugh and play backgammon, and I would sadden her as usual by bringing no girlfriend, no prospective producer of little brutes.

"Why, my love," she'd said to me once a few years earlier in near despair, "do you take out these perfectly presentable girls and never marry them?"

"There's always something I don't want to spend my life with."

"But you do *sleep* with them?"

"Yes, darling, I do."

"You're too choosy."

"I expect so," I said.

"You haven't had a single one that's lasted," she complained. "Everyone else's sons have live-in girlfriends, sometimes going on for years even if they don't marry, so why can't you?"

I'd smiled at the encouragement to what would once have been called sin, and kissed her, and told her I preferred living alone, but that one day I'd find the perfect girl to love forever; and it hadn't even fleetingly occurred to me that when I found her she would be married to someone else.

Sunday came and I went to Clapham: bittersweet hours, as ever.

Over lunch I told them tentatively that I'd seen the boy who had tried to kill Calder, and they reacted as strongly as I'd expected, Gordon saying, "You've told the police, of course," and Judith adding, "He's dangerous, Tim."

I shook my head. "No. I don't think so. I hope not." I smiled wryly and told them all about Ricky Barnet and Indian Silk, and the pressure which had led to the try at stabbing. "I don't think he'll do anything like that again. He's grown so far away from it already that he feels a different person."

"I hope you're right," Gordon said.

"Fancy it being Dissdale who bought Indian Silk," Pen said. "Isn't it amazing?"

"Especially as he was saying he was short of cash and wanting to sell box-space at Ascot," Judith added.

"Mm," I said. "But after Calder had cured the horse Dissdale sold it again pretty soon, and made a handsome profit, by what I gather."

"Typical Dissdale behavior," Gordon said without criticism. "Face the risk, stake all you can afford, take the loot if you're lucky, and get out fast." He smiled. "By Ascot I guess he'd blown the Indian Silk profit and was back to basics. It doesn't take someone like Dissdale any longer to lose thousands than it does to make them."

"He must have colossal faith in Calder," Pen said musingly.

"Not colossal, Pen," Gordon said. "Just twice what a knacker would pay for a carcass."

"Would *you* buy a sick-to-death horse?" Judith asked. "I mean, if Calder said buy it and I'll cure him, would you believe it?"

Gordon looked at her fondly. "I'm not Dissdale, darling, and I don't think I'd buy it."

"And that is precisely," I pointed out, "why Fred Barnet lost Indian Silk. He thought Calder's powers were all rubbish and he wouldn't lay out good money to put them to the test. But Dissdale *did*. Bought the horse and presumably also paid Calder . . . who boasted about his success on television and nearly got himself killed for it."

"Ironic, the whole thing," Pen said, and we went on discussing it desultorily over coffee.

I stayed until six, when Pen went off to her shop for a Sunday-evening stint and Gordon began to look tired, and I drove back to Hampstead in the usual post-Judith state; half-fulfilled, half-starved.

Towards the end of November, and at Oliver Knowles' invitation, I traveled to another Sunday lunch, this time at the stud farm in Hertfordshire.

It turned out, not surprisingly, to be one of Ginnie's

days home from school, and it was she, whistling to Squibs, who set off with me through the yards.

"Did you know we had a hundred and fifty-two mares here all at the same time, back in May?" she said.

"That's a lot," I said, impressed.

"They had a hundred and fourteen foals among them, and only one of the mares and three of the foals died. That's a terrifically good record, you know."

"Your father's very skilled."

"So is Nigel," she said grudgingly. "You have to give him his due."

I smiled at the expression.

"He isn't here just now," she said. "He went off to Miami yesterday to lie in the sun."

"Nigel?"

She nodded. "He goes about this time every year. Sets him up for the winter, he says."

"Always Miami?"

"Yes, he likes it."

The whole atmosphere of the place was back to where I'd known it first, to the slow chill months of gestation. Ginnie, snuggling inside her padded jacket, gave carrots from her pocket to some of the mares in the first yard and walked me without stopping through the empty places, the second yard, the foaling yard, and past the breeding shed.

We came finally, as always, to the stallion yard where the curiosity of the residents brought their heads out the moment they heard our footsteps. Ginnie distributed carrots and pats with the aplomb of her father, and Sandcastle graciously allowed her to stroke his nose.

"He's quiet now," she said. "He's on a much lower diet at this time of year."

I listened to the bulk of knowledge behind the calm words and I said, "What are you going to do when you leave school?"

"This, of course." She patted Sandcastle's neck. "Help Dad. Be his assistant."

"Nothing else?"

She shook her head. "I love the foals. Seeing them

born and watching them grow. I don't want to do anything else, ever."

We left the stallions and walked between the paddocks with their foals and dams, along the path to the Watcherleys', Squibs trotting on ahead and marking his fenceposts. The neighboring place, whose ramshackle state I'd only glimpsed on my pursuit of the loose five million, proved now to be almost as neat as the parent spread, with much fresh paint in evidence and weeds markedly absent.

"Dad can't bear mess," Ginnie said when I remarked on the spit-and-polish. "The Watcherleys are pretty lucky, really, with Dad paying them rent *and* doing up their place *and* employing them to look after the animals in this yard. Bob may still gripe a bit at not being on his own, but Maggie was telling me just last week that she would be everlastingly thankful that Calder Jackson stole their business."

"He hardly stole it," I said mildly.

"Well, you know what I mean. Did better at it, if you want to be pedantic." She grinned. "Anyway, Maggie's bought some new clothes at last, and I'm glad for her."

We opened and went into a few of the boxes, where she handed out the last of the carrots and fondled the inmates, both mares and growing foals, talking to them, and all of them responded amiably to her touch, nuzzling her gently. She looked at peace and where she belonged, all growing pains suspended.

The Third Year

April

Alec had bought a bunch of yellow tulips when he went out for *What's Going On,* and they stood on his desk in a beer mug, catching a shaft of spring sunshine and standing straight like guardsmen.

Gordon was making notes in a handwriting growing even smaller, and the two older colleagues were counting the weeks to their retirement. Office life: an ordinary day.

My telephone rang, and with eyes still bent on a letter from a tomato grower asking for more time to repay his original loan because of needing a new greenhouse (half an acre) right this minute, I slowly picked up the receiver.

"Oliver Knowles," the voice said. "Is that you, Tim?"

"Hello," I replied warmly. "Everything going well?"

"No." The word was sickenly abrupt, and both mentally and physically I sat up straighter.

"What's the matter?"

"Can you come down here?" he asked, not directly answering. "I'm rather worried. I want to talk to you."

"Well . . . I could come on Sunday," I said.

"Could you come today? Or tomorrow?"

I reviewed my work load and a few appointments. "Tomorrow afternoon, if you like," I said. "If it's bank business."

"Yes, it is." The anxiety in his voice was quite plain, and communicated itself with much ease to me.

"Can't you tell me what's the trouble?" I asked. "Is Sandcastle all right?"

"I don't know," he said. "I'll tell you when you come."

"But Oliver . . ."

"Listen," he said. "Sandcastle is in good health and he hasn't escaped again or anything like that. It's too difficult to explain on the telephone. I want your advice, that's all."

He wouldn't say any more and left me with the dead receiver in my hand and some horrid suspenseful question marks in my mind.

"Sandcastle?" Gordon asked.

"Oliver says he's in good health."

"That horse is insured against everything—those enormous premiums—so don't worry too much," Gordon said. "It's probably something minor."

It hadn't sounded like anything minor, and when I reached the stud farm the next day I found that it certainly wasn't. Oliver came out to meet me as I braked to a standstill by his front door, and there were new deep lines on his face that hadn't been there before.

"Come in," he said, clasping my hand. "I'm seriously worried. I don't know what to do."

He led the way through the house to the office-sitting room and gestured me to a chair. "Sit down and read this," he said, and gave me a letter.

There had been no time for "nice day" or "how is Ginnie?" introductory noises, just this stark command. I sat down, and I read, as directed.

The letter, dated April twenty-first, said,

Dear Oliver,

I'm not complaining, because of course one pays one's fee and takes one's chances, but I'm sorry to tell you that the Sandcastle foal out of my mare Spiral Binding has been born with a half of one ear missing. It's a filly, by the way, and I daresay it won't affect her speed, but her looks are ruined.

So sad.

I expect I'll see you one day at the sales.

Yours,

Jane

"Is that very bad?" I asked, frowning.

In reply he wordlessly handed me another letter. This one said:

Dear Mr. Knowles,

You asked me to let you know how my mare Girandette, whom you liked so much, fared on foaling. She gave birth safely to a nice colt foal, but unfortunately he died at six days. We had a post mortem, and it was found that he had malformed heart valves, like hole-in-heart-babies.

This is a great blow to me, financially as well as all else, but that's life I suppose.

Yours sincerely,

George Page

"And now this," Oliver said, and handed me a third.

The heading was that of a highly regarded and well-known stud farm, the letter briefly impersonal.

Dear Sir,

Filly foal born March 31st to Poppingcorn.
Sire: Sandcastle.
Deformed foot, near fore.
Put down.

I gave him back the letters and with growing misgiving asked, "How common are these malformations?"

Oliver said intensely, "They happen. They happen occasionally. But those letters aren't all. I've had two telephone calls—one last night. Two more foals have died of holes in the heart. Two more! That's five with something wrong with them." He stared at me, his eyes like dark pits. "That's far too many." He swallowed. "And what about the others, the other thirty-five? Suppose . . . suppose there are more . . ."

"If you haven't heard, they're surely all right."

He shook his head hopelessly. "The mares are scattered all over the place, dropping Sandcastle's foals where they are due to be bred next. There's no automatic reason for those stud managers to tell me when a foal's born, or what it's like. I mean, some do it out of courtesy but they just don't usually bother, and nor do I. I tell the owner of the mare, not the manager of the stallion."

"Yes, I see."

"So there may be other foals with deformities . . . that I haven't heard about."

There was a long, tense pause in which the enormity of the position sank coldly into my banking consciousness. Oliver developed sweat on his forehead and a tic beside his mouth, as if sharing his anxiety had doubled rather than halved it.

The telephone rang suddenly, making us both jump.

"You answer it," he said. "Please."

I opened my mouth to protest that it would be only some routine call about anything else on earth, but then merely picked up the receiver.

"Is that Oliver Knowles?" a voice said.

"No . . . I'm his assistant."

"Oh. Then will you give him a message?"

"Yes, I will."

"Tell him that Patrick O'Marr rang him from Limballow, Ireland. Have you got that?"

"Yes," I said. "Go ahead."

"It's about a foal we had born here three or four weeks ago. I thought I'd better let Mr. Knowles know that we've had to put it down, though I'm sorry to give him bad news. Are you listening?"

"Yes," I said, feeling hollow.

"The poor little fellow was born with a sort of curled-in hoof. The vet said it might straighten out in a week or two, but it didn't, so we had it X-rayed, and the lower pastern bone and the coffin bone were fused and tiny. The vet said there was no chance of them developing properly, and the little colt would never be able to walk, let alone race. A beautiful little fella too, in all other ways. Anyway, I'm telling Mr. Knowles because of course he'll be looking out for Sandcastle's first crop to win for him, and I'm explaining why this one won't be there. Pink Roses, that's the mare's name. Tell him, will you? Pink Roses. She's come here to be bred to Dallaton. Nice mare. She's fine herself, tell Mr. Knowles."

"Yes," I said. "I'm very sorry."

"One of those things." The cultured Irish accent sounded not too despairing. "The owner of Pink Roses is cut up about it, of course, but I believe he's insured against a dead or deformed foal, so it's a case of wait another year and better luck next time."

"I'll tell Mr. Knowles," I said. "And thank you for letting us know."

"Sorry and all," he said. "But there it is."

I put the receiver down slowly and Oliver said dully, "Another one? Not another one."

I nodded and told him what Patrick O'Marr had said.

"That's six," Oliver said starkly. "And Pink Roses . . . that's the mare you saw Sandcastle cover, this time last year."

"Was it?" I thought back to that majestic mating, that moment of such promise. Poor little colt, conceived in splendor and born with a club foot.

"What am I going to do?" Oliver said.

"Get out Sandcastle's insurance policy."

He looked blank. "No, I mean, about the mares. We have all the mares here who've come this year to Sandcastle. They've all foaled except one, and nearly all of them have already been covered. I mean . . . there's another crop already growing, and suppose those . . . suppose all of those . . . ." He stopped as if he simply couldn't make his tongue say the words. "I was awake all night," he said.

"The first thing," I said again, "is to look at that policy."

He went unerringly to a neat row of files in a cupboard and pulled out the needed document, a many-paged affair, partly printed, partly typed. I spread it open and said to Oliver, "How about some coffee? This is going to take ages."

"Oh. All right." He looked around him vaguely. "There'll be some put ready for me for dinner. I'll go and plug it in." He paused. "Percolator," he explained.

I knew all the symptoms of a mouth saying one thing while the mind was locked on to another. "Yes," I said. "That would be fine." He nodded with the same unmeshed mental gears, and I guessed that when he got to the kitchen he'd have trouble remembering what for.

The insurance policy had been written for the trade and not for the customer, a matter of jargon-ridden sentences full of words that made plain sense only to people who used them for a living. I read it very carefully for that reason; slowly and thoroughly from start to finish.

There were many definitions of the word "accident," with stipulations about the number of veterinary surgeons who should be consulted and should give their signed opinions before Sandcastle (hereinafter called the horse) could be humanely destroyed for any reason whatsoever. There were stipulations about fractures, naming those bones that should commonly be held to be repairable, and about common muscle, nerve and tendon troubles that would not be considered grounds for destruction, unless of such severity that the horse actually couldn't stand up.

Aside from these restrictions the horse was to be considered to be insured against death from any natural causes whatsoever, to be insured against accidental death occurring while the horse was free (such a contingency to be guarded against with diligence, gross negligence being a disqualifying condition), to be insured against death by fire should the stable be consumed, and against death caused maliciously by human hand. He was insured fully against malicious or accidental castration and against such accidental damage being caused by veterinarians acting in good faith to treat the horse. He was insured against infertility on a sliding scale, his full worth being in question only if he proved one hundred percent infertile (which laboratory tests had shown was not the case).

He was insured against accidental or malicious poisoning and against impotence resulting from nonfatal illness, and against incapacitating or fatal injuries inflicted upon him by any other horse.

He was insured against death caused by the weather (storm, flood, lightning, etc.) and also, surprisingly, against death or incapacity caused by war, riot or civil commotion, causes usually specifically excluded from insurance.

He was insured against objects dropped from the sky and against being driven into by mechanical objects on the ground and against trees falling on him and against hidden wells opening under his feet.

He was insured against every foreseeable disaster except one. He was not insured against being put out of business because of congenital abnormalities among his progeny.

Oliver came back carrying a tray on which sat two kitchen mugs containing tea, not coffee. He put the tray on the desk and looked at my face, which seemed only very slightly to deepen his despair.

"I'm not insured, am I," he said, "against possessing a healthy potent stallion to whom no one will send their mares."

"I don't know."

"Yes . . . I see you do." He was shaking slightly. "When the policy was drawn up about six people, including myself and two vets, besides the insurers themselves, tried to think of every possible contingency, and to guard against it. We threw in everything we could think of." He swallowed. "No one . . . no one thought of a whole crop of deformed foals."

"No," I said.

"I mean, breeders usually insure their own mares, if they want to, and the foal, to protect the stallion fee, but many don't because of the premiums being high. And I . . . I'm paying this enormous premium . . . and the one thing . . . the one thing that happens is something we never . . . no one ever imagined . . . could happen.''

The policy, I thought, had been too specific. They should have been content with something like "any factor resulting in the horse not being considered for stud purposes"; but perhaps the insurers themselves couldn't find underwriters for anything so open to interpretation and opinion. In any case, the damage was done. All-risk policies all too often were not what they said; and insurance companies never paid out if they could avoid it.

My own skin felt clammy. Three million pounds of the bank's money and two million subscribed by private people were tied up in the horse, and if Oliver couldn't repay it was we who would lose.

I had recommended the loan. Henry had wanted the adventure and Val and Gordon had been willing, but it was my own report that had carried the day. I couldn't have foreseen the consequences any more than Oliver, but I felt most horribly and personally responsible for the mess.

"What shall I do?" he said again.

"About the mares?"

"And everything else."

I stared into space. The disaster that for the bank would mean a loss of face and a sharp dip in the profits and to the private subscribers just a painful financial setback meant in effect total ruin for Oliver Knowles.

If Sandcastle couldn't generate income, Oliver would be bankrupt. His business was not a limited company, which meant that he would lose his farm, his horses, his house; everything he possessed. To him too, as to my mother, the bailiffs would come, carrying off his furniture and his treasures and Ginnie's books and toys. . . .

I shook myself mentally and physically and said, "The first thing to do is nothing. Keep quiet and don't tell anyone what you've told me. Wait to hear if any more of the foals are . . . wrong. I will consult with the other directors at Ekaterin's and see what can be done in the way of providing time. I mean . . . I'm not promising . . . but we might consider suspending repayments while we look into other possibilities."

He looked bewildered. "What possibilities?"

"Well . . . of having Sandcastle tested. If the original tests of his fertility weren't thorough enough, for instance, it might be possible to show that his sperm had always been defective in some way, and then the insurance policy would protect you. Or at least it's a very good chance."

The insurers, I thought, might in that case sue the laboratory that had originally given the fertility all-clear, but that wasn't Oliver's problem, nor mine. What did matter was that all of a sudden he looked a fraction more cheerful, and drank his tea absentmindedly.

"And the mares?" he said.

I shook my head. "In fairness to their owners you'll have to say that Sandcastle's off-color."

"And repay their fees," he said gloomily.

"Mm."

"He'll have covered two today," he said. "I haven't mentioned any of this to Nigel. I mean, it's his job to organize the breeding sessions. He has a great eye for those mares, he knows when they are feeling receptive. I leave it to his judgment a good deal, and he told me this morning that two were ready for Sandcastle. I just nodded. I felt sick. I didn't tell him."

"So how many does that leave, er, uncovered?"

He consulted a list, fumbling slightly. "The one that hasn't foaled, and . . . four others."

Thirty-five more mares, I thought numbly, could be carrying that seed.

"The mare that hasn't yet foaled," Oliver said flatly, "was bred to Sandcastle last year."

I stared. "You mean . . . one of his foals will be born *here?*"

"Yes." He rubbed his hand over his face. "Any day."

There were footsteps outside the door and Ginnie came in, saying on a rising, inquiring inflection, "Dad?"

She saw me immediately and her face lit up. "Hello! How lovely. I didn't know you were coming."

I stood up to give her a customarily enthusiastic greeting, but she sensed at once that the action didn't match the climate. "What's the matter?" She looked into my eyes and then at her father. "What's happened?"

"Nothing," he said.

"Dad, you're lying." She turned again to me. "Tell me. I can see something bad has happened. I'm not a child anymore. I'm seventeen."

"I thought you'd be at school," I said.

"I've left. At the end of last term. There wasn't any point in me going back for the summer when all I'm interested in is here."

She looked far more assured, as if the schooldays had been a chrysalis and she were now the imago, flying free. The beauty she had longed for hadn't quite arrived, but her face was full of character and far from plain, and she would be very much liked, I thought, throughout her life.

"What is it?" she said. "What's happened?"

Oliver made a small gesture of despair and capitulation. "You'll have to know sometime." He swallowed. "Some of Sandcastle's foals . . . aren't perfect."

"How do you mean, not perfect?"

He told her about all six and showed her the letters, and she went slowly, swaying, pale. "Oh, Dad, no. No. It can't be. Not Sandcastle. Not that beautiful boy."

"Sit down," I said, but she turned to me instead, burying her face against my chest and holding on to me tightly. I put my arms round her and kissed her hair and comforted her for an age as best I could.

I went to the office on the following morning, Friday, and with a slight gritting of teeth told Gordon the outcome of my visit to Oliver.

He said, "My God," several times, and Alec came over from his desk to listen also, his blue eyes for once solemn behind the gold-rimmed spectacles, the blond eyelashes blinking slowly and the laughing mouth grimly shut.

"What will you do?" he said finally, when I stopped.

"I don't really know."

Gordon stirred, his hands trembling unnoticed on his blotter in his overriding concern. "The first thing, I suppose," he said, "is to tell Val and Henry. Though what any of us can do is a puzzle. As you said, Tim, we'll have to wait to assess quite how irretrievable the situation is, but I can't imagine anyone with a top-class broodmare having the confidence to send her to Sandcastle in future. Can you, really, Tim? Would *you?*"

I shook my head. "No."

"Well, there you are," Gordon said. "No one would."

Henry and Val received the news with undisguised dismay and told the rest of the directors at lunch. The man who had been against the project from the beginning reacted with genuine anger and gave me a furious dressing-down over the grilled sole.

"No one could foresee this," Henry protested, defending me.

"Anyone could foresee," said the dissenting director caustically, "that such a scatterbrained scheme would blow up in our faces. Tim has been given too much power too soon, and it's his judgment that's at fault here, his alone. If he'd had the common *nous* to recognize the dangers, you would have listened to him and turned the proposal down. It's certainly because of his stupidity and immaturity that the bank is facing this loss, and I shall put my views on record at the next board meeting."

There were a few uncomfortable murmurs round the table, and Henry with unruffled geniality said, "We are all to blame, if blame there is, and it is unfair to call Tim stupid for not foreseeing something that escaped the imaginations of all the various experts who drew up the insurance policy."

The dissenter, however, repeated his "I told you so" remarks endlessly through the cheese and coffee, and I sat there depressedly enduring his digs because I wouldn't give him the satisfaction of seeing me leave before he did.

"What will you do next?" Henry asked me, when at

long last everyone rather silently stood up to drift back to their desks. "What do you propose?"

I was grateful that by implication he was leaving me in the position I'd reached and not taking the decisions out of my hands. "I'm going down to the farm tomorrow," I said, "to go through the financial situation. Add up the figures. They're bound to be frightful."

He nodded with regret. "Such a marvelous horse. And no one, Tim, whatever anyone says, could have dreamed he'd have such a flaw."

I sighed. "Oliver has asked me to stay tomorrow night and Sunday night. I don't really want to, but they do need support."

"They?"

"Ginnie, his daughter, is with him. She's only just seventeen. It's very hard on them both. Shattering, in fact."

Henry patted my arm and walked with me to the lift. "Do what you can," he said. "Let us know the full state of affairs on Monday."

Before I left home that Saturday morning I had a telephone call from Judith.

"Gordon's told me about Sandcastle. Tim, it's so terrible. Those poor, poor people."

"Wretched," I said.

"Tim, tell Ginnie how sorry I am. Sorry . . . how hopeless words are, you say sorry if you bump someone in the supermarket. That dear child . . . she wrote to me a couple of times from school, just asking for feminine information, like I'd told her to."

"Did she?"

"Yes. She's such a nice girl. So sensible. But this . . . this is too much. Gordon says they're in danger of losing *everything.*"

"I'm going down there today to see where he stands."

"Gordon told me. Do please give them my love."

"I will." I paused fractionally. "My love to you, too."

"Tim . . ."

"I just wanted to tell you. It's still the same."

"We haven't seen you for weeks. I mean . . . I haven't."

"Is Gordon in the room with you?" I asked.

"Yes, that's right."

I smiled twistedly. "I do hear about you, you know," I said. "He mentions you quite often, and I ask after you . . . it makes you feel closer."

"Yes," she said in a perfectly natural voice. "I know exactly what you mean. I feel the same about it exactly."

"Judith . . ." I took a breath and made my own voice calm to match hers. "Tell Gordon I'll telephone him at home, if he'd like, if there is anything that needs consultation before Monday."

"I'll tell him. Hang on." I heard her repeating the question and Gordon's distant rumble of an answer, and then she said, "Yes, he says please do, we'll be at home this evening and most of tomorrow."

"Perhaps you'll answer when the telephone rings."

"Perhaps."

After a brief silence I said, "I'd better go."

"Goodbye then, Tim," she said. "And do let us know. We'll both be thinking of you all day, I know we will."

"I'll call," I said. "You can count on it."

The afternoon was on the whole as miserable as I'd expected and in some respects worse. Oliver and Ginnie walked about like pale automatons making disconnected remarks and forgetting where they'd put things, and lunch, Ginnie version, had consisted of eggs boiled too hard and packets of potato chips.

"We haven't told Nigel or the lads what's happening," Oliver said. "Fortunately there is a lull in Sandcastle's program. He's been very busy because nearly all his mares foaled in mid-March, close together, except for four and the one who's still carrying." He swallowed. "And the other stallions, of course, their mares are all here too, and we have their foals to deliver and their matings to be seen to. I mean . . . we have to go on. We have to."

Towards four o'clock they both went out into the

yards for evening stables, visibly squaring their shoulders to face the stablehands in a normal manner, and I began adding the columns of figures I'd drawn up from Oliver's records.

The tally when I'd finished was appalling and meant that Oliver could be an undischarged bankrupt for the rest of his life. I put the results away in my own briefcase and tried to think of something more constructive; and Oliver's telephone rang.

"Oliver?" a voice said, sounding vaguely familiar.

"He's out," I said. "Can I take a message?"

"Get him to ring me. Ursula Young. I'll give you the number."

"Ursula!" I said in surprise. "This is Tim Ekaterin."

"Really?" For her it was equally unexpected. "What are *you* doing there?"

"Just staying the weekend. Can I help?"

She hesitated slightly but then said, "Yes, I suppose you can. I'm afraid it's bad news for him, though. Disappointing, you might say." She paused. "I've a friend who has a small stud farm, just one stallion, but quite a good one, and she's been so excited this year because one of the mares booked to him was in foal to Sandcastle. She was thrilled, you see, to be having a foal of that caliber born on her place."

"Yes," I said.

"Well, she rang me this morning, and she was crying." Ursula herself gulped: she might appear tough but other people's tears always moved her. "She said the mare had dropped the Sandcastle foal during the night and she hadn't been there. She said the mare gave no sign yesterday evening, and the birth must have been quick and easy, and the mare was all right, but . . ."

"But what?" I said, scarcely breathing.

"She said the foal—a filly—was on her feet and suckling when she went to the mare's box this morning, and at first she was overjoyed, but then . . . but then . . ."

"Go on," I said hopelessly.

"Then she saw. She says it's dreadful."

"Ursula . . ."

"The foal has only one eye."

Oh, my God, I thought: dear *God.*

"She says there's nothing on the other side," Ursula said, "no proper socket." She gulped again. "Will you tell Oliver? I thought he'd better know. He'll be most disappointed. I'm so sorry."

"I'll tell him."

"These things happen, I suppose," she said. "But it's so upsetting when they happen to your friends."

"You're very right."

"Goodbye then, Tim. See you soon, I hope, at the races."

I put down the receiver and wondered how I would ever tell them, and in fact I didn't tell Ginnie, only Oliver, who sat with his head in his hands, despair in every line of his body.

"It's hopeless," he said.

"Not yet," I said encouragingly, though I wasn't as certain as I sounded. "There are still the tests to be done on Sandcastle."

He merely slumped lower. "I'll get them done, but they won't help. The genes that are wrong will be minute. No one will ever see them, however powerful the microscope."

"You can't tell. If they can see D.N.A., why not a horse's chromosomes?"

He raised his head slowly. "Even then . . . it's such a long shot." He sighed deeply. "I think I'll ask the Equine Research Establishment at Newmarket to have him there, to see what they can find. I'll ring them on Monday."

"I suppose," I said tentatively, "well, I know it sounds silly, but I suppose it couldn't be anything as simple as something he'd *eaten?* Last year, of course."

He shook his head. "I thought of that. I've thought of bloody well everything, believe me. All the stallions had the same food, and none of the others' foals are affected . . . or at least we haven't heard of any. Nigel feeds the stallions himself out of the feed room in that yard, and we're always careful what we give them because of keeping them fit."

"Carrots?" I said.

"I give carrots to every horse on the place. Everyone here does. Carrots are good food. I buy them by the hundredweight and keep them in the first big yard where the main feed room is. I put handfuls in my pockets every day. You've seen me. Rotaboy, Diarist and Parakeet all had them. It can't possibly be anything to do with carrots."

"Paint: something like that? Something new in the boxes, when you put in all the security? Something he could chew?"

He again shook his head. "I've been over it and over it. We did all the boxes exactly the same as each other. There's nothing in Sandcastle's box that wasn't in the others. They're all exactly alike." He moved restlessly. "I've even been down there to make sure there's nothing Sandcastle could reach to lick if he put his head right over the half-door as far as he could get. There's nothing, nothing at all."

"Drinking pails?"

"No. They don't always use the same pails. I mean, when Lenny fills them he doesn't necessarily take them back to the particular boxes they came from. The pails don't have the stallion's name on, if that's what you mean."

I didn't mean anything much: just grabbing at straws.

"Straw . . ." I said. "How about an allergy? An allergy to something around him? Could an allergy have such an effect?"

"I've never heard of anything like that. I'll ask the Research people, though, on Monday."

He got up to pour us both a drink. "It's good to have you here," he said. "A sort of net over the bottomless pit." He gave me the glass with a faint half-smile, and I had the definite impression that he would not in the end go to pieces.

I telephoned then to the Michaels' house and Gordon answered at the first ring, as if he'd been passing nearby. Nothing good to report, I said, except that Ginnie sent Judith her love. Gordon said Judith was in the garden picking parsley for supper, and he would tell her. "Call tomorrow," he said, "if we can help."

Our own supper, left ready in the refrigerator by Oliver's part-time housekeeper, filled the hollows left by lunch, and Ginnie went to bed straight afterwards, saying she would be up at two o'clock and out with Nigel in the foal yard.

"She goes out most nights," Oliver said. "She and Nigel make a good team. He says she's a great help, particularly if three or four mares are foaling at the same time. I'm often out there myself, but with all the decisions and paperwork as well I get very tired if I do it too much. Fall asleep over meals, that sort of thing."

We ourselves went to bed fairly early, and I awoke in the large high-ceilinged guest room while it was still blackly dark. It was one of those fast awakenings that mean that sleep won't come back easily, and I got out of bed and went to the window, which looked out over the yard.

I could see only roofs and security lights and a small section of the first yard. There was no visible activity, and my watch showed four-thirty.

I wondered if Ginnie would mind if I joined her in the foaling yard; and got dressed and went.

They were all there, Nigel and Oliver as well as Ginnie, all in one open-doored box where a mare lay on her side on the straw. They all turned their heads as I approached but seemed unsurprised to see me and gave no particular greeting.

"This is Plus Factor," Oliver said. "In foal to Sand-castle."

His voice was calm and so was Ginnie's manner, and I guessed that they still hadn't told Nigel about the deformities. There was hope, too, in their faces, as if they were sure that this one, after all, would be perfect.

"She's coming," Nigel said quietly. "Here we go."

The mare gave a grunt and her swelling sides heaved. The rest of us stood silent, watching, taking no part. A glistening half-transparent membrane with a hoof showing within it appeared, followed by the long slim shape of the head, followed very rapidly by the whole foal, flopping out onto the straw, steaming, the membrane breaking open, the fresh air reaching the head, new life beginning with the first fluttering gasp of the lungs.

Amazing, I thought.

"Is he all right?" Oliver said, bending down, the anxiety raw, unstifled.

"Sure," Nigel said. "Fine little colt. Just his foreleg's doubled over . . ."

He knelt beside the foal, who was already making the first feeble efforts to move his head, and he stretched out both hands gently to free the bent leg fully from the membrane, and to straighten it. He picked it up . . . and froze.

We could all see.

The leg wasn't bent. It ended in a stump at the knee. No cannon bone, no fetlock, no hoof.

Ginnie beside me gave a choking sob and turned abruptly towards the open door, towards the dark. She took one rocky pace and then another, and then was running: running nowhere, running away from the present, the future, the unimaginable. From the hopeless little creature on the straw.

I went after her, listening to her footsteps, hearing them on gravel and then losing them, guessing she had reached the grass. I went more slowly in her wake down the path to the breeding pen, not seeing her, but sure she was out somewhere in the paths around the paddocks. With eyes slowly acclimatizing I went that way and found her not far off, on her knees beside one of the posts, sobbing with the deep sound of a wholly adult desperation.

"Ginnie," I said.

She stood up as if to turn to me was natural and clung to me fiercely, her body shaking from the sobs, her face pressed hard against my shoulder, my arms tightly round her. We stook like that until the paroxysm passed; until, dragging a handkerchief from her jeans, she could speak.

"It's one thing knowing it in theory," she said, her voice full of tears and her body still shaking spasmodically from aftersobs. "I read those letters. I did know. But *seeing* it . . . that's different."

"Yes," I said.

"And it means . . ." She took gulps of air, trying hard for control. "It means, doesn't it, that we'll lose our farm. Lose everything?"

"I don't know yet. Too soon to say that."

"Poor Dad." The tears were sliding slowly down her cheeks, but like harmless rain after a hurricane. "I don't see how we can bear it."

"Don't despair yet. If there's a way to save you, we'll find it."

"Do you mean . . . your bank?"

"I mean everybody."

She wiped her eyes and blew her nose, and finally moved away a pace, out of my arms, strong enough to leave shelter. We went slowly back to the foaling yard and found nobody there except horses. I undid the closed top half of Plus Factor's box and looked inside; looked at the mare standing there patiently without her foal and wondered if she felt any fretting sense of loss.

"Dad and Nigel have taken him, haven't they?" Ginnie said.

"Yes."

She nodded, accepting that bit easily. Death to her was part of life, as to every child brought up close to animals. I closed Plus Factor's door and Ginnie and I went back to the house while the sky lightened in the east to the new day, Sunday.

The work of the place went on.

Oliver telephoned to various owners of the mares who had come to the other three stallions, reporting the birth of foals alive and well and one dead before foaling, very sorry. His voice sounded strong, civilized, controlled, the competent captain at the helm, and one could almost see the steel creeping back, hour by hour, into his battered spirit. I admired him for it; and I would fight to give him time, I thought, to come to some compromise to avert permanent ruin.

Ginnie, showered, breakfasted, tidy in sweater and shirt, went off to spend the morning at the Watcherleys' and came back smiling; the resilience of youth.

"Both of those mares are better from their infections," she reported, "and Maggie says she's heard Calder Jackson's not doing so well lately, his yard's half-empty. Cheers Maggie up no end, she says."

For the Watcherleys too, I thought briefly, the fall of Oliver's business could mean a return to rust and weeds, but I said, "Not enough sick horses just now, perhaps."

"Not enough sick horses with rich owners, Maggie says."

In the afternoon Ginnie slept on the sofa looking very childlike and peaceful, and only with the awakening did the night's pain roll back.

"Oh, dear . . ." The slow tears came. "I was dreaming it was all right. That that foal was a dream, only a dream . . ."

"You and your father," I said, "are brave people."

She sniffed a little, pressing her nose with the back of her hand. "Do you mean," she said slowly, "that whatever happens, we mustn't be defeated?"

"Mm."

She looked at me, and after a while nodded. "If we have to, we'll start again. We'll work. He did it all before, you know."

"You both have the skills," I said.

"I'm glad you came." She brushed the drying tears from her cheeks. "God knows what it would have been like without you."

I went with her out into the yards for evening stables, where the muck-carrying and feeding went on as always. Ginnie fetched the usual pocketful of carrots from the feed room and gave them here and there to the mares, talking cheerfully to the lads while they bent to their chores. No one, watching and listening, could ever have imagined that she feared the sky was falling.

"Evening, Chris, how's her hoof today?"

"Hi, Danny, Did you bring this one in this morning?"

"Hello, Pete. She looks as if she'll foal any day now."

"Evening, Shane. How's she doing?"

"Hi, Sammy, is she eating now OK?"

The lads answered her much as they spoke to Oliver himself, straightforwardly and with respect, and in most cases without stopping what they were doing. I looked back as we left the first big yard for the second, and for a moment took one of the lads to be Ricky Barnet.

"Who's that?" I said to Ginnie.

She followed my gaze to where the lad walked across to the yard tap, swinging an empty bucket with one hand and eating an apple with the other.

"Shane. Why?"

"He reminded me of someone I knew."

She shrugged. "He's all right. They all are, when Nigel's looking, which he doesn't do often enough."

"He works all night," I said mildly.

"I suppose so."

The mares in the second yard had mostly given birth already and Ginnie that evening had special eyes for the foals. The lads hadn't reached those boxes and Ginnie didn't go in to any of them, warning me that mares with young foals could be protective and snappy.

"You never know if they'll bite or kick you. Dad doesn't like me going in with them alone." She smiled. "He still thinks I'm a baby."

We went on to the foaling yard, where a lad greeted as Dave was installing a heavy slow-walking mare in one of the boxes.

"Nigel says she'll foal tonight," he told Ginnie.

"He's usually right."

We went on past the breeding pen and came down to the stallions, where Lenny and Don were washing down Diarist (who appeared to have been working) in the center of the yard, using a lot of water, energy and oaths.

"Mind his feet," Lenny said. "He's in one of his moods."

Ginny gave carrots to Parakeet and Rotaboy, and we came finally to Sandcastle. He looked as great, as charismatic as ever, but Ginnie gave him his tidbit with her own lips compressed.

"He can't help it all, I suppose," she said, sighing. "But I do wish he'd never won any races."

"Or that we'd let him die that day on the main road?"

"Oh, no!" She was shocked. "We couldn't have done that, even if we'd known . . ."

Dear girl, I thought; many people would personally have mown him down with a truck.

We went back to the house via the paddocks, where she fondled any heads that came to the railings and parted with the last of the crunchy orange goodies. "I can't believe that this will all end," she said, looking over the horse-dotted acres. "I just *can't* believe it."

I tentatively suggested to both her and Oliver that they might prefer it if I went home that evening, but they both declared themselves against.

"Not yet," Ginnie said anxiously and Oliver nodded forcefully. "Please do stay, Tim, if you can."

I nodded, and rang the Michaels', and this time got Judith.

"Do let me speak to her," Ginnie said, taking the receiver out of my hand. "I do so want to."

And I, I thought wryly, I too want so much to talk to her, to hear her voice, to renew my own soul through her: I'm no one's universal pillar of strength, I need my comfort too.

I had my crumbs, after Ginnie. Ordinary words, all else implied; as always.

"Take care of yourself," she said finally.

"You, too," I said.

"Yes." The word was a sigh, faint and receding, as if she'd said it with the receiver already away from her mouth. There was the click of disconnection, and Oliver was announcing briskly that it was time for whisky, time for supper; time for anything, perhaps, but thinking.

Ginnie decided that she felt too restless after supper to go to bed early, and would go for a walk instead.

"Do you want me to come?" I said.

"No. I'm all right. I just thought I'd go out. Look at the stars." She kissed her father's forehead, pulling on a thick cardigan for warmth. "I won't go off the farm. You'll probably find me in the foal yard, if you want me."

He nodded to her fondly but absentmindedly, and with a small wave to me she went away. Oliver asked me gloomily, as if he'd been waiting for us to be alone, how soon I thought the bank would decide his fate, and we talked in snatches about his daunting prospects, an hour or two sliding by on possibilities.

Shortly before ten, when we had probably twice repeated all there was to say, there came a heavy hammering on the back door.

"Whoever's that?" Oliver frowned, rose to his feet and went to find out.

I didn't hear the opening words, but only the goose-pimpling urgency in the rising voice.

"She's where?" Oliver said loudly, plainly, in alarm. "Where?"

I went quickly into the hallway. One of the lads stood in the open doorway, panting for breath, wide-eyed and scared.

Oliver glanced at me over his shoulder, already on the move. "He says Ginnie's lying on the ground unconscious."

The lad turned and ran off, with Oliver following and myself close behind: and the lad's breathlessness, I soon found, was owing to Ginnie's being on the far side of the farm, away down beyond Nigel's bungalow and the lads' hostel, right down on the far drive, near the gate to the lower road.

We arrived there still running, the lad now doubling over in his fight for breath, and found Ginnie lying on her side on the hard asphalt surface with another of the lads on his knees beside her, dim figures in the weak moonlight, blurred outlines of shadow.

Oliver and I too knelt there and Oliver was saying to the lads, "What happened, what happened? Did she fall?"

"We just found her," the kneeling lad said. "We

were on our way back from the pub. She's coming round, though, sir, she's been saying things."

Ginny in fact moved slightly, and said, "Dad."

"Yes, Ginnie, I'm here." He picked up her hand and patted it. "We'll soon get you right." There was relief in his voice, but short-lived.

"Dad," Ginnie said, mumbling. "Dad."

"Yes, I'm here."

"Dad . . ."

"She isn't hearing you," I said worriedly.

He turned his head to me, his eyes liquid in the dark of his face. "Get an ambulance. There's a telephone in Nigel's house. Tell him to get an ambulance here quickly. I don't think we'll move her . . . Get an ambulance."

I stood up to go on the errand but the breathless lad said, "Nigel's out. I tried there. There's no one. It's all locked."

"I'll go back to the house."

I ran as fast on the way back and had to fight to control my own gulping breaths there to make my words intelligible. "Tell them to take the lower road from the village . . . the smaller right fork . . . where the road divides. Nearly a mile from there . . . wide metal farm gate, on the left."

"Understood," a man said impersonally. "They'll be on their way."

I fetched the padded quilt off my bed and ran back across the farm and found everything much as I'd left it. "They're coming," I said. "How is she?"

Oliver tucked the quilt round his daughter as best he could. "She keeps saying things. Just sounds, not words."

"Da . . ." Ginnie said.

Her eyelids trembled and slightly opened.

"Ginnie," Oliver said urgently. "This is Dad."

Her lips moved in a mumbling unformed murmur. The eyes looked at nothing, unfocused, the gleam just reflected moonlight, not an awakening.

"Oh, God," Oliver said. "What's happened to her? What can have happened?"

The two lads stood there, awkward and silent, not knowing the answer.

"Go and open the gate," Oliver told them. "Stand on the road. Signal to the ambulance when it comes."

They went as if relieved; and the ambulance did come, lights flashing, with two brisk men in uniform who lifted Ginnie without much disturbing her onto a stretcher. Oliver asked them to wait while he fetched the Land Rover from Nigel's garage, and in a short time the ambulance set off to the hospital with Oliver and me following.

"Lucky you had the key," I said, indicating it in the ignition. Just something to say: anything.

"We always keep it in that tin on the shelf."

The tin said "Blackcurrant Coughdrops. Take as Required."

Oliver drove automatically, following the rear lights ahead. "Why don't they go faster?" he said, though their speed was quite normal.

"Don't want to jolt her, perhaps."

"Do you think it's a stroke?" he said.

"She's too young."

"No. I had a cousin . . . an aneurysm burst when he was sixteen."

I glanced at his face: lined, grim, intent on the road.

The journey seemed endless, but ended at a huge bright hospital in a sprawling town. The men in uniform opened the rear doors of the ambulance while Oliver parked the Land Rover and we followed them into the brightly lit emergency reception area, seeing them wheel Ginnie into a curtained cubicle, watching them come out again with their stretcher, thanking them as they left.

A nurse told us to sit on some nearby chairs while she fetched a doctor. The place was empty, quiet, all readiness but no bustle. Ten o'clock on Sunday night.

A doctor came in a white coat, stethoscope dangling. An Indian, young, black-haired, rubbing his eyes with forefinger and thumb. He went behind the curtains with the nurse and for about a minute Oliver clasped and unclasped his fingers, unable to contain his anxiety.

The doctor's voice reached us clearly, the Indian accent making no difference.

"They shouldn't have brought her here," he said. "She's dead."

Oliver was on his feet, bounding across the shining floor, pulling back the curtains with a frantic sweep of the arm.

"She's not dead. She was talking. Moving. She's not dead."

In dread I followed him. She couldn't be dead, not like that, not so fast, not without the hospital fighting long to save her. She *couldn't* be.

The doctor straightened up from bending over her, withdrawing his hand from under Ginnie's head, looking at us across the small space.

"She's my daughter," Oliver said. "She's not dead."

A sort of weary compassion drooped in the doctor's shoulders. "I am sorry," he said. "Very sorry. She is gone."

"No!" The word burst out of Oliver in an agony. "You're wrong. Get someone else."

The nurse made a shocked gesture but the young doctor said gently, "There is no pulse. No heartbeat. No contraction of the pupils. She has been gone for perhaps ten minutes, perhaps twenty. I could get someone else, but there is nothing to be done."

"But *why?*" Oliver said. "She was talking."

The dark doctor looked down to where Ginnie was lying on her back, eyes closed, brown hair falling about her head, face very pale. Her jerseys had both been unbuttoned for the stethoscope, the white bra showing, and the nurse had also undone the waistband of the skirt, pulling it loose. Ginnie looked very young, very defenseless, lying there so quiet and still, and I stood numbly, not believing it, unable, like Oliver, to accept such a monstrous change.

"Her skull is fractured," the doctor said. "If she was talking, she died on the way here, in the ambulance. With head injuries it can be like that. I am sorry."

There was a sound of an ambulance's siren wailing outside, and sudden noise and rushing people by the doors where we had come in, voices raised in a jumble of instructions.

"Traffic accident," someone shouted, and the doctor's eyes moved beyond us to the new need, to the future, not the past.

"I must go," he said, and the nurse, nodding, handed me a flat white plastic bottle that she had been holding.

"You may as well take this," she said. "It was tucked into the waistband of her skirt, against the stomach."

She made as if to cover Ginnie with a sheet, but Oliver stopped her.

"I'll do it," he said. "I want to be with her."

The young doctor nodded, and he and I and the nurse stepped outside the cubicle, drawing the curtains behind us. The doctor looked in a brief pause of stillness towards the three or four stretchers arriving at the entrance, taking a breath, seeming to summon up energy from deep reserves.

"I've been on duty for thirty hours," he said to me. "And now the pubs are out. Ten o'clock, Sundays. Drunk drivers, drunk pedestrians. Always the same."

He walked away to his alive and bleeding patients and the nurse pinned a "Do not Enter" sign onto the curtains of Ginnie's cubicle, saying she would be taken care of later.

I sat drearily on a chair, waiting for Oliver. The white plastic bottle had a label stuck onto one side saying "Shampoo." I put it into my jacket pocket and wondered if it was just through overwork that the doctor hadn't asked how Ginnie's skull had been fractured, asked whether she'd fallen onto a rock or a curb . . . or been hit.

The rest of the night and all the next day were in their own way worse, a truly awful series of questions, answers, forms and officialdom, with the police slowly taking over from the hospital and Oliver trying to fight against a haze of grief.

It seemed to me wicked that no one would leave him alone. To them he was just one more in a long line of bereaved persons, and although they treated him with perfunctory sympathy, it was for their own paperwork and not for his benefit that they wanted signatures, information and guesses.

Large numbers of policemen descended on the farm early in the morning, and it gradually appeared that that area of the country was being plagued by a stalker of young girls who jumped out of bushes, knocked them unconscious and sexually assaulted them.

"Not Ginnie . . ." Oliver protested in deepening horror.

The most senior of the policemen shook his head. "It would appear not. She was still wearing her clothing. We can't discount, though, the possibility that it was the same man, and that he was disturbed by your grooms. When young girls are knocked unconscious at night, it's most often a sexual attack."

"But she was on my own land," he said, disbelieving.

The policeman shrugged. "It's been known in suburban front gardens."

He was a fair-haired man with a manner that was not exactly brutal but spoke of long years of acclimatization to dreadful experiences. Detective Chief Inspector Wyfold, he'd said, introducing himself. Forty-fivish, I guessed, sensing the hardness within him at sight and judging him through that day more dogged than intuitive, looking for results from procedure, not hunches.

He was certain in his own mind that the attack on Ginnie had been sexual in intent and he scarcely considered anything else, particularly since she'd been carrying no money and had expressly said she wouldn't leave the farm.

"She could have talked to someone over the gate," he said, having himself spent some time on the lower drive. "Someone walking along the road. And there are all your grooms that we'll need detailed statements from, though from their preliminary answers it seems they weren't in the hostel but down at the village, in the pubs."

He came and went and reappeared again with more questions at intervals through the day and I lost track altogether of the hours. I tried, in his presence and out, and in Oliver's the same, not to think much about Ginnie herself. I thought I would probably have wept if I had, of no use to anyone. I thrust her away into a defensive compartment knowing that later, alone, I would let her out.

Some time in the morning one of the lads came to the house and asked what they should do about one of the mares who was having difficulty foaling, and Lenny also arrived wanting to know when he should take Rotaboy to the breeding pen. Each of them stood awkwardly, not knowing where to put their hands, saying they were so shocked, so sorry, about Ginnie.

"Where's Nigel?" Oliver said.

They hadn't seen him, they said. He hand't been out in the yards that morning.

"Didn't you try his house?" Oliver was annoyed rather than alarmed: another burden on a breaking back.

"He isn't there. The door's locked and he didn't answer."

Oliver frowned, picked up the telephone and pressed the buttons. Listened: no reply.

He said to me, "There's a key to his bungalow over there on the board, third hook from the left. Would you go and look . . . would you mind?"

"Sure."

I walked down there with Lenny, who told me repeatedly how broken up the lads were over what had happened, particularly Dave and Sammy, who'd found her. They'd all liked her, he said. All the lads who lived in the hostel were saying that perhaps if they'd come back sooner, she wouldn't have been attacked.

"You don't live in the hostel, then?" I said.

"No. Down in the village. Got a house. Only the ones who come just for the season, they're the ones in the hostel. It's shut up, see, all winter."

We eventually reached Nigel's bungalow, where I rang the doorbell and banged on the knocker without result. Shaking my head slightly I fitted the key in the lock, opened the door, went in.

Curtains were drawn across the windows, shutting out a good deal of daylight. I switched on a couple of lights and walked into the sitting room, where papers, clothes and dirty cups and plates were strewn haphazardly and the air smelled faintly of horse.

There was no sign of Nigel. I looked into the equally untidy kitchen and opened a door, which proved to be that of a bathroom, and another, which revealed a room with bare-mattressed twin beds. The last door in the small inner hall led to Nigel's own bedroom . . . and there he was, face down, fully clothed, lying across the counterpane.

Lenny, still behind me, took two paces back.

I went over to the bed and felt Nigel's neck behind the ear. Felt the pulse going like a steam hammer. Heard the rasp of air in the throat. His breath would have anesthetized a crocodile, and on the floor beside him lay an empty gin bottle. I shook his shoulder unsympathetically with a complete lack of result.

"He's drunk," I said to Lenny. "Just drunk."

Lenny looked all the same as if he was about to vomit. "I thought . . . I thought."

"I know," I said: and I'd feared it also, instinctively, the one because of the other.

"What will we do, then, out in the yard?" Lenny asked.

"I'll find out."

We went back to the sitting room, where I used Nigel's telephone to call Oliver and report.

"He's flat out," I said. "I can't wake him. Lenny wants instructions."

After a brief silence Oliver said dully, "Tell him to take Rotaboy to the breeding shed in half an hour. I'll see to things in the yards. And Tim?"

"Yes?"

"Can I ask you . . . would you mind . . . helping me here in the office?"

"Coming straight back."

The disjointed, terrible day wore on. I telephoned to

Gordon in the bank explaining my absence and to Judith also, at Gordon's suggestion, to pass on the heartbreak, and I took countless incoming messages as the news spread. Outside on the farm nearly two hundred horses got fed and watered, and birth and procreation went inexorably on.

Oliver came back stumbling from fatigue at about two o'clock, and we ate some eggs, not tasting them, in the kitchen. He looked repeatedly at his watch, and said finally, "What's eight hours back from now? I can't even *think*."

"Six in the morning," I said.

"Oh." He rubbed a hand over his face. "I suppose I should have told Ginnie's mother last night." His face twisted. "My wife . . . in Canada . . ." He swallowed. "Never mind, let her sleep. In two hours I'll tell her."

I left him alone to that wretched task and took myself upstairs to wash and shave and lie for a while on the bed. It was in taking my jacket off for those purposes that I came across the plastic bottle in my pocket, and I took it out and stood it on the shelf in the bathroom while I shaved.

An odd sort of thing, I thought, for Ginnie to have tucked into her waistband. A plastic bottle of shampoo; about six inches high, four across, one deep, with a screw cap on one of the narrow ends. The white label saying "Shampoo" had been handwritten and stuck on the top of the bottle's original dark-brown, white-printed label, of which quite a bit still showed around the edges.

Instructions, part of the underneath label said. *Shake well. Be careful not to get the shampoo in the dog's eyes. Rub well into the coat and leave for ten or fifteen minutes before rinsing.*

At the bottom, below the stuck-on label, were the words, in much smaller print, *Manufactured by Eagle, Inc., Michigan, U.S.A. List number 29931.*

When I'd finished shaving I unscrewed the cap and tilted the bottle gently over the basin.

A thick greenish liquid appeared, smelling powerfully of soap.

Shampoo: what else.

The bottle was to all intents full. I screwed on the cap again and put it on the shelf, and thought about it while I lay on the bed with my hands behind my head.

Shampoo for dogs.

After a while I got up and went down to the kitchen, and in a high cupboard found a small collection of empty, washed, screw-top glass jars, the sort of thing my mother had always saved for herbs and picnics. I took one that would hold perhaps a cupful of liquid and returned upstairs, and over the washbasin I shook the bottle well, unscrewed the cap and carefully poured more than half the shampoo into the jar.

I screwed the caps onto both the bottle and the jar, copied what could be seen on the original label into the small engagement diary I carried with me everywhere, and stowed the now half-full round glass container from Oliver's kitchen inside my own sponge-bag: and when I went downstairs again I took the plastic bottle with me.

"Ginnie had it?" Oliver said dully, picking it up and squinting at it. "Whatever for?"

"The nurse at the hospital said it was tucked into the waistband of her skirt."

A smile flickered. "She always did that when she was little. Plimsols, books, bits of string, anything. To keep her hands free, she said. They all used to slip down into her little knickers, and there would be a whole shower of things sometimes when we undressed her." His face went hopelessly bleak at this memory. "I can't believe it, you know," he said. "I keep thinking she'll walk through the door." He paused. "My wife is flying over. She says she'll be here tomorrow morning." His voice gave no indication whether that was good news or bad. "Stay tonight, will you?"

"If you want."

"Yes."

Chief Inspector Wyfold turned up again at that point and we gave him the shampoo bottle, Oliver explaining about Ginnie's habit of carrying things in her clothes.

"Why didn't you give this to me earlier?" he asked me.

"I forgot I had it. It seemed so paltry at the time, compared with Ginnie dying."

The Chief Inspector picked up the bottle by its serrated cap and read what one could see of the label, and to Oliver he said, "Do you have a dog?"

"Yes."

"Would this be what you usually use, to wash him?"

"I really don't know. I don't wash him myself. One of the lads does."

"The lads being the grooms?"

"That's right."

"Which lad washed your dog?" Wyfold asked.

"Um . . . any. Whoever I ask."

The Chief Inspector produced a thin white folded paper bag from one of his pockets and put the bottle inside it. "Who to your knowledge has handled this, besides yourselves?" he asked.

"I suppose," I said, "the nurse at the hospital . . . and Ginnie."

"And it spent from last night until now in your pocket?" He shrugged. "Hopeless for prints, I should think, but we'll try." He fastened the bag shut and wrote on a section of it with a ball pen. To Oliver, almost as an aside, he said, "I came to ask you about your daughter's relationships with men."

Oliver said wearily, "She didn't have any. She's only just left school."

Wyfold made small negative movements with head and hands as if amazed at the naiveté of fathers. "No sexual relationship to your knowledge?"

Oliver was too exhausted for anger. "No," he said.

"And you sir?" he turned to me. "What were your relations with Virginia Knowles?"

"Friendship."

"Including sexual intercourse?"

"No."

Wyfold looked at Oliver, who said tiredly, "Tim is a business friend of mine. A financial adviser, staying here for the weekend, that's all."

The policeman frowned at me with disillusion as if he didn't believe it. I gave him no amplified answer because I simply couldn't be bothered, and what could I have said? That with much affection I'd watched a child grow into an attractive young woman and yet not wanted to sleep with her? His mind ran on carnal rails, all else discounted.

He went away in the end taking the shampoo with him, and Oliver with immense fortitude said he had better go out into the yards to catch the tail end of evening stables. "Those mares," he said. "Those foals . . . they still need the best of care."

"I wish I could help," I said, feeling useless.

"You do."

I went with him on his rounds, and when we reached the foaling yard, Nigel, resurrected, was there.

His stocky figure leaned against the doorpost of an open box as if without its support he would collapse, and the face he slowly turned towards us had aged ten years. The bushy eyebrows stood out starkly over charcoal-shadowed eyes, puffiness in his skin swelling the eyelids and sagging in deep bags on his cheeks. He was also unshaven, unkempt and feeling ill.

"Sorry," he said. "Heard about Ginnie. Very sorry." I wasn't sure whether he was sympathizing with Oliver or apologizing for the drunkenness. "A big noise of a policeman came asking if I'd killed her. As if I would." He put a shaky hand on his head, almost as if physically to support it on his shoulders. "I feel rotten. My own fault. Deserve it. This mare's likely to foal tonight. That shit of a policeman wanted to know if I was sleeping with Ginnie. Thought I'd tell you . . . I wasn't."

Wyfold, I reflected, would ask each of the lads, individually, the same question. A matter of time, perhaps, before he asked Oliver himself; though Oliver and I, he had had to concede, gave each other a rock-solid alibi.

We walked on towards the stallions and I asked Oliver if Nigel often got drunk, since Oliver hadn't shown much surprise.

"Very seldom," Oliver said. "He's once or twice turned out in that state but we've never lost a foal because of it. I don't like it, but he's so good with the mares." He shrugged. "I overlook it."

He gave carrots to all four stallions but scarcely glanced at Sandcastle, as if he could no longer bear the sight.

"I'll try the Research people tomorrow," he said. "Forgot about it, today."

From the stallions he went, unusually, in the direction of the lower gate, past Nigel's bungalow and the hostel, to stand for a while at the place where Ginnie had lain in the dark on the night before.

The asphalt driveway showed no mark. Oliver looked to where the closed gate sixty feet away led to the road, and in a drained voice said, "Do you think she could have talked to someone out there?"

"She might have, I suppose."

"Yes." He turned to go back. "It's all so *senseless*. And unreal. Nothing feels real."

Exhaustion of mind and body finally overtook him after dinner and he went gray-faced to bed, but I in the first quiet of the long day went out again for restoration: for a look at the stars, as Ginnie had said.

Thinking only of her I walked slowly along some of the paths between the paddocks, the way lit by a half-moon with small clouds drifting, and stopped eventually at the place where, on the previous morning, I'd held her tight in her racking distress. The birth of the deformed foal seemed so long ago, yet it was only yesterday: the morning of the last day of Ginnie's life.

I thought about that day, about the despair in its dawn and the resolution of its afternoon. I thought of her tears and her courage, and of the waste of so much goodness. The engulfing, stupefying sense of loss that had hovered all day swamped into my brain until my body felt inadequate, as if it wanted to burst, as if it couldn't hold in so much feeling.

When Ian Pargetter had been murdered I had been angry on his behalf and had supposed that the more one loved the dead person the greater one's fury against the killer. But now I understood that anger could simply be crowded out by something altogether more overwhelming. As for Oliver, he had displayed shock, daze, desolation and disbelief in endless quantities all day, but of anger, barely a flicker.

It was too soon to care who had killed her. The fact of her death was too much. Anger was irrelevant, and no vengeance could give her life.

I had loved her more than I'd known, but not as I loved Judith, not with desire and pain and longing. I'd loved Ginnie as a friend; as a brother. I'd loved her, I thought, right back from the day when I'd returned her to school and listened to her fears. I'd loved her up on the hill, trying to catch Sandcastle, and I'd loved her for her expertise and for her growing adult certainty that here, in these fields, was where her future lay.

I'd thought of her young life once as being a clear stretch of sand waiting for footprints, and now there would be none, now only a blank, chopping end to all she could have been and done, to all the bright love she had scattered around her.

"Oh . . . *Ginnie*," I said aloud, calling to her hopelessly in tearing body-shaking grief. "Ginnie . . . little Ginnie . . . come back."

But she was gone from there. My voice fled away into darkness, and there was no answer.

May

On and off for the next two weeks I worked on Oliver's financial chaos at my desk in the bank, and at a special board meeting argued the case for giving him time before we foreclosed and made him sell all he had.

I asked for three months, which was considered scandalously out of the question, but got him two, Gordon chuckling over it quietly as we went down together afterwards in the lift.

"I suppose two months was what you wanted?" he said.

"Er . . . yes."

"I know you," he said. "They were talking of twenty-one days maximum before the meeting, and some wanted to bring in liquidators at once."

I telephoned Oliver and told him. "For two months you don't have to pay any interest or capital repayments, but this is only temporary, and it is a special, fairly unusual concession. I'm afraid, though, that if we can't find a solution to Sandcastle's problem or come up with a cast-iron reason for the insurance company to pay out, the prognosis is not good."

"I understand," he said, his voice sounding calm. "I haven't much hope, but thank you, all the same, for the respite—I will at least be able to finish the programs for the other stallions, and keep all the foals here until they're old enough to travel safely."

"Have you heard anything about Sandcastle?"

"He's been at the Research Establishment for a week, but so far they can't find anything wrong with him. They don't hold out much hope, I'd better tell you, of being able to prove anything one way or another about his sperm, even though they're sending specimens to another laboratory, they say."

"They'll do their best."

"Yes, I know. But . . . I walk around here as if this place no longer belongs to me. As if it isn't mine. I know, inside, that I'm losing it. Don't feel too badly, Tim. When it comes, I'll be prepared."

I put the receiver down not knowing whether such resignation was good because he would face whatever came without disintegration, or bad because he might be surrendering too soon. A great host of other troubles still lay ahead, mostly in the shape of breeders demanding the return of their stallion fees, and he needed energy to say that in most cases he couldn't return them. The money had already been lodged with us, and the whole situation would have to be sorted out by lawyers.

The news of Sandcastle's disgrace was so far only a doubtful murmur here and there, but when it all broke open with a screech it was, I supposed predictably, in *What's Going On Where It Shouldn't.*

The bank's six copies were read to rags before lunch on the day Alec fetched them, eyes lifting from the page with anything from fury to a wry smile.

Three short paragraphs, headed *"House on Sand,"* said:

Build not your house on sand. Stake not your banking house on a Sandcastle.

The five million pounds advanced by a certain prestigious merchant bank for the purchase of the stallion Sandcastle now look like being washed away by the tide.

Sadly, the investment has produced faulty stock, or in plain language, several deformed foals.

Speculation now abounds as to what the bank can do to minimize its losses, since Sandcastle himself must be considered as half a ton of highly priced dog-meat.

"That's done it," Gordon said, and I nodded: and the dailies, who always read *What's Going On* as a prime news source, came up in the racing columns the next day with a more cautious approach, asking "Sandcastle's Progeny Flawed?" and saying things like "rumors have reached us" and "we are reliably informed."

Since our own home-grown leaker for once hadn't mentioned the bank by name, none of the dailies did either, and for them, of course, the bank itself was unimportant compared with the implications of the news.

Oliver, in the next weekday issues, was reported as having been asked how many, precisely, of Sandcastle's foals were deformed, and as having answered that he didn't know. He had heard of some, certainly, yes. He had no further comment.

A day later still the papers began printing reports telephoned in to them by the stud farms where Sandcastle's scattered progeny had been foaled, and the tally of disasters mounted. Oliver was reported this time as having said the horse was at the Equine Research Establishment at Newmarket, and everything possible was being done.

"It's a mess," Henry said gloomily at lunch, and even the dissenting director had run out of insults, beyond saying four times that we were the laughingstock of the City and it was all my fault.

"Have they found out who killed Knowles' daughter?" Val Fisher asked.

"No." I shook my head. "He says the police no longer come to the house."

Val looked regretful. "Such a sadness for him, on top of the other."

There were murmurs of sympathy and I didn't think I'd spoil it by telling them what the police thought of Oliver's lads.

"That man Wyfold," Oliver had said on the telephone during one of our almost daily conversations, "he more or less said I was asking for trouble, having a young girl on the place with all those lads. What's more, it seems many of them were halfway drunk that night, and with three pubs in the village they weren't even all together and have no idea of who was where at what time, so one of Wyfold's theories is that one of them jumped her and Dave and Sammy interrupted him. Alternatively Nigel did it. Alternatively some stranger walking down the road did it. Wyfold's manner is downright abrasive but I'm past caring. He despises my discipline. He says I shouldn't let my lads get drunk—as if anyone could stop them. They're free men. It's their business, not mine, what they do with their money and time on Sunday nights. I can only take action if they don't turn up on Monday morning. And as for Nigel being paralytic!" Words momentarily failed him. "How can Nigel possibly expect the lads to stay more or less sober if he gets like that? And he says he can't remember anything that happened the night Ginnie died. Nothing at all. Total alcoholic blackout. He's been very subdued since."

The directors, I felt, would not be any more impressed than the Detective Chief Inspector with the general level of insobriety, and I wondered whether Nigel's slackness with the lads in general had always stemmed from a knowledge of his own occasional weakness.

The police had found no weapon, Oliver said on another day. Wyfold had told him that there was no way of knowing what had been used to cause the depressed fracture at the base of her brain. Her hair over the fracture bore no traces of anything unexpected. The forensic surgeon was of the opinion that there had been a single very heavy blow. She would have been knocked unconscious instantly. She wouldn't even have known. The period of apparent semiconsciousness had been illusory: parts of her brain would have functioned but she would not have been aware of anything at all.

"I suppose it's a mercy," Oliver said. "With some girls you hear of . . . how do their parents bear it?"

His wife, he said, had gone back to Canada. Ginnie's death seemed not to have brought mother and father together, but to have made the separation complete.

"The dog shampoo?" Oliver repeated, when I asked. "Wyfold says that's just what it was, they checked it. He asked Nigel and all the lads if it was theirs, if they'd used it for washing Squibs, but none of them had. He seems to think Ginnie may have seen it lying in the road and picked it up, or that she got into conversation over the gate with a man who gave her the shampoo for Squibs as a come-on and then killed her afterwards."

"No," I said.

"Why not?"

"Because he'd have taken the shampoo away again with him."

"Wyfold says not if he couldn't find it, because of its being dark and her having hidden it to all intents and purposes under her skirt and two jumpers, and not if Dave and Sammy arrived at that point."

"I suppose it's possible," I said doubtfully.

"Wyfold says that particular shampoo isn't on sale at all in England, it's American, and there's absolutely no way at all of tracing how it got here. There weren't any fingerprints of any use; all a blur except a few of yours and mine."

Another day he said, "Wyfold told me the hardest murders to solve were single blows on the head. He said the case would remain open, but they are busy again with another girl who was killed walking home from a dance, and this time she definitely is one of that dreadful series, poor child . . . I was lucky, Tim, you know, that Dave and Sammy came back when they did."

There came a fine May day in the office when Alec, deciding we needed some fresh air, opened one of the windows that looked down to the fountain. The fresh air duly entered but like a lion, not a lamb, and blew papers off all the desks.

"That's a hurricane," I said. "For God's sake shut it."

Alec closed off the gale and turned round with a grin. "Sorry and all that," he said.

We all left our chairs and bent down like gleaners to

retrieve our scattered work, and during my search for
page 3 of a long assessment of a proposed sports com-
plex I came across a severe and unwelcome shock in the
shape of a small, pale blue sheet off a memo pad.

There were words penciled on it and crossed out with
a wavy line, with other words underneath.

Build your castle not on Sand was crossed out, and so
was *Sandcastle gone with the tide,* and underneath was
written *Build not your house on sand. Build not your
banking house on a Sandcastle.*

"What's that?" Alec said quickly, seeing it in my
hand and stretching out his own. "Let's see."

I shook my head and kept it in my own hand while I
finished picking up the sportsdrome, and when order
was restored throughout the office I said, "Come along
to the interview room."

"Right now?"

"Right now."

We went into the only room on our floor where any
real privacy was possible and I said without any shilly-
shallying, "This is your handwriting. Did you write the
article in *What's Going On?*"

He gave a theatrical sigh and a tentative smile and a
large shrug of the shoulders.

"That's just doodling," he said. "It means nothing."

"It means, for a start," I said, "that you shouldn't
have left it round the office."

"Didn't know I had."

"Did you write the article?"

The blue eyes unrepentantly gleamed at me from behind the gold rims. "It's a fair cop, I suppose."

"But *Alec . . .*" I protested.

"Yeah."

"And the others," I said, "those other leaks, was that
you?"

He sighed again, his mouth twisting.

"Was it?" I repeated, wanting above all things to
hear him deny it.

"Look," he said, "what harm did it do? Yes, all right,
the stories did come from me. I wrote them myself, actually, like that one." He pointed to the memo paper in

my hand. "And don't give me any lectures on disloyalty because none of them did us any harm. Did us good, if anything."

"Alec . . ."

"Yes," he said, "but just think, Tim, what did those pieces really do? They stirred everyone up, sure, and it was a laugh a minute to see all their faces, but what else? I've been thinking about it, I assure you. It wasn't why I did it in the first place, that was just wanting to stir things, I'll admit, but *because* of what I wrote we've now got much better security checks than we had before."

I listened to him open-mouthed.

"All that work you did with the computer, making us safer against frauds, that was because of what I wrote. And the Corporate Finance boys, they now go around with their mouths zipped up like suitcases so as not to spill the beans to the investment managers. I did *good*, do you see, not harm."

I stood and looked at him, at the tight tow-colored curls, the cream-colored freckled skin, the eyes that had laughed with me for eight years. I don't want to lose you, I thought: I wish you hadn't done it.

"And what about this piece about Sandcastle? What good has that done?" I said.

He half-grinned. "Too soon to say."

I looked at the damaging scrap in my hands and almost automatically shook my head.

"You're going to say," Alec said, "that I'll have to leave."

I looked up. His face was wholly calm.

"I knew I'd have to leave if any of you ever found out."

"But don't you *care?*" I said frustratedly.

He smiled. "I don't know. I'll miss *you*, and that's a fact. But as for the job . . . well, I told you, it's not my whole life, like it is yours. I loved it, I grant you, when I came here. All I wanted was to be a merchant banker, it sounded great. But to be honest it was the glamour I suppose I wanted, and there's honesty for you, I never thought I'd admit that, even to myself."

"But you do it well."

"Up to a point. We discussed all that."

"I'm sorry," I said helplessly.

"Yeah, well, so am I in a way, and in a way I'm not. I've been dithering for ages, and now that it isn't my choice I'm as much relieved as anything."

"But . . . what will you do?"

He gave a full cherubic smile. "I don't suppose you'll approve."

"What, then?"

"What's Going On," he said, "have offered me a whole-time job." He looked at my shattered expression. "I've written quite a bit for them, actually. About other things, of course, not us. But in most editions there's something of mine, a paragraph or two or a whole column. They've asked me several times to go, so now I will."

I thought back to all those days when Alec had bounded out for the six copies and spent his next hour chuckling. Alec, the gatherer of news, who knew all the gossip.

"They get masses of information in," Alec said, "but they need someone to evaluate it all properly, and there aren't so many merchant bankers looking for that sort of job."

"No," I said dryly. "I can imagine. For a start, won't your salary be much less?"

"A bit," he admitted, cheerfully. "But my iconoclastic spirit will survive."

I moved restlessly, wishing things had been different.

"I'll resign from here," he said. "Make it easier."

Rather gloomily I nodded. "And will you say why?"

He looked at me thoughtfully. "If you really want me to, yes," he said finally. "Otherwise not. You can tell them yourself, though, after I've gone, if you want to."

"You're a damned fool," I said explosively, feeling the loss of him acutely. "The office will be bloody dull without you."

He grinned, my long-time colleague, and pointed to the piece of memo paper. "I'll send you pinpricks now and then. You won't forget me. Not a chance."

Gordon, three days later, said to me in surprise, "Alec's leaving, did you know?"

"I knew he was thinking of it."

"But why? He's good at his job, and he always seemed happy here."

I explained that Alec had been unsettled for some time and felt he needed to change direction.

"Amazing," Gordon said. "I tried to dissuade him, but he's adamant. He's going in four weeks."

Alec, indeed, addressed his normal work with the bounce and zealousness of one about to be liberated, and for the rest of his stay in the office was better company than ever. Chains visibly dropped from his spirits, and I caught him several times scribbling speculatively on his memo pad with an anything-but-angelic grin.

Oliver had sent me, at my request, a list of all the breeders who had sent their mares to Sandcastle the previous year, and I spent two or three evenings on the telephone asking after those foals we didn't know about. Oliver himself, when I'd asked him, said he frankly couldn't face the task, and I didn't in the least blame him: my inquiries brought forth an ear-burning amount of blasphemy.

The final count came to:

Five foals born outwardly perfect but dead within two weeks because of internal abnormalities.

One foal born with one eye. (Put down.)

Five foals born with deformed legs, deformation varying from a malformed hoof to the absent half-leg of Plus Factor's colt. (All put down.)

Three foals born with part of one or both ears missing. (All still living.)

One foal born with no tail. (Still living.)

Two foals born with malformed mouths, the equivalent of human harelips. (Both put down.)

One foal born with a grossly deformed head. (Foaled with heartbeat but couldn't breathe; died at once.)

Apart from this horrifying tally, four mares who had been sent home as in foal had subsequently "slipped" and were barren: one mare had failed to conceive at all;

three mares had not yet foaled (breeders' comments incendiary); and fourteen had produced live, healthy foals with no defects of any sort.

I showed the list to Gordon and Henry, who went shockedly silent for a while as if in mourning for the superb racer they had so admired.

"There may be more to come," I said, not liking it. "Oliver says thirty mares covered by Sandcastle this year are definitely in foal. Some of those will be all right . . . and some may not."

"Isn't there a test you can do to see if a baby is abnormal?" Henry said. "Can't they do that with the mares, and abort the deformed foals now, before they grow?"

I shook my head. "I asked Oliver that. He says amniocentesis—that's what that process is called—isn't possible with mares. Something to do with not being able to reach the target with a sterile needle because of all the intestines in the way."

Henry listened with the distaste of the nonmedical to these clinical realities. "What it means, I suppose," he said, "is that the owners of all of these thirty mares will have the foals aborted and demand their money back."

"I'd think so, yes."

He shook his head regretfully. "So sad, isn't it. Such a shame. Quite apart from the financial loss, a tragedy in racing terms."

Oliver said on the telephone one morning, "Tim, I need to talk to you. Something's happened."

"What?" I said, with misgivings.

"Someone has offered to buy Sandcastle."

I sat in a mild state of shock, looking at Alec across the room sucking his pencil while he wrote his future.

"Are you there?" Oliver said.

"Yes. What for and for how much?"

"Well, he says to put back into training. I suppose it's possible. Sandcastle's only five. I suppose he could be got fit to race by August or September, and he might still win races for a few more years."

"Good heavens."

"He's offering twenty-five thousand pounds."

"Um," I said. "Is that good or bad?"

"Realistically, it's as much as he's worth."

"I'll consult with my seniors here," I said. "It's too soon, this minute, to say yes or no."

"I did tell him that my bankers would have to agree, but he wants an answer fairly soon, because the longer the delay the less time there is for training and racing this season."

"Yes," I said, understanding. "Where is he? Sandcastle, I mean."

"Still in Newmarket. But it's pointless him staying there any longer. They haven't found any answers. They say they just don't know what's wrong with him, and I think they want me to take him away."

"Well," I pondered briefly. "You may as well fetch him, I should think."

"I'll arrange it," he said.

"Before we go any further," I said, "are you sure it's a bonafide offer and not just some crank?"

"I had a letter from him and I've talked to him on the telephone, and to me he sounds genuine," Oliver answered. "Would you like to meet him?"

"Perhaps, yes."

We fixed a provisional date for the following Saturday morning, and almost as an afterthought I asked the potential buyer's name.

"Smith," Oliver said. "A Mr. Dissdale Smith."

I went to Hertfordshire on that Saturday with a whole host of question marks raising their eyebrows in my mind, but it was Dissdale, as it happened, who had the deeper astonishment.

He drove up while I was still outside Oliver's house, still clasping hands in greeting and talking of Ginnie. Dissdale had come without Bettina, and the first thing he said, emerging from his car, was "Hello, Tim, what a surprise, didn't know you knew Oliver Knowles."

He walked across, announced himself, shook hands with Oliver, and patted me chubbily on the shoulder. "How's things, then? How are you doing, Tim?"

"Fine," I said mildly.

Oliver looked from one of us to the other. "You know each other already?"

Dissdale said, "How do you mean, already?"

"Tim's my banker," Oliver said in puzzlement. "It was his bank, Ekaterin's, which put up the money for Sandcastle."

Dissdale stared at me in stunned amazement and looked bereft of speech.

"Didn't you know?" Oliver said. "Didn't I mention it?"

Dissdale blankly shook his head and finally found his voice. "You just said your banker was coming . . . I never for a moment thought . . ."

"It doesn't make much odds," Oliver said. "If you know each other it may simply save some time. Let's go indoors. There's some coffee ready." He led the way through his immaculate house to the sitting room—office, where a tray stood on the desk with coffee hot in a pot.

Oliver himself had had four weeks by then in that house without Ginnie, but to me, on my first visit back, she seemed still most sharply alive. It was I, this time, who kept expecting her to walk into the room; to give me a hug, to say hello with her eyes crinkling with welcome. I felt her presence vividly, to an extent that to start with I listened to Dissdale with only surface attention.

"It might be better to geld him," he was saying. "There are some good prizes, particularly overseas, for geldings."

Oliver's instinctive response of horror subsided droopingly to defeat.

"It's too soon," I said, "to talk of that."

"Tim, face facts," Dissdale said expansively. "At this moment in time that horse is a walking bomb. I'm making an offer for him because I'm a bit of a gambler, you know that, and I've a soft spot for him, whatever his faults, because of him winning so much for me that day the year before last, when we were all in my box at Ascot. You remember that, don't you?"

"I do indeed."

"He saved my life, Sandcastle did."

"It was partly because of that day," I said, nodding, "that Ekaterin's loaned the money for him. When the request came in from Oliver, it was because Henry Shipton—our chairman, if you remember—and Gordon and I had all seen the horse in action that we seriously considered the proposition."

Dissdale nodded his comprehension. "A great surprise, though," he said. "I'm sorry it's you and Gordon. Sorry it's your bank, I mean, that's been hit so hard. I read about the deformed foals in the papers, of course, and that's what gave me the idea of buying Sandcastle in the first place, but it didn't say which bank . . ."

I wondered fleetingly if Alec could claim that omission as a virtue along with everything else.

Oliver offered Dissdale more coffee, which he accepted with cream and sugar, drinking almost absentmindedly while he worked through the possible alterations he would need in approach now he'd found he was dealing with semifriends. Having had time myself over several days to do it, I could guess at the speed he was needing for reassessment.

"Dissdale," I said neutrally, deciding to disrupt him, "did the idea of buying Sandcastle come from your profitable caper with Indian Silk?"

His rounded features fell again into shock. "How . . . er . . . did you know about that?"

I said vaguely, "Heard it on the racecourse, I suppose. But didn't you buy Indian Silk for a pittance because he seemed to be dying, and then sent him to Calder?"

"Well . . ."

"And didn't Calder cure him? And then you sold him again, but well this time, no doubt needing the money, as don't we all, since when Indian Silk's won the Cheltenham Gold Cup? Isn't that right?"

Dissdale raised a plump hand palm upwards in a gesture of mock defeat. "Don't know where you heard it, but yes, there's no secret, that's what happened."

"Mm." I smiled at him benignly. "Calder said on television, didn't he, that buying Indian Silk was his idea originally, so I wondered . . . I'm wondering if this is his idea too. I mean, did he by any chance suggest a repeat of the gamble that came off so happily last time?"

Dissdale looked at me doubtfully.

"There's nothing wrong in it," I said. "Is it Calder's idea?"

"Well, yes," he said, deciding to confide. "But it's my money, of course."

"And, um, if you do buy Sandcastle, will you send him too along to Calder, like Indian Silk?"

Dissdale seemed not to know whether to answer or not, but appearing to be reassured by my friendly interest said finally, "Calder said he could give him a quick pepping-up to get him fit quickly for racing, yes."

Oliver, having listened restlessly up to this point, said, "Calder Jackson can't do anything for Sandcastle that I can't."

Both Dissdale and I looked at Oliver in the same way, hearing the orthodox view ringing out with conviction and knowing that it was very likely untrue.

"I've been thinking these past few days," I said to Dissdale, "first about Indian Silk. Didn't you tell Fred Barnet, when you offered him a rock-bottom price, that all you were doing was providing a dying horse with a nice quiet end in some gentle field?"

"Well, Tim," he said knowingly. "You know how it is. You buy for the best price you can. Fred Barnet, I know he goes round grousing that I cheated him, but I didn't, he could have sent his horse to Calder the same as I did."

I nodded. "So now, be honest, Dissdale, are you planning again to buy for the best price you can? I mean, does twenty-five thousand pounds for Sandcastle represent the same sort of bargain?"

"Tim," Dissdale said, half-affronted, half in sorrow, "what a naughty suspicious mind. That's not friendly, not at all."

I smiled. "I don't think I'd be wise, though, do you, to recommend to my board of directors that we should accept your offer without thinking it over very carefully?"

For the first time there was a shade of dismay in the

chubby face. "Tim, it's a fair offer, anyone will tell you."

"I think my board may invite other bids," I said. "If Sandcastle is to be sold, we must recoup the most we can."

The dismay faded: man-of-the-world returned. "That's fair," he said. "As long as you'll come back to me, if anyone tops me."

"Sure," I said. "An auction, by telephone. When we're ready, I'll let you know."

With a touch of anxiety he said, "Don't wait too long. Time's money, you know."

"I'll put your offer to the board tomorrow."

He made a show of bluff contentment, but the anxiety was still there underneath. Oliver took the empty coffee cup that Dissdale still held and asked if he would like to see the horse he wanted to buy.

"But isn't he in Newmarket?" Dissdale said, again looking disconcerted.

"No, he's here. Came back yesterday."

"Oh. Then yes, of course, yes, I'd like to see him."

He's out of his depth, I thought abruptly: for some reason Dissdale is very very unsettled.

We went on the old familiar walk through the yards, with Oliver explaining the layout to the new visitor. To me there was now a visible thinning out of numbers, and Oliver, with hardly a quiver in his voice, said that he was sending the mares home with their foals in an orderly progression as usual, with in consequence lower feed bills, fewer lads to pay wages to, smaller expenses all round: he would play fair with the bank, he said, matter-of-factly, making sure to charge what he could and also to conserve what he could towards his debt. Dissdale gave him a glance of amused incredulity, as if such a sense of honor belonged to a bygone age, and we came in the end to the stallion yard, where the four heads appeared in curiosity.

The stay in Newmarket hadn't done Sandcastle much good, I thought. He looked tired and dull, barely arching his neck to lift his nose over the half-door, and it was he, of the four, who turned away first and retreated into the gloom of his box.

"Is that Sandcastle?" Dissdale said, sounding disappointed. "I expected something more, somehow."

"He's had a taxing three weeks," Oliver said. "All he needs is some good food and fresh air."

"And Calder's touch," Dissdale said with conviction. "That magic touch most of all."

When Dissdale had driven away Oliver asked me what I thought, and I said, "If Dissdale's offering twenty-five thousand he's certainly reckoning to make much more than that. He's right, he is a gambler, and I'll bet he has some scheme in mind. What we need to do is guess what the scheme is, and decide what we'll do on that basis, such as doubling or trebling the ante."

Oliver was perplexed. "How can we possibly guess?"

"Hm," I said. "Did you know about Indian Silk?"

"Not before today."

"Well, suppose Dissdale acts to a pattern, which people so often do. He told Fred Barnet he was putting Indian Silk out to grass, which was diametrically untrue; he intended to send him to Calder and with luck put him back in training. He told *you* he was planning to put Sandcastle back into training, so suppose that's just what he *doesn't* plan to do. And he suggested gelding, didn't he?"

Oliver nodded.

"Then I'd expect gelding to be furthest from his mind," I said. "He just wants us to believe that's his intention." I reflected. "Do you know what I might do if I wanted to have a real gamble with Sandcastle?"

"What?"

"It sounds pretty crazy," I said. "But with Calder's reputation it might just work."

"What are you talking about?" Oliver said in some bewilderment. "What gamble?"

"Suppose," I said, "that you could buy for a pittance a stallion whose perfect foals would be likely to win races."

"But no one would risk . . ."

"Suppose," I interrupted, "there was nearly a fifty-percent chance, going on this year's figures, that you'd get a perfect foal. Suppose Dissdale offered Sandcastle as a sire at say a thousand pounds, the fee only payable if the foal was born perfect and lived a month."

Oliver simply stared.

"Say Sandcastle's perfect progeny do win, as indeed they should. There are fourteen of them so far this year, don't forget. Say that in the passage of time his good foals proved to be worth the fifty-percent risk. Say Sandcastle stands in Calder's yard, with Calder's skill on the line. Isn't there a chance that over the years Dissdale's twenty-five-thousand-pound investment would provide a nice steady return for them both?"

"It's impossible," he said weakly.

"No, not impossible. A gamble." I paused. "You wouldn't get people sending top mares, of course, but you might get enough dreamers among the breeders who'd chance it."

"Tim . . ."

"Just think of it," I said. "A perfect foal by Sandcastle for peanuts. And if you get a malformed foal, well, some years your mare might slip or be barren anyway."

He looked at his feet for a while, and then into the middle distance, and then he said, "Come with me. I've something to show you. Something you'd better know."

He set off towards the Watcherleys', and would say nothing more on the way. I walked beside him down the familiar paths and thought about Ginnie because I couldn't help it, and we arrived in the next-door yard that was now of a neatness to be compared with all the others.

"Over here," Oliver said, going across to one of the boxes. "Look at that."

I looked where directed: at a mare with a colt foal suckling, not unexpected in that place.

"He was born three days ago," Oliver said. "I do so wish Ginnie had seen him."

"Why that one, especially?"

"The mare is one of my own," he said. "And that foal is Sandcastle's."

It was my turn to stare. I looked from Oliver to the foal and back again. "There's nothing wrong with him," I said.

"No."

"But . . ."

Oliver smiled twistedly. "I was going to breed her to Diarist. She was along here at the Watcherleys' because the foal she had then was always ailing, but she herself was all right. I was along here looking at her one day when she'd been in season awhile, and on impulse I led her along to the breeding pen and told Nigel to fetch Sandcastle, and we mated them there and then. That foal's the result." He shook his head regretfully. "He'll be sold, of course, with everything else. I wish I could have kept him, but there it is."

"He should be worth quite a bit," I said.

"I don't think so," Oliver said. "And that's the flaw in your gamble. It's not just the racing potential that raises prices at auction, it's the chance of breeding. And no one could be sure, breeding from Sandcastle's stock, that the genetic trouble wouldn't crop up for evermore. It's not on, I'm afraid. No serious breeder would send him mares, however great the bargain."

We stood for a while in silence.

"It was a good idea," I said, "while it lasted."

"My dear Tim . . . we're clutching at straws."

"Yes." I looked at his calm strong face; the captain whose ship was sinking. "I'd try anything, you know, to save you," I said.

"And to save the bank's money?"

"That too."

He smiled faintly. "I wish you could, but time's running out."

The date for bringing in the receiver had been set, the insurance company had finally ducked, the lawyers were closing in and the respite I'd gained for him was trickling away with no tender plant of hope growing in the ruins.

We walked back towards the house, Oliver patting the mares as usual as they came to the fences.

"I suppose this may all be here next year," he said,

"looking much the same. Someone will buy it . . . it's just I who'll be gone."

He lifted his head, looking away over his white-painted rails to the long line of the roofs of his yards. The enormity of the loss of his life's work settled like a weight on his shoulders and there was a haggard set to his jaw.

"I try not to mind," he said levelly. "But I don't quite know how to bear it."

When I reached home that evening my telephone was ringing. I went across the sitting room expecting it to stop the moment I reached it, but the summons continued, and on the other end was Judith.

"I just came in," I said.

"We knew you were out. We've tried once or twice."

"I went to see Oliver."

"The poor, poor man." Judith had been very much distressed over Ginnie and still felt that Oliver needed more sympathy because of his daughter than because of his bankruptcy, which I wasn't sure was any longer the case. "Anyway," she said, "Pen asked me to call you as she's tied up in her shop all day and you were out when she tried . . . She says she's had the reply from America about the shampoo and are you still interested?"

"Yes, certainly."

"Then . . . if you're not doing anything else . . . Gordon and I wondered if you'd care to come here for the day tomorrow, and Pen will bring the letter to show you."

"I'll be there," I said fervently, and she laughed.

"Good, then. See you."

I was at Clapham with alacrity before noon, and Pen, over coffee, produced the letter from the drug company.

"I sent them a sample of what you gave me in that little glass jar," she said. "And, as you asked, I had some of the rest of it analyzed here, but honestly, Tim, don't hope too much from it for finding out who killed Ginnie, it's just shampoo, as it says."

I took the official-looking letter, which was of two pages clipped together, with impressive headings.

Dear Ms. Warner,

We have received the inquiry from your pharmacy and also the sample you sent us, and we now reply with this report, which is a copy of that which we recently sent to the Hertfordshire police force on the same subject.

The shampoo in question is our "Bannitch," which is formulated especially for dogs suffering from various skin troubles, including eczema. It is distributed to shops selling goods to dog owners and offering cosmetic canine services, but would not normally be used except on the advice of a veterinarian.

We enclose the list of active ingredients and excipients, as requested.

"What are excipients?" I asked, looking up.

"The things you put in with the active drug for various reasons," she said. "Like for instance chalk for bulk in pills."

I turned the top page over and read the list on the second.

> Bannitch
> Excipients
>   Bentonite
>   Ethylene glycol monostearate
>   Citric acid
>   Sodium phosphate
>   Glyceryl monoricinoleate
>   Perfume
> Active ingredients
>   Captan
>   Amphoteric
>   Selenium

"Terrific," I said blankly. "What do they all mean?"

Pen, sitting beside me on the sofa, explained.

"From the top . . . bentonite is a thickening agent so that everything stays together and doesn't separate out. Ethylene glycol monostearate is a sort of wax, probably there to add bulk. Citric acid is to make the whole mixture acid, not alkaline, and the next one, sodium phosphate, is to keep the acidity level more or less constant. Glyceryl monoricinoleate is a soap, to make lather, and perfume is there so that the dog smells nice to the owner when she's washing him."

"How do you know so much?" Gordon asked, marveling.

"I looked some of them up," said Pen frankly, with a smile. She turned back to me and pointed to the short lower column of active ingredients. "Captan and amphoteric are both drugs for killing fungi on the skin, and selenium is also antifungal and is used in shampoos to cure dandruff." She stopped and looked at me doubtfully. "I did tell you not to hope too much. There's nothing there of any consequence."

"And nothing in the sample that isn't on the manufacturer's list?"

She shook her head. "The analysis from the British lab came yesterday, and the shampoo in Ginnie's bottle contained exactly what it should."

"What do you expect, Tim?" Gordon asked.

"It wasn't so much expect, as hope," I said regretfully. "Hardly hope, really. Just a faint outside chance."

"Of what?"

"Well . . . the police thought—think—that the purpose of killing Ginnie was sexual assault, because of those other poor girls in the neighborhood."

They all nodded.

"But it doesn't *feel* right, does it? Not when you know she wasn't walking home from anywhere, like the others, and not when she wasn't actually, well, interfered with. And then she had the shampoo . . . and the farm was in such trouble, and it seemed to me possible, just slightly possible, that she had somehow discovered that something in that bottle was significant . . ." I paused, and then said slowly to Pen, "I suppose what I was looking for was something that could have been put into Sandcastle's food or water that affected his reproductive organs. I don't know if that's possible. I don't know anything about drugs . . . I just *wondered*."

They sat in silence with round eyes, and then Gordon, stirring, said with an inflection of hope, "Is that possible, Pen? Could it be something like that?"

"Could it *possibly?*" Judith said.

"My loves," Pen said. "I don't know." She looked also as if whatever she said would disappoint us. "I've never heard of anything like that, I simply haven't."

"That's why I took the shampoo and gave it to you," I said. "I know it's a wild and horrible idea, but I told Oliver I'd try everything, however unlikely."

"What you're suggesting," Judith said plainly, "is that someone might *deliberately* have given something to Sandcastle to make him produce deformed foals, and that Ginnie found out . . . and was killed for it."

There was silence.

"I'll go and get a book or two," Pen said. "We'll look up the ingredients, just in case. But honestly, don't *hope.*"

She went home, leaving the three of us feeling subdued. For me this had been the last possibility, although since I'd heard from Oliver that the police check had revealed only the expected shampoo in the bottle, it had become more and more remote.

Pen came back in half an hour with a thick tome, a piece of paper, and worried creases across her forehead. "I've been reading," she said. "Sorry to be so long. I've been checking up on sperm deformities, and it seems the most likely cause is radiation."

"I said instantly, "Let's ring Oliver."

They nodded and I got through to him with Pen's suggestion.

"Tim!" he said. "I'll see if I can get anyone in Newmarket . . . even though it's a Sunday . . . I'll ring you back."

"Though how a stallion could get anywhere near a radioactive source," Pen said while we were waiting, "would be a first-class mystery in itself." She looked down at the paper she carried. "This is the analysis report from the British lab, bill attached, I'm afraid.

Same ingredients, though written in the opposite order, practically, with selenium put at the top, which means that that's the predominant drug, I should think."

Oliver telephoned again in a remarkably short time. "I got the chief researcher at home. He says they did think of radiation but discounted it because it would be more likely to result in total sterility, and there's also the improbability of a horse being near any radioactive isotopes." He sighed. "Sandcastle has never even been X-rayed."

"See if you can check," I said. "If he ever was irradiated in any way it could come into the category of accidental or even malicious damage, and we'd be back into the insurance policy."

"All right," he said. "I'll try."

I put down the receiver to find Pen turning the pages of her large pharmacological book with concentration.

"What's that?" Judith asked, pointing.

"Toxicity of minerals," Pen answered absentmindedly. "Ethylene glycol . . ." She turned pages, searching. "Here we are." She read down the column, shaking her head. "Not that, anyway." She again consulted the index, read the columns, shook her head. "Selenium . . . selenium . . ." She turned the pages, read the columns, pursed her lips. "It says that selenium is poisonous if taken internally, though it can be beneficial on the skin." She read some more. "It says that if animals eat plants that grow in soil that has much selenium in it, they can die."

"What is selenium?" Judith asked.

"It's an element," Pen said. "Like potassium and sodium." She read on, "It says here that it is mostly found in rocks of the Cretaceous age—such useful information—and that it's among the most poisonous of elements but also an essential nutrient in trace quantities for both animals and plants." She looked up. "It says it's useful for flower-growers because it kills insects, and that it accumulates mostly in plants that flourish where there's a low annual rainfall."

"Is that all?" Gordon asked, sounding disappointed.

"No, there's pages of it. I'm just translating the gist into understandable English."

She read on for a while, and then it seemed to me that she totally stopped breathing. She raised her head and looked at me, her eyes wide and dark.

"What is it?" I said.

"Read it." She gave me the heavy book, pointing to the open page.

I read: *Selenium is absorbed easily from the intestines and affects every part of the body, more lodging in the liver, spleen, and kidneys than in brain and muscle. Selenium is teratogenic.*

"What does teratogenic mean?" I asked.

"It means," Pen said, "that it produces deformed offspring."

"What?" I exclaimed. "You don't mean . . ."

Pen was shaking her head. "It couldn't affect Sandcastle. It's impossible. It would simply poison his system. Teratogens have nothing to do with males."

"Then what . . . ?"

"They act on the developing embryo," she said. Her face crumpled almost as if the knowledge was too much and would make her cry. "You could get deformed foals if you fed selenium *to the mares.*"

I went on the following morning to see Detective Chief Inspector Wyfold, both Gordon and Henry concurring that the errand warranted time off from the bank. The forceful policeman shook my hand, gestured me to a chair and said briskly that he could give me fifteen minutes at the outside, as did I know that yet another young girl had been murdered and sexually assaulted the evening before, which was now a total of six, and that his superiors, the press and the whole flaming country were baying for an arrest? "And we are no nearer now," he added with anger, "than we were five months ago, when it started."

He listened all the same to what I said about selenium, but in conclusion shook his head.

"We looked it up ourselves. Did you know it's the main ingredient in an antidandruff shampoo sold off open shelves all over America in the drugstores? It used to be on sale here too, or something like it, but it's been discontinued. There's no mystery about it. It's not rare, nor illegal. Just ordinary."

"But the deformities . . ."

"Look," he said restively. "I'll bear it in mind. But it's a big jump to decide from one bottle of ordinary dog shampoo that *that's* what's the matter with these foals. I mean, is there any way of proving it?"

With regret I said, "No, there isn't." No animal, Pen's book had inferred, would retain selenium in its system for longer than a day or two if it was eaten only once or twice and in nonfatal amounts.

"And how, anyway," Wyfold said, "would you get a whole lot of horses to drink anything as nasty as shampoo?" He shook his head. "I know you're very anxious to catch Virginia Knowles' killer, and don't think we don't appreciate your coming here, but we've been into the shampoo question thoroughly, I assure you."

His telephone buzzed and he picked up the receiver, his eyes still turned in my direction but his mind already elsewhere. "What?" he said. "Yes, all right. Straightaway." He put down the receiver. "I'll have to go."

"Listen," I said, "isn't it possible that one of the lads was giving selenium to the mares this year also, and that Ginnie somehow found out . . ."

He interrupted. "We tried to fit that killing onto one of those lads, don't think we didn't, but there was no evidence, absolutely none at all." He stood up and came round from behind his desk, already leaving me in mind as well as body. "If you think of anything else, Mr. Ekaterin, by all means let us know. But for now—I'm sorry, but there's a bestial man out there we've got to catch—and I'm still of the opinion he tried for Virginia Knowles too, and was interrupted."

He gave me a dismissing but not impatient nod, holding open the door and waiting for me to leave his office ahead of him. I obliged him by going, knowing that realistically he couldn't be expected to listen to any further unsubstantiated theories from me while another victim lay more horribly and recently dead.

Before I went back to him, I thought, I had better dig further and come up with connected, believable facts, and also a basis, at least, for proof.

Henry and Gordon heard with gloom in the bank before lunch that at present we were "insufficient data" in a Wyfold pigeonhole.

"But you still believe, do you, Tim . . . ?" Henry said inquiringly.

"We have to," I answered. "And yes, I do."

"Hm." He pondered. "If you need more time off from the office, you'd better take it. If there's the slightest chance that there's nothing wrong with Sandcastle after all, we must do our absolute best not only to prove it to our own satisfaction but also to the world in general. Confidence would have to be restored to breeders, otherwise they wouldn't send their mares. It's a tall order altogether."

"Yes," I said. "Well . . . I'll do all I can"; and after lunch and some thought I telephoned Oliver, whose hopes no one had so far raised.

"Sit down," I said.

"What's the matter?" He sounded immediately anxious. "What's happened?"

"Do you know what teratogenic means?" I said.

"Yes, of course. With mares one always has to be careful."

"Mm . . . Well, there was a teratogenic drug in the bottle of dog shampoo that Ginnie had."

"What?" His voice rose an octave on the word, vibrating with instinctive unthinking anger.

"Yes," I said. "Now calm down. The police say it proves nothing either way, but Gordon and Henry, our chairman, agree that it's the only hope we have left."

"But Tim . . ." The realization hit him. "That would mean . . . that would mean . . ."

"Yes," I said. "It would mean that Sandcastle was always breeding good and true and could return to goldmine status."

I could hear Oliver's heavily disturbed breathing and could only guess at his pulse rate.

"No," he said. "No. If shampoo had got into a batch of feed, all the mares who ate it would have been affected, not just those covered by Sandcastle."

"If the shampoo got into the feed accidentally, yes. If it was given deliberately, no."

"I can't . . . I can't . . ."

"I did tell you to sit down," I said reasonably.

"Yes, so you did." There was a pause. "I'm sitting," he said.

"It's at least possible," I said, "that the Equine Research people could find nothing wrong with Sandcastle because there actually *isn't* anything wrong with him."

"Yes," he agreed faintly.

"It is possible to give teratogenic substances to mares."

"Yes."

"But horses wouldn't drink shampoo."

"No, thoroughbreds especially are very choosy."

"So how would you give them shampoo, and when?"

After a pause he said, still breathlessly, "I don't know how. They'd spit it out. But when it is easier, and that could probably be no more than three or four days after conception. That's when the body tube is forming in the embryo . . . that's when a small amount of teratogenic substance could do a lot of damage."

"Do you mean," I said, "that giving a mare selenium just *once* would insure a deformed foal?"

"Giving a mare what?"

"Sorry. Selenium. A drug for treating dandruff."

"Good . . . heavens." He rallied towards his normal self. "I suppose it would depend on the strength of the dose, and its timing. Perhaps three or four doses . . . No one could really *know,* because no one would have tried . . . I mean, there wouldn't have been any research."

"No," I agreed. "But supposing that in this instance someone got the dosage and the timing right, and also found a way of making the shampoo palatable, then *who was it?*"

There was a long quietness during which even his breathing abated.

"I don't know," he said finally. "Theoretically it could have been me, Ginnie, Nigel, the Watcherleys or any of the lads who were here last year. No one else was on the place often enough."

"Really no one? How about the vet or the blacksmith or just a visiting friend?"

"But there were *eighteen* deformed foals," he said. "I would think it would have to have been someone who could come and go here all the time."

"And someone who knew which mares to pick," I said. "Would that knowledge be easy to come by?"

"Easy!" he said explosively. "It is positively thrust at everyone on the place. There are lists in all the feed rooms and in the breeding pen itself saying which mares are to be bred to which stallion. Nigel has one, there's one in my office, one at the Watcherleys'—all over. Everyone is supposed to double-check the lists all the time, so that mistakes aren't made."

"And all the horses," I said slowly, "wear head collars with their names on."

"Yes, that's right. An essential precaution."

All made easy, I thought, for someone intending mischief to particular mares and not to any others.

"Your own Sandcastle foal," I said. "He's perfect . . . and it may be because on the lists your mare was down for Diarist."

"Tim!"

"Look after him," I said. "And look after Sandcastle."

"I will," he said fervently.

"And Oliver . . . is that lad called Shane still with you?"

"No, he's gone. So have Dave and Sammy, who found Ginnie."

"Then could you send me at the bank a list of the names and addresses of all the people who were working for you last year, and also this year? And I mean *everyone,* even your housekeeper and anyone working for Nigel or cleaning the lads' hostel, things like that."

"Even my part-time secretary girl?"

"Even her."

"She only comes three mornings a week."

"That might be enough."

"All right," he said. "I'll do it straightaway."

"I went to see Chief Inspector Wyfold this morning," I said. "But he thinks it's just a coincidence that Ginnie had shampoo with a foal-deforming drug in it. We'll have to come up with a whole lot more, to convince him. So anything you can think of . . ."

"I'll think of nothing else."

"If Dissdale Smith should telephone you, pressing for an answer," I said, "just say the bank are deliberating and keeping you waiting. Don't tell him anything about this new possibility. It might be best to keep it to ourselves until we can prove whether or not it's true."

"Dear God," he said fearfully, "I hope it is."

In the evening I talked to Pen, asking her if she knew of any way of getting the selenium out of the shampoo.

"The trouble seems to be," I said, "that you simply couldn't get that stuff into a horse as it is."

"I'll work on it," she said, "but of course the manufacturer's chemists will have gone to a good deal of trouble to make sure the selenium stays suspended throughout the mixture and doesn't all fall to the bottom."

"It did say 'Shake well' on the bottle."

"Mm, but that might be for the soap content, not for the selenium."

I thought. "Well, could you get the soap out, then? It must be the soap the horses wouldn't like."

"I'll try my hardest," she promised. "I'll ask a few friends." She paused. "There isn't much of the shampoo left. Only what I kept after sending the samples off to America and the British lab."

"How much?" I said anxiously.

"Half an egg-cupful. Maybe less."

"Is that enough?"

"If we work in test tubes . . . perhaps."

"And Pen . . . Could you or your friends make a guess, as well, as to how much shampoo you'd need to provide enough selenium to give a teratogenic dose to a mare?"

"You sure do come up with some difficult questions, dearest Tim, but we'll certainly try."

Three days later she sent a message with Gordon, saying that by that evening she might have some answers, if I would care to go down to her house after work.

I cared and went, and with a smiling face she opened her front door to let me in.

"Like a drink?" she said.

"Well, yes, but . . ."

"First things first." She poured whisky carefully for me and Cinzano for herself. "Hungry?"

"Pen . . ."

"It's only rolls with ham and lettuce in. I never cook much, as you know." She disappeared to her seldom-used kitchen and returned with the offerings, which turned out to be nicely squelchy and much what I would have made for myself.

"All right," she said finally, pushing away the empty plates, "now I'll tell you what we've managed."

"At last."

She grinned. "Yes. Well then, we started from the premise that if someone had to use shampoo as the source of selenium then that someone didn't have direct or easy access to poisonous chemicals, which being so he also wouldn't have sophisticated machinery available for separating one ingredient from another—a centrifuge, for instance. OK so far?"

I nodded.

"So what we needed, as we saw it, was a *simple* method that involved only everyday equipment. Something anyone could do anywhere. So the first thing we did was to let the shampoo drip through a paper filter, and we think you could use almost anything for that purpose, like a paper towel, a folded tissue or thin blotting paper. We actually got the best and fastest results from a coffee filter, which is after all specially designed to retain very fine solids while letting liquids through easily."

"Yes," I said. "Highly logical."

Pen smiled. "So there we were with some filter papers in which, we hoped, the microscopic particles of selenium were trapped. The filters were stained bright green by the shampoo. I brought one here to show you . . . I'll get it." She whisked off to the kitchen taking the empty supper plates with her, and returned carrying a small tray with two glasses on it.

One glass contained cut pieces of green-stained coffee filter lying in what looked like oil, and the second glass contained only an upright test tube, closed at the top with a cork and showing a dark half-inch of solution at the bottom.

"One of my friends in the lab knows a lot about horses," Pen said, "and he reckoned that all racehorses are used to the taste of linseed oil, which is given them in their feed quite often as a laxative. So we got some linseed oil and cut up the filter and soaked it." She pointed to the glass. "The selenium particles floated out of the paper into the oil."

"Neat," I said.

"Yes. So then we poured the result into the test tube and just waited twenty-four hours or so, and the selenium particles slowly gravitated through the oil to the bottom." She looked at my face to make sure I understood. "We transferred the selenium from the wax-soap base, in which it would remain suspended, into an oil base, in which it *wouldn't* remain suspended."

"I do understand," I assured her.

"So here in the test tube," she said with a conjuror's flourish, "we have concentrated selenium with the surplus oil poured off." She picked the tube out of the glass, keeping it upright, and showed me the brownish shadowy liquid lying there, darkest at the bottom, almost clear amber at the top. "We had such a small sample to start with that this is all we managed to collect. But that dark stuff is definitely selenium sulfide. We checked it on a sort of scanner called a gas chromatograph." She grinned. "No point in not using the sophisticated apparatus when it's there right beside you—and

we were in a research lab of a teaching hospital, incidentally."

"You're marvelous."

"Quite brilliant," she agreed with comic modesty.
"We also calculated that that particular shampoo was
almost ten percent selenium, which is a very much
higher proportion than you'd find in shampoos for humans. We all agree that this much, in the test tube, is
enough to cause deformity in a foal—or in any other spe-
cies, for that matter. We found many more references in
other books—lambs born with deformed feet, for instance, where the sheep had browsed off plants growing
on selenium-rich soil. We all agree that it's the *time*
when the mare ingests the selenium that's most cru-
cial, and we think that to be sure of getting the desired
result you'd have to give selenium every day for three
or four days, starting two or three days after conception."

I slowly nodded. "That's the same sort of time-scale
that Oliver said."

"And if you gave too much," she said, "too large a
dose, you'd be more likely to get abortions than really
gross deformities. The embryo would only go on growing at all, that is, if the damage done to it by selenium
was relatively minor."

"There were a lot of *different* deformities," I said.

"Oh, sure. It could have affected any developing cell,
regardless."

I picked up the test tube and peered closely at its
murky contents. "I suppose all you'd have to do would
be stir this into a cupful of oats."

"That's right."

"Or . . . could you enclose it in a capsule?"

"Yes, if you had the makings. We could have done it
quite easily in the lab. You'd need to get rid of as much
oil as possible, of course, in that case, and just scrape
concentrated selenium into the capsules."

"Mm. Calder could do it, I suppose?"

"Calder Jackson? Why yes, I guess he could if you
wanted him to. He had everything there that you'd

need." She lifted her head, remembering something. "He's on the television tomorrow night, incidentally."

"Is he?"

"Yes. They were advertising it tonight just after the news, before you came. He's going to be a guest on that chat show . . . Mickey Bonwith's show . . . Do you ever see it?"

"Sometimes," I said, thoughtfully. "It's transmitted live, isn't it?"

"Yes, that's right." She looked at me with slight puzzlement. "What's going on in that computer brain?"

"A slight calculation of risk," I said slowly, "and of grasping unrepeatable opportunities. And tell me, dearest Pen, if I found myself again in Calder's surgery, what should I look for, to bring out?"

_ She stared at me literally with her mouth open. Then, recovering, she said, "You can't mean . . . *Calder?*"

"Well," I said soberly, "what I'd really like to do is to make sure one way or another. Because it does seem to me, sad though it is to admit it, that if you tie in Dissdale's offer for Sandcastle with someone deliberately poisoning the mares, and then add Calder's expertise with herbs—in which selenium-soaked plants might be included—you do at least get a *question mark*. You do want to know for sure, don't you think, whether or not Calder and Dissdale set out deliberately to debase Sandcastle's worth so that they could buy him for peanuts . . . So that Calder could perform a well-publicized 'miracle cure' of some sort on Sandcastle, who would thereafter always sire perfect foals, and gradually climb back into favor. Whose fees might never return to forty thousand pounds, but would over the years add up to a fortune."

"But they couldn't," Pen said, aghast. "I mean . . . Calder and Dissdale . . . we *know* them."

"And you in your trade, as I in mine, must have met presentable, confidence-inspiring crooks."

She fell silent, staring at me in a troubled way, until finally I said, "There's one other thing. Again nothing I could swear to—but the first time I went to Calder's place he had a lad there who reminded me sharply of the boy with the knife at Ascot."

"Ricky Barnet," Pen said, nodding.

"Yes. I can't remember Calder's lad's name, and I couldn't identify him at all now after all this time, but at Oliver's I saw another lad, called Shane, who *also* reminded me of Ricky Barnet. I've no idea whether Shane and Calder's lad are one and the same person, though maybe not, because I don't think Calder's lad was called Shane, or I *would* have remembered, if you see what I mean."

"Got you," she said.

"But *if*—and it's a big if—if Shane did once work for Calder, he might *still* be working for him . . . feeding selenium to mares."

Pen took her time, with gravity in the experienced eyes, and at last said, *"Someone* would have had to be there on the spot to do the feeding, and it certainly couldn't have been Calder or Dissdale. But couldn't it have been that manager, Nigel? It would have been easy for him. Suppose Dissdale and Calder paid him . . . ? Suppose they promised to employ him, or even give him a share of Sandcastle, once they'd got hold of the horse."

I shook my head. "I did wonder. I did think of Nigel. There's one good reason why it probably isn't him, though, and that's because he, and only he besides Oliver, knew that one of the mares down for Diarist was covered by Sandcastle." I explained about Oliver's impulse mating. "The foal is perfect, but might very likely not have been if it was Nigel who was doing the feeding."

"Not conclusive," Pen said, slowly.

"No."

She stirred. "Did you tell the police all this?"

"I meant to," I said, "but when I was there with Wyfold on Monday it seemed impossible. It was all so insubstantial. Such a lot of guesses. Maybe wrong conclusions. Dissdale's offer could be genuine. And a lad I'd seen for half a minute eighteen months ago . . . it's difficult to remember a strange face for half an hour, let alone all that time. I have only an impression of blankness and of sunglasses . . . and I don't have the same impression of Oliver's lad Shane. Wyfold isn't the sort of man to be vague to. I thought I'd better come up with something more definite before I went back to him."

She bit her thumb. "Can't you take another good look at this Shane?"

I shook my head. "Oliver's gradually letting lads go, as he does every year at this time, and Shane is one who has already left. Oliver doesn't know where he went and has no other address for him, which he doesn't think very unusual. It seems that lads can drift from stable to stable forever with their papers always showing only the address of their last or current employer. But I think we *might* find Shane, if we're lucky."

"How?"

"By photographing Ricky Barnet, side view, and asking around on racetracks."

She smiled. "It might work. It just might."

"Worth a try."

My mind drifted back to something else worth a try, and it seemed that hers followed.

"You don't really mean to break into Calder's surgery, do you?" she said.

"Pick the lock," I said. "Yes."

"But . . ."

"Time's running out, and Oliver's future and the bank's money with it, and yes, sure, I'll do what I can."

She curiously looked into my face. "You have no real conception of danger, do you?"

"How do you mean?"

"I mean . . . I saw you, that day at Ascot, simply hurl yourself at that boy, at that knife. You could have been badly stabbed, very easily. And Ginnie told us that you frightened her to tears jumping at Sandcastle the way you did, to catch him. She said it was suicidal . . . and yet you yourself seemed to think nothing of it. And at Ascot, that evening, I remember you being *bored* with the police questions, not stirred up high by a brush with death . . ."

Her words petered away. I considered them and found in myself a reason and an answer.

"Nothing that has happened so far in my life," I said seriously, "has made me fear I might die. I think . . . I know it sounds silly . . . I am unconvinced of my own mortality."

June

On the following day, Friday, June first, I took up a long-offered invitation and went to lunch with the board of a security firm to which we had lent money for launching a new burglar alarm on the market. Not greatly to their surprise I was there to ask a favor, and after a repast of five times the calories of Ekaterin's they gave me, with some amusement, three keys that would unlock almost anything but the crown jewels, and also a concentrated course on how to use them.

"Those pickers are strictly for opening doors in emergencies," the locksmiths said, smiling. "If you end up in jail, we don't know you."

"If I end up in jail, send me another set in a fruit-cake."

I thanked them and left, and practiced discreetly on the office doors in the bank, with remarkable results. Going home I let myself in through my own front door with them, and locked and unlocked every cupboard and drawer that had a keyhole. Then I put on a dark roll-neck jersey over my shirt and tie and with scant trepidation drove to Newmarket.

I left my car at the side of the road some distance from Calder's house and finished the journey on foot, walking quietly into his yard in the last of the lingering summer dusk, checking against my watch that it was almost ten o'clock, the hour when Mickey Bonwith led his guests to peacock chairs and dug publicly into their psyches.

Calder would give a great performance, I thought: and the regrets I felt about my suspicions of him redoubled as I looked at the outline of his house against the sky and remembered his uncomplicated hospitality.

The reserve that had always at bottom lain between us I now acknowledged as my own instinctive and stifled doubt. Wanting to see worth, I had seen it: and the process of now trying to prove myself wrong gave me more sadness than satisfaction.

His yard was dark and peaceful, all lads long gone. Within the hall of the house a single light burned, a dim point of yellow glimpsed through the bushes fluttering in a gentle breeze. Behind the closed doors of the boxes the patients would be snoozing, those patients with festering sores and bleeding guts and all manner of woes awaiting the touch.

Sandcastle, if I was right, had been destined to stand there, while Calder performed his "miracle" without having to explain how he'd done it. He never had explained: he'd always broadcast publicly that he didn't know *how* his power worked, he just knew it did. Thousands, perhaps millions, believed in his power. Perhaps even breeders, those dreamers of dreams, would have believed, in the end.

I came to the surgery, a grayish block in the advancing night, and fitted one of the lock-pickers into the keyhole. The internal tumblers turned without protest, much oiled and used, and I pushed the door open and went in.

There were no windows to worry about. I closed the door behind me and switched on the light, and immediately began the search for which I'd come: to find selenium in homemade capsules, or in a filtering device, or in bottles of shampoo.

Pen had had doubts that anyone would have risked giving selenium a second year if the first year's work had proved so effective, but I'd reminded her that Sandcastle had already covered many new mares that year before the deformed foals had been reported.

"Whoever did it couldn't have known at that point that he'd been successful. So to make sure, I'd guess he'd go on, and maybe with an increased dose . . . and if no selenium was being given this year, *why did Ginnie have it?*"

Pen had reluctantly given in. "I suppose I'm just trying to find reasons for you not to go to Calder's."

"If I find anything, Chief Inspector Wyfold can go there later with a search warrant. Don't worry so."

"No," she'd said, and gone straight on looking anxious.

The locked cabinets at both ends of Calder's surgery proved a cinch for the picks, but the contents were a puzzle, as so few of the jars and boxes were properly labeled. Some indeed had come from commercial suppliers, but these seemed mostly to be the herbs Calder had talked of: hydrastis, comfrey, fo-ti-tieng, myrrh, sarsaparilla, licorice, passiflora, papaya, garlic; a good quantity of each.

Nothing was obligingly labeled selenium.

I had taken with me a thickish polyethylene bag that had a zip across one end and had formerly enclosed a silk tie and handkerchief, a present from my mother at Christmas. Into that I systematically put two or three capsules from each bottle, and two or three pills of each sort, and small sachets of herbs: and Pen, I thought, was going to have a fine old time sorting them all out.

With the bag almost half full of samples I carefully locked the cabinets again and turned to the refrigerator, which was of an ordinary domestic make with only a magnetic door fastening.

Inside there were no bottles of shampoo. No coffee filters. No linseed oil. There were simply the large plastic containers of Calder's cure-all tonic.

I thought I might as well take some to satisfy Pen's curiosity, and rooted around for a small container, finding some empty medicine bottles in a cupboard below the workbench. Over the sink I poured some of the tonic into a medicine bottle, screwed on the cap, and returned the plastic container carefully to its place in the fridge. I stood the medicine bottle on the workbench ready to take away, and turned finally to the drawers where Calder kept things like hops and also his antique pill-making equipment.

Everything was clean and tidy, as before. If he had made capsules containing selenium there, I could see no trace.

With mounting disappointment I went briefly through every drawer. Bags of seeds: sesame, pumpkin, sunflower. Bags of dried herbs: raspberry leaves, alfalfa. Boxes of the empty halves of gelatin capsules, waiting for contents. Empty unused pill bottles. All as before: nothing I hadn't already seen.

The largest bottom drawer still contained the plastic sacks of hops. I pulled open the neck of one of them and found only the expected strong-smelling crop: closed the neck again, moving the bag slightly to settle it back into its place, and saw that under the bags of hops lay a brown leather briefcase, ordinary size, six inches deep.

With a feeling of wasting time I hauled it out onto the working surface on top of the drawers, and tried to open it.

Both catches were locked. I fished for the keys in my trousers pocket and with the smallest of the picks delicately twisted until the mechanisms clicked.

Opened the lid. Found no bottles of dog shampoo, but other things that turned me slowly to a state of stone.

The contents looked at first sight as if the case belonged to a doctor: stethoscope, pen torch, metal instruments, all in fitted compartments. A cardboard box without its lid held four or five small tubes of antibiotic ointment. A large bottle contained only a few small white pills, the bottle labeled with a long name I could scarcely read, let alone remember, with "diuretic" in brackets underneath. A pad of prescription forms, blank, ready for use.

It was the name and address rubber-stamped onto the

prescription forms and the initials heavily embossed in gold into the leather beneath the case's handle that stunned me totally.

I.A.P. on the case.

Ian A. Pargetter on the prescriptions.

Ian Pargetter, veterinary surgeon, address in Newmarket.

His case had vanished the night he died.

This case . . .

With fingers beginning to shake I took one of the tubes of antibiotics and some of the diuretic pills and three of the prescription forms and added them to my other spoils, and then with a heart at last beating at about twice normal speed checked that everything was in its place before closing the case.

I felt as much as heard the surgery door open, the current of air reaching me at the same instant as the night sounds. I turned, thinking that one of Calder's lads had come on some late hospital rounds and wondering how I could ever explain my presence; and I saw that no explanation at all would do.

It was Calder himself crossing the threshold. Calder with the light on his curly halo, Calder who should have been a hundred miles away talking to the nation on the tube.

His first expression of surprise turned immediately to grim assessment, his gaze traveling from the medicine bottle of tonic mixture on the workbench to the veterinary case lying open. Shock, disbelief and fury rose in an instantly violent reaction, and he acted with such speed that even if I'd guessed what he would do I could hardly have dodged.

His right arm swung in an arc, coming down against the wall beside the door and pulling from the bracket that held it a slim scarlet fire extinguisher. The swing seemed to me continuous. The red bulbous end of the fire extinguisher in a split second filled my vision and connected with a crash against my forehead, and consciousness ceased within a blink.

The world came back with the same sort of on–off

switch: one second I was unaware, the next, awake. No gray area of daze, no shooting stars, simply on–off, off–on.

I was lying on my back on some smelly straw in an electrically lit horse box with a brown horse peering at me suspiciously from six feet above. I couldn't remember for a minute how I'd got there; it seemed such an improbable position to be in. Then I had a recollection of a red ball crashing above my eyes, and then, in a snap, total recall of the evening.

Calder.

I was in a box in Calder's yard. I was there because, presumably, Calder had put me there.

Pending? I wondered.

Pending what?

With no reassuring thoughts I made the moves to stand up, but found that though consciousness was total, recovery was not. A whirling dizziness set the walls tilting, the gray concrete blocks seeming to want to lean in and fall on me. Cursing slightly I tried again more slowly and made it to one elbow with eyes balancing precariously in their sockets.

The top half of the stable door abruptly opened with the sound of an unlatching bolt. Calder's head appeared in the doorway, his face showing shock and dismay as he saw me awake.

"I thought," he said, "that you'd be unconscious . . . that you wouldn't know. I hit you so hard . . . you're supposed to be out." His voice saying these bizarre words sounded normal.

"Calder . . ." I said.

He was looking at me no longer with anger but almost with apology. "I'm sorry, Tim," he said. "I'm sorry you came."

The walls seemed to be slowing down.

"Ian Pargetter . . ." I said. "Did *you* . . . kill him? Not you?"

Calder produced an apple and fed it almost absentmindedly to the horse. "I'm sorry, Tim. He was so stubborn. He refused . . ." He patted the horse's neck. "He wouldn't do what I wanted. Said it was over, he'd had enough. Said he'd stop me, you know." He looked for a moment at the horse and then down to me. "Why did you come? I've liked you. I wish you hadn't."

I tried again to stand up and the whirling returned as before. Calder took a step backwards, but only one, stopping when he saw my inability to arise and charge.

"Ginnie," I said. "Not Ginnie . . . Say it wasn't you who hit Ginnie . . ."

He simply looked at me, and didn't say it. In the end he said merely, and with clear regret, "I wish I'd hit you harder . . . but it seemed . . . enough." He moved another step backwards so that I could see only the helmet of curls under the light and dark shadows where his eyes were; and then while I was still struggling to my knees he closed the half-door and bolted it, and from outside switched off the light.

Night-blindness made it even harder to stand up but at least I couldn't *see* the walls whirl, only feel they were spinning. I found myself leaning against one of them and ended more or less upright, spine supported, brain at last settling into equilibrium.

The gray oblong of window gradually detached itself from the blackness, and when my equine companion moved his head I saw the liquid reflection of an eye.

Window . . . way out.

I slithered round the walls to the window and found it barred on the inside, not so much to keep horses in, I supposed, but to prevent them breaking the glass. Five strong bars, in any case, were set in concrete top and bottom, as secure as any prison cell, and I shook them impotently with two hands in proving them immovable.

Through the dusty windowpanes I had a sideways view across the yard towards the surgery, and while I stood there and held onto the bars and watched, Calder went busily in and out of the open lighted doorway, carrying things from the surgery to his car. I saw what I was sure was Ian Pargetter's case go into the trunk, and remembered with discomfiture that I'd left the bunch of picks in one of its locks. I saw him carry also an armful of the jars that contained unlabeled capsules and several boxes of unguessable contents, stowing them in the trunk carefully and closing them in.

Calder was busy obliterating his tracks.

I yelled at him, calling his name, but he didn't even hear or turn his head. The only result was startled movement in the horse behind me, a stamping of hooves and a restless swinging round the box.

"All right," I said soothingly. "Steady down. All right. Don't be frightened."

The big animal's alarm abated, and through the window I watched Calder switch off the surgery light, lock the door, get into his car and drive away.

He drove away out of his driveway, towards the main road, not towards his house. The lights of his car passed briefly over the trees as he turned out through the gates, and then were gone: and I seemed suddenly very alone, imprisoned in that dingy place for heaven knew how long.

Vision slowly expanded so that from the dim light of the sky I could see again the outlines within the box: walls, manger, horse. The big dark creature didn't like me being there and wouldn't settle, but I could think of no way to relieve him of my presence.

The ceiling was solid, not as in some stables open through the rafters to the roof. In many it would have been possible for an agile man to climb the partition from one box to the next, but not here; and in any case there was no promise of being better off next door. One would be in a different box but probably just as simply and securely bolted in.

There was nothing in my trousers pockets but a handkerchief. Penknife, money and house keys were all in my jacket in the trunk of my own unlocked car out on the road. The dark jersey, which had seemed good for speed, quiet and concealment, had left me without even a coin for a screwdriver.

I thought concentratedly of what a man could do with his fingers that a horse couldn't do with superior strength, but found nothing in the darkness of the door to unwind or unhinge; nothing anywhere to pick loose.

It looked most annoyingly as if that was where I was going to stay until Calder came back.

And then . . . what?

If he'd intended to kill me, why hadn't he already made sure of it? Another swipe or two with the fire extinguisher would have done . . . and I would have known nothing about it.

I thought of Ginnie, positive now that that was how it had been for her, that in one instant she had been thinking, and in the next . . . not.

Thought of Ian Pargetter, dead from one blow of his own brass lamp. Thought of Calder's shock and grief at that event, probably none the less real despite his having killed the man he mourned. Calder shattered over the loss of a business friend . . . the friend he had himself struck down.

He must have killed him, I thought, on a moment's ungovernable impulse, for not . . . what had he said? . . . for not wanting to go on, for wanting to stop Calder doing . . . what Calder planned.

Calder had struck at me with the same sort of speed: without pause for consideration, without time to think of consequences. And he had lashed at me as a friend too, without hesitation, while saying shortly after that he liked me.

Calder, swinging the fire extinguisher, had ruthlessly aimed at killing the man who had saved his life.

Saved Calder's life . . . Oh, God, I thought, why ever did I do it?

The man in whom I had wanted to see only goodness had after that day killed Ian Pargetter, killed Ginnie: and if I hadn't saved him they would both have lived.

The despair of that thought filled me utterly, swelling with enormity, making me feel, as the simpler grief for Ginnie had done, that one's body couldn't hold so much emotion. Remorse and guilt could rise like dragons' teeth from good intentions, and there were in truth unexpected paths to hell.

I thought back to that distant moment that had affected so many lives: to that instinctive reflex, faster than thought, which had launched me at Ricky's knife.

If I could have called it back I would have been looking away, not seeing, letting Calder die . . . letting Ricky take his chances, letting him blast his young life to fragments, destroy his caring parents.

One couldn't help what came after.

A fireman or a lifeboatman or a surgeon might fight to the utmost stretch of skill to save a baby and find he had let loose a Hitler, a Nero, Jack the Ripper. It couldn't always be Beethoven or Pasteur whose life one extended. All one asked was an ordinary, moderately sinful, normally well-intentioned, fairly harmless human. And if he cured horses . . . all the better.

Before that day at Ascot Calder couldn't even have thought of owning Sandcastle, because Sandcastle at that moment was in mid-career with his stud value uncertain. But Calder had seen, as we all had, the majesty of that horse, and I had myself listened to the admiration in his voice.

At some time after that he must have thought of selenium, and from there the wickedness had grown to encompass us all: the wickedness that would have been extinguished before birth if I'd been looking another way.

I knew logically that I couldn't have not done what I did; but in heart and spirit that didn't matter. It didn't stop the engulfing misery or allow me any ease.

Grief and sorrow came to us all, Pen had said: and she was right.

The horse became more restive and began to paw the ground.

I looked at my watch, the digital figures bright in the darkness: twenty minutes or thereabouts since Calder had left. Twenty minutes that already seemed like twenty hours.

The horse swung round suddenly in the gloom with unwelcome vigor, bumping against me with his rump.

"Calm down, boy," I said soothingly. "We're stuck with each other. Go to sleep."

The horse's reply was the equivalent of unprintable: the crash of a steel-clad hoof against a wall.

Perhaps he didn't like me talking, I thought, or indeed even moving about. His head swung round towards the window, his bulk stamping restlessly from one side of the box to the other, and I saw that he, unlike Oliver's horses, wore no head collar: nothing with which to hold him, while I calmed him, patting his neck.

His head reared up suddenly, tossing violently, and with a foreleg he lashed forward at the wall.

Not funny, I thought. Horrific to have been in the firing-line of that slashing hoof. For heaven's sake, I said to him mentally, I'll do you no harm. Just stay quiet. Go to sleep.

I was standing at that time with my back to the door, so that to the horse I must have been totally in shadow: but he would know I was there. He could smell my presence, hear my breathing. If he could see me as well, would it be better?

I took a tentative step towards the dim oblong of window, and had a clear, sharp, and swiftly terrifying view of one of his eyes.

No peace. No sleep. No prospect of anything like that. The horse's eye was stretched wide with white showing all round the usual darkness, staring not at me but as if blind, glaring wildly at nothing at all.

The black nostrils looked huge. The lips as I watched were drawing back from the teeth. The ears had gone flat to the head and there was froth forming in the mouth. It was the face, I thought incredulously, not of unrest or alarm . . . but of madness.

The horse backed suddenly away, crashing his hindquarters into the rear wall and rocking again forwards, but this time advancing with both forelegs off the ground, the gleams from thrashing hooves curving in silvery streaks in the gloom, the feet hitting the wall below the window with sickening intent.

I pressed in undoubted panic into the corner made by wall and door, but it gave no real protection. The box was roughly ten feet square by eight feet high, a space even at the best of times half-filled by horse. For that horse at that moment it was a straightjacket confine-

ment out of which he seemed intent on physically
smashing his way.

The manger, I thought. Get in the manger.

The manger was built at about waist height diago-
nally across one of the box's rear corners; a smallish
metal trough set into a sturdy wooden support. As a
shelter it was pathetic, but at least I would be off the
ground. . . .

The horse turned and stood on his forelegs and let fly
backwards with an almighty double kick that thudded
into the concrete wall six inches from my head, and it
was then, at that moment, that I began to fear that the
crazed animal might not just hurt but kill me.

He wasn't purposely trying to attack; most of his
kicks were in other directions. He wasn't trying to bite,
though his now-open mouth looked savage. He was un-
controllably wild, but not with me . . . though that, in
so small a space, made little difference.

He seemed in the next very few seconds to go utterly
berserk. With speeds I could only guess at in the scur-
rying shadows he whirled and kicked and hurled his
bulk against the walls, and I, still attempting to jump
through the tempest into the manger, was finally
knocked over by one of his flailing feet.

I didn't realize at that point that he'd actually broken
one of my arms because the whole thing felt numb. I
made it to the manger, tried to scramble up, got my foot
in . . . sat on the edge . . . tried to raise my other, now
dangling foot . . . and couldn't do it fast enough. Another direct hit crunched on my ankle and I knew, that
time, that there was damage.

The air about my head seemed to hiss with hooves
and the horse was beginning a high bubbling whinny.
Surely someone, I thought desperately, someone would
hear the crashing and banging and come. . . .

I could see him in flashes against the window, a
rearing, bucking, kicking, rocketing nightmare. He
came wheeling round, half-seen, walking on his hind
legs, head hard against the ceiling, the forelegs thrashing as if trying to climb invisible walls . . . and he
knocked me off my precarious perch with a swiping

punch in the chest that had half a ton of weight behind it and no particular aim.

I fell twisting onto the straw and tried to curl my head away from those lethal feet, to save instinctively my face and gut . . . and leave backbone and kidneys to their fate. Another crushing thud landed on the back of my shoulder and jarred like a hammer through every bone, and I could feel a scream forming somewhere inside me, a wrenching cry for mercy, for escape, for an end to battering, for release from terror.

His mania if anything grew worse, and it was he who was finally screaming, not me. The noise filled my ears, bounced off the walls, stunning, mind-blowing, the roaring of furies.

He somehow got one hoof inside my rolled body and tumbled me fast over, and I could see him arching above me, the tendons like strings, the torment in him too, the rage of the gods bursting from his stretched throat, his forelegs so high that he was hitting the ceiling.

This is death, I thought. This is dreadful, pulverizing extinction. Only for this second would I see and feel . . . and one of his feet would land on my head and I'd go . . . I'd go . . .

Before I'd even finished the thought his forelegs came crashing down with a hoof so close it brushed my hair; and then again, as if driven beyond endurance, he reared dementedly on his hind legs, the head going up like a reverse thunderbolt towards the sky, the skull meeting the ceiling with the force of a ram. The whole building shook with the impact, and the horse, his voice cut off, fell in a huge collapsing mass across my legs, spasms shuddering through his body, muscles jerking in stiff kicks, the air still ringing with the echoes of extremity.

He was dying in stages, unconscious, reluctant, the brain finished, the nerve messages still passing to convulsing muscles, turmoil churning without direction in stomach and gut, the head already inert on the straw.

An age passed before it was done. Then the heavy

body fell flaccid, all systems spent, and lay in perpetual astonishing silence, pinning me beneath.

The relief of finding him dead and myself alive lasted quite a long time, but then, as always happens with the human race, simple gratitude for existence progressed to discontent that things weren't better.

He had fallen with his spine towards me, his bulk lying across my legs from my knees down; and getting out from under him was proving an impossibility.

The left ankle, which felt broken, protested screechingly at any attempted movement. I couldn't lift my left arm for the same reason. There was acute soreness in my chest, making breathing itself painful and coughing frightful; and the only good thing I could think of was that I was lying on my back and not face down in the straw.

A very long time passed very slowly. The crushing weight of the horse slowly numbed my legs altogether and transferred the chief area of agony to the whole of my left arm, which I might have thought totally mangled if I hadn't been able to see it dimly lying there looking the same as usual, covered in blue sweater, white cuff slightly showing, hand with clean nails, gold watch on wrist.

Physical discomfort for a while shut out much in the way of thought, but eventually I began to add up memories and ask questions, and the biggest, most immediate question was what would Calder do when he came back and found me alive.

He wouldn't expect it. No one could really expect anyone to survive being locked in with a mad horse, and the fact that I had was a trick of fate.

I remembered him giving the horse an apple while I'd struggled within the spinning walls to stand up. Giving his apple so routinely, and patting the horse's neck.

I remembered Calder saying on my first visit that he gave his remedies to horses in hollowed-out apples. But this time it had been no remedy, this time something opposite, this time a drug to make crazy, to turn a normal steel-shod horse into a killing machine.

What had he said when he'd first found me conscious? Those bizarre words ... "I thought you'd be out. I thought you wouldn't know. ..." And something else ... "I wish I'd hit you harder, but it seemed enough."

He had said also that he was sorry, that he wished I hadn't come. ... He hadn't meant, I thought, that I should be aware of it when the horse killed me. At the very least, he hadn't meant me to see and hear and suffer that death. But also, when he found me awake, it hadn't prevented him from *then* giving the apple, although he knew that I *would* see, *would* hear, would ... suffer.

The horse hadn't completed the task. When Calder returned, he would make good the deficit. It was certain.

I tried, on that thought, again to slide my legs out, though how much it would have helped if I had succeeded was debatable. It was as excruciating as before, since the numbness proved temporary. I concluded somewhat sadly that dragging a broken ankle from beneath a dead horse was no jolly entertainment, and in fact, given the state of the rest of me, couldn't be done.

I had never broken any bones before, not even skiing. I'd never been injured beyond the transient bumps of childhood. Never been to hospital, never troubled a surgeon, never slept from anesthetic. For thirty-four years I'd been thoroughly healthy and, apart from chicken pox and such, never ill. I even had good teeth.

I was unprepared in any way for the onslaught of so much pain all at once, and also not quite sure how to deal with it. All I knew was that when I tried to pull out my ankle the protests throughout my body brought actual tears into my eyes and no amount of theoretical resolution could give me the power to continue. I wondered if what I felt was cowardice. I didn't much care if it was. I lay with everything stiffening and getting cold and worse, and I'd have given a good deal to be as oblivious as the horse.

The oblong of window at length began to lighten towards the new day; Saturday, June second. Calder would come back and finish the job, and no reasonable pathologist would swear the last blow had been delivered hours after the first. Calder would say in bewilderment, "But I had no idea Tim was coming to see me. . . . I was in London for the television . . . I have no idea how he came to shut himself into one of the boxes . . . because it's just possible to do that, you know, if you're not careful . . . I've no idea why the horse should have panicked, or kicked him, because he was a placid old boy . . . as you can see . . . the whole thing's a terrible accident, and I'm shattered . . . most distressed. . . ." And anyone would look at the horse from whose bloodstream the crazing drug would have departed and conclude that I'd been pretty unintelligent and also unlucky, and too bad.

Ian Pargetter's veterinary case had gone to a securer hiding place or to destruction, and there would be only a slight chance left of proving Calder a murderer. Whichever way one considered it, the outlook was discouraging.

I couldn't be bothered to roll my wrist over to see the time. The sun rose and shone slantingly through the bars with the pale brilliance of dawn. It had to be five o'clock, or after.

Time drifted. The sun moved away. The horse and I lay in intimate silence, dead and half-dead; waiting.

A car drove up fast outside and doors slammed.

It will be now, I thought. Now. Very soon.

There were voices in the distance, calling to each other. Female and male. *Strangers.*

Not Calder's distinctive, loud, edgy, public voice. Not his at all.

Hope thumped back with a tremendous surge and I called out myself, saying "Here . . . Come here," but it was at best a croak, inaudible beyond the door.

Suppose they were looking for Calder, and when they didn't find him, drove away . . . I took all possible breath into my lungs and yelled "Help . . . Come here."

Nothing happened. My voice ricocheted off the walls and mocked me, and I dragged in another grinding lungful and shouted again . . . and again . . . and again.

The top half of the door swung outward and let in a dazzle of light, and a voice yelled incredulously, "He's *here*. He's in here. . . ."

The bolt on the lower half-door clattered and the daylight grew to an oblong, and against the light three figures appeared, coming forward, concerned, speaking with anxiety and joy and bringing life.

Judith and Gordon and Pen.

Judith was gulping and so I think was I.

"Thank God," Gordon said. "Thank God."

"You didn't go home," Pen said. "We were worried."

"Are you all right?" Judith said.

"Not really . . . but everything's relative. I've never been happier, so who cares."

"If we put our arms under your shoulders," Gordon said, surveying the problem, "we should be able to pull you out."

"Don't do that," I said.

"Why not?"

"One shoulder feels broken. Get a knacker."

"My dear Tim," he said, puzzled.

"They'll come with a truck . . . and a winch. Their job is dead horses."

"Yes, I see."

"And an ambulance," Pen said, "I should think."

I smiled at them with much love, my fairly incompetent saviors. They asked how I'd got where I was, and to their horror I briefly told them: and I in turn asked why they'd come, and they explained that they'd been worried because Calder's television program had been canceled.

"Mickey Bonwith was taken ill," Pen said. "They just announced it during the evening. There would be no live Mickey Bonwith show, just an old recording, very sorry, expect Calder Jackson at a later date."

"Pen telephoned and told us where you were going, and why," Judith said.

"And we were worried," Gordon added.

"You didn't go home . . . didn't telephone," Pen said.

"We've been awake all night," Gordon said. "The

girls were growing more and more anxious . . . so we came."

They'd come a hundred miles. You couldn't ask for better friends.

Gordon drove away to find a public telephone and Pen asked if I'd found what I'd come for.

"I don't know," I said. "Half the things had no labels."

"Don't talk any more," Judith said. "Enough is enough."

"I might as well."

"Take your mind off it," Pen nodded, understanding.

"What time is it?" I asked.

Judith looked at her watch. "Ten to eight."

"Calder will come back . . ." And the lads too, I thought. He'd come when the lads turned up for work. About that time. He'd need witnesses to the way he'd found me.

"Tim," Pen said with decision, "if he's coming . . . did you take any samples? Did you get a chance?"

I nodded weakly.

"I suppose you can't remember what they were . . ."

"I hid them."

"Wouldn't he have found them?" She was gentle and prepared to be disappointed; careful not to blame.

I smiled at her. "He didn't find them. They're here."

She looked blankly round the box and then at my face. "Didn't he search you?" she said in surprise. "Pockets . . . of course he would."

"I don't know . . . but he didn't find the pills."

"Then where *are* they?"

"I learned from Ginnie about keeping your hands free," I said. "They're in a plastic bag . . . below my waistband . . . inside my pants."

They stared incredulously, and then they laughed, and Judith with tears in her eyes said, "Do you mean . . . all the time . . ."

"All the time," I agreed. "And go easy getting them out."

Some things would be best forgotten but are impossible to forget, and I reckon one could put the next half-hour into that category: at the end of it I lay on a table-like stretcher in the open air, and my dead-weight pal was half up the ramp of the knacker's van that Gordon with exceptional persuasiveness had conjured out at that hour of the morning.

The three lads who had at length arrived for work stood around looking helpless, and the two ambulance men, who were not paramedics, were farcically trying to get an answer on a radio with transmission troubles as to where they were supposed to take me.

Gordon was telling the knackers' men that I said it was essential to remove a blood sample from the horse and that the carcass was not to be disposed of until that was done. Judith and Pen both looked tired, and were yawning. I wearily watched some birds wheeling high in the fair blue sky and wished I were up there with them, as light as air; and into this riveting tableau drove Calder.

Impossible to know what he thought when he saw all the activity, but as he came striding from his car his mouth formed an oval of apprehension and shock.

He seemed first to fasten his attention on Gordon, and then on the knackers' man who was saying loudly, "If you want a blood sample you'll have to give us a written authorization, because of calling in a vet and paying him."

Calder looked from him to the dead horse still half-way up the ramp, and from there towards the horse's normal box, where the door stood wide open.

From there he turned with bewilderment to Judith, and then with horror saw the bag Pen held tightly, the transparent plastic bag with the capsules, pills and other assorted treasures showing clearly inside.

Pen remarkably found her voice and in words that must have sounded like doom to Calder said, "I didn't tell you before . . . I'm a pharmacist."

"Where did you get that?" Calder said, staring at the bag as if his eyes would burn it. "Where . . ."

"Tim had it."

Her gaze went to me and Calder seemed finally to realize that my undoubted stillness was not that of death. He took two paces towards the stretcher and looked down at my face and saw me alive, awake, aware.

Neither of us spoke. His eyes seemed to retreat in the sockets and the shape of the upper jaw stood out starkly. He saw in me, I daresay, the ravages of the night, and I saw in him the realization become certainty that my survival meant his ruin.

I thought: you certainly should have hit harder; and maybe he thought it too. He looked at me with searing intensity that defied analysis and then turned abruptly away and walked with jerky steps back to his car.

Gordon took two or three hesitant steps towards perhaps stopping him, but Calder without looking back started his engine, put his foot on the accelerator and with protesting tires made a tight semicircular turn and headed for the gate.

"We should get the police," Gordon said, watching him go.

Judith and Pen showed scant enthusiasm and I none at all. I supposed we would have to bring in the police in the end, but the longer the boring rituals could be postponed, from my point of view, the better. Britain was a small island, and Calder too well-known to go far.

Pen looked down at the plastic storehouse in her hands and then without actual comment opened her handbag and put the whole thing inside. She glanced briefly at me and smiled faintly, and I nodded with relief that she and her friends would have the unraveling of the capsules to themselves.

On that same Saturday, at about two-thirty in the afternoon, a family of picnickers came across a car that had been parked out of sight of any road behind some clumps of gorse bushes. The engine of the car was running and the children of the family, peering through the windows, saw a man slumped on the back seat with a tube in his mouth.

They knew him because of his curly hair, and his beard.

The children were reported to be in a state of hysterical shock and the parents were angry, as if some authority, somewhere or other, should prevent suicides' spoiling the countryside.

Tributes to Calder's miracle-working appeared on television that evening, and I thought it ironic that the master who had known so much about drugs should have chosen to gas his way out.

He had driven barely thirty miles from his yard. He had left no note. The people who had been working with him on the postponed Mickey Bonwith show said they couldn't understand it, and Dissdale telephoned Oliver to say that in view of Calder's tragic death he would have to withdraw his offer for Sandcastle.

I, by the time I heard all this, was half-covered in infinitely irritating plaster of paris, there being more grating edges of bone inside me than I cared to hear about, and horseshoe-shaped crimson bruises besides.

I had been given rather grudgingly a room to myself, privacy in illness being considered a sinful luxury in the national health service, and on Monday evening Pen came all the way from London again to report on the laboratory findings.

She frowned after she'd kissed me. "You look exhausted," she said.

"Tiring place, hospital."

"I suppose it must be. I'd never thought . . ."

She put a bunch of roses in my drinking-water jug and said they were from Gordon and Judith's garden.

"They send their love," she said chattily, "and their garden's looking lovely."

"Pen . . ."

"Yes. Well." She pulled the visitor's chair closer to the bed upon which I half-sat, half-lay in my plaster and borrowed dressing gown on top of the blankets. "You have really, as they say, hit the jackpot."

"Do you mean it?" I exclaimed.

She grinned cheerfully. "It's no wonder that Calder killed himself, not after seeing you alive and hearing you were going to get the dead horse tested, and knowing that after all you had taken all those things from his surgery. It was either that or years in jail and total disgrace."

"A lot of people would prefer disgrace."

"Not Calder, though."

"No."

She opened a slim briefcase on her knees and produced several typewritten pages.

"We worked all yesterday and this morning," she said, "but first I'll tell you that Gordon got the dead horse's blood test done immediately at the Equine Research Establishment, and they told him on the telephone this morning that the horse had been given ethyl isobutrazine, which was contrary to normal veterinary practice."

"You don't say."

Her eyes gleamed. "The Research people told Gordon that any horse given ethyl isobutrazine would go utterly berserk and literally try to climb the walls."

"That's just what he did," I said soberly.

"It's a drug that is used all the time as a tranquilizer to stop dogs barking or getting carsick, but it has an absolutely manic effect on horses. One of its brand names is Diquel, in case you're interested. All the veterinary books warn against giving it to horses."

"But normally . . . in a horse . . . it would wear off?"

"Yes, in six hours or so, with no trace."

Six hours, I thought bleakly. *Six hours* . . .

"In your bag of goodies," Pen said, "guess what we found? Three tablets of Diquel."

"Really?"

She nodded. "Really. And now pin back your ears, dearest Tim, because when we found what Calder had been doing, words simply failed us."

They seemed indeed to fail her again, for she sat looking at the pages with a faraway expression.

"You remember," she said at last, "when we went to Calder's yard that time at Easter, we saw a horse that had been bleeding in its urine . . . crystalluria was what he called it . . . that antibiotics hadn't been able to cure?"

"Yes," I said. "Other times too, he cured horses with that."

"Mm. And those patients had been previously treated by Ian Pargetter before he died, hadn't they?"

I thought back. "Some of them, certainly."

"Well . . . you know you told me before they carted you off in the ambulance on Saturday that some of the jars of capsules in the cupboards were labled only with letters like *a plus w, b plus w,* and *c plus s?*"

I nodded.

"Three capsules each with one transparent and one blue end, *did* contain *c* and *s.* Vitamin C, and sulfanilamide." She looked at me for a possible reaction, but vitamin C and sulfanilamide sounded quite harmless, and I said so.

"Yes," she said, "separately they do nothing but good, but *together they can cause crystalluria.*"

I stared at her.

"Calder had made those capsules expressly to *cause the horse's illness* in the first place, so that he could 'cure' it afterwards. And then the only miracle he'd have to work would be to stop giving the capsules."

"My God," I said.

She nodded. "We could hardly believe it. It meant, you see, that Ian Pargetter almost certainly *knew.* Because it was he, you see, who could have given the horse's trainer or owner or lad or whatever a bottle of capsules labeled 'antibiotic' to dole out every day. And those capsules were precisely what was making the horse ill."

"Pen!"

"I'd better explain just a little, if you can bear it," she said. "If you give sulfa drugs to anyone—horse or person—who doesn't need them, you won't do much harm because urine is normally slightly alkaline or only slightly acid and you'll get rid of the sulfa safely. But vitamin C is ascorbic acid and makes the urine *more* acid, and the acid works with sulfa drugs to form crystals, and the crystals cause pain and bleeding . . . like powdered glass."

There was a fairly long silence, and then I said, "It's diabolical."

She nodded. "Once Calder had the horse in his yard he could speed up the cure by giving him bicarbonate of soda, which will make the urine alkaline again and also dissolve the crystals, and with plenty of water to drink the horse would be well in no time. Miraculously fast, in fact." She paused and smiled, and went on, "We tested a few more things that were perfectly harmless herbal remedies and then we came to three more home-made capsules, with pale green ends this time, and we reckon that they were your *a plus w.*"

"Go on, then," I said. "What's *a,* and what's *w?*"

"*A* is antibiotic, and *w* is warfarin. And before you ask, warfarin is a drug used in humans for reducing the clotting ability of the blood."

"That peach-colored pill you found on the surgery floor," I said. "That's what you said."

"Oh, yes." She looked surprised. "So I did. I'd forgotten. Well . . . if you give certain antibiotics *with* warfarin you increase the effect of the warfarin to the extent that blood will hardly clot at all . . . and you get severe bleeding from the stomach, from the mouth, from anywhere where a small blood vessel breaks . . . when normally it would clot and mend at once."

I let out a held breath. "Every time I went, there was a bleeder."

She nodded. "Warfarin acts by drastically reducing the effect of vitamin K, which is needed for normal clotting, so all Calder had to do to reverse things was feed lots of vitamin K . . . which is found in large quantities in alfalfa.

"And *b plus w?*" I asked numbly.

"Barbiturate and warfarin. Different mechanism, but if you used them together and then stopped just the barbiturate, you could cause a sort of delayed bleeding about three weeks later." She paused. "We've all been looking up our pharmacology textbooks, and there are warnings there, plain to see if you're looking for them, about prescribing antibiotics or barbiturates or indeed phenylbutazone or anabolic steroids for people on warfarin without carefully adjusting the warfarin dosage. And you see," she went on, "putting two drugs together in one capsule was really brilliant, because no one would think they were giving a horse two drugs, but just one . . . and we reckon Ian Pargetter could have put Calder's capsules into any regular bottle, and the horse's owner would think that he was giving the horse what it said on the label."

I blinked. "It's incredible."

"It's easy," she said. "And it gets easier as it goes on."

"There's more?"

"Sure there's more." She grinned. "How about all those poor animals with extreme debility who were so weak they could hardly walk?"

I swallowed. "How about them?"

"You said you found a large bottle in Ian Pargetter's case with only a few pills in it? A bottle labeled 'diuretic,' or in other words, pills designed to increase the passing of urine?"

I nodded.

"Well, we identified the ones you took, and if you simply gave those particular thiazide diuretic pills over a long period to a horse you would cause *exactly* the sort of general progressive debility shown by those horses."

I was past speech.

"And to cure the debility," she said, "you just stop the diuretics and provide good food and water. And hey presto!" She smiled blissfully. "Chemically, it's so elegant. The debility is caused by constant excessive excretion of potassium, which the body needs for strength, and the cure is to restore potassium as fast as safely possible . . . with potassium salts, which you can buy anywhere."

I gazed at her with awe.

She was enjoying her revelations. "We come now to the horses with nonhealing ulcers and sores."

Always those, too, in the yard, I thought.

"Ulcers and sores are usually cleared up fairly quickly by applications of antibiotic cream. Well . . . by this time we were absolutely bristling with suspicions, so last of all we took that little tube of antibiotic cream you found in Ian Pargetter's case, and we tested it. And lo and behold, it didn't contain antibiotic cream at all."

"What then?"

"Cortisone cream."

She looked at my noncomprehension and smiled. "Cortisone cream is fine for eczema and allergies, but *not* for general healing. In fact, if you scratched a horse and smeared some dirt into the wound to infect it and then religiously applied cortisone cream twice a day you would get a nice little ulcer that would never heal. Until, of course, you sent your horse to Calder, who would lay his hands upon your precious . . . and apply antibiotics at once, to let normal healing begin."

"Dear God in heaven."

"Never put cortisone cream on a cut," she said. "A lot of people do. It's stupid."

"I never will," I said fervently.

Pen grinned. "They always fill toothpaste from the blunt end. We looked very closely and found that the end of the tube had been unwound and then resealed. Very neat."

She seemed to have stopped, so I asked, "Is that the lot?"

"That's the lot."

We sat for a while and pondered.

"It does answer an awful lot of questions," I said finally.

"Such as?"

"Such as why Calder killed Ian Pargetter," I said. "Ian Pargetter wanted to stop something . . . which must have been this illness caper. Said he'd had enough. Said also that he would stop Calder too, which must have been his death warrant."

Pen said, "Is that what Calder actually told you?"

"Yes, that's what he said, but at the time I didn't understand what he meant."

"I wonder," Pen said, "why Ian Pargetter wanted to stop altogether? They must have had a nice steady income going between the two of them. Calder must have recruited him years ago."

"Selenium," I said.

"What?"

"Selenium was different. Making horses ill in order to cure them wasn't risking much permanent damage, if any at all. But selenium would be forever. The foals would be deformed. I'd guess when Calder suggested it the idea sickened Ian Pargetter. Revolted him, probably, because he was after all a vet."

"And Calder wanted to go on with it all . . . enough to kill."

I nodded. "Calder would have had his sights on a fortune as well as an income. And but for Ginnie somehow getting hold of that shampoo, he would very likely have achieved it."

"I wonder how she did," Pen said.

"Mm." I shifted uncomfortably on the bed. "I've remembered the name of the lad Calder had who looked like Ricky Barnet. It was Jason. I remembered it the other night . . . in that yard . . . funny the way the mind works."

"What about him?" Pen said sympathetically.

"I remembered Calder saying he gave the pills to Jason for Jason to give the horses. The herb pills, he meant. But with Ian Pargetter gone, Calder would have needed someone else to give those double-edged capsules to horses . . . because he still had horses in his yard with those same troubles long after Ian Pargetter was dead."

"So he did," she said blankly. "Except . . ."

"Except what?"

"Only that when we got to the yard last Saturday, before I heard you calling, we looked into several other boxes, and there weren't many horses there. The place wasn't full, like it had been."

"I should think," I said slowly, "that it was because Jason had been busy working for three months or more at Oliver's farm, feeding selenium in apples."

A visual memory flashed in my brain. *Apples* . . . Shane, the stable lad, walking across the yard, swinging a bucket and eating an apple. Shane, Jason: one and the same.

"What is it?" Pen said.

"Photos of Ricky Barnet."

"Oh, yes."

"They say I can leave here tomorrow," I said, "if I insist."

She looked at me with mock despair. "What exactly did you break?"

"They said this top lot was scapula, clavicle, humerus, sternum and ribs. Down there," I pointed, "they lost me. I didn't know there *were* so many bones in one ankle."

"Did they pin it?"

"God knows."

"How will you look after yourself?"

"In my usual clumsy fashion."

"Don't be silly," she said. "Stay until it stops hurting."

"That might be weeks . . . there's some problem with ligaments or tendons or something."

"What problem?"

"I didn't really listen."

"Tim." She was exasperated.

"Well . . . it's so boring," I said.

She gave an eyes-to-heaven laugh. "I brought you a present from my shop." She dug into her handbag. "Here you are, with my love."

I took the small white box she offered, and looked at the label on its side.

Comfrey, it said.

She grinned. "You might as well try it," she said. "Comfrey does contain allantoin, which helps to knit bones. And you never know . . . Calder really was an absolute expert with all sorts of drugs."

On Tuesday, June fifth, Oliver Knowles collected me from the hospital to drive me on some errands and then take me to his home, not primarily as an act of compassion but mostly to talk business. I had expected him to accept my temporary disabilities in a straightforward and unemotional manner, and so he did, although he did say dryly when he saw me that when I had invited myself over the telephone I had referred to a "crack or two" and not to half an acre of plaster with clothes strung on in patches.

"Never mind," I said. "I can hop and I can sit and my right arm is fine."

"Yes. So I see."

The nurse who had wheeled me in a chair to his car said, however, "He can't hop, it jars him," and handed Oliver a slip of paper. "There's a place along that road"—she pointed—"where you can hire wheelchairs." To me she said, "Get a comfortable one. And one that lets your leg lie straight out, like this one. You'll ache less. All right?"

"All right," I said.

"Hm. Well . . . take care."

She helped me into the car with friendly competence and went away with the hospital transport, and Oliver and I did as she advised, storing the resulting cushioned and chromium comfort in the trunk of his car.

"Right," I said. "Then the next thing to do is buy a good instant camera and a stack of films."

Oliver found a shop and bought the camera while I sat in the front passenger seat as patiently as possible.

"Where next?" he said, coming back with parcels.

"Cambridge. An engineering works. Here's the address." I handed him the piece of paper on which I'd written Ricky Barnet's personal directions. "We're meeting him when he comes out of work."

"Who?" Oliver said. "Who are we meeting?"

"You'll see."

We parked across the road from the firm's gate and waited, and at four-thirty on the dot the exodus occurred.

Ricky Barnet came out and looked this way and that in searching for us, and beside me I heard Oliver stir and say, "But that's Shane," in surprise, and then relax and add doubtfully, "No, it isn't."

"No, it isn't." I leaned out of the open window and called to him, "Ricky . . . over here."

He crossed the road and stopped beside the car.

"Hop in," I said.

"You been in an accident?" he said disbelievingly.

"Sort of."

He climbed into the back of the car. He hadn't been too keen to have his photograph taken for the purpose I'd outlined, but he was in no great position to refuse; and I'd made my blackmailing pressure sound like honey, which I wasn't too bad at, in my way. He still wasn't pleased, however, which had its own virtues, as the last thing I wanted was forty prints of him grinning.

Oliver drove off and stopped where I asked at a suitably neutral background—a gray-painted factory wall—and he said he would himself take the photographs if I explained what I wanted.

"Ricky looks like Shane," I said. "So take pictures of Ricky in the way he *most* looks like Shane. Get him to turn his head slowly like he did when he came out of work, and tell him to hold it where it's best."

"All right."

Ricky got out of the car and stood in front of the wall, with Oliver focusing at head-and-shoulder distance. He took the first picture and we waited for it to develop.

Oliver looked at it, grunted, adjusted the light meter, and tried again.

"This one's all right," he said, watching the colors emerge. "Looks like Shane. Quite amazing."

With a faint shade of sullenness Ricky held his pose for as long as it took to shoot four boxes of film. Oliver passed each print to me as it came out of the camera, and I laid them in rows along the seat beside me while they developed.

"That's fine," I said, when the films were finished. "Thank you, Ricky."

He came over to the car window and I asked him without any great emphasis, "Do you remember, when Indian Silk got so ill with debility, which vet was treating him?"

"Yeah, sure, that fellow that was murdered. Him and his partners. The best, Dad said."

I nodded noncommittally. "Do you want a ride to Newmarket?"

"Got my motorbike, thanks."

We took him back to his engineering works, where I finally cheered him up with payment for his time and trouble, and watched while he roared off with a flourish of self-conscious bravado.

"What now?" Oliver said. "Did you say Newmarket?"

I nodded. "I've arranged to meet Ursula Young."

He gave me a glance of bewilderment and drove without protest, pulling duly into the midtown car park where Ursula had said to come.

We arrived there first, the photography not having taken as long as I'd expected, and Oliver finally gave voice to a long-restrained question.

"Just what," he said, "are the photographs *for?*"

"For finding Shane."

"But why?"

"Don't explode."

"No."

"Because I think he gave the selenium to your mares."

Oliver sat very still. "You asked about him before," he said. "I did wonder . . . if you thought . . . he killed Ginnie."

It was my own turn for quiet.

"I don't know if he did," I said at last. "I don't know."

Ursula arrived in her car with a rush, checking her watch and apologizing all the same, although she was on time. She, like Oliver and Ricky, looked taken aback at my unorthodox attire, but rallied in her usual nononsense fashion and shuffled into the back seat of Oliver's car, leaning forward to bring her face on a level with ours.

I passed her thirty of the forty pictures of Ricky Barnet, who of course she knew immediately.

"Yes, but," I explained, "Ricky looks like a lad who worked for Oliver, and it's *that* lad we want to find."

"Well, all right. How important is it?"

Oliver answered her before I could. "Ursula, if you find him, we might be able to prove there's nothing wrong with Sandcastle. And don't ask me how, just believe it."

Her mouth had opened.

"And Ursula," Oliver said, "if you find him—Shane, that lad—I'll put business your way for the rest of my life."

I could see that to her, a middle-rank bloodstock agent, it was no mean promise.

"All right," she said briskly. "You're on. I'll start spreading the pictures about at once, tonight, and call you with results."

"Ursula," I said, "if you find where he is now, make sure he isn't frightened off. We don't want to lose him."

She looked at me shrewdly. "This is roughly police work?"

I nodded. "Also, if you find anyone who employed him in the past, ask if by any chance a horse he looked after fell ill. Or any horse in the yard, for that matter. And don't give him a name . . . he isn't always called Shane."

"Is he dangerous?" she said straightly.

"We don't want him challenged," I said. "Just found."

"All right. I trust you both, so I'll do my best. And I suppose one day you'll explain what it's all about?"

If he's done what we think," I said, "we'll make sure the whole world knows. You can count on it."

She smiled briefly and patted my unplastered shoulder. "You look gray," she said, and to Oliver, "Tim told me a horse kicked him and broke his arm. Is that right?"

"He told me that, too."

"And what else?" she asked me astringently. "How did you get in this state?"

"The horse didn't know its own strength." I smiled at her. "Clumsy brute."

She knew I was dodging in some way, but she lived in a world where the danger of horse kicks was ever-present and always to be avoided, and she made no more demur. Stowing the photographs in her capacious handbag she wriggled her way out of the car, and with assurances of action drove off in her own.

"What now?" Oliver said.

"A bottle of Scotch."

He gave me an austere look, which then swept over my general state and softened to understanding.

"Can you wait until we get home?" he said.

That evening, bit by bit, I told Oliver about Pen's analysis of the treasures from Calder's surgery and of Calder's patients' drug-induced illnesses. I told him that Calder had killed Ian Pargetter, and why, and I explained again how the idea of first discrediting, then buying and rebuilding Sandcastle had followed the pattern of Indian Silk.

"There may be others besides Indian Silk that we haven't heard of," I said thoughtfully. "Show jumpers, eventers, even prize ponies. You never know. Dissdale might have gone along more than twice with his offer to buy the no-hoper."

"He withdrew his offer for Sandcastle the same night Calder died."

"What exactly did he say?" I asked.

"He was very upset. Said he'd lost his closest friend, and that without Calder to work his miracles there was no point in buying Sandcastle."

I frowned. "Do you think it was genuine?"

"His distress? Yes, certainly."

"And the belief in miracles?"

"He did *sound* as if he believed."

I wondered if it was in the least possible that Dissdale was an innocent and duped accomplice and hadn't known that his bargains had been first made ill. His pride in knowing the Great Man had been obvious at Ascot, and perhaps he had been flattered and foolish but not wicked after all.

Oliver asked in the end how I'd found out about the drug-induced illnesses and Ian Pargetter's murder, and I told him that too, as flatly as possible.

He sat staring at me, his gaze on the plaster.

"You're very lucky to be in a wheelchair, and not a coffin," he said. "Damn lucky."

"Yes."

He poured more of the brandy we had progressed to after dinner. Anesthesia was coming along nicely.

"I'm almost beginning to believe, " he said, "that somehow or other I'll still be here next year, even if I do have to sell Sandcastle and whatever else is necessary."

I drank from my replenished glass. "Tomorrow we'll make a plan contingent upon Sandcastle's being reinstated in the eyes of the world. Look at the figures, see what the final damage is likely to be, draw up a time scale for recovery. I can't promise because it isn't my final say-so, but if the bank gets all its money in the end, it'll most likely be flexible about when."

"Good of you," Oliver said, hiding emotion behind his clipped martial manner.

"Frankly," I said, "you're more use to us salvaged than bust."

He smiled wryly. "A banker to the last drop of blood."

Because of stairs' being difficult I slept on the sofa where Ginnie had dozed on her last afternoon, and I dreamed of her walking up a path towards me looking happy. Not a significant dream, but an awakening of fresh regret. I spent a good deal of the following day thinking of her instead of concentrating on profit and loss.

In the evening Ursula telephoned with triumph in her strong voice and also a continual undercurrent of amazement.

"You won't believe it," she said, "but I've already found three racing stables in Newmarket where he worked last summer and autumn, and in *every case* one of the horses in the yard fell sick!"

I hadn't any trouble at all with belief and asked what sort of sickness.

"They all had crystalluria. That's crystals . . ."

"I know what it is," I said.

"And . . . it's absolutely incredible . . . but all three

were in stables that had in the past sent horses to
Calder Jackson, and these were sent as well, and he
cured them straightaway. Two of the trainers said they
would swear by Calder, he had cured horses for them
for years."

"Was the lad called Shane?" I asked.

"No. Bret. Bret Williams. The same in all three
places."

She dictated the addresses of the stables, the names
of the trainers, and the dates (approximate) when
Shane-Jason-Bret had been in their yards.

"These lads just come and go," she said. "He didn't
work for any of them for as long as a month. Just didn't
turn up one morning. It happens all the time."

"You're marvelous," I said.

"I have a feeling," she said with less excitement,
"that what I'm telling you is what you expected to
hear."

"Hoped."

"The implications are unbelievable."

"Believe them."

"But *Calder*," she protested. "He couldn't . . ."

"Shane worked for Calder," I said. "All the time. Permanently. Wherever he went, it was to manufacture
patients for Calder."

She was silent so long that in the end I said, "Ursula?"

"I'm here," she said. "Do you want me to go on with
the photos?"

"Yes, if you would. To find him."

"Hanging's too good for him," she said grimly. "I'll
do what I can."

She disconnected, and I told Oliver what she'd said.

"Bret Williams? He was Shane Williams here."

"How did you come to employ him?" I asked.

Oliver frowned, looking back. "Good lads aren't that
easy to find, you know. You can advertise until you're
blue in the face and only get third- or fourth-rate appli-
cants. But Nigel said Shane impressed him at the interview and that we should give him a month's trial, and
of course after that we kept him on, and took him back

gladly this year when he telephoned asking, because he was quick and competent and knew the job backwards, and was polite and a good time-keeper . . ."

"A paragon," I said dryly.

"As lads go, yes."

I nodded. He would have to have been good; to have taken pride in his deception, with the devotion of all traitors. I considered those fancy names and thought that he must have seen himself as a sort of macho hero, the great foreign agent playing out his fantasies in the day-to-day tasks, feeling superior to his employers while he tricked them with contempt.

He could have filled the hollowed cores of apples with capsules, and taken a bite or two round the outside to convince, and fed what looked like remainders to his victims. No one would ever have suspected, because suspicion was impossible.

I slept again on the sofa and the following morning Oliver telephoned Detective Chief Inspector Wyfold and asked him to come to the farm. Wyfold needed persuading; reluctantly agreed; and nearly walked out in a U turn when he saw me waiting in Oliver's office.

"No. Look," he protested. "Mr. Ekaterin's already approached me with his ideas and I simply haven't time . . ."

Oliver interrupted. "We have a great deal more now. Please do listen. We quite understand that you are busy with all those other poor girls, but at the very least we can take Ginnie off that list for you."

Wyfold finally consented to sit down and accept some coffee and listen to what we had to say: and as we told him in turns and in detail what had been happening his air of impatience dissipated and his natural sharpness took over.

We gave him copies of Pen's analyses, the names of "Bret's" recent employers and the last ten photographs of Ricky. He glanced at them briefly and said, "We interviewed this groom, but . . ."

"No, you didn't," Oliver said. "The photo is of a boy who looks like him if you don't know either of them well."

Wyfold pursed his lips, but nodded. "Fair enough."

"We do think he may have killed Ginnie, even if you couldn't prove it," Oliver said.

Wyfold began putting together the papers we'd given him. "We will certainly redirect our inquiries," he said, and giving me a dour look added, "if you had left it to the police to search Calder's surgery, sir, Calder Jackson would not have had the opportunity of disposing of Ian Pargetter's case and any other material evidence. These things are always mishandled by amateurs." He looked pointedly at my plaster jacket. "Better have left it to the professionals."

I gave him an amused look but Oliver was gasping. "Left to you," he said, "there would have been no search at all . . . or certainly not in time to save my business."

Wyfold's expression said plainly that saving people's business wasn't his prime concern, but beyond mentioning that picking locks and stealing medicinal substances constituted a breach of the law he kept any further disapproval to himself.

He was on his feet, ready to go, when Ursula rang again, and he could almost hear every word she said because of her enthusiasm.

"I'm in Gloucestershire," she shouted. "I thought I'd work from the other end, if you see what I mean. I remembered Calder had miraculously cured Binty Rockingham's utterly brilliant three-day-eventer who was so weak he could hardly totter, so I came here to her house to ask her, and guess what?"

"What?" I asked obligingly.

"That lad worked for her!" The triumph exploded. "A good lad, she says, would you believe it? He called himself Clint. She can't remember his last name, it was more than two years ago and he was only here a few weeks."

"Ask her if it was Williams," I said.

There was some murmuring at the other end and then Ursula's voice back again, "She thinks so, yes."

"You're a dear, Ursula," I said.

She gave an unembarrassed laugh. "Do you want me

to go on down the road to Rube Golby's place? He had a show pony Calder cured a fair time ago of a weeping wound that wouldn't heal."

"Just one more, then, Ursula. It's pretty conclusive already, I'd say."

"Best to be sure," she said cheerfully. "And I'm enjoying myself, actually, now I'm over the shock."

I wrote down the details she gave me and when she'd gone off the line I handed the new information to Wyfold.

"Clint," he said with disillusion. "Elvis next, I shouldn't wonder."

I shook my head. "A man of action, our Shane."

Perhaps through needing to solve at least one murder while reviled for not catching his rapist, Wyfold put his best muscle into the search. It took him only two weeks to find Shane, who was arrested on leaving a pub in the racing village of Malton, Yorkshire, where he had been heard boasting several times about secret exploits of undisclosed daring.

Wyfold told Oliver, who telephoned me in the office, to which I'd returned via a newly installed wheelchair ramp up the front steps.

"He called himself Dean," Oliver said. "Dean Williams. It seems the police are transferring him from Yorkshire back here to Hertfordshire, and Wyfold wants you to come to his police headquarters to identify Shane as the man called Jason at Calder's yard."

I said I would.

I didn't say that with honesty I couldn't.

"Tomorrow," Oliver added. "They're in a hurry because of holding him without a good enough charge, or something."

"I'll be there."

I went in a chauffeur-driven hired car, a luxury I seemed to have spent half my salary on since leaving Oliver's house.

I was living nearer the office than usual, with a friend whose apartment was in a block with an elevator, not up stairs like my own. The pains in my immobile joints refused obstinately to depart, but owing to a further gift from Pen (via Gordon) were forgettable most of the time. A new pattern of "normal" life had evolved, and all I dearly wanted was a bath.

I arrived at Wyfold's police station at the same time as Oliver, and together we were shown into an office, Oliver pushing me as if born to it. Two months minimum, they'd warned me to expect of life on wheels. Even if my shoulder would be mended before then, it wouldn't stand my weight on crutches. Patience, I'd been told. Be patient. My ankle had been in bits and they'd restored it like a jigsaw puzzle and I couldn't expect miracles, they'd said.

Wyfold arrived, shook hands briskly (an advance) and said that this was not a normal identity parade, as of course Oliver knew Shane very well, and I obviously knew him also, because of Ricky Barnet.

"Just call him Jason," Wyfold told me, "if you are sure he's the same man you saw at Calder Jackson's."

We left the office and went along a fiercely lit institutional corridor to a large interview room, which contained a table, three chairs, a uniformed policeman standing . . . and Shane, sitting down.

He looked cocky, not cowed.

When he saw Oliver he tilted his head almost jauntily, showing not shame but pride, not apology but a sneer. On me he looked with only a flickering glance, neither knowing me from our two very brief meetings nor reckoning on trouble from my direction.

Wyfold raised his eyebrows at me to indicate the need for action.

"Hello, Jason," I said.

His head snapped round immediately and this time he gave me a full stare.

"I met you at Calder Jackson's yard," I said.

"You never did."

Although I hadn't expected it, I remembered him clearly. "You were giving sun-lamp treatment to a horse and Calder Jackson told you to put on your sunglasses."

He made no more effort to deny it. "What of it, then?" he said.

"Conclusive evidence of your link with the place, I should think," I said.

Oliver, seeming as much outraged by Shane's lack of contrition as by his sins, turned with force to Wyfold and in half-controlled bitterness said, "Now prove he killed my daughter."

"What!"

Shane had risen in panic to his feet, knocking his chair over behind him and losing in an instant the smart-alec assurance. "I never did," he said.

We all watched him with interest, and his gaze traveled fast from one face to another, seeing only assessment and disbelief and nowhere admiration.

"I didn't kill her," he said, his voice hoarse and rising. "I didn't. Straight up, I didn't. It was him. He did it."

"Who?" I said.

"Calder. Mr. Jackson. He did it. It was him, not me." He looked across at all of us with desperation. "Look, I'm telling you the truth, straight up I am. I never killed her, it was him."

Wyfold began telling him in a flat voice that he had a right to remain silent and that anything he said might be written down and used in evidence, but Shane wasn't clever and fright had too firm a hold. His fantasy world had vanished in the face of unimaginable reality, and I found myself believing every word he said.

"We didn't know she was there, see. She heard us talking, but we didn't know. And when I carried the stuff back to the hostel he saw her moving so he hit her. I didn't see him do it, I didn't, but when I went back there he was with Ginnie on the ground and I said she was the boss's daughter, which he didn't even know, see, but he said all the worse if she was the boss's daughter because she must have been standing there in the shadow listening and she would have gone straight off and told everybody."

The words, explanations, excuses came tumbling out in self-righteous urgency and Wyfold thankfully showed no signs of regulating the flow into the careful officialese of a formal statement. The uniformed police-man, now sitting behind Shane, was writing at speed in a notebook, recording, I imagined, the gist.

"I don't believe you," Wyfold said impatiently. "What did he hit her with?"

Shane redoubled his efforts to convince, and from then on I admired Wyfold's slyly effective interrogatory technique.

"With a fire extinguisher," Shane said. "He kept it in his car, see, and he had it in his hand. He was real fussy about fire always. Would never let anyone smoke any-where near the stables. That Nigel . . ." the sneer came back temporarily ". . . the lads all smoked in the feed room, I ask you, behind his back. He'd no idea what went on."

"Fire extinguisher . . ." Wyfold spoke doubtfully, shaking his head.

"Yeah, it was. It was. One of them red things about this long." Shane anxiously held up his hands about fif-teen inches apart. "With the nozzle, sort of, at the top. He was holding it by that, sort of swinging it. Ginnie was lying flat on the ground, face down, like, and I said, 'What have you gone and done?' and he said she'd been listening."

Wyfold sniffed.

"It was like that, straight up," Shane said urgently.

"Listening to what?"

"We were talking about the stuff, see."

"The shampoo . . ."

"Yeah." He seemed only briefly to feel the slightest alarm at the mention of it. "I told him, see, that the stuff had really worked because there'd been a foal born that morning with half a leg, that Nigel he tried to hush it up but by afternoon he was half cut and he told one of the lads so we all knew. So I told Mr. Jackson and he said great, because it was time we'd heard, and there hadn't been a murmur in the papers and he was getting worried he hadn't got the dose right, or something. So anyway when I told him about the foal with half a leg he laughed, see, he was so pleased, and he said this was probably the last lot I'd have to do, just do the six bottles he'd brought, and then scarper."

Oliver looked very pale, with sweat along his hairline and whitely clenched fists. His mouth was rigidly closed with the effort of self-control, and he listened throughout without once interrupting or cursing.

"I took the six bottles off to the hostel but when I got there I'd only got five, so I went back to look for the one I'd dropped, but I forgot it, see, when I saw him standing there over Ginnie and him saying she'd heard us talking, and then he said for me to come with him down to the village in his car and he'd drop me at a pub where the other lads were, so as I couldn't have been back home killing the boss's daughter, see? I remembered about the bottle I'd dropped when we were on our way to the village but I didn't think he'd be best pleased and anyway I reckoned I'd find it all right when I went back, but I never did. I didn't think it would matter much, because no one would know what it was for, it was just dog shampoo, and anyway I reckoned I'd skip using the new bottles after all because of the fuss there would be over Ginnie. But if it hadn't been for that bottle I wouldn't have gone out again at all, see, and I wouldn't know it was him that killed her, and it wasn't me, it *wasn't*."

He came to what appeared in his own mind to be a halt, but as far as Wyfold, Oliver and myself were concerned he had stopped short of enough.

"Are you saying," Wyfold said, "that you walked back from the village with the other grooms, knowing what you would find?"

"Well, yeah. Only Dave and Sammy, see, they'd got back first, and when I got back there was an ambulance there and such, and I just kept in the background."

"What did you do with the other five bottles of shampoo?" Wyfold asked. "We searched all the rooms in the hostel. We didn't find any shampoo." '

The first overwhelming promptings of fear were beginning to die down in Shane, but he answered with only minimal hesitation, "I took them down the road a ways and threw them in a ditch. That was after they'd all gone off to the hospital." He nodded in the general direction of Oliver and myself. "Panicked me a bit, it did, when Dave said she was talking, like. But I was glad I'd got rid of the stuff after, when she was dead after all, with everyone snooping around."

"You could show me which ditch?" Wyfold said.

"Yeah, I could."

"Good."

"You mean," Shane said, with relief, "you believe what I told you . . ."

"No, I don't mean that," Wyfold said repressively. "I'll need to know what you ordinarily did with the shampoo."

"What?"

"How you prepared it and gave it to the mares."

"Oh." An echo of the cocky cleverness came back: a swagger to the shoulders, a curl to the lip. "It was dead easy, see. Mr. Jackson showed me how. I just had to put a coffee filter in a wash basin and pour the shampoo through it, so's the shampoo all ran down the drain and there was that stuff left on the paper, then I just turned the coffee filter inside out and soaked it in a little jar with some linseed oil from the feed shed, and then I'd stir a quarter of it into the feed if it was for a mare I was looking after anyway, or let the stuff fall to the bottom and scrape up a teaspoonful and put it in an apple for the others. Mr. Jackson showed me how. Dead easy, the whole thing."

"How many mares did you give it to?"

"Don't rightly know. Dozens, counting last year. Some I missed. Mr. Jackson said better to miss some than be found out. He liked me to do the oil best. Said too many apples would be noticed." A certain amount of anxiety returned. "Look, now I've told you all this, you know I didn't kill her, don't you?"

Wyfold said impassively, "How often did Mr. Jackson bring you bottles of shampoo?"

"He didn't. I mean, I had a case of it under my bed. Brought it with me when I moved in, see, same as last year. But this year I ran out, like, so I rang him up from the village one night for some more. So he said he'd meet me at the back gate at nine on Sunday when all the lads would be down in the pub."

"That was a risk he wouldn't take," Wyfold said skeptically.

"Well, he did."

Wyfold shook his head.

Shane's panic resurfaced completely. "He was there," he almost shouted. "He was. He *was*."

Wyfold still looked studiedly unconvinced and told Shane that it would be best if he now made a formal statement, which the sergeant would write down for him to sign when he, Shane, was satisfied that it represented what he had already told us: and Shane in slight bewilderment agreed.

Wyfold nodded to the sergeant, opened the door of the room, and gestured to Oliver and me to leave. Oliver in undiluted grimness silently pushed me out. Wyfold, with a satisfied air, said in his plain uncushioning way, "There you are then, Mr. Knowles, that's how your daughter died, and you're luckier than some. That little sod's telling the truth. Proud of himself, like a lot of crooks. Wants the world to know." He shook hands perfunctorily with Oliver and nodded briefly to me, and walked away to his unsolved horrors where the papers called for his blood and other fathers choked on their tears.

Oliver pushed me back to the outside world but not directly to where my temporary chauffeur had said he would wait. I found myself making an unscheduled turn into a small public garden, where Oliver abruptly left me beside the first seat we came to and walked jerkily away.

I watched his back, ramrod-stiff, disappearing behind bushes and trees. In grief, as in all else, he would be tidy.

A boy came along the path on roller skates and wheeled round to a stop in front of me.

"You want pushing?" he said.

"No. But thanks all the same."

He looked at me judiciously. "Can you make that chair go straight, using just one arm?"

"No. I go round in a circle and end where I started."

"Thought so." He considered me gravely. "Just like the earth," he said.

He pushed off with one foot and sailed away straight on the other and presently, walking firmly, Oliver came back.

He sat on the bench beside me, his eyelids slightly reddened, his manner calm.

"Sorry," he said, after a while.

"She died happy," I said. "It's better than nothing."

"How do you mean?"

"She heard what they were doing. She picked up the shampoo Shane dropped. She was coming to tell you that everything was all right, there was nothing wrong with Sandcastle and you wouldn't lose the farm. At the moment she died she must have been full of joy."

Oliver raised his face to the pale summer sky.

"Do you think so?"

"Yes, I do."

"Then I'll believe it," he said.

October

Gordon was coming up to sixty, the age at which everyone retired from Ekaterin's, like it or not. The bustle of young brains, the founder Paul had said, was what kept money moving, and his concept still ruled in the house.

Gordon had his regrets but they were balanced, it seemed to me, by a sense of relief. He had battled for three years now against his palsy and had finished the allotted work span honorably in the face of the enemy within. He began saying he was looking forward to his leisure, and that he and Judith would go on a celebratory journey as soon as possible. Before that, however, he was to be away for a day of medical tests in hospital.

"Such a bore," he said, "but they want to make these checks and set me up before we travel."

"Very sensible," I said. "Where will you go?"

He smiled with enthusiasm. "I've always wanted to see Australia. Never been there, you know."

"Nor have I."

He nodded and we continued with our normal work in the accord we had felt for so many years. I would miss him badly for his own sake, I thought, and even more because I would no longer have, through him, constant news of and contact with Judith. The days seemed to gallop towards his birthday and my spirits grew heavy as his lightened.

Oliver's problems were no longer the day-to-day communiqués at lunch. The dissenting director had conceded that even blue-chip certainties weren't always proof against well-planned malice and no longer grumbled about my part in things, particularly since the day that Henry in his mild-steel voice made observations about defending the bank's money beyond the call of duty.

"And beyond the call of common sense," Val murmured in my ear. "Thank goodness."

Oliver's plight had been extensively aired by Alec in *What's Going On Where It Shouldn't*, thanks to comprehensive leaks from one of Ekaterin's directors; to wit, me.

Some of the regular newspapers had danced round the subject, since with Shane still awaiting trial the business of poisoning mares was sub judice. Alec's paper, with its usual disrespect for secrecy, had managed to let everyone in the bloodstock industry know that Sandcastle himself was a rock-solid investment, and that any foals already born perfect would not be carrying any damaging genes.

As for the mares covered this year, the paper continued, *there is a lottery as to whether they will produce deformed foals. Breeders are advised to let their mares go to term, because there is a roughly fifty percent chance that the foal will be perfect. Breeders of mares who produce deformed or imperfect foals will, we understand, have their stallion fees refunded and expenses reimbursed.*

The bloodstock industry is drawing up its own special guidelines to deal with this exceptional case.

Meanwhile, fear not. Sandcastle is potent, fertile and fully reinstated. Apply without delay for a place in next year's program.

* * *

Alec himself telephoned me in the office two days after the column appeared.

"How do you like it?" he said.

"Absolutely great."

"The editor says the newsagents in Newmarket have been ringing up like mad for extra copies."

"Hm," I said. "I think perhaps I'll get a list of all breeders and bloodstock agents and personally—I mean anonymously—send each of them a copy of your column, if your editor would agree."

"Do it without asking him," Alec said. "He would probably prefer it. We won't sue you for infringement of copyright, I'll promise you."

"Thanks a lot," I said. "You've been really great."

"Wait till you get an eyeful of the next issue. I'm working on it now. *Do-It-Yourself Miracles,* that's the heading. How does it grab you?"

"Fine."

"The dead can't sue," he said cheerfully. "I just hope I spell the drugs right."

"I sent you the list," I protested.

"The typesetters," he said, "can scramble eggs, let alone sulfanilamide."

"See you someday," I said, smiling.

"Yeah. Pie and beer. We'll fix it."

His miracle-working column in the next issue demolished Calder's reputation entirely and made further progress towards restoring Sandcastle's, and after a third bang on the Sandcastle-is-tops gong in the issue after that, Oliver thankfully reported that confidence both in his stallion and in his stud farm was creeping back. Two thirds of the nominations were filled already, and inquiries were arriving for the rest.

"One of the breeders whose mare is in foal now is threatening to sue me for negligence, but the bloodstock associations are trying to dissuade him. He can't do anything, anyway, until after Shane's trial and after the foal is born, and I just hope to God it's one that's perfect."

From the bank's point of view his affairs were no longer in turmoil. The board had agreed to extend the period of the loan for three extra years, and Val, Gordon and I had worked out the rates at which Oliver could repay without crippling himself. All finally rested on Sandcastle, but if his progeny should prove to have inherited his speed, Oliver should in the end reach the prosperity and prestige for which he had aimed.

"But let's not," Henry said, smiling one day over roast lamb, "let's not make a habit of going to the races."

Gordon came to the office one Monday saying he had met Dissdale the day before at lunch in a restaurant that they both liked.

"He was most embarrassed to see me," Gordon said. "But I had quite a talk with him. He really didn't know, you know, that Calder was a fake. He says he can hardly believe, even now, that the cures weren't cures, or that Calder actually killed two people. Very subdued, he was, for Dissdale."

"I suppose," I said diffidently, "you didn't ask him if he and Calder had ever bought, cured and sold sick animals before Indian Silk."

"Yes, I did, actually, because of your thoughts. But he said they hadn't. Indian Silk was the first, and Dissdale rather despondently said he supposed Calder and Ian Pargetter couldn't bear to see all their time and trouble go to waste, so when Ian Pargetter couldn't persuade Fred Barnet to try Calder, Calder sent Dissdale to buy the horse outright."

"And it worked a treat."

Gordon nodded. "Another thing Dissdale said was that Calder was as stunned as he was himself to find it was Ekaterin's who had loaned the money for Sandcastle. There had been no mention of it in the papers. Dissdale asked me to tell you that when he told Calder who it was who had actually put up the money, Calder said 'My God' several times and walked up and down all evening and drank far more than usual. Dissdale didn't know why, and Calder wouldn't tell him, but Dissdale says he thinks now it was because Calder was feeling remorse at hammering Ekaterin's after an Ekaterin had saved his life."

"Dissdale," I said dryly, "is still trying to find excuses for his hero."

"And for his own admiration of him," Gordon agreed. "But perhaps it's true. Dissdale said Calder had liked you very much."

Liked me, and apologized, and tried to kill me: that too.

Movement had slowly returned to my shoulder and arm once the body-restricting plaster had come off, and via electrical treatment, exercise and massage normal strength had returned.

In the ankle department things weren't quite so good: I still after more than four months wore a brace, though now of removable aluminum and strapping, not plaster. No one would promise I'd be able to ski on the final outcome and meanwhile all but the shortest journeys required sticks. I had tired of hopping up and down my Hampstead stairs, on my return there, to the extent of renting an apartment of my own with an elevator to take me aloft and a garage in the basement, and I reckoned life had basically become reasonable again on the day I drove out of there in my car: automatic gear change, no work for the left foot, perfect.

A day or two before he was due to go into hospital for his check-up Gordon mentioned in passing that Judith was coming to collect him from the bank after work to go with him to the hospital, where he would be spending the night so as to be rested for the whole day of tests on Friday.

She would collect him again on Friday evening and they would go home together, and he would have the weekend to rest in before he returned to the office on Monday.

"I'll be glad when it's over," he said frankly. "I hate all the needles and the pulling and pushing about."

"When Judith has settled you in, would she like me to give her some dinner before she goes home?" I said.

He looked across with interest, the idea taking root. "I should think she would love it. I'll ask her."

He returned the next day saying Judith was pleased,

and we arranged between us that when she left him in
the hospital she would come to join me in a convenient
restaurant that we all knew well: and on the following
day, Thursday, the plan was duly carried out.

She came with a glowing face, eyes sparkling, white
teeth gleaming; wearing a blue full-skirted dress and
shoes with high heels.

"Gordon is fine, apart from grumbling about tomorrow," she reported, "and they gave him almost no supper, to his disgust. He says to think of him during our
filet steaks."

I doubt if we did. I don't remember what we ate. The
feast was there before me on the other side of the small
table, Judith looking beautiful and telling me nonsensi-
cal things like what happens to a blasé refrigerator
when you pull its plug out.

"What, then?"

"It loses its cool."

I laughed at the stupidity of it and brimmed over with
the intoxication of having her there to myself, and I
wished she was my own wife so fiercely that my muscles ached.

"You'll be going to Australia . . ." I said.

"Australia?" She hesitated. "We leave in three
weeks."

"So soon."

"Gordon's sixty the week after next," she said. "You
know he is. There's the party."

Henry, Val and I had clubbed together to give Gordon
a small sending-off in the office after his last day's
work, an affair to which most of Banking's managers
and their wives had been invited.

"I hate him going," I said.

"To Australia?"

"From the bank."

We drank wine and coffee and told each other much
without saying a word. Not until we were nearly leaving did she say tentatively, "We'll be away for months,
you know."

My feelings must have shown. "Months . . . How
many?"

"We don't know. We're going to all the places Gordon or I have wanted to see that couldn't be fitted into an ordinary vacation. We're going to potter. Bits of Europe, bits of the Middle East, India, Singapore, Bali, then Australia, New Zealand, Tahiti, Fiji, Hawaii, America." She fell silent, her eyes not laughing now but full of sadness.

I swallowed. "Gordon will find it exhausting."

"He says not. He passionately wants to go, and I know he's always yearned to have the time to see things . . . and we're going slowly, with lots of rests."

The restaurant had emptied around us and the waiters hovered with polite faces willing us to go. Judith put on her blue coat and we went outside onto the cold pavement.

"How do you plan to go home now?" I asked.

"Underground."

"I'll drive you," I said.

She gave me a small smile and nodded, and we walked slowly across the road to where I'd left the car. She sat in beside me and I did all the automatic things like switching on the lights and letting off the handbrake, and I drove all the way to Clapham without consciously seeing the road.

Gordon's house behind the big gates lay quiet and dark. Judith looked up at its bulk and then at me, and I leaned across in the car and put my arms round her and kissed her. She came close to me, kissing me back with a feeling and a need that seemed as intense as my own, and for a while we stayed in that way, floating in passion, dreaming in deep unaccustomed touch.

As if of one mind we each at the same time drew back and slowly relaxed against the seat. She put her hand on mine and threaded her fingers through, holding tight.

I looked ahead through the windshield, seeing trees against the stars: seeing nothing.

A long time passed.

"We can't," I said eventually.

"No."

"Especially not," I said, "in his own house."

"No."

After another long minute she let go of my hand and opened the door beside her, and I too opened mine.

"Don't get out," she said, "because of your ankle."

I stood up, however, on the driveway and she walked round the car towards me. We hugged each other but without kissing, a long hungry minute of body against body; commitment and farewell.

"I'll see you," she said, "at the party"; and we both knew how it would be, with Lorna Shipton talking about watching Henry's weight and Henry flirting roguishly with Judith whenever he could, and everyone talking loudly and clapping Gordon on the back.

She walked over to the front door and unlocked it, and looked back, briefly, once, and then went in, putting the walls between us in final, mutual, painful decision.

December

I felt alone and also lonely, which I'd never been before, and I telephoned to Pen one Sunday in December and suggested taking her out to lunch. She said to come early as she had to open her shop at four, and I arrived at eleven-thirty to find coffee percolating richly and Pen trying to unravel the string of the Christmas kite.

"I found it when I was looking for some books," she said. "It's so pretty. When we've had coffee, let's go out and fly it."

We took it onto the common, and she let the string out gradually until the dragon was high on the wind, circling and darting and fluttering its frilly tail. It took us slowly after it across the grass, Pen delightedly intent and I simply pleased to be back there in that place.

She glanced at me over her shoulder. "Are we going too far for your ankle? Or too fast?"

"No and no," I said.

"Still taking the comfrey?"

"Religiously."

The bones and other tissues round my shoulder had

mended fast, I'd been told, and although the ankle still lagged I was prepared to give comfrey the benefit of the doubt. Anything that would restore decent mobility attracted my enthusiasm: life with brace and walking stick, still boringly necessary, made even buying groceries a pest.

We had reached a spot on a level with Gordon and Judith's house when a gust of wind took the kite suddenly higher, setting it weaving and diving in bright-colored arcs and stretching its land-line to tautness. Before anything could be done the string snapped and the dazzling butterfly wings soared away free, rising in a spiral, disappearing to a shape, to a black dot, to nothing.

"What a pity," Pen said, turning to me with disappointment and then pausing, seeing where my own gaze had traveled, downwards to the tall cream gates, firmly shut.

"Let her go," Pen said soberly, "like the kite."

"She'll come back."

"Take out some other girl," she urged.

I smiled lopsidedly. "I'm out of practice."

"But you can't spend your whole life . . ." She stopped momentarily, and then said, "Parkinson's disease isn't fatal. Gordon could live to be eighty or more."

"I wouldn't want him dead," I protested. "How could you think it?"

"Then what?"

"Just to go on, I suppose, as we are."

She took my arm and turned me away from the gates to return to her house.

"Give it time," she said. "You've got months. You both have."

I glanced at her. "Both?"

"Gordon and I don't go around with our eyes shut."

"He's never said anything . . ."

She smiled. "Gordon likes you better than you like him, if possible. Trusts you, too." She paused. "Let her go, Tim, for your own sake."

We went silently back to her house and I thought of

all that had happened since the day Gordon stood in the fountain, and of all I had learned and felt and loved and lost. Thought of Ginnie and Oliver and Calder, and of all the gateways I'd gone through to grief and pain and the knowledge of death. So much—too much—compressed into so small a span.

"You're a child of the light," Pen said contentedly. "Both you and Judith. You always take sunshine with you. I don't suppose you know it, but everything brightens when people like you walk in." She glanced down at my slow foot. "Sorry. When you limp in. So carry the sunlight to a new young girl who isn't married to Gordon and doesn't break your heart." She paused. "That's good pharmacological advice, so take it."

"Yes, doctor," I said: and knew I couldn't.

On Christmas Eve, when I had packed to go to Jersey and was checking around the flat before leaving, the telephone rang.

"Hello," I said.

There was a series of clicks and hums and I was about to put the receiver down when a breathless voice said, "Tim . . ."

"Judith?" I said incredulously.

"Yes."

"Where are you?"

"Listen, just listen. I don't know who else to ask, not at Christmas . . . Gordon's ill and I'm alone and I don't know, I don't know . . ."

"Where are you?"

"India . . . He's in hospital. They're very good, very kind, but he's so ill . . . unconscious . . . they say cerebral hemmorrhage . . . I'm so afraid . . . I do so love him . . ." She was suddenly crying, and trying not to, the words coming out at intervals when control was possible. "It's so much to ask . . . but I need . . . help."

"Tell me where," I said. "I'll come at once."

"Oh . . ."

She told me where. I was packed and ready to go, and I went.

Because of the date and the off-track destination

there were delays and it took me forty hours to get there. Gordon died before I reached her, on the day after Christmas, like her mother.

ABOUT THE AUTHOR

Dick Francis is a former champion steeplechase jockey who rode for some years for Queen Elizabeth, the Queen Mother. When age and injury grounded him at thirty-six, he was asked to write a weekly racing column for the London *Sunday Express*. From this experience he branched out into fiction, using the inside world of horses as the background for his novels. Dick Francis is married, lives in Oxfordshire, England, and still rides whenever he can.

A Special Blend...

MYSTERY, ADVENTURE and THE WORLD of RACING

DICK FRANCIS